MARKED
FOR
DEATH

MARKED FOR DEATH

A DEATH & TEXAS WESTERN

WILLIAM W. JOHNSTONE

AND J. A. JOHNSTONE

PINNACLE BOOKS

Kensington Publishing Corp.

www.kensingtonbooks.com

PINNACLE BOOKS are published by

Kensington Publishing Corp.
119 West 40th Street
New York, NY 10018

PUBLISHER'S NOTE

Following the death of William W. Johnstone, the Johnstone family is working with a carefully selected writer to organize and complete Mr. Johnstone's outlines and many unfinished manuscripts to create additional novels in all of his series like The Last Gunfighter, Mountain Man, and Eagles, among others. This novel was inspired by Mr. Johnstone's superb storytelling.

ISBN-13: 978-0-7860-4741-3
ISBN-10: 0-7860-4741-0

First Pinnacle paperback printing: April 2021

10 9 8 7 6 5 4 3 2 1

Printed in the United States of America

Electronic edition:

ISBN-13: 978-0-7860-4742-0 (e-book)
ISBN-10: 0-7860-4742-9 (e-book)

CHAPTER ONE

It was about an hour before the Two Forks Kitchen would open for the midday meal when Cullen McCabe slow-walked the dun gelding down the street to Dr. Malcolm Taylor's office. His sorrel packhorse followed, tied with a lead rope to his saddle. He had bought the dun from Art Becker in East City at a ridiculously low price, but Art refused to accept any amount higher than the twenty dollars he quoted. Cullen understood that Art wanted to show his appreciation for the job Cullen had done to clean out the undesirables in that town. The dun was a good strong horse, but Cullen was of the opinion that no horse could replace Jake, the bay gelding that had been his partner for almost six years. He had not been inspired to name the dun yet, thinking that he might still trade him if he found another horse that approached Jake's talents. He was thinking about Jake's final moments on the dark trail where he was ambushed. The gunman who put the fatal shots in Jake, also put two rounds in Cullen before Cullen sent him to hell.

Arriving at Dr. Taylor's office, Cullen dismounted, using only one hand, since his left arm was riding in a sling. The wound in his side had been a grazing shot and was little more than a discomfort at this point. But the wound in his left shoulder needed a doctor's attention, since the slug was still in there and causing quite a bit of pain. For that reason, he had come straight back to Two Forks after his job for the governor was completed, instead of going to Austin and a possible new assignment. He looped his reins over the hitching rail in front of the doctor's office and walked in the small waiting room. A little bell on the top of the door announced his arrival.

In a few minutes, Grace Taylor, the doctor's wife, came into the room. "Looks like you've got a little problem," she said cheerfully. From the looks of the imposing man with his arm in a sling, she wondered if he might be the mysterious stranger who had a cabin on the river south of town somewhere. Clara Thornton had told her of her husband Ron's and Leon Armstrong's ongoing speculation about Cullen McCabe, who received telegrams from the governor from time to time. "How did you hurt it?" Grace asked. "Is it a sprain or something?"

"No, ma'am," Cullen replied. "There's a bullet in it and I think it might be infected. I'd like for the doctor to get it out."

"Oh," she said. "I guess you'd better come with me." He followed her into a short hall to an examining room. "If you'll just sit down there, I'll go get the doctor, Mr. . . ."

"McCabe," he finished her statement, and sat down in the chair she had indicated.

"You've got a gunshot patient, Malcolm," Grace said when she found her husband still sitting at the kitchen table, drinking coffee. He was puzzled by her look of amusement until she explained in a whisper, in case the imposing Mr. McCabe had supersensitive hearing. "Cullen McCabe," Grace announced, "the fellow that shot Sonny Tice, the mysterious man that Ron Thornton and Leon Armstrong are always talking about. He's got a bullet in his shoulder."

"No foolin'?" Doc Taylor responded, a hint of sarcasm in his tone. He was aware of Ron's and Leon's fascination with the man who seldom came to town, and when he did, it was usually to get a telegram that sent him off somewhere. As for Doc, he figured that was McCabe's business and he didn't particularly care what the man's business was. "You want me to get his autograph for ya? That is, if he can write." He got up from the table and started for the door. "Might as well heat up some water."

"Mr. McCabe," Doc greeted him when he walked into the examining room. "Understand you've got a gunshot wound. Let's take a look at it." He helped Cullen untie his sling. "Somebody bandaged it up pretty good for you," he remarked. "How long ago did they put this bandage on?"

"Three days ago, last night," Cullen replied.

After taking a good look at the wound, Doc said, "It needs to come outta there, all right. Looks like it's trying to set up a little infection. I expect it was getting a little tender, wasn't it? Well, I'll cut it right outta there. You want me to give you a little ether?"

"Druther you just go ahead and cut it on outta there," Cullen said. "I've got some things I need to tend to this afternoon, so I'd like to keep a clear head."

"Whatever you say, but it might be a little unpleasant."

"I expect so," Cullen agreed.

Grace brought in a pan of hot water and Doc cleaned the wound up as well as he could. "I'll clean it now with carbolic acid to try to keep the infection down," he said. After that, he went to work with his scalpel. He was quick, which Cullen appreciated because it hurt like hell. "There it is," Doc said after only about ten minutes. "It oughta heal up with no problem, but if it doesn't, come back to see me." He redressed the wound with clean bandages and advised, "Best leave your arm in that sling to give that incision time to heal." Cullen paid him and thanked him, tipped his hat to Grace on his way out the door, then headed for the telegraph office, leading the dun horse and the sorrel.

"Mr. McCabe!" Leon Armstrong sang out when Cullen walked in. "Ain't seen you in a while. Looks like you had a little bad luck," he said, pointing to his arm. "I ain't got no telegrams for you right now."

"I didn't expect any," Cullen replied. "I wanna send one to the same place you get all mine from."

"The governor's office in Austin?" Leon asked, and handed him a pencil and a blank pad.

Cullen wrote down the message. *Won't be ready to go to work for about a week. Need time for wound to heal. McCabe.* "That oughta do," he said.

"Are you gonna be in town awhile, in case you get a reply right back from the governor?"

"Not long," Cullen answered. "I'm gonna go have some dinner at the Two Forks Kitchen, then I'm headin' down the river."

"If I get a reply right away, I'll send Jimmy down there to tell you," Leon said. He wanted to ask Cullen what happened to his shoulder, but he hesitated, afraid he might tell him it was none of his business.

"'Preciate it," McCabe said as he walked out. He decided to ride to the hotel and the little eating establishment next to it. When he grabbed the saddle horn with his right hand, preparing to step up into the saddle, the horse turned his head to give him a forlorn look. "What's that for?" Cullen asked. "We ain't goin' far. You're lookin' at me like an orphan." He reached over and scratched the horse's ears. "That's a good name for you, Orphan." It occurred to him that he had been responsible for the dun's previous owner's demise, making the horse a sure-enough orphan. "So I reckon I oughta take you in for a while till I come across another Jake." Even as he said it, he knew there was but one Jake. "But, you'll do, so I won't be lookin' for a horse right away." The horse nodded his head up and down several times as if he understood the agreement and Cullen climbed aboard.

Up at the upper end of the street, two young men walked out of the River House Saloon after spending what little money they had on a few shots of Garland Wilson's whiskey. Suddenly, one of them caught sight of the formidable figure riding toward the hotel, leading a pack-horse. It was an image they had seen before and one they would never forget. "It's him!" Joe Tice blurted, excitedly.

Joe's brother, Samson, looked where Joe pointed. "It's him, all right!" The question before them was what to do about it. Their father, Jesse Tice, was not with them on this trip to town. In fact, Jesse didn't even know they had gone to town. They were supposed to be scouting a small herd of horses owned by a rancher six miles from town.

"Whaddaya reckon we oughta do?" Joe asked. Both of them remembered all too well the complete disaster that was the result of the last time they, along with their father, had attempted to call McCabe out. It was Joe who challenged him to a shootout and McCabe succeeded in relieving both brothers of their guns and knocking their father senseless. The incident was enough to convince Joe that no good could ever come in facing McCabe man-to-man. They were forced to retreat from the town, carrying old Jesse with a broken nose. "We ain't supposed to be in town. You reckon Pa would give us a lickin' if we was to try to get a shot at McCabe?"

"He oughta be proud of us, if we was to kill McCabe," Samson said. "I bet he'd forget all about us comin' to town when we was supposed to be scoutin' them horses."

"Let's go get him, then," Joe said, still trying to match his brother's cocky attitude, even though his honest preference was to take a wide path around Cullen McCabe. "It's time he paid for killin' Sonny," he continued, talking the talk. "Watch him. Where's he goin'?"

They watched until McCabe reached the dining room next to the hotel and dismounted. "He's goin' to the Kitchen. He's fixin' to eat," Samson said. "Look yonder, does it look to you like he's got his arm in a sling?" They both strained harder to see more clearly at the distance they were watching from. "Well, I'll be go to hell," Samson uttered, "he's totin' his arm in a bandanna. We ain't gonna get no better chance than right now. Pa would skin us, if we passed this up." They climbed on their horses and rode toward the Two Forks Kitchen at a lope.

When they got there, Samson told his brother to hold up a minute. "You know they started makin' you take your gun off when you go in there to eat. Let's wait a minute or two and give him plenty of time to get rid of his gun."

Inside the dining room Cullen was talking to Alma Brown just inside the door. "It's been a long time since you've been back to see us," she said. "Looks like you've had a little bad luck."

"Yeah, nothin' serious, just a nuisance to have to mess with," Cullen replied. "I'm gonna leave my gun belt on, if you don't mind. I'll lay my gun on the table, but the belt is hard to strap on when you don't have but one hand, so I'll leave it on."

Alma laughed. "Well, the bullets ain't the problem, it's the gun that shoots 'em that Porter's concerned with, so I reckon that'll be fine." He laid the weapon on the table, put there for that purpose, and followed her to a small table near the kitchen. "I expect you'll be wanting coffee with your dinner," she said, and he nodded. "Gracie's made up a big pot of beef stew for dinner today. How's that sound?"

"I think that suits my taste just fine," Cullen said, and looked to his sling to make sure it was riding like he wanted when she left to fetch his dinner. In a few seconds, she was back with his coffee and told him Gracie was filling a big plate for him, since he was such a big man. "Much obliged," he said, and when she turned to go to another table, he saw the trouble entering the door. *The Tice boys! Why, oh why, am I cursed with these idiots?* They walked inside and closed the door behind them. He realized then that the old man, Jesse, was not with them. There were only a few diners in the room at this particular time, but all conversation stopped when they noticed the two young men standing just inside the door. A glance told the patrons the two cocky-looking visitors were not there to have dinner. Both men wore smirks as they zeroed their gaze in on the somber man with his arm in a sling.

When she spotted them from the kitchen door, Alma hurried out to confront them. "You gentlemen must not have seen the sign asking you to leave your weapons here on the table, if you wanna eat dinner."

"We ain't come in here to eat no dinner," Samson responded. "And we'll be needin' our guns. We got some business to take care of with Cullen McCabe. So you just keep your nose out of it and nobody else will get hurt." She started to protest, but he shoved her aside and drew his .44. "Cullen McCabe, it's time to settle up for the last time you was in town. You broke our pappy's nose."

Cullen released a long, patient sigh before answering. "Your pappy oughta learn to keep his nose outta other people's business. And I'm gonna advise you two to just forget about this business of vengeance for your brother's death. He forced it on himself. There were witnesses that told you he gave me no choice and I'm tryin' to keep you two from making the same mistake he did. So get on out of here and go on about your business."

"You ain't gettin' off that easy, McCabe," Samson said. "You're gonna pay up for killin' our brother."

"You made up your mind," Cullen said. "You wanna settle up for good?"

"That's right," a smiling Samson Tice answered him.

"All right, if that's the way you want it. Just step outside, so you'll quit botherin' these people tryin' to eat their dinner. I'll be out as soon as I finish my food and we'll have at it. You can practice your quick-draw while you're waitin'."

Still smiling, Samson replied, "I don't think so. I think we druther get it done right here, right now." He took a couple of steps forward to be sure McCabe's gun was well behind him on the table. Joe followed his lead.

"You're sayin' you wanna call my hand while my gun

is on the table behind you and I got one arm in a sling. Well, I can't say as how I blame you. But that ain't gonna do much to build your reputation as a fast gun. That's just gonna get you arrested by Sheriff Woods for murder."

"Damn, he might be right about that, Samson," Joe whispered. Up to now, he had tried to talk as cocky about facing McCabe as Samson did. At this point, however, it seemed like he and Samson had good reason to back off.

Overhearing him, Cullen said, "Better listen to your brother and get on outta here. It ain't gonna do much for your reputation if you come after a man with his arm in a sling."

"Don't listen to him," Samson told his brother. "He's just tryin' to talk his way outta gettin' shot, like he did last time. Only this time it ain't gonna work. This time, you're gonna pay for shootin' Sonny." He took several more steps closer to be sure he placed his shot right where he wanted it.

McCabe put his fork down. "You sure you wanna do this?" Samson's answer was a widening of the smirk on his face as he slowly raised his .44 and took deliberate aim. Cullen reached into the sling supporting his arm, almost casually, and withdrew the vest-pocket Remington derringer he had tucked against the inside of his forearm. The .41 short bullet struck Samson in the forehead, preserving his expression of surprise for eternity and rendering younger brother, Joe, motionless, his drawn six-gun hanging at his side. Wasting no time, Cullen quickly got up and took the pistol from Joe's hand while the young man stared in shocked disbelief at his brother's body on the floor.

Shocked as well, the other patrons in the dining room sat speechless as Cullen turned Joe around and led him out the door. "Your brother made a mistake and I don't want you to make one, too. You saw that he gave me no choice, right? Now it's time for this vengeance business to stop. You need to take your brother home and when you tell your pa what happened, you need to be a man about it and tell him the truth. I'll get some help to load your brother's body on his horse and I'll tell Sheriff Woods that you didn't have any part in it. All right?" Joe made no response, but he let Cullen lead him out to the horses. "You wait right here and I'll be back with your brother."

Cullen left the confused young man there and went back inside, where the conversation had at last resumed. "I need a hand here," he announced. "I ain't got but one arm." A couple of men answered his call and the three of them carried Samson out to the horses. While Joe watched motionless, they hefted the body across his saddle. "All right," Cullen said to Joe. "Climb on your horse and take your brother home. He oughta ride all right, if you take it slow." He thanked the two men who helped with the body and stood there watching Joe until he was sure he was not going to turn around and come back. Then he went back inside to finish his dinner, only to find his plate and cup gone from the table. Satisfied that he had just received a refusal-for-service notice for breaking the dining room firearms policy, he picked up his hat and prepared to leave.

"Hey, where are you going?" Alma questioned as she came out the kitchen door carrying a fresh plate and a fresh cup of coffee. "You let your dinner get cold."

Surprised, he had to chuckle. "I thought you kicked me out for that boot pistol I hid in my sling. I don't reckon it'd do much good to say I forgot about it."

"Not a bit of good," Alma replied. "I'd have to say it's

a doggone good thing you hid that pistol in there, though."
She paused to study his face for a few seconds. "I don't
know what your line of work is." She gave a little chuckle.
"Nobody in town does. But do you have a lot of problems
like this one today?"

"Sometimes," he answered.

She waited for him to expound on that, but when he
didn't, she shrugged and started toward the kitchen. "Don't
forget to pick up your grown-up pistol on your way out."

Knowing he was short of most all supplies, his next
stop before heading for his cabin on the river was Thornton's General Merchandise. Ronald Thornton was behind
the counter when he went inside. "Hey-yo, Mr. McCabe,"
Thornton greeted him. "I thought I saw you ride by a little
while ago." Like everyone else, he asked about the arm
in the sling and Cullen told him it was a minor injury and
the doctor had advised him to wear the sling for a while.

When her husband failed to ask McCabe how he had
injured his arm and well aware of how badly he wanted
to know, Clara Thornton asked the question. "What happened to your arm?" She glanced at Ronald in time to
catch him wincing at her boldness. He and Leon Armstrong had built up a mysterious identity for the solemn
stranger because of his telegrams from the governor.

"It's not my arm. It's my shoulder," Cullen said.

"Bullet wound?" Clara asked, not to be denied.

"Yes, ma'am," Cullen answered, puzzled by her interest. He called off some items he needed as he could think
of them. Satisfied he hadn't forgotten anything, he paid
Thornton and carried his purchases out to his horses.

"I knew it!" Ronald exclaimed. "I gotta ask Leon if he got another telegram." He looked at his wife, who was shaking her head impatiently. "Bein' a woman, you can have the gall to ask a man like him if he's been shot. If I hadda asked him, he'da probably told me it was none of my business."

"You and Leon are two sick men," Clara charged. "Just because a man is quiet and doesn't talk about himself, you make up fairy tales about him. He isn't any different than most other men in town."

Outside, Sheriff Calvin Woods approached Cullen as he was tying on the supplies he had just bought. "Hello, McCabe. I just heard about the trouble at the hotel dinin' room. It looks to me like you ain't ever gonna be free of the Tice boys until you kill 'em all off."

"It does look that way, doesn't it?" McCabe answered. "I tried to talk him out of it, but he was determined he was gonna shoot me."

"I know, I just came from there. Everybody who saw it said you did everything you could to prevent it. Are you thinkin' I oughta go out to Tice's and arrest Joe?"

"No, I don't reckon," Cullen replied. "He was talkin' big when they first walked in the dinin' room, but he didn't have any stomach for finishin' what his brother started. I'm sorry I'm the bait for their foolishness and I'm gonna stay outta town, so I don't cause anybody else to get hurt."

"It's a damn shame that you're the one who has to keep outta town to prevent trouble, when it's Tice and his sons who are the cause of it all. You keep a sharp eye around you. I don't think Jesse Tice has sense enough to give it up."

CHAPTER TWO

Jesse Tice took a long pull out of the whiskey jug beside his rocking chair on the platform that served as his front porch. He had spent a good part of the day working on the jug of corn whiskey while Samson and Joe were following a small herd of horses that he had plans for, for tomorrow or the next day. He planned to convert that rancher's horses into more jugs of corn whiskey and supplies to last a few months. "Shut up!" he yelled when one of his two hounds suddenly started barking. He craned his neck to see what the dog was barking at and in a few minutes, the lone rider came into view at the edge of the creek. Jesse dropped his hand to the handle of the Colt Peacemaker he wore and waited to see who was calling. He didn't expect the boys back until the next morning. "Now, who the hell . . . ?" he murmured to himself, straining to identify the rider through eyes blurred by the cheap whiskey he drank. The rider continued on toward the cabin and now Jesse could see that he was leading another horse that figured to be a packhorse, for it appeared to be loaded with some form of packs.

It was not until the rider had reached the edge of the

yard that Jesse realized it was his son Joe. "Joe!" he called out. "What the hell are you doin' back here tonight? Where's your brother?" He pushed himself up out of the rocker to stand wavering on unsteady legs. Before Joe could answer, Jesse realized what Joe was hauling on the horse he was leading. "What happened?" he cried out, and charged off the porch, stumbling as he did to go down on his hands and knees on the ground. Joe jumped down from his horse to help his father up, but Jesse pushed him away and crawled up to Samson's horse. He reached up and grabbed the stirrup to help himself up, only to come face-to-face with his dead son and the black hole in his forehead that stared back at him like an evil eye. The shock of it almost caused him to fall backward, but Joe caught him by the elbow to steady him. "Who did it?" Jesse demanded, thinking at once that his sons had been caught around the rancher's horses. "I told you to scout the horses and we'd steal 'em at night."

"It weren't that rancher that shot Samson," Joe confessed. "We didn't go down the river like you said." Seeing the anger building up in his father's eyes, he sought to shift some of the blame. "It was Samson's idea. He said we didn't need to go scout them horses. We knew where they'd be and we could go get 'em anytime we was ready."

Even in his drunken state, Jesse was aware that Joe was avoiding the question. "Who shot him?" he demanded, suspicious of Joe's reluctance to come out with it.

"Cullen McCabe," Joe croaked, almost choking on the name. Prepared for his father's explosion of rage, he held his arm up to shield himself from the blows he knew were to descend upon him. Instead, he was stunned by the trancelike silence that suddenly overcame the angry old man, who was rapidly becoming sober by the minute.

"He's back again," Jesse stated. Then he turned his head away from the body lying across the saddle to fix his gaze on his remaining son. "Did you go to town?"

"Yes, sir," Joe said. "Samson still had a dollar and he wanted a drink of likker." Jesse continued to stare at him, waiting for more of an explanation, so Joe went on. "He said he didn't think you'd mind if we just had a couple of drinks, so we went to the River House."

"And that's where you ran into McCabe?" Jesse pressed.

Joe started to lie about it but feared that his father would find out the truth about the shooting. "No, sir, we ran into him in the hotel dinin' room."

"You said Samson didn't have but a dollar and he spent it in the saloon. What were you doin' in the hotel dinin' room?"

"I don't know," Joe replied. "We saw him go in there and he was wounded. He had one arm in a sling. We thought it'd be a good chance to kill him! Thought you'd be proud of us!"

"Is he dead?" Jesse asked. When Joe didn't answer right away, Jesse demanded, "Is Cullen McCabe dead?"

Joe did not want to tell his father that he had been struck helpless by the sudden execution of his brother. He wished now that he had been able to shoot McCabe in retaliation for Samson's death. He could not bring himself to tell Jesse that McCabe had been armed with nothing more than a vest-pocket gun and he wasn't sure if the weapon was a single-shot or not. All he would have had to do was raise his Colt and shoot him, but he had somehow been so cowered by the intimidating man that he couldn't act. "No, sir, he ain't dead. He had a gun hid in that sling he was wearin'. He pulled it out and shot Samson. I wasn't where I could help Samson," he lied.

From Joe's accounting of the shooting, Jesse couldn't get a clear picture of how it had actually happened. "You tellin' me you and Samson followed him into the dinin' room and McCabe just whipped out a pistol and shot Samson, without no reason a-tall?"

"No, sir, Samson had his gun out, but he didn't shoot it."

"Why the hell not?" Jesse bellowed. "There ain't nobody in this family who can pull a trigger on that devil, but I've took all I'm gonna take from him. We're goin' back into town right now and kill him."

"What about Samson?" Joe asked.

In his anger, Jesse had forgotten the body lying across the saddle. He sputtered briefly before he said, "We'll get him off that horse and tote him in the house. We can bury him when we get back. We need to take care of McCabe first."

After laying Samson's body in a corner of the front room in the cabin, Jesse climbed on Samson's horse and he and Joe headed back to Two Forks. The first stop they made was at the River House. The saloon was fairly busy when Jesse boldly pushed through the swinging doors and stood surveying the room, his hand resting on the handle of his Peacemaker. When he didn't see McCabe anywhere in the room, he walked over to the bar. Joe followed behind him. "Whaddle it be?" Toby Watson asked, his eyes shifting back and forth between Jesse and his son. Like everyone else in town, the bartender knew about the shooting at the dining room earlier that day. He also remembered that Joe and Samson had been in before that shooting. It was not hard to guess what Jesse Tice had on his mind right now.

"I'm lookin' for Cullen McCabe," Jesse replied.

"McCabe?" Toby asked. Again, like almost everyone in town, Toby didn't know much about the somber man who rode into town occasionally for supplies and sometimes a telegram. He was not a regular customer of the River House. "I ain't seen him in here today, but that ain't unusual."

Jesse turned to take another look around the saloon, not quite sure what to do now. "Come on," he said, finally deciding. "We'll go take a look up and down the street. He might be in one of the stores." He promptly headed for the door. When they got outside, Jesse said, "Keep an eye out for that big bay horse he rides." He had no way of knowing that Cullen's horse, Jake, had been killed and Cullen was now riding a dun.

Their search resulted in no success, since Cullen had long since left Two Forks to head for his cabin down the river. "Maybe he went back to the dinin' room," Jesse said. "There's still some people in there."

"I wouldn't hardly think he'd go back there after he done that shootin' in there," Joe was anxious to suggest. He was not keen in returning to the place where someone might give his pa a more complete picture of the incident than he had.

"Won't hurt to take a look," Jesse ordered. They walked up to the hotel and went around to the side and the outside entrance to the dining room. When they found the door locked, Jesse peered through the glass panes. "There's people still settin' at the tables, eatin'." He rapped hard on the locked door, but no one inside appeared to notice. So he rapped harder then, literally rattling the door.

Standing to one side of the door, Sheriff Calvin Woods stood talking to Porter Johnson, the owner of the Two Forks Kitchen. "Sounds like somebody's hungry," Porter said, and stepped over where he could see who was at the door. "Well, I'll be . . ." he marveled. "Speak of the devil, it's ol' Jesse Tice. What in the world is he doin' here?"

"I expect he's here about the same thing we're talkin' about," the sheriff said. Woods had come by to get the story of the shooting from Porter's perspective, but Porter was just in the process of telling the sheriff he wasn't there at the time it happened. "Let's see what he wants."

Porter unlocked the door and held it open. "Mr. Tice, ain't it?" Tice had never been a customer of the dining room as far as Porter knew. "The kitchen's closed for supper," he informed him.

"I didn't come here for supper," Tice replied. "I come lookin' for that no-account drifter that shot my boy Samson. Is he in here?"

"No, he ain't in here," Porter replied, "but the sheriff is. Maybe you'd wanna talk to him about what caused your son to get killed in here today, 'cause it sounds to me like you're lookin' for trouble."

"I don't need to talk to no damn sheriff," Tice responded. "Joe, here, was with Samson. He told me McCabe shot my boy down. If the sheriff was doin' his job, he'd already have McCabe in jail right now."

The sheriff stepped over beside Porter then. "Mr. Tice,

I don't believe you've got the straight story on what caused your son to lose his life. The fact of the matter is, I don't arrest people in this town for defending themselves. As far as me doin' my job, I didn't witness the shootin'. Neither did Mr. Johnson, so I had to check with the folks who actually saw what happened. Your boys decided they were gonna kill Cullen McCabe while he was already wounded and his handgun was layin' on the table here. Outright murder is what they planned. They walked in here with guns drawn and witnesses said Samson raised his pistol and aimed it at McCabe. But McCabe had a little boot pistol he carried in the sling on his arm and he got off a shot before Samson did. Now that's what happened. Is that the way you heard it?"

"That's exactly the way it happened," Alma Brown interrupted. Having seen the confrontation at the dining room door, she had moved close enough to hear the discussion.

Woods nodded toward Joe, standing behind his father. "Your other boy walked in with his gun drawn, too, but he never raised it or aimed it at anybody. And that's the reason he ain't in jail right now. McCabe said to let him go 'cause he didn't make a move on him." It was obvious by the expression on Tice's face that it was not the report he had gotten from his son. It did little to smother the flames of hatred he had fanned into a rage of vengeance for the damage McCabe had done to his family, however. When no words came to him at that moment, he stood, silently fuming, his fists clenched. Sheriff Woods made another appeal. "Mr. Tice, Cullen McCabe has made every effort to avoid trouble with you and your sons. It's best you just let this be the end of it while you still have your one son left."

"Hah!" Tice blurted. "You're awful worried about protectin' that killer, ain'tcha?"

Woods looked Tice in the eye and slowly shook his head. "I'm worried about you and Joe, there. Cullen McCabe ain't no man to mess around with. I'd think you had learned that by now. I'm sorry about your son. I'm hopin' you'll take my advice and let this feud you've worked up with McCabe end right here tonight. You're wastin' your time comin' to town lookin' for him. He doesn't hang around town, he keeps to himself. He only comes in town once in a while."

"Yeah, well, thank you for your advice," Tice sneered sarcastically. "Come on, Joe." He turned around and walked away from the door, back to the horses at the rail. When Joe came up beside him, Jesse struck him with a hard backhand on the side of his face, causing the boy to stagger backward a couple of steps. "You rotten weasel," he scorned. "You stood there and watched your brother die and you didn't shoot McCabe? What kind of yellow dog have I raised, who won't stand by his own brother? There ain't no Tice blood in your veins a-tall. I reckon you got nothin' but that sorry Simpson blood on your mother's side. I oughta knocked you in the head when I saw how much you looked like her family, same as I did with her. I reckon I'm stuck with you now. I ain't got nobody else to help me do what I gotta do and you'll be better'n nothin', but not much." He stuck his foot in the stirrup. "Get on your horse. There ain't nothin' else we can do here tonight," he said as he climbed up into the saddle. "You've got a grave to dig for your brother." He wheeled Samson's horse around and started out the north road.

His face still stinging, Joe wheeled his horse and followed, thinking of how different things would have been, had he only had the nerve to pull that trigger. He was also thinking of the many times his father had said he had taken after his mother's family, which to Jesse was the ultimate insult. But tonight was the first time his father had claimed to have knocked his mother in the head. He remembered the afternoon when his father had come from the stable carrying his mother in his arms. One of the horses had kicked her, Jesse said. He said he had warned her about getting behind that particular horse when he was in the stall. Joe was only thirteen years old, second youngest to Sonny, who was twelve. None of the brothers ever doubted their father's version of her death. But now, Joe believed that in his drunken rage, his father had blurted out the truth about that day in the stable. He realized that he could come to the same fate as his mother, especially now, when there was no one left to know if he was dead or alive. At best, he guessed his father still had uses for him, like digging Samson's grave. But he also got an idea that Jesse was going after McCabe and he needed his help with whatever he planned to do. He wanted to run away from Jesse and Two Forks as far as he could get, but he was afraid. He knew Jesse would come after him.

Jesse rode in silence all the way back home and Joe followed along the dark trail behind him, wondering how violent his father's mood might be when they got to their destination. When they reached the run-down cabin that served as the Tice homestead, Jesse appeared to be calm. "Take care of these horses," were the last words he spoke after leaving the hotel dining room. "Then get a shovel outta the barn and dig a grave for Samson over yonder beside Sonny's grave. Dig it nice and deep, like we did for Sonny. When you get done with it, we'll carry Samson out there and bury him."

"Yes, sir," Joe responded. "I'll dig him a deep one." He took the reins of the two horses and led them toward the barn to relieve them of their saddles before turning them out with the other few horses by the creek. Jesse went inside the cabin to see if there was any whiskey left in the jug he had been working on. Finding some left in it, he pulled a chair over a few feet from the corpse lying against the front wall and sat down to contemplate the loss of another son. This was where Joe found him a little over an hour later, slumped in the chair, the empty jug resting on the floor beside him, his finger still in the handle of the jug. The fire in the fireplace was little more than a few live coals, so he decided he'd better revive it, so that was the first thing he did. Then he turned to his father.

"Pa," Joe called softly. "I got the grave dug. You ready to bury Samson?" A drunken grunt was the only reply he got from his father. Thinking Jesse had told him to let him know when the grave was ready, Joe tried again with the same response. So he gave Jesse a couple of nudges on his shoulder, only to have him unconsciously fling his arm at him. Joe had seen his father in this state often enough to know he was out until morning when he would wake up with a head that felt three sizes bigger than normal. He turned to consider the body lying on the floor then, wondering how hard it was going to be to drag it out to the grave. *I shoulda left one of the horses saddled,* he thought. Lucky for him, Samson, like his two brothers and his father, was not a big man, so Joe figured he could drag him without help. Knowing he was going to be up all night, if he didn't get at it, he went to work stripping the body of everything he could use. The last to go were Samson's boots, which he decided he would trade for his and he was confident his father wouldn't know he had swapped them.

When he had stripped the body of everything that added weight, he took hold of Samson's ankles and started dragging him toward the door. Moving the body, already stiff, was much like dragging a heavy log as Joe grunted and strained to pull it across the porch. "Damn!" he swore as he pulled the body off the step and paused to take a breath before dragging it across the yard to the freshly dug hole in the ground. After a lengthy struggle with his late brother's remains, he arrived at the grave. He dragged Samson up parallel with the hole that now appeared to be just a little too short. He stood there, breathing heavily and sweating profusely in spite of the chilly night air, as he compared the difference between the length of the grave and the length of the body. After a moment's consideration, he shrugged, and rolled Samson's body over to drop into the grave. Unfortunately, due to the extra length of the body, his brother fell only halfway down before becoming wedged head and foot, his middle sagging only slightly.

"Damn," Joe swore again, and looked around for some large rocks to drop on the body, hopefully to drive him on down to the bottom. He could find only a few of any size at all, but he dropped them onto the body in hopes they would amass enough weight to do the job. When they failed to collapse the body, he had no alternative but to start shoveling dirt onto Samson. At first, he tried to land most of the dirt on the suspended body, hoping to add enough weight to force it on down. He soon found he was simply filling the hole around the body with a small portion filling under it. His objective soon changed to simply filling the hole over before his father saw it, regardless of how deep Samson was buried. Nearing exhaustion, Joe went back to the cabin to try to salvage a little sleep from what was left of the night. His father appeared not to have moved from the position he had found him in before, the only difference, a gravel-throated snore. Joe built up the fire again and crawled into his bedroll.

"Get up!" Jesse Tice blared, and gave the sleeping body a sharp couple of kicks with his boot. "We got things to do. You can't lay around here sleepin' all day!"

Joe crawled out of his bedroll, trying to blink some light into his eyes, but it was still dark inside the cabin. Feeling as if he had just crawled into his bedroll, he asked, "What time is it?"

"It's time you got your lazy hide outta that blanket and got up. That's what time it is."

"Whadda we gettin' up so early for?" Joe asked.

"We're goin' huntin'," Jesse answered. "And we ain't comin' back till we get Cullen McCabe's head on a stake. We're gonna track him down just like we track down a coyote."

This was not what Joe wanted to hear from his father. Although he knew it was futile, he had hoped nevertheless that Jesse had finally given up his feud with McCabe and realized it would bring only more death to what was left of his family. Now, it appeared, if anything, Jesse's craze for revenge was stronger than before. "We gonna go back to hangin' around Two Forks to try to catch him when he comes to town?"

"No, we ain't," Jesse replied. "You heard what that chicken-livered sheriff said. McCabe don't come to town 'less he just has to. But he must have a place that's close enough to go to town and go back home without havin' to camp overnight. He's southeast of Two Forks, if he's somewhere on the river. Has to be, 'cause our place is northwest of Two Forks and we've rode every inch of that land between here and Austin and we ain't never run across his cabin. We need to hunt southeast of Two Forks and we need to get ready to be out a few days. So, we need to take a packhorse and enough chuck to feed us for a while."

"Yes, sir," Joe said, obediently, and left at once to do his father's bidding.

CHAPTER THREE

It had been two days since Cullen's confrontation with Jesse Tice's two sons in the dining room in the hotel. He thought about the useless feud between himself and the Tices. Already, it had resulted in the deaths of two of Tice's sons and he was feeling the helpless frustration of having the role of executioner forced upon him. There was no doubt in his mind that the world, or at least this part of Texas, would be a better place without Jesse Tice and his sons. But he did not appreciate the fact that, somehow, he had been picked to exterminate them. With every confrontation, he had made every effort to spare Tice and his sons. But the evil old man seemed determined to sacrifice his sons and himself in his quest to kill him. "It's just bad luck," he muttered to the dun gelding watching him as he knelt beside the creek on this chilly and windy day, washing the cloth that had served as the sling for his wounded shoulder. He had decided he could manage without the sling now, although the wound itself was still tender. He glanced up at the horse he had named Orphan. "I expect my shoulder is gonna have to heal up completely before it doesn't always remind me of Jake. Ain't your fault, but

Jake was a damn good horse and the fellow that put a bullet in my shoulder put Jake down for good." Orphan looked at him as if he almost understood. Then he suddenly jerked to the side when a strip of dirt was ripped from the ground between them.

Both man and horse reacted immediately, almost before the sound of the shot that struck the bank of the creek between them rang out. Cullen scrambled away from the water's edge to take cover behind the creek bank, while his horse bolted across the creek to the other side. The first order of business was to try to find out where the shot had come from. So he crawled along behind the short creek bank until he reached an oak with a double trunk that allowed him to raise up high enough to take a look. Judging by the angle of the strip of dirt taken out by the bullet, he figured that the shooter must be somewhere on a low ridge some fifty yards away. He could only guess who and how many he might be dealing with and what their motive was for attacking him. The first thought that came to mind, however, was Jesse Tice and the bad news that the revenge-driven old man had succeeded in finding his cabin.

"Damn wind! We shoulda got closer," Jesse complained when his shot had missed. "I couldn't see enough of him because of that bank." To get any closer, however, they would have had to cross a wide treeless flat stretch between the ridge and the heavy growth of trees along the creek. Their spotting of the cabin sitting among the trees was accidental. Had it not been for the wind gust that suddenly swept across the tree branches to create a window that revealed a corner of the cabin, they might not have seen it at all.

"How do we know that's McCabe over yonder?" Joe felt compelled to ask. As his father had just said, they were able to see only part of a man squatting beside the creek. It could have been anyone.

"I know it's him," Jesse insisted. "Ain't nobody else."

"What if we kill him, then find out it ain't McCabe?" Joe was still concerned.

"Then it'll just be some dumb sodbuster's bad luck to be in the wrong place at the wrong time," Jesse answered him impatiently. "And maybe he's got somethin' we can use. So, shoot him first and then we'll worry about the rest." He strained in an effort to see any movement in the trees on the creekbank. "I expect we'd best move away from this spot before he figures out where we are."

While Jesse and his son moved to another location on the ridge, Cullen made his way back toward his cabin, still using the low bank for cover. He wanted to get his rifle from the cabin, if he was going to play hide-and-seek with Jesse and Joe. So, when he crawled up the creek opposite the door of his cabin, he braced himself to make a run for the cabin door, not sure if his progress had been followed. *One way to find out,* he thought as he pushed away from the bank and ran across the shallow creek. Bullets were flying as soon as he broke cover, the shots snapping as they passed close beside him. He ran in the front door and slammed it shut behind him. The shots continued to hammer the log walls of his cabin as both father and son tried to shoot the structure to pieces. Cullen wasted little time in pulling his rifle from his saddle and checking to see that he had a full magazine. Satisfied, he went into the kitchen and squeezed through the small back window. Dropping to the ground, he hurried into the trees behind the cabin. He had no intentions of holing up inside while they continued to pepper the cabin with gunshots. He much preferred to move around outside in an attempt to find his attackers.

"He's built himself a pretty stout cabin," Joe commented. "It's gonna take a whole lot more cartridges to run him outta there."

"We may have to burn him outta there," Jesse said, and pointed to a fire Cullen had built in the front yard. "Right now, we need to run across that open area while he's in the cabin. We get in them trees and we can work right in close enough to shoot that cabin to pieces. Come on," he ordered, and they started out across the grassy slope, leaving the horses on the back side of the ridge.

Taking cover in the trees, they threw a few more shots at the door and windows of the cabin but soon saw that Joe's assessment of the cabin was accurate. It was a well-built cabin. So Jesse's plan to burn McCabe out appeared to be their best bet. "We can set a little fire on two corners of that cabin," he said. "You gather up some of these dead limbs and sticks and anything that'll burn easy. Make two piles under the back corners of the cabin. I'll keep throwin' enough bullets up against that cabin, so he won't be comin' outta there while you're doin' it. There ain't no windows on the sides, so he can't see what you're doin'. When you're ready, I'll start plunkin' away at that cabin while you pull some of them burnin' logs off his fire and stick 'em under the dead limbs. When we get that cabin to smokin' real good, he's gonna have to come out." Joe wasn't convinced that he could start a big enough fire to actually set the cabin to blaze. But at this point, he was afraid to argue the point, so he did as he was told.

After gaining the cover of the trees behind his cabin, Cullen moved quickly upstream until he could safely cross over the creek and start to work his way back down to a spot about thirty yards above the cabin. Soon, he spotted a couple of muzzle flashes from the trees in front of the cabin. He pulled the Winchester up to his shoulder and brought the front sight down on the spot where he saw the flashes. About to squeeze the trigger, he paused when a figure ran out of the trees, carrying a double armload of sticks, limbs, and what looked like dead brush. Cullen recognized the figure as Joe Tice. He was not surprised, but still reluctant to shoot him down, he decided to wait to see what Joe was going to do. While he watched, Joe disappeared behind the cabin, only to reappear at the right-rear corner. He proceeded to drop his armload of dead sticks, then stuff them under the corner. *He's gonna try to set my cabin on fire,* Cullen thought as Joe returned to the trees to gather up another load of tinder for his fire. Meanwhile Jesse kept a slow but continuous rain of gunfire on the cabin. *To make sure I stay inside,* Cullen thought.

When that was done, Joe went back into the trees for a minute or two, *probably to consult with his papa,* Cullen thought. When Joe came back out, he went to the fire still burning strong in the front yard and pulled a sizable piece of a burning log from it. Cullen watched as Joe went to the left-rear corner and inserted the burning wood into the kindling he had piled there. A feeling of sheer disgust came over Cullen as he watched, knowing he had no choice now. He had made every effort to keep from killing Jesse Tice and his sons, but they would not stop coming after him. The time had come to rid the earth of the Tice curse. Joe was getting to his feet when Cullen's bullet struck him in the chest. He went over backward to lie dead on the ground.

In the trees across the creek from the front of the cabin, Jesse Tice rose from his kneeling position, staring in shock from the sight of the killing of his last son. Instead of anguish and sorrow, his brain was filled with anger at his son for failing to carry out the job he had been given to do without getting shot. McCabe had gotten out of the cabin, that much was clear. *Joe should have allowed for that possibility,* he thought, even though he, himself, had been sure McCabe was holed up inside. It was Joe's fault. He ran around behind the cabin to set the fires up. He should have noticed if there was a back door or window. *I'd best get myself away from this spot,* he thought at once when it struck him that McCabe had no doubt seen his muzzle flashes. He, on the other hand, didn't know where McCabe was because he was looking at Joe when he was hit. That thought caused an instant panic and he backed quickly away into the trees, realizing that it was now a stalk-and-kill contest between the two of them. *It's what I wanted,* he told himself in an effort to bolster his courage. *Now I'll kill the murdering dog!* In his haste to retreat, he stumbled over a log as he backed away and wound up on the seat of his pants in the branches of a small berry bush.

A couple dozen yards away, Cullen paused to listen when he heard the thrashing in the bushes between the trees. It was enough to give him a general idea where Tice was. He knew the bushes were thickest almost directly in line with his front door, so he cranked a series of three quick shots into the midst of them. When there was no answering fire, he yelled out, "Tice! You've forced me to kill the last of your sons. You ready to call that enough bloodshed? Let that be the end of it. I don't wanna have to kill you, too, but I will if you keep this up."

"You murderin' devil!" Tice shouted back. "I'll say it's over when you meet me face-to-face to see who's right and who's wrong."

"All right, if that's the only way you'll have it," Cullen answered, although he was not convinced that Tice really wanted to settle with him face-to-face in a duel.

"That's the way I want it," Tice yelled back while trying to untangle himself from the berry bushes. "Man-to-man, face-to-face, in a fair fight. But how do I know I can trust you to fight fair?"

"You don't," Cullen called back, "any more than I can trust you. So you just tell me how you wanna do this and we'll see who's still standin' when we're done."

"I'll count to three," Tice yelled. "On three, we'll both step outta these trees and face each other on the open bank, guns still in the holsters. Agreed?"

"Agreed," Cullen replied. He had a pretty good idea then where Tice was after hearing him suggest the rules. "Whenever you're ready."

"All right," Tice said. "Guns in the holster."

"My six-gun's in my holster," Cullen reported.

Tice began the count. At the count of three, Cullen left the tree he was hiding behind and took a knee, his rifle aimed at the general spot where he had decided Tice to be. Tice came out at the same time, his six-gun in hand. He managed to get off one wild shot before Cullen cut him down with a round in his gut. His pistol dropped from his hand to fall on the bank before bouncing into the water's edge. With both hands gripping his stomach, Tice sank slowly to the ground when Cullen walked up to him. "I'm gut-shot, you cheatin' devil," Tice moaned mournfully, his face twisting with each agonizing thrust of pain. "You weren't supposed to use a rifle."

"I figured it'd be more accurate than my six-gun at that range," Cullen replied. "And I figured you'd come outta there shootin'."

Tice grimaced with the pain that was like a flame in his gut, then managed to say, "You've kilt my whole family now. I hope you're satisfied."

"All I ever wanted from you and your family was to leave me alone. Why in hell could you not do that?"

"I'll see you in hell," Jesse swore.

"When you do, I'd appreciate it if you'd pretend you don't know me," Cullen said, and walked around behind him. He was thinking he was glad he had already cranked a fresh round into the chamber of the Winchester, so Tice wouldn't hear him cock the rifle. He hesitated only a moment before pulling the trigger that sent Tice on his way to hell, but he didn't like to see any animal suffer the painful death that was to be Tice's, had he not. He felt some regret about Tice's son Joe, however. It was his opinion that Joe might have been salvaged if he could have separated himself from his father and brothers. He told himself that he had rid the community of a cancer called Jesse Tice and his sons, but he didn't feel very good about the way it had to be done. "Well, it is the way it is," he announced to the corpse lying at his feet. "And now, there's the job of cleanin' up the mess it left."

First, he had to find their horses and the obvious place to begin would be the ridge across the open area. Not bothering with a saddle, he put the bridle on Orphan and rode across the grass plain to the low ridge. Riding up on top, he saw the horses tied on the other side. He led them back to his cabin and used them to carry the bodies of their owners off a good distance from the cabin to deposit them near the foot of the same low ridge. He left father and son to the buzzards, thinking they should perform at least one helpful act on this earth.

When he had removed the bodies, he took inventory of anything of value he found on them, as well as anything they carried on the packhorse. There wasn't much he had any use for except .44 cartridges and weapons. The three horses were in fairly good shape and were worth something, so he figured to sell them to Jim Tilly, who owned the stable in Two Forks. If he didn't want them, he could always sell them to Burnett in Austin. He'd prefer not to have to drive the horses to Austin, however, so he intended to offer them to Tilly at a price he couldn't refuse.

He was in the process of putting out the small blaze Joe Tice had succeeded in creating under one corner of his cabin when he decided it might be best to inform Sheriff Woods about the events that had just taken place. He might suggest to Woods that it could be worth his while to ride out to Jesse Tice's place in the event that Tice had horses corralled there. Cullen was not interested in acquiring any more horses, but he didn't like the thought of the horses left penned up to die. If the sheriff was not interested, Cullen was sure that Jim Tilly would be. *Might as well go ahead and ride into Two Forks,* he thought as he took a look at the heavy logs at the back-left corner of his cabin. "It woulda took a helluva lot bigger fire than this to set those logs on fire," he commented. "It's almost suppertime now, so I'll wait and go in the mornin'," he decided aloud.

As was his usual practice, he locked his log cabin up tight after putting the few weapons and extra ammunition in a cache he had built into the ground a couple hundred feet downstream. Although he had wired the governor that he was taking a week to recover from his wounds, he packed his packhorse like he always did when he was going on an assignment. That way, he was always ready to head north to Austin without having to return home for his packhorse. He decided to make the stable his first stop in case the sheriff might get the idea that Tice's horses should be turned over to him. So he rode up the middle of the street to Jim Tilly's stable, leading Tice's three horses on a rope behind his packhorse. He knew who Jim Tilly was, but he had never had occasion to do any business with him. Of course, Tilly knew who Cullen was. In a town the size of Two Forks, it's difficult to kill two men and go unnoticed.

"Well, Mr. McCabe, ain't it?" Tilly said when Cullen pulled up in front of the stable. He took a glance at the string of horses. "What can I do for you?"

"Mr. Tilly," Cullen responded. "I've got three horses I don't need and I thought I'd see if you're in the horse-buyin' business."

Tilly took another look at the horses. "I do buy and sell horses now and then. I ain't really been lookin' for any stock lately. Those three behind your packhorse?"

"That's right," Cullen replied. "The saddles go with 'em. The one without a saddle had a packsaddle on him, but it was better'n mine, so I kept it." Tilly shook his head, looking like he wasn't really interested, so before he could say as much, Cullen said, "Sixty dollars will buy the three of 'em."

That had the desired effect upon Jim Tilly. "Sixty dollars for all three? Saddles, too?" Cullen nodded. "Are they stolen?" Tilly asked. "Are the two previous owners likely to come in here lookin' for 'em?"

"That ain't very likely," Cullen answered. "Are you interested?"

"Lemme take a closer look," Tilly said, and promptly gave the three horses a good inspection, looking for the reason for the low asking price. After he had finished and could find no serious defect, he said, "Hell, the saddles are worth that much."

"That's what I figure," Cullen said.

"I'll be right back," Tilly said, and hurried inside the stable. In a short minute, he was back with sixty dollars cash and he and Cullen shook on it to close the deal. Cullen stuck the money in a pocket of his vest and turned to leave. "If you come up with any more you wanna sell, I'm always interested," Tilly called after him, and Cullen acknowledged with a wave of his hand. Like most of the folks in Two Forks, Tilly knew nothing at all about the big, quiet man before this morning's transaction. If anything, he was more a mystery afterward.

Cullen's next stop was the sheriff's office, where he found Woods about to lock his office door in preparation to go to the hotel dining room for breakfast. "Howdy, McCabe. What brings you into town? I thought you said you were plannin' to stay away for a while, so you wouldn't run into the Tice boys."

"Ain't no need to anymore," Cullen said, "and that's what I came to tell you. Figured you oughta know. Jesse and his boy Joe finally found my cabin yesterday. I didn't have much choice, either shoot them, or let them shoot me. So I picked my first choice. I brought you their guns and rifles and belts and such. I didn't fire the first shots, but when they tried to set my cabin on fire, I had to put a stop to it. If you wanna see the bodies, I can show you where they are."

"I ain't got no reason to see their bodies," Woods replied. "I ain't got no reason to doubt your word. Tell you the truth, I figured it was just a matter of time before ol' Tice got hisself killed, if he kept comin' after you." He shrugged. "Hell, it ain't nothin' to me, anyway, I'm just responsible for what happens in town. How 'bout some breakfast?" he asked, changing the subject abruptly. "That's where I was just fixin' to go when you came up."

"Sounds like a good idea to me," Cullen replied. He walked out with Woods and waited while the sheriff closed the padlock on his office door. Cullen led Orphan and the packhorse as he walked beside Woods. "You know, you might wanna ride out to Tice's place to take a look around. Most likely, he's got some more horses there and they might be in a corral."

"Like I said, I'm responsible for what goes on inside the city limits," Woods informed him. "I don't care what he's got out there on his place. I'm just glad I'm not gonna have him to worry about anymore."

It was obvious to Cullen that Woods was blatantly truthful about his lack of concern for what happened to Jesse Tice, or anything he might have owned. So Cullen felt pretty confident that Jim Tilly would be more than willing to go out to Tice's cabin to check on any horses he might have left uncared for. The subject was dropped long before they reached the Two Forks Kitchen, next to the hotel.

"Mornin', Sheriff," Alma Brown greeted them. "I see you brought somebody with you for breakfast," she joked. "Is he a prisoner?" She laughed at her joke, then said, "Mornin', McCabe, didn't expect to see you back in town so soon."

"Didn't expect it, myself," Cullen said as he unbuckled his gun belt and placed it on the table placed there for that purpose.

Alma couldn't resist japing him. "It's a good thing you haven't got that sling on this morning 'cause I was ready to search it, if you did." She looked at Woods and laughed. "Maybe I oughta have a table ready for the Tice boys, too."

"I wouldn't think that will be any problem this mornin'," Woods told her. "Now, how 'bout some coffee?"

"You want your usual?" Alma asked Woods. When he said he did, she turned her attention to Cullen. "How 'bout you, McCabe? What do you want for breakfast?"

"I don't get eggs very often. I think I'd like about four of 'em, scrambled up with some sausage, if you've got any, and some potatoes—biscuits, with some honey, if you've got any of that."

"Looks like you brought an appetite fittin' for a man your size," Alma remarked.

"I'm not always sure when I'll get another breakfast like that, so when I get the chance, I always make sure I don't pass up the opportunity," he said.

Alma left to tell Gracie what to fix and to get their coffee. She was sharp enough to know that something had happened by their very attitude this morning. McCabe was as silent as a stone statue, but she knew she could get it out of the sheriff when she caught him alone. That opportunity came quicker than she expected in the form of Jimmy Armstrong, Leon's young son. In the midst of their breakfast, Jimmy came in the door and headed straight for Cullen and the sheriff. "Mr. McCabe, Papa saw you ride by this mornin'. He said to bring you this telegram. Said it might be important."

"Thank you, son," Cullen said, and dug into his pocket for a coin for the boy when he took the telegram. "If I need to send a reply, I'll come by when I'm done eatin' breakfast. Tell your pa that."

"Yes, sir," Jimmy replied, "and thank you, sir." He ran back out the door. Woods stopped eating and along with Alma, who came to stand over the table, waited anxiously for Cullen to open the wire and read it.

Aware of their curiosity, Cullen said to Alma, "I could use a little more of that coffee." He folded the telegram and put it in his inside vest pocket. Both Alma and Woods looked disappointed. "Just some business to take care of, most likely," he said, and continued eating his breakfast. Curious himself, but not to the point where he would interrupt a breakfast as good as the one he was presently enjoying, he cleaned his plate, drained the last gulp of coffee from his cup, and took his leave. After he paid for his meal, he was standing at the weapons table, buckling on his gun belt when Alma made one last attempt to feed her curiosity.

"Don't forget to read your telegram," she reminded him. "It might be something important."

"Right," Cullen replied. "Thanks for remindin' me."

He settled his hat squarely on his head and went out the door. He wasn't certain, but he thought he heard a definitely unladylike word uttered after the door had closed behind him.

Outside, he stepped up into the saddle and headed Orphan in the direction of the railroad station. He pulled the dun gelding to a halt just short of the telegraph office to read his telegram. It was from the only place he ever got telegrams, the governor's office in Austin. It read:

RECEIVED YOUR WIRE OF 5/22 STOP
UNDERSTAND YOUR NEED TO HEAL
WOUNDS STOP URGENT NEED FOR YOUR
SERVICES IF AT ALL POSSIBLE STOP

It was from Michael O'Brien and requested a reply.

"Well, that's the reason I always bring my packhorse," he said to the telegram in his hand, and nudged Orphan to start again.

"Hope Jimmy didn't interrupt your breakfast," Leon Armstrong said in way of greeting when Cullen walked in the telegraph office. "But I thought you might want that telegram right away. I'm thinkin' it was sure good luck you were in town today."

"Reckon so," Cullen said. "It said he wants a reply, so here it is. I'm on my way. Be in your office in a couple of days."

When he left the telegraph office, he went to Thornton's store to replenish his supplies and load them on his packhorse. Then he had one last stop on his way out of town. He saw Jim Tilly out by the corral, so he rode up beside him. "I might be able to point you toward a better deal than the one for those three horses," he said to Tilly.

"Yeah? How's that?" Tilly replied, interested at once.

So Cullen told him that odds were pretty favorable that there might be horses abandoned out at Jesse Tice's place. And they would be there for the first person to come along and claim them. "I already told Sheriff Woods about the horses and he said he wasn't interested in 'em. So there won't be any problem in claimin' 'em."

"Ain't Tice likely to object?" Tilly asked, although he suspected something had happened to Jesse Tice.

"Reckon not," Cullen replied. "Tice and his son ain't there no more." He wheeled the dun and left Tilly to wonder.

CHAPTER FOUR

Cullen arrived in Austin in time to catch the man he knew only as Burnett before he closed his stable for the night. "You're ridin' a different horse this time," Burnett commented. So Cullen told him about his bad luck to have had Jake killed. "Well, this 'un looks like a pretty stout replacement," Burnett said.

"Yeah, he'll do," Cullen allowed, "but it's still too early to tell for sure. He's got a lot to live up to."

"You et your supper yet?" Burnett inquired.

"Nope, I figured I'd go pay a visit to the Pot Luck Restaurant and see what Rose Bettis is servin' for supper."

"Good idea. I'll go with you, soon as we take care of your horses," Burnett said. "You gonna sleep with your horses this time?" Cullen said that he was, so Burnett helped him unload his horses and pile his saddle and supplies in a corner of the stall. When they were finished, Burnett locked up the stable and they walked up the street to the little eating establishment next to the hardware store. When they walked in, Rose Bettis remembered Cullen, as most people did.

"Well, look who's back in town," Rose greeted him. "I remember you were in here before, but I can't recollect your name. I thought maybe you found a better place to eat."

"Cullen McCabe," he said. "No, ma'am, I ain't ever found any food to beat yours. This is just the first time I've been back to Austin in a while."

"Well, welcome back. You got back on pork chop night. I hope you like pork chops."

"I reckon I hit you just right, then," Cullen replied. "I like pork chops." Rose piled two plates high with food and topped off their coffee. Then, since they were the last two customers to come in, she sat down with them and had a cup of coffee, herself. Curious about the big quiet man who came into her kitchen only once in a while, she asked, "What brings you into town tonight?"

"I figured this would be the best place to get some pork chops," Cullen replied, his face so expressionless that she almost believed him.

"Ask a foolish question, get a foolish answer," she responded. "Right, Burnett?" Burnett shrugged. He had no idea what Cullen's business in Austin was, Cullen had never volunteered the information. Burnett had prudently avoided asking the stoic-looking man any personal questions at all.

Realizing that Rose was uncomfortable with the thought that she might have asked something that he considered nobody's business, Cullen formed a smile and said, "I'm just passin' through on my way back from visitin' some friends. Going back to my place down below Two Forks." When he and Burnett finished supper, he said, "I expect I'll be here for breakfast in the mornin' before I head out."

* * *

As he had said, he was there again the next morning for breakfast after he had saddled Orphan and loaded his packhorse. Burnett didn't accompany him, saying that he never ate much breakfast. He would just make some coffee and that would do for him. Cullen took his time eating breakfast, knowing Michael O'Brien wouldn't be in his office until eight. So, after he had drained his cup for the last time, he rode on over to the governor's office to make Benny Thacker nervous while he waited for O'Brien to appear.

As usual, Cullen McCabe arrived about thirty minutes before Michael O'Brien arrived at his office. Benny had to be at the office before O'Brien got there because O'Brien wanted coffee ready when he walked in. This was in spite of the fact that he always came directly from the Capitol Diner after just having eaten breakfast. Ordinarily, this was of no concern to Benny, but he knew that Cullen McCabe had wired that he would be there, and he always arrived before it was time to go to work. Although he had never given him reason to fear him, Benny was nevertheless uncomfortable when he was alone with McCabe, for even a short time. The governor's special agent was so big and looked so deadly powerful that the frail clerk feared McCabe might suddenly revert back to his caveman ancestry and maul him, just to entertain himself. "Mr. O'Brien should be here at eight," Benny forced himself to say. "Shall I fix you a cup of coffee while you wait?"

"No, thanks," Cullen replied. "I think I musta drank a barrel of coffee over at Pot Luck." Benny looked at once relieved. "You just go on about your business. Don't pay any attention to me," Cullen said.

When O'Brien got there about fifteen minutes earlier than usual, Benny ran to meet him at the door. "Mr. McCabe is waiting for you, sir. I offered him coffee, but he didn't want any."

"Mr. McCabe!" O'Brien exclaimed, ignoring Benny's remarks. "Good to see you, man. Governor Hubbard was really pleased with your last assignment. Is the governor in yet?" He aimed that question at Benny and Benny shook his head rapidly. "Well, he shouldn't be long," O'Brien continued. "We got your wire about taking some time to heal some wounds. I hope it's not asking too much to bring you in right now." He paused to give him a smile. "You look like you're in pretty good shape."

"It's really only the one wound in my shoulder," Cullen said, "but it seems to be healin' up all right."

"Good, good," O'Brien responded. "Let's go on in the office and I'll get you started on this next job." Again looking at Benny. "Bring us in some coffee. Did you offer McCabe any?"

"He did," Cullen said. "I don't want any more."

"All right. It'll just be one for me, Benny, and you can get the governor's when you see him." He walked over to his office door and held it open for Cullen. Inside, they took seats at a conference table and O'Brien asked, "You know where Reid's Mill is?"

"Can't say as I do," Cullen replied.

"It's about one hundred and twenty miles due north of Austin," O'Brien said, "about twenty-five miles northwest of Waco. I didn't know where it was, myself, before we got a letter asking for help. A fellow by the name of Lucien

Reid built a flour mill up there on the Bosque River. That's who the town is named for and he's the one we got the letter from. A couple of years ago a community of religious folks from somewhere in Louisiana journeyed west into Texas and they settled on the Bosque River where Reid built his mill. There was plenty of open land for their farms and their cattle, and they've built up a good-sized little town. Reid said in his letter that everything was pointing to their success. But they've got some trouble now and think the state should help. We don't know much more than what I've just told you, but the governor thinks you oughta ride up there and find out what the trouble is. You know, they're a churchgoing community and Governor Hubbard wants to help them out."

"So, you just want me to find out what their problem is and report back to you?" Cullen asked.

"Basically, yes," O'Brien hesitated, "but I'm gonna bet the governor expects the same thing from you as you have done on every assignment so far. When you identify the problem, if you can fix it yourself, then do what you have to do." He hesitated again. "Inside the law, of course, just like you always have. You've shown discretion in the past, so the governor trusts you will continue to do so."

"I understand," Cullen said. "I'll see what I can do."

"Good. I know we can depend on you. I've got some names of the town council who all signed off on the letter. Might be handy to know them when you get to town." He handed Cullen the list of names. The governor hurried in the door just as Cullen started toward it.

"McCabe!" Governor Hubbard exclaimed. "I'm sorry I'm running late this morning. I had a breakfast meeting that ran a little longer than it should have. Did Michael bring you up to date on why we called you in?"

"Yes, sir, I think he did," Cullen replied, then stood patiently while the governor did a quick summary of what O'Brien had told him.

"Good, good," Hubbard said when Cullen assured him he understood his mission. "These jobs you're handling for me are saving the state from spreading the Rangers so thin they can't effectively cover everything. How soon can you get started to Reid's Mill?"

"Well, I was on my way when you walked in the door," Cullen answered.

"Then I'll get out of your way," Hubbard chuckled, and held the door for him. "Good hunting. Hope to hear from you soon."

Out in the reception area, Cullen went to the large state map on the wall to look for Reid's Mill. O'Brien came up behind him to help out. "Reid's Mill isn't on the map yet, but you'll find it right about here." He put his finger on a spot south of a town called Clifton, right on the Bosque River. "At least, that's where it's supposed to be. That river runs right down the middle of Bosque County."

"That river's not very far west of the Brazos," Cullen remarked.

"That's right," O'Brien said. "Matter of fact, the Brazos forms the eastern boundary of the county."

Studying the map, Cullen observed, "Like you said, looks like I could head straight north to strike this place. Might be a little bit farther, but it might be easier, though, to head up to Waco, then cut over to the northwest to strike Reid's Mill. Looks like the Bosque River empties into the Brazos at Waco. I could just follow the Bosque back till I come to Reid's Mill." He felt some doubt that there was a trail leading from Austin directly north to Reid's Mill. So he figured it might even be quicker to go by way of Waco, instead of relying on following his nose across unknown territory. With that decided, he said, "Much obliged," and took his leave, acknowledging Benny with a nod of his head as he went out the door.

As was his usual custom, he went at once to the bank on the corner to pick up his expense money for the trip. Then he set out on the well-traveled road to Waco, figuring to make that part of the trip in two days. As he rode through the outskirts of Austin, his head was full of thoughts and speculation about what might be waiting for him in a little town he had never heard of, on a river he'd never heard of, in a county he'd never heard of.

He met an occasional wagon on its way into Austin when the morning was still early, but by the time he thought his horses needed to rest, he had the road all to himself. As a matter of habit, he pulled off the road when he came to a small creek and followed it upstream for about fifty yards before he released his horses to drink and rest. When they were ready again, he started out, heading for a spot about twenty miles farther where he intended to camp for the night. By the time he reached that spot, which was a popular camping ground where the road crossed the Lampasas River, his stomach was reminding him that he had not eaten since breakfast. So after his horses were taken care of, he had a healthy fire going and got water for his coffee. He was happy to find there were no other campers on this particular night as he sat watching his horses grazing down near the water's edge. He found himself thinking longingly of Rose Bettis's pork chops as he turned his bacon over in the frying pan and dropped some hardtack in with it to cook in the grease. *Mary Kate was a fine cook*. The thought caught him by surprise, for he had made it a point not to think about his late wife, nor Lucy, Cullen junior, or William, who was only five when Cullen's family was taken away from him. He had forced himself to push memories of his family back into a locked vault in his brain, for he had realized there was no relief from the pain of their loss. It had taken almost six months to track down every one of the five men who murdered his family and burned his house. But their deaths had brought no peace and he soon learned that he could not escape certain insanity if he did not let his family go. So he directed his thoughts back to the bacon and hardtack in his frying pan and shifted his concern to the question of whether or not Orphan was going to prove to be a satisfactory replacement for Jake. Any other thoughts belonged to another world in which he didn't exist.

He was awake early the next morning and on his way again. Orphan seemed to be aware that he was still being evaluated, so he showed a spirited attitude as he responded to Cullen's commands. There was one more stop to rest his horses before reaching Waco that evening. Not sure what the next few days were going to offer, he decided to put his horses in a stable for the night. He had put Jake up in a stable near the south side of town once before when he had ridden through on a trip to Fort Worth. It was close to a small hotel called the Smith House and he re-membered that the dining room served a good supper, as best as he could remember. So he figured that was his best bet tonight. The horses could use some grain and he could use a good meal, himself.

Pete Hargett remembered the imposing stranger of few words, even if he couldn't recall his name. "Evenin'," he said. "Ain't seen you in a while. What brings you back to Waco?" He was scratching his chin, trying to recall the first visit.

"I'm just passin' through on my way to a town called Reid's Mill," Cullen said. "I never been there before. You ever hear of it?" He paused, then said, "My name's Cullen McCabe. I'd like to leave my horses with you tonight."

"Pete Hargett," he replied. "I've heard tell of a little community called Reid's Mill, but I couldn't tell you much about it. I don't know if it's a real town or not. It ain't supposed to be very far from Waco, but I've never been there."

"Well, I'm gonna head up that way in the mornin'," Cullen declared, "providin' I can find the Bosque River."

Pete laughed. "Well, I can tell you where to find the Bosque."

"Good. Does that little woman still have that dinin' room in the Smith House?"

"Violet? Sure does. She's still goin' strong. She oughta be servin' supper right now."

"I reckon that's all I need, then," Cullen decided. "If you'd give both my horses a portion of grain, I'd appreciate it. Last time I was here, I slept in the stall with my horses. Is that still all right with you?"

"That's fine by me," Hargett declared, "but I'll lock up in a couple of hours from now. So if you're thinkin' about visitin' the Reservation after supper, you'd best make it quick."

Cullen had to pause, confused, but then he remembered

Waco had a lively *red-light* district and it was called the Reservation. "Nope, that won't be a problem. I'll be back here as soon as I finish up supper." That settled, Hargett helped him unload his packhorse and pile it with his saddle in a corner of a stall. He told him that while Cullen was eating supper he would put some fresh hay in the stall to give him a more comfortable bed.

The Smith House looked a little more run-down than he had remembered it, which gave him pause about eating in the dining room. But Hargett said Violet Buckley was still going strong, so he decided he'd take a chance. When he stepped inside the door, he couldn't help but notice the room looked spotlessly clean. There were only a few people seated at the long table in the middle of the room and they all stopped eating to gawk at the imposing figure seeming to fill the doorway. Cullen thought at once of the Pot Luck Restaurant in Austin, for this was a one-woman operation also. He must have lingered a few long moments, looking the room over because the scrawny little gray-haired woman standing behind a short counter asked, "You wantin' to eat, or did you just come by to count the customers?"

"I thought I might have some supper," Cullen replied. "What are you servin' tonight?"

"Beef stew with baked potato and biscuits," she replied rather curtly. "Will that suit you?"

"I reckon," Cullen answered, matching her bluntness, "if it's fit to eat." He couldn't help wondering if this was the same woman who had been there the time before when he was here.

"You can always try someplace else," she suggested. "There's plenty of other places to eat in Waco."

Thinking it a wonder she had the few customers he saw with the attitude she displayed, he was tempted to take her suggestion and go someplace else. The trouble with that was the fact that he had left his horse in the stable and the busiest part of town was a good walk from there. So he said, "I'll take a gamble on your stew." Then as an afterthought, he asked, "Is your name Violet?" He couldn't help thinking that he possibly had misunderstood Hargett when he said her name and he may have said, "Violent." She was wearing a sizable bruise on her cheekbone. Maybe that had something to do with her disposition.

She nodded in answer to his question and asked, "You want coffee?"

He said that he did. She turned abruptly and went to a pot on the stove to fill a cup. The few customers seemed to make it a point not to catch his eye as he pulled a chair back at the long table. *Friendly town*, he thought, *they must not welcome strangers*—but it was fine with him. He wasn't one to chatter away with strangers while he ate his supper. He quickly jerked his hand away then to avoid being splashed with hot coffee that spilled over the cup when Violet set it down rather carelessly on the table. *Thank you, Violent,* he thought to himself.

"Sorry," she mumbled, "musta slipped." She hesitated then as if making a decision before she announced, "We got a new policy here. You have to pay in advance for your supper."

"Oh, is that so?" Cullen responded. "How much?" he asked, reaching in his pocket for some money.

Violet glanced quickly at the other people at the table, then back at Cullen. "Dollar and a half," she said.

"Dollar and a half?" he repeated, surprised. "Lady, you

sure must be proud of your beef stew." He noticed that most of the other customers looked up in surprise also. It made him wonder if she was quoting a special price for him only.

"Like I said," she replied. "There's lots of other places to eat in town and they're all cheaper than we are."

He had to think about it for a few moments but decided against going to all the trouble to find another place to get his supper. "Good thing I ain't gonna be here but one night. I couldn't afford another night." He gave her two dollars. "You owe me fifty cents and a damn good supper." She seemed disappointed but took his money to the cash drawer behind the counter and returned with his change. He glanced over at the man closest to him, but the man looked away at once. He got a definite impression that he, as a stranger, was being taken for a ride and they were all in on it. *That stew better be damn good,* he thought, *or I'm gonna be getting my money back. That is, if she ever brings the stew.* It seemed it was taking an awful long time to bring his plate, since everybody else at the table was already eating. He was about to inquire about that when the door opened and two men walked in. Laughing loudly at a remark one of them had said as they came in the room, they attracted Violet's attention and she hurried from the kitchen immediately to confront them.

"There she is, Shorty!" one of the two men exclaimed, his speech slurred by the alcohol he had apparently imbibed before coming to eat. "Shriveled-up little old magpie. Whatcha got to eat, Magpie?"

"Nothin' for you and the sorry bunch you ride with," Violet shot back at him. "I told you not to come back here after you ran off all my customers and made a mess of my dinin' room night before last."

"Me and Shorty need somethin' to eat," the belligerent man stated, "and we ain't gonna go lookin' all over town for it when we can get it right here. You think we raised a little hell in here the other night? You wait till you see this dump if you don't get us somethin' to eat right now."

"This is my place of business," Violet insisted, "and I've got the right to refuse to serve anybody I want. And I refuse to serve anybody that rides with the Crooked-T. So, I'd like you to leave now and you can take that one with you." She indicated Cullen with a nod of her head.

Shorty took a look at Cullen seated at the end of the long table and noticed that he was the only one at that table who dared to look back at him. "I don't know, Clive," he said. "I don't know if we oughta trust her to fix our supper. Maybe we oughta go on back to the Reservation and find the other boys. We're pullin' outta here in the mornin'. I don't wanna waste tonight settin' around here."

"We'll do that," Clive said, "after I get some food in my belly. Right now, I'm thinkin' ol' Magpie, here, is lookin' for another knot on her cheekbone to match the one I give her the other night."

"I think it'd be a good idea to listen to your friend Shorty," Cullen spoke up then, thinking he had a pretty good picture of what happened. "There's a lot more of what you boys are lookin' for down at the Reservation."

All eyes turned then to the wide-shouldered man sitting at the table waiting for a plate of stew. It was the heavyset bully named Clive who responded. "What did you say?" He turned to give Cullen his full attention.

"I think you heard what I said. The lady told you she'd rather you go somewhere else to spoil somebody else's suppertime. And I know damn well I ain't in the mood for any nonsense tonight. So, why don't you do everybody a favor and take off."

"Why, you . . ." Clive started, sputtering in disbelief, obviously not accustomed to being challenged. "You must be lookin' to get your back broke and I can take care of that for you."

Shorty, not quite as drunk as his belligerent friend, took a closer look at the stone-cold gaze of the stranger. It was the gaze of a mountain lion moments before attacking. Something told him they did not want to mess with this man. "Hell, Clive," he said, "I don't think I wanna have that woman messin' around with my food, anyway. To hell with this jasper, let's get on down to the Reservation before the rest of the boys drink all the whiskey up. We can get somethin' to eat there." He glanced at Cullen, who continued to watch them carefully, still with the look of a great cat prepared to strike.

"Maybe you're right," Clive allowed, thinking of any number of things Violet might slip into his stew. "Food ain't that good here, anyway." He turned his attention back to the expressionless man still staring at him. "Right after I give this jasper a little lesson on keepin' his nose outta business that ain't none of his." Before Shorty could protest, Clive stepped over in front of Cullen's chair and demanded, "Get up outta that chair. I got somethin' I wanna give you."

Cullen remained seated. "I don't have time to waste on blowhards like you," he announced. "You'd best get out that door while you can still walk."

"Ha!" Clive exclaimed. "You hear that, Shorty?" He turned back around in time to catch the full force of the sudden assault as Cullen drove his shoulder into his stomach. The force of the attack drove Clive backward until they collided with the front wall of the dining room, knocking the wind out of him. Gasping for air, Clive fumbled to draw his pistol from his holster, only to have Cullen wrench it from his hand and use it to rap him across his nose hard enough to drop him senseless on the floor. Without hesitation, Cullen turned to hold the .44 on Shorty.

Still standing motionless, stunned by the violence of the explosion from the deadly calm of the stranger, Shorty immediately raised his hands. "You got no problem with me, mister. I got no part in this."

"Get him away from here before I kill him," Cullen ordered.

"Yes, sir," Shorty said, and immediately went to Clive to try to get him up on his feet. But Cullen had rapped him hard enough to render him helpless and he was too big a man for Shorty to pick up easily. So Cullen picked up Clive's feet and told Shorty to get his shoulders. Together, they carried the senseless man out and lifted him up across his saddle.

"You take him back to wherever your friends are," Cullen said. "If he's wantin' to have another go with me, I won't be here by the time he gets back. And it ain't got nothin' to do with these people who run this hotel. I'm a stranger, just like you. So if he wants to get even, he'll have to pick up my trail and I'll be happy to accommodate him."

"I understand," Shorty assured him, "and like I said, I didn't want no part in this."

Cullen remained outside and watched until they disappeared from his sight before going back into the dining room, where he found Violet and most of the customers crowded around the one small window in the front. He didn't say anything, but simply walked to the chair and took his hat off the back of it, turned around, and went back out the door. Surprised, Violet ran out the door after him. "Hey!" she yelled. "Where you goin'? You ain't ate your supper!"

He stopped and turned back to face her. "I thought you wanted me to go somewhere else to eat."

"No, no," she at once apologized. "I'm sorry, mister, when you came in, I thought you were another one of that Crooked-T bunch of troublemakers. I don't know why. I just did. Please, come on back inside and I'll fix you up a plate. After what you just did, I can't let you go off hungry." She held the door open for him. "I owe you some money, too," she said as he passed by her. "I don't charge a dollar and a half for supper. I just told you that 'cause I was hopin' you'd say that was too much and go somewhere else." She laughed. "I'm sorry I took you for one of that crowd. Hell, I'm givin' you all your money back. Your supper's on the house and that includes a slice of pie."

"Well, I am gettin' kinda hungry," he said, and took his hat off again. "But I'm happy to pay you for my supper." He paused, then added, "Your regular price."

She laughed at that, as did the other customers, who no longer avoided his gaze. "What is your name?"

"Cullen McCabe," he answered. "And yours is Violet, like the flower, right?" She said that was correct and he said to himself, *and not Violent*.

CHAPTER FIVE

After some simple directions from Pete Hargett, Cullen found the confluence of the Bosque River with the Brazos. He guided Orphan down onto a common wagon road that appeared to follow the river to the northwest. *Maybe I was wrong,* he thought, *maybe there is a road from Waco to Reid's Mill.* At any rate, it should make his trip a lot easier, so he nudged the dun gently with his heels and Orphan set the pace, already accustomed to Cullen's usually desired gait. He had been tempted to have breakfast with Violet Buckley this morning, since he knew he was now welcome. But if Reid's Mill was only about twenty-five miles, as he had been told by Michael O'Brien, he decided to wait until he arrived there. He continued along the little river with its narrow channels and low water in many places through a gently rolling prairie. The land looked all right for grazing cattle as long as the river never dried up completely. And the thick growth of post oak, elm, and sycamores along the bank seemed to indicate that it was a year-round river.

He had ridden for what he estimated to have been at least twenty-five miles and had not come to the town. So, he was about to decide to stop to rest his horses when he caught sight of the first building on the horizon. "Little farther, boy," he said to his horse, "and you'll get a rest." A few minutes later and he could determine that the building he was looking at was the flour mill. "Lucien Reid," he recited the name of the man who owned the mill and the author of the letter written to the governor asking for help.

As he walked Orphan slowly into the yard of the mill, he saw the small log house behind it. Seeing a hitching rail in front of a door into the mill, he figured that to be the office where Reid's sales of flour were transacted. There was a barnlike door on the side as well, and Cullen guessed that was where the farmers' wheat was brought to be ground into flour. As he neared the office door, it opened and a boy of about fourteen or fifteen started out but stopped when he saw Cullen approaching. He turned and appeared to be talking to someone inside. By the time Cullen reached the hitching rail, the boy reappeared, this time with a man behind him. "Mornin'," Cullen said. "Mind if I step down?"

"Mornin'," the short, stocky man with a bald pate and a full gray beard, returned. "Somethin' I can help you with?"

His attitude seemed somewhat guarded, causing Cullen to remember Violet Buckley's initial reception. He was beginning to wonder if his appearance needed some help, but there wasn't much he could do about that. "My name's Cullen McCabe. I just came up this way from Waco and I'm fixin' to rest my horses and cook myself a little breakfast. Fellow in Waco told me you had a flour mill up here on the river and I ain't ever seen one before. So, I was just ridin' up closer to take a look at it."

Reid seemed to ease up a little then. "Well, you didn't get here when the wheel was in operation."

"Is it broke down?" Cullen asked.

Reid smiled. "No, sir, it's runnin' fine. There just ain't anything to grind right now. Just about all the winter wheat's done been harvested, so we won't be too busy for a little while."

"I reckon I just got here at the wrong time," Cullen said. "But if it's all right with you, I'll take my horses downstream a little ways and let 'em drink some water and rest 'em up while I cook myself some bacon."

"Where are you headed?" Reid asked.

Cullen chuckled. "Well, I reckon I'm already where I'm goin', unless there's another mill on the river farther along. Reid's Mill is the name of the town I'm headin' for." Just like every job he had done for the governor, he purposefully kept the reason for his appearance a secret. He figured that way he more easily got a better picture of the problem. This was often in contrast to the story he heard from someone's version of the problem.

"Reid's Mill, huh?" Reid responded. "That's not much of a town. What brings you to Reid's Mill?"

"Cattle," Cullen replied. "I hear it's good land for cattle and it ain't too crowded so far. I thought it'd be worth my while to take a look around before it is. Might not be what I want, but I won't know that unless I look at it."

That seemed to satisfy Reid that there was nothing to fear from the big stranger, even if he wasn't dressed like the typical cowhand. "Well, you've found Reid's Mill, all right, and when you ride past that clump of oak trees yonder, you'll see what there is of the rest of the town.

My name's Lucien Reid and this is my son, Lucien junior. We call him Luke."

"Well, I'll be . . ." Cullen faked surprise as he shook Reid's extended hand. "They musta named the town after you."

"There wasn't any town a-tall before I built the mill, but now we're gettin' more and more every day. And we're mostly all farmers with families. Like I said, there wasn't anybody here when I decided to build my mill. Then the first group of settlers came together to build a good churchgoin' community. And little by little, there's been other like-minded families that have moved in until we've got a right nice town growin'. One of the first buildings in town was our church, Presbyterian, and we mostly built the town around it."

"Well, I'll have to say that's mighty admirable," Cullen said. "I'd like to hear more about your plans for your town, but I need to take care of my horses. I'll get outta your way, go down the river a ways, build me a little fire, and cook something to put in my stomach. I'll clean up my mess before I go, leave the riverbank just like I found it."

"No need for you to go down the river," Reid said. "Luke, go tell your mother to put on a fresh pot of coffee and see if she's got something she can whip up real quick to go with it."

"Oh, I 'preciate the offer," Cullen protested, "but I couldn't put your wife to that much trouble. It might put you in the doghouse for a spell, too, springin' something like that on her." He had counted on Reid's desire to tell him all about Reid's Mill. He might learn most of everything he wanted to report to the governor—and get breakfast to boot.

"Nonsense," Reid insisted. "Hannah would be put out with me if I didn't bring you up to the house. We're always happy to welcome folks who are interested in becoming part of what we're hopin' will be the best town in Texas. I wouldn't mind a cup of coffee, myself. Now, you can lead your horses right over there between the mill and the house. There's grass on that bank and they can get water from the river. When you get 'em took care of, come on up to the back door."

"All right, if you're sure she won't come after both of us with a shotgun," Cullen japed. "You're sure bein' mighty neighborly." He led his horses to the spot Reid pointed to and stripped the saddle off Orphan and the packs off the sorrel. When that was done, he walked across the short expanse of yard to the back of the house and knocked on the kitchen door.

"Come on in, Cullen," Reid yelled from inside. Cullen walked into the kitchen to meet a slender woman standing a head taller than her husband. She was not a pretty woman, but she had a pleasant smile for their visitor. "Hannah, this is Cullen McCabe. He's come over from Waco to take a look at what we're buildin' here in Reid's Mill."

"Welcome, Mr. McCabe. How do you like your eggs? I'm thinking by the size of you that you'll need at least four. My pan's hot, so how do you want 'em?"

"Thank you, Mrs. Reid, but I didn't expect you to make breakfast for me. Coffee woulda been a gracious plenty."

"Well, my pan's hot and I'm gonna cook 'em whether you want 'em or not, so you might as well have 'em the way you like 'em," she said. When he didn't make a choice right away, she cracked an egg and dropped it in the bacon grease in the pan, much to the amusement of Reid and their son, Luke.

"I'll take 'em scrambled, then," Cullen quickly blurted when the second egg was cracked and emptied into the frying pan. "And three oughta be plenty."

"Are you sure?" Hannah asked. "You're a pretty good-sized man. I don't want you to leave my table hungry just because you're tryin' to be polite. I fried some bacon to go with these eggs, but it'll be about fifteen minutes before you can finish 'em off with some biscuits. I rolled out some dough while you were taking care of your horses. My oven was already hot, so they shouldn't take too long to bake."

Cullen was almost overwhelmed by the hospitality shown a stranger who had just ridden up out of nowhere. It was quite a contrast to the first impression he had made on Violet Buckley when he walked into her kitchen. He felt he should offer to pay for the food Hannah was preparing for him, but he knew that would be as much as an insult to them. So he made a show of his enjoyment of his breakfast and claimed that he had never eaten biscuits as good as hers before, which pleased her greatly. "I've got to quit before I get too heavy for my horse to tote me," Cullen finally announced. "I've got to admit it, Mrs. Reid, you whipped me with your cookin'. Luke, here, is gonna have to roll me out the door."

While she picked up the dishes from the table, Lucien and Cullen sat there awhile longer, drinking coffee and talking about the short history of the town of Reid's Mill. Cullen learned that there had been a core group of four families who split off from the Presbyterian church in Louisiana and drove their wagons west, looking for enough open land to build a new church where there was room to grow. The original plan, according to Lucien, was for those four families to build their church in Clifton, where one of the four, Paul Dickson, had a cousin who owned a general store in that town. "Trouble was," Lucien continued, "when they got out here, they found out there wasn't any suitable land left for all their farmin' needs. It was the same problem I had when I wanted to locate my mill there. I ended up buildin' my mill five miles from Clifton. It was just pure luck they stumbled upon my mill. And the land was open for what they needed, so they decided to build their community right here."

"So you weren't part of the original four families that came from Louisiana," Cullen said.

"That's a fact, but we might as well be, since we found we belonged in the same pews as they did. Right, Mama?" Hannah smiled and nodded. They had talked for some time before Cullen was able to determine any troubles the town might have. "Sounds to me like you've found your own little Eden right here in Texas," he commented.

The smile on Reid's face stayed in place as he glanced at his wife after Cullen's remark. "I reckon it does sound that way. But like the Eden in the Bible, Reid's Mill has its devil, too."

"Only this devil goes by the name of Harman Gill," Hannah commented as she walked by the table to pick up the last of the dishes.

Lucien shrugged as if he wished he hadn't made the remark about the devil. Cullen figured Reid had not wanted to bring up any negatives when he thought he was selling the town to a potential investor. When Cullen gave him a questioning look, Reid forced a chuckle and said,

"Harman Gill just opened our first and only saloon. And most of us who built this town would rather he had built it somewhere else."

Standing in the middle of the kitchen, where she had paused to listen, Hannah said, "He built his saloon right across the river from the church. When you walk out of church on Sunday morning, you can see the early-morning drunks sitting on the porch of that saloon."

Afraid now that his wife was painting a negative picture of the town, Lucien was quick to comment, "It's not as big a problem as Hannah makes it sound. Harman Gill doesn't get enough business from the residents of Reid's Mill to make it worthwhile for him to keep his door open. The town folk don't want the saloon, so it's just a matter of time before he closes down here and moves the saloon to Clifton. They've already got a saloon there and it ain't but five miles from Reid's Mill."

Almost as if arguing the other side of the issue, Hannah continued. "He doesn't need the business from the town folk," she insisted. "He gets enough business from that rowdy bunch of outlaws who ride for the Crooked-T."

"What's the Crooked-T?" Cullen asked, pretending he had never heard of it. "Is that a cattle ranch near here?"

"It's a cattle operation between the Bosque and the Brazos to the east," Lucien answered. "I doubt if they've ever raised a cow. Most of their stock just sorta moves in and out in the middle of the night, if you know what I mean." Then he hastened to say, "But there's plenty of good grazin' land west of the Bosque. Ol' Marvin Creed likes to keep his stock closer to Waco, so his ranch is east of here on the Brazos. I reckon we oughta be thankful for that."

Cullen was already getting a pretty good picture of the trouble the town of Reid's Mill had written the governor about. It was the same trouble many cow towns in Texas had, the mixture of unruly cowhands and alcohol, and there wasn't much anybody could do about it. There might be some help from the state, if the Crooked-T was, in fact, as crooked as its name, and was a cattle-rustling organization.

"But you need to take a good look at Reid's Mill and see all the good things we've got goin' in our town," Lucien said, afraid his family had succeeded in scaring off a potential settler.

"I intend to do that," Cullen assured him. "I'm gonna hang around for a few days, so I can take a good look. Is there a hotel where I could get a room for a few days?"

"There's no hotel yet," Reid replied, "but there's a first-class rooming house, run by Harvey and Becca Stoddard. They'll fix you up with a nice room and Becca's almost as good a cook as Hannah." He looked at his wife and winked. Back to Cullen then, he said, "You tell Becca that we sent you to see her. She's the one who actually runs the place. Harvey built the house and he was plannin' to build a hotel when the town got big enough to support one. But he slipped when he was finishin' the roof on the boardin'house and fell two stories to the ground. He musta landed hard on his chest 'cause Doc Stevens said Harvey's heart has been actin' crazy ever since. He ain't been able to do a lick of work without feelin' wore out. So Becca runs things and Harvey just mostly sits in his chair and talks about runnin' things."

"So the folks came here from Louisiana to build their

own little town around their church," Cullen remarked, "and they don't want anybody sellin' whiskey as part of it."

"That ain't exactly the way we had it planned, when we decided to create this little community," Reid was quick to respond. "There's more'n a few of us that like a drink of likker now and then. As a matter of fact, that was one of the things Harvey Stoddard was plannin' to build, a gentleman's drinkin' club. What we didn't want was a likker mill with gamblin' and saloon gals and all the things that go with it. And Harman Gill brought all that with him. So, instead of a community built around our church, Reid's Mill is just like all the other little cow towns, with all the same problems."

The discussion about the town's hopes and plans continued on until Cullen felt his horses had enough rest, especially since they were to journey only a short distance after leaving the flour mill. "I expect I've kept you from your work and used up enough of yours and Hannah's hospitality," he announced.

"We've been pleased to make your acquaintance, Cullen," Hannah responded. "I hope you find Reid's Mill is to your likin' and you decide to join our community." She had made up her mind, and would tell Lucien later, that she sensed a good man in Cullen McCabe. She felt sure that the core inside the rugged physical countenance was that of a man of honesty and compassion.

Lucien and Luke walked down behind the mill with Cullen when he went to saddle up for his ride into town. "Moss Pringle's the man who owns the stable," Reid reminded him. "He'll take good care of your horses, if you decide to leave 'em with him."

"Much obliged," Cullen said when he stepped up on

Orphan, "for the breakfast and the hospitality. I'm sure I'll be seein' you later." He nodded politely to Hannah as he rode out of the yard. Standing in the kitchen door to watch him leave, she acknowledged his nod with a little wave of her hand. When he was gone, she waited for her husband and son to return to the house.

"With all the talking that went on, he never said much about himself," Hannah remarked. "He never said whether he had a family or where he came from."

"Seems to be a nice enough fellow," Lucien said. "Tell you the truth, though, when he first rode up, I thought for sure he was lookin' for the Crooked-T. If he's a cattleman, like he says, he looks more like the type that rides for Marvin Creed." He paused a moment, then said, "But if he is, he sure don't talk like it."

As far as Cullen's thoughts about gaining the information he was sent to Reid's Mill to gather, he figured he probably had enough to report to the governor already. But to be sure, he figured he needed to verify the picture he had just gotten from his breakfast with the Reids. That meant seeing for himself how big a problem the saloon presented and more about operations at the Crooked-T.

Almost immediately after leaving Lucien Reid's place, he saw Moss Pringle's stable. It was on the opposite side of the narrow river from the mill and next to it was a blacksmith. When he came up even with the blacksmith, he looked up the main street and saw that the town was actually on the eastern side of the river. It was linked to the few businesses on the western side by two small bridges, one by the stable, the other by the saloon. Lucien had told him the rooming house was up at the north end of town, so he walked Orphan slowly up the street to make that his first stop. Just past the general store, he came to the church at just about the center of the street. He remembered Hannah's comment about Sunday mornings when he looked to see the Whiskey Mill Saloon almost directly across from the church. He chuckled to himself when he thought, *Whiskey Mill, so it won't get confused with the flour mill, I reckon.* He continued on toward the end of the street and the large, two-story house with a wide porch all the way across the front. It looked to be a well-built house, a testament to Harvey Stoddard's skill as a carpenter, he thought.

"Howdy," the man sitting in a rocking chair right beside the front door offered as Cullen pulled his horse to a stop in front of the house. It seemed a chilly day to be sitting on the porch, but the man wasn't even wearing a coat. "Help ya?" he inquired.

Cullen had a notion he was talking to Harvey Stoddard. "I've come to see about rentin' a room," he replied.

The man reached over, grasped the doorknob, and opened it partway. Then he yelled, "Becca! Man about a room! Becca!"

After a few moments, during which the man said nothing, even though he looked Cullen up and down quite blatantly, a pleasant-looking woman wearing an apron opened the door wide. "Can I help you, sir?"

"Yes, ma'am, I hope so," Cullen replied.

She gave him a quick look and volunteered, "The noon meal isn't quite ready yet. It won't be long, though. You can wait out here on the porch with my husband, if you want to."

"Ah, no, ma'am," Cullen said. "Tell you the truth, I just ate a big breakfast with Lucien and Hannah Reid. They sent me here. Said I might be able to rent a room here for a few days while I'm in town."

"Oh, why certainly," Becca responded at once. "I just took you for one of those cowhands who come by here once in a while to eat. Come on inside, Mr. . . ." She paused and waited for his name, then continued when he supplied it. ". . . McCabe and I'll show you the rooms I have vacant. You say you're just looking for a room for a few days?"

"Yes, ma'am," Cullen answered, and followed her inside.

"It's just for yourself, right?" He said that it was. "This is the parlor," she continued. "As a guest, you're welcome to use it whenever you like." Continuing to walk, she said, "This is the dining room where we serve three meals a day." She paused to stick her head in the kitchen. "I'll be back in a minute, Cora, I'm showing a room to a gentleman." She led him back to the front hall and up the stairway to the second floor. "I've got two vacant rooms now, this large one at the head of the stairs. Mr. Morrison and his wife shared that room until their house was finished. And there's a small room at the end of the hall. Of course, the rent is cheaper for that one, but you're such a big man, you might want a bigger room."

"Let's take a look at the small one," Cullen said. "Most of the time when I'm travelin', I don't have anything bigger'n a bedroll." They looked in the small room, Becca quoted him a rate, and Cullen said it would do just fine.

"Good," she said, and gave him a key. "We usually ask for a night's rent in advance." He paid her for three and told her he might decide to stay longer after he had a chance to look around the town. He followed her back downstairs while she told him where the washroom was and which hours were reserved for the women. "Of course, we have the outhouses out behind the house, one for the women and one for the men." She seemed quite proud of that. "Welcome to Stoddard House," she said. "It's too bad you've just eaten, but you can see how good the food is at supper." She left him then to get his saddlebags and personal belongings off his horses and leave them in his room. The next item on his list was to settle his horses in the stable.

CHAPTER SIX

After he was finished moving into his room, he stepped up into the saddle and rode back down the street to the little bridge across the river and the stable on the other side. He didn't see anyone around when he pulled up in front and dismounted, so he walked inside, where he saw a man leaning over a grain bin, his head and shoulders inside the bin. "Mr. Pringle?" Cullen asked.

Startled, Moss Pringle jumped in response, banging his head on the lid of the bin in the process. When he rolled around to see who spoke, his eyes gaped wide open as he saw the imposing figure of Cullen McCabe in the dark alleyway. Astonished by his stunned reaction, Cullen said, "I'm sorry if I spooked you. I reckon I shoulda made more noise before I came in."

"You scared the bejeebers outta me," Moss confessed. "I swear, I thought you were somebody else."

"Who'd you think I was?" Cullen asked.

"Clive Dawkins," Moss answered, then looking uncertain again he asked, "You ain't one of them from the Crooked-T, are you? 'Cause I didn't have nothin' to do with his horse showin' up here at my stable."

Well, it's a small world, all right, Cullen thought. It appeared he was not the only one unfortunate to have had dealings with Clive Dawkins. It might not be the same man. He had not heard Clive's last name during his engagement with Clive and Shorty at the Smith House in Waco. But his first name wasn't that common and both Clives rode for the Crooked-T. "No," Cullen said, "I don't have anything to do with the Crooked-T. Sorry if I gave you a start. All I want is to see about puttin' my horses up here for a few days. I'm stayin' at the roomin' house at the other end of the street and I was told by Lucien Reid that you'd take good care of my horses."

"Oh . . . Well, Lucien told you the truth. I'll surely take good care of your horses."

"I'll need to leave my packsaddle and packs here, too," Cullen said. "Any problem with that?"

"No, sir, mister. What's your name?" Cullen answered and Moss said, "I'll give 'em both a portion of grains, Mr. McCabe, and I won't charge you for it. And that's just for you not bein' Clive Dawkins."

"Sounds like this Clive Dawkins is causin' a lot of trouble for you. What's he botherin' you for? You say something about his horse showin' up here in your stable? What was that all about?"

"Some of that saddle trash he rides with decided to play a little joke on him," Moss said. "They were drinkin' and raisin' hell at the Whiskey Mill Saloon and a couple of his friends stole his horse and brought it down here and put it in my corral. It was late at night. I was locked up, I didn't know nothin' about it. So the big joke was him stalkin' all over town, lookin' for his horse. Like I said, I was asleep when they put his horse in my corral, but I sure as hell woke up when he found his horse. He took to shootin' his gun in the air and hollerin' for me to come outside and face him. I just grabbed my shotgun and sat down in front of the stable door and waited for him to break in. I don't know what I woulda done if some of his Crooked-T pals hadn't finally told him I didn't take his horse. It was all a joke they played on him. For some reason, he was still mad at me, like I had somethin' to do with it. He hollered that he was gonna deal with me later. When you walked in just now, I thought it was him, already back, and I didn't have my shotgun with me." When he thought he saw some concern in Cullen's expression, he hastened to add, "And I'm gonna be damn sure nothin' happens to these horses I'm responsible for."

"I'm glad to hear you say that," Cullen said, even though that was not really the reason for the concern Moss saw on his face. He had thought when he left Waco that he had seen the last of Clive Dawkins. But now he was aware that he had moved right into Clive's backyard. "I thought the Crooked-T headquarters was on the Brazos River. At least, that's what I was told. That must be fifteen miles from here. How come Reid's Mill sees their hands over here that often?"

"'Cause there ain't no place closer," Moss replied. "They used to go to Clifton till Harman Gill built the Whiskey Mill."

"Yeah, but that's still fifteen miles to ride for a drink of whiskey," Cullen stressed. "I could understand maybe once a week, but you say it's more than that?"

"It's unusual for an honest, hardworkin' cowhand," Moss allowed, "but we ain't talkin' about that kinda cow-hand. Those boys who ride for Marvin Creed ain't done an honest day's work in their lives and there's stray cows all over that range between here and the Brazos. Funny thing, though, seems like they've all got money to spend on Harman Gill's whiskey and women. There's four or five of 'em that like to stay two or three nights at a time in those rooms upstairs over the saloon. Jim Duncan, he's the blacksmith, he says they stay in a line shack halfway between here and the ranch a lot of the time, so it ain't that far a ride into town. When they're in town, they don't bring their horses here for me to take care of. They just leave 'em tied up at a hitchin' rail somewhere." He shrugged in disgust. "Anyway, that's how Clive Dawkins's horse ended up in my corral."

"When was that?" Cullen asked, for his run-in with Clive Dawkins was just last night and that was in Waco.

"Three nights ago," Moss answered, "but I gotta admit, I've been expectin' him to show up here ever since."

"Have you got any form of law enforcement in town?" Cullen asked. "Sheriff, vigilantes, anything like that?"

"No, when we pulled up stakes in Louisiana and came out here, we were just lookin' to build our own community around our church. We never figured we would need a sheriff or a vigilance committee."

Cullen found it hard to believe grown people could be so naive to think they could build a garden of peace and innocence in the middle of a raw country like Texas and expect everybody to respect their peace. He didn't say as much to Moss because he couldn't blame him and his neighbors for wanting such a place. Back to his purpose for coming to the stable, he finished unloading his horses and turning them over to Moss to take care of. "Now, I think I'll take a little walk around town," he told him.

* * *

Since the blacksmith had set up his forge next door to the stable, Cullen decided to call on him next, so he didn't cross the bridge back over to the main street. When he walked in, he found Jim Duncan in the midst of repairing a couple of wagon wheels for a settler who worked a small farm not far from town. A burly bear of a man with forearms the size of small tree trunks, he paused to give Cullen a quick look-over when he glanced up to discover the stranger. With no verbal greeting, he remained silent and waited for Cullen to state his business.

"I reckon you'd be Jim Duncan," Cullen said.

"I am," Duncan replied. "What can I do for you?" His demeanor remained passive and guarded, if not cautious. He paused again to pull a rag from his hip pocket to wipe the sweat from his forehead, never taking his eyes off Cullen.

It occurred to Cullen that he might again be mistaken for one of Marvin Creed's riders from the Crooked-T. So he said, "Don't need anything right now, but I might need some new shoes on my horses sometime in the next day or two. I'll be stayin' in town for a few days and I left my horses next door with Moss Pringle."

"You stayin' at the Whiskey Mill?" Duncan asked, with still no change in his facade of disinterest.

"No, I took a room at Stoddards' roomin' house," Cullen replied. His answer caused a raising of Duncan's eyebrows.

"You work for the Crooked-T?" Duncan asked bluntly.

"'Fraid not," Cullen said, "and I'm gettin' kinda tired

of everybody assumin' I do. I just decided to take a look at Reid's Mill to see what kinda town it is."

Duncan threw his head back and released a deep belly laugh. "I swear, I reckon everybody in town has got suspicious of every stranger that passes through." He paused then, just to be sure. "You ain't got nothin' to do with the Crooked-T?"

"I ain't."

Duncan laughed again. "Well, welcome to Reid's Mill, partner. I'd be pleased to shoe your horses whenever you're ready to have it done. But I gotta be honest with you, mister, you don't look like no ordinary farmer or storekeeper. What line of work are you in?"

"I reckon you could say I'm a scout for some folks that are lookin' for the right kind of land to raise cattle," Cullen said. "Lucien Reid was tellin' me the story behind the foundin' of Reid's Mill. Are you one of the original members who came here from Louisiana to build your church?"

"Yes, sir, I am," Duncan proclaimed proudly, and wiped the sweat from the broad bald spot on the top of his head, the only spot apparently devoid of thick black hair on his body.

"Hannah Reid told me that everything was goin' fine until your neighbor came along and built the saloon right across from the church." Cullen chuckled when he thought of Hannah's remark. "She complained about comin' outta Sunday services and havin' to see the drunks comin' outta the saloon."

"That's a fact, all right," Duncan responded. "But that kinda works both ways. A feller has to be careful, if he wants to take a little drink, and be sure the folks at the church don't spot him comin' outta the saloon. I'll tell you the truth, I'm strong on my religious faith, but I like to take a little drink once in a while. And I ain't the only one of the brothers that do, either. We'd talked about a gentleman's club when we first got here. Then Harman Gill came in and built his saloon and nobody wants to compete with that. It wouldn'ta been so bad, if he hadn't attracted that Crooked-T bunch of saddle trash. A nice quiet little saloon wouldn'ta been that bad. But the fact is, if I want a little drink of likker, I have to go to the Whiskey Mill." He paused abruptly then, realizing he had been rambling on and on. "I'm sorry. I've been just a-runnin' my mouth like I ain't got good sense. I ain't even asked your name."

"Cullen McCabe," he answered. "No problem a-tall." He had only talked to a handful of people in town, but they all had the same complaints. At this early stage in his investigation, he could see nothing the state could do about Reid's Mill's bad luck. He was inclined to take that report back to the governor with the recommendation that the town should get themselves a sheriff to throw the hell-raisers in jail. Reid's Mill was not unlike any number of lawless towns in Texas. But to be a little more thorough, he decided to stick around a few days to be sure he saw everything he needed to see. So he told Jim Duncan he'd be back with his horses in a day or two and continued walking toward the saloon.

"Who's that big fellow?" Harman Gill asked his bartender, Archie Wells, when Cullen walked in the door of the Whiskey Mill.

"Damned if I know," Archie answered. "I ain't ever seen him before."

Cullen paused just inside the batwing doors of the saloon to look the room over. There was no one seated at any of the tables except two bored women sitting together drinking coffee near the back of the room. So, he walked over to the bar, where one man was talking to the bartender. "Howdy, stranger," Archie greeted him. "Whatcha gonna have?"

"Have you got some good rye whiskey?" Cullen asked.

"Sure have," Archie replied. "You're in the Whiskey Mill. We've got everything you need." He poured Cullen a drink from a bottle of rye and watched as Cullen threw it back. "Ain't seen you in town before. You hire on with the Crooked-T?"

"Nope," Cullen replied, accustomed to the familiar greeting, "never heard of 'em."

"Welcome to the Whiskey Mill," the man who had been leaning on the bar talking to the bartender said. "My name's Harman Gill. I'm the owner. What brings you to our little town?"

"Nothin' much," Cullen said. "Just never been here before. Thought I'd take a look around."

"What are you lookin' for?" Gill asked. "Maybe I can help you." When Cullen merely shrugged in response, Gill asked, "What line of work are you in?"

"Oh, first one thing and then another. Just depends on what looks interestin' at the time."

"You sound like the kinda man a friend of mine hires," Gill said. "Marvin Creed, owns the Crooked-T."

Cullen shrugged again. "Like I said, never heard of it. What is it, a ranch? I ain't lookin' for work tendin' no damn cows."

"It's a cattle operation, the biggest in these parts." He

glanced up at the clock behind the bar. "Won't be long now you'll see some of Marvin's boys start to show up in town. A couple of hours from now, that's when this dead little town will start to come alive."

"Well, I reckon I'd like to see that," Cullen said. "Maybe I'll come back in a couple of hours to see if you're right."

"You do that." He stuck out his hand. "I'm Harman Gill," he repeated, then nodded toward the bartender. "That's Archie Wells."

"Cullen McCabe," he said, taking Gill's hand. "I expect I'll see you after supper."

When he crossed back over the second bridge, he looked back down the main street and noticed a barber pole on a small building beside the general store. It reminded him that he was overdue for a haircut. The town barber was usually a good source for what was happening in a town, so he decided to take advantage of his services. *Might as well get a shave, too, while I'm at it,* he thought. Although the barbershop was small, Cullen noticed a larger building that looked like a barn right behind it. A couple hundred feet beyond the barn, he saw a small house, apparently just recently built, for he could see part of the porch was still unfinished.

A tiny bell over the door announced his arrival when he walked in the barbershop. In a few seconds, Joe Morrison walked in from another room. He was stopped by the sight of the imposing man in his doorway, but only for an instant before greeting him. "Yes, sir, can I help you?"

"Shave and a haircut," Cullen answered. "Whaddaya charge?"

When Joe answered, "Two bits," Cullen took his hat off and hung it on a hook, one of six put on the wall for that purpose. Then he seated himself in the barber chair. "Joe Morrison," he said, introducing himself. "I know you ain't ever been in before. I'da sure remembered if I'd ever worked on you before."

"That's a fact," Cullen said. "Just rode into town this mornin'. Cullen McCabe's my name." Then he remembered something Becca Stoddard had said that morning when he was looking at rooms. "Morrison," he said. "You, by any chance, just move out of the roomin' house?"

"Matter of fact, I did," Joe replied, looking surprised. "My wife, Hope, and I stayed with Becca while we were finishing building our house. Did you move into our old room?"

"No, I moved into a small room down at the end of the hall," Cullen answered. "That's why I stopped here to get a little spruced up for my first appearance at the supper table. I reckon my hair is gettin' kinda shaggy and it could use some shearin'. Most of the time I just cut it off, myself, but I wanna make a good impression on the folks at the boardin'house. Might as well get a shave, too, while I'm at it."

"I guarantee you you'll like the food. That woman, Cora, she's got cookin' for her, is one jim-dandy cook. I miss the cookin' ever since we moved out, but I sure as the devil don't ever tell my wife that." He tied an apron around Cullen's neck and started working up some lather in a shaving mug. "What brings you to Reid's Mill?"

"I just wanna see what's goin' on in this little town," Cullen answered honestly. Then, before Joe could interrogate him further, he asked a question. "Ain't none of my business, but it seems like it'd be kinda hard to make it as a barber in a town this small, chargin' two bits for a shave and a haircut."

Joe laughed. "You're right about that, Mr. McCabe. Although I get a little bit of business from the closest farms and ranches, I had to take on the job as undertaker to support Hope and me. It was kinda funny the way that landed in my lap. To start with, there wasn't any real need for an undertaker. When somebody in the family died, the rest of the family buried 'em and that was that. That changed, though, when the likes of the Crooked-T riders decided to make Reid's Mill their pleasure mill. And with a rough bunch of men like that overrunning the place, the town had to find somebody to take care of the bodies. They went to Doc Stevens first, but he didn't want any part of it, so I took the job." He began applying the shaving lather to Cullen's face. "The town pays me a small fee to take care of the bodies and sometimes I find money or something of value on the deceased. It makes it worthwhile. If the town grows like we think it might, I'm thinkin' about gettin' into the funeral home business. Harvey Stoddard said he'd help me build coffins. He's a pretty good carpenter, but he doesn't do any heavy work anymore."

"That's what I heard," Cullen said. He decided he liked the barber's attitude about things in general and he appreciated the fact that he didn't ask him if he rode for the Crooked-T.

He decided he had time to make one more call before

returning to the rooming house for supper, so he walked into the general store. He was greeted cordially by Paul Dickson, the owner of the store. His friendly greeting was due to the fact that by this time Dickson had already heard about the formidable-looking stranger who had taken a room at Stoddards' and did not ride for the Crooked-T.

"I understand you're in town for a few days to see what we're all about here in Reid's Mill, Mr. McCabe," Dickson said. When Cullen seemed a little surprised, Dickson continued. "Doesn't take long for word to get around in a town this size. I'm Paul Dickson. I'm the mayor of our little community. I'm sure you might have heard that we have some little problems, but overall, I hope you'll appreciate the good Christian core that this town is built on. As we continue to grow, we'll have more control over problems that won't seem so big as they may seem now. Just last week, I was in contact with the U.S. Postal Service about building a post office here in Reid's Mill. I think we may have our own post office pretty soon, although they might want us to change the name of the town to Reidsville." He chuckled and commented, "Lucien Reid might object, but I don't think anybody else will." He paused then and called out, "Sarah, come in here and meet Mr. McCabe." In a few seconds, she came in from the storeroom, where she had been listening at the door. "This is my wife, Sarah," he said to Cullen.

"Cullen McCabe," he said. "Pleased to meet you, ma'am."

"Mr. McCabe," she returned politely while staring up into the chiseled features of the powerful man towering above her. She could understand at once why everyone's first impression of him was that he belonged to that devil's crew that called themselves the Crooked-T. "What do you think of the town so far?" Sarah asked.

He hesitated a moment, then said, "Let me put it this way, I ain't met anybody but nice folks since I got here. I can see why you're proud of your town." *Even though Lucien Reid wrote the governor that your town has been invaded by the devil's forces,* he thought. He regretted the fact that he could see no way to save them so far. "I'm mighty proud to meet both of you and I'm sure I'll be back to buy some things I need before I leave town. So I'll let you get back to your business." He made a quick exit before the questions continued.

"Well, Mr. McCabe, I see you made it back for supper," Becca Stoddard greeted him when he appeared in the dining room.

"Yes, ma'am," Cullen replied. "I wasn't gonna miss it. I ran into Joe Morrison . . ." That was as far as he got before she interrupted him.

"I see you did," she said, causing him to reach up to stroke his smooth-shaven chin self-consciously.

"Yes, ma'am. I didn't wanna make too bad an impression on your boarders. Joe told me he didn't want his wife to know how much he missed Cora's cookin'."

His remark caused a chuckle from the diners at the table. It obviously pleased Becca, prompting her to call out, "Did you hear that, Cora?"

"I always knew Joe Morrison was one of the smartest men I ever met," Cora called back from the kitchen.

"For anyone who hasn't already found out, Mr. Cullen McCabe has just moved into room number six at the end of the hall and will be with us for a few days. Isn't that right, Mr. McCabe?"

"Yes, ma'am," he answered, and exchanged nods with most of them. "Least, that's my plan right now." He sat down between Johnny Mitchell, who printed a newspaper for the little town, and Stumpy Morgan, who had a harness shop near Dickson's store. Cullen was glad there were no questions about his reasons for a visit to Reid's Mill. His attention was soon captured by the plate of food Becca placed before him. It looked to him to be piled higher than everyone else's. And he could only guess it was because of his size, or because Becca wanted to impress her new boarder. It was good food. Joe Morrison had been right. As the boarders finished their supper and began to leave the table, Cullen lingered to talk to Stumpy Morgan. "I might have you take a look at my saddle," he told Stumpy. "I think I might need some stitchin' reinforced."

"You need me to look at it right now?" Stumpy asked. "I'm headin' back toward the shop before I turn in for the night."

"No, it's not that big a hurry," Cullen told him.

"Ha," Harvey Stoddard huffed. "Headed back to the shop, but won't likely make it past the Whiskey Mill, I'd bet."

"Ain't nothin' wrong with one little shot of likker to help you sleep," Stumpy replied.

"Nothin' wrong a-tall," Cullen agreed. "If you don't mind company, I'll go with you. I ain't quite ready to turn in, myself."

"Why, you're welcome to join me," Stumpy said at once. Cullen figured this wasn't the first time the bald little man with the drooping mustache had to defend his desire to have a drink of whiskey. "Whenever you're ready."

"No reason to wait," Cullen said, and they got up from the table, pausing only when Cullen stuck his head in the kitchen door to compliment Cora on the cooking.

After they had gone, Johnny Mitchell looked at Harvey and remarked, "The last time Stumpy tried to get a drink in that damn saloon, a couple of Crooked-T men ran him out."

"Looks like he's takin' a big enough bodyguard with him this time," Harvey said.

"It ain't gonna be too long before ol' Stumpy gets as old as I am," Johnny said, "and gives up that drink of likker."

CHAPTER SEVEN

Unnoticed by his formidable companion, Stumpy Morgan literally swaggered as he and Cullen walked into the Whiskey Mill. When they walked up to the bar, Archie Wells grinned and said, "Howdy, Stumpy, glad to see you back again."

"Howdy, Archie," Stumpy returned. "Me and my friend need a couple of shots of whiskey, somethin' that ain't too watered down."

"Right," Archie responded, and glanced at Cullen. "Rye, if I remember. Right?" Cullen nodded in answer.

"Rye," Stumpy repeated. "We'll take 'em over and set down at a table. I'm buyin'."

"That's mighty big of you," Cullen said. "I'll buy the second one." He said to Archie then, "If we're gonna sit down to drink 'em, why don't you just pour us four and we'll take 'em over to a table."

"Good idea," Stumpy said, and reached for his money while Archie poured and they both paid for two drinks. Cullen let Stumpy pick out a table and followed him over to one close to the wall. Then he sat down with his back to the wall.

Although still early in the evening, Cullen noticed a few more customers in the saloon, just as Harman Gill had predicted, but it was still a light crowd. His glance darted to a couple of cowhands from a ranch close by, no doubt, to a poker game of older men, to two obvious underage farm boys. The two women he had seen in there earlier were working the card players and the cowhands, knowing that any money the farm boys had was probably gone already. Noticing Cullen then, one of the women walked over to check him out. "You was in here earlier, big feller," Mae Davis said. "You always wear that expression on your face, like you ain't had nothin' to smile about in a month? How'd you like to take a little trip up to see my room? I can give you somethin' to smile about."

"Reckon not," Cullen answered frankly.

It seemed to offend the woman. "Well, ain't you the particular one?" She huffed, then sneered once in Stumpy's direction, snorted, then promptly returned to badger the young cowhands.

Stumpy couldn't help chuckling and sought to inform Cullen. "Them two women are tougher'n any bronc rider in here. The young one that just invited you up to her paradise is Mae Davis. The older one pesterin' the card players is Molly Dugan. The Molly-Maes is what the Crooked-T boys call 'em. They's both whores and both their initials is MD, and you're more likely to need to see the doctor after you try to saddle-break either one of 'em."

"Is that a fact?" Cullen responded. "How did you come by that information? Did you hop in the saddle, or is that just what you've been told?"

Stumpy grinned, unashamed. "That's what those Crooked-T coyotes say. I'm too old to think about such things, but when I was a younger man . . ." His voice trailed off as he spotted a couple of men coming in the door and he reached up to pull the brim of his hat down a little lower on his forehead.

Noticing his reaction, Cullen glanced toward the door, too. "Somebody you know?" he asked.

"Somebody I wish to hell I didn't know," Stumpy answered. "Rob Gillespie and Skeeter Shaw."

"Crooked-T?" Cullen guessed.

"That's right," Stumpy answered, "and two of the biggest loudmouths in the territory when they get to drinkin'. I had a little run-in with 'em last Saturday when they got to tusslin' around with Archie at the bar and knocked my whiskey over. I told 'em I'd appreciate it if they'd buy me another one and they didn't like that. They told me they thought I oughta get outta here and they weren't too polite about how they said it. Archie told me it'd be best if I was to go ahead and leave, so I did. I'll admit, I didn't wanna have no trouble with the two of 'em. I don't even wear a gun." He watched the two men as they walked up to the bar and ordered whiskey. "They were pretty drunk that night. They might not even remember me. I'll just keep settin' here by the wall and they might not notice us." He gave Cullen an apologetic look and said, "I don't wanna cause you no trouble."

"No problem," Cullen replied. "You're right, though, we'll just sit here and mind our own business. I doubt if they'll bother us. Looks like they're more interested in givin' Archie a hard time."

Cullen had no sooner said it when the two men turned their backs to the bar and started to look the room over. Their interest seemed to be attracted more toward the card game and the cowhands. Most likely because that was where the women were, Cullen figured. After a few minutes, the woman named Mae walked over to the bar to talk to them. They talked for only a moment or two before they turned to look in Cullen and Stumpy's direction. "Uh-oh," Stumpy muttered as the two men continued to stare at them. "That witch, she's told 'em 'bout me and you over here. I swear, Cullen, I never thought those two would be here this early in the evenin'."

"Don't worry about it, Stumpy. You've got as much right to drink in this place as they have. We'll take care of any trouble they start." He couldn't keep his thoughts from going back to his time in the little town of Sundown where he was the sheriff. Saturday nights in Sundown often found his jail filled with cowhands from nearby ranches, sleeping off their drunks. *This town desperately needs a strong sheriff,* he thought. *Maybe these two will behave themselves,* he thought. All he wanted to see was how busy the saloon became as the night wore on. So far, it was not out of the ordinary business he would expect for any town. He released a tired sigh then when the two Crooked-T men pushed away from the bar and swaggered nonchalantly toward them.

They walked up to stand right in front of the table, saying nothing for a few moments but grinning foolishly. "Would you lookee here, Skeeter. Damned if it ain't our old friend Stumpy."

"Nah, Rob, that can't be," Skeeter replied. "You told him not to drag his sorry butt in here again, so maybe he just looks like Stumpy."

"That's right," Rob said, continuing the game. "Why

did I tell him not to come back in here? I swear, I can't remember." His grin never left his face.

"The way I recollect it," Skeeter came back, "it was because you was gonna have to whip him like a baby if he ever showed up here again. You gave him a choice, though, don't you remember? If he didn't want to take his whuppin', he could face you with a gun in his hand."

"That's right. That's what I said. And I told him not to come back in here unless he was wearin' a gun, and look at him, he ain't wearin' no gun. Looks like he's brung him some protection this time, though. What about him?" Rob turned his sneering grin on Cullen. "He looks like he don't like the way this is goin'."

Skeeter immediately whipped out his .44 and aimed it directly at Cullen's face. "Oh, he ain't gonna be no trouble."

"All right." Rob turned back to face Stumpy. "You're too yellow to stand up to me in a face-off with handguns, so now you're gonna pull them britches down, lay across that table, and feel my belt on your backside like a naughty little young 'un."

Silent throughout their whole performance, Cullen decided it was time to do something before Stumpy panicked and got himself in a jam. "I've gotta admit you two jackasses put on an entertainin' show, all about two damn fools in a saloon shootin' their mouths off. You oughta go find you a stage to play that little act on. Now, I'm gonna tell you a fact that ain't playactin'. A man sticks a gun in my face is a dead man, if he doesn't put it in his holster by the time I count to three. One, two . . ." At the count of two, Skeeter grinned and cocked the hammer back, preparing to pull the trigger. That was as far as he got before the bullet from under the table slammed into his gut. Cullen didn't wait. While Skeeter doubled up and sank to the floor, Cullen came up from his chair, bringing the table with him. Rob was struggling to draw his gun when he was knocked to the floor by the table with Cullen on top of it. He continued to fight desperately in an effort to pull his .44 until Cullen struck him across the temple with his six-gun, rendering him senseless.

On his feet then, Cullen made a quick scan of the room to make sure everyone else was a spectator and nothing more. "Archie," he called to the bartender while he reached down and removed the pistol from Rob's holster, "that shotgun you're inchin' over to, reach under there and grab it by the barrel. Then lay it on the bar." When he did so, Cullen told Stumpy to get it. "Take the shells out of it and leave the gun on the bar. Archie, you can come out from behind the bar now and stand in front of it, just in case you've got another weapon hidden back there."

Rapidly recovering his senses, Stumpy did as Cullen directed, ready to help now. He took a look at Skeeter lying on the floor and asked, "You want me to go get Doc Stevens or Joe Morrison?"

Cullen took another look as well and decided Skeeter didn't look likely to recover. "Get Joe Morrison. He can cart him over to his place. The doctor can go to see him there, if he's still alive. And, Stumpy, get some rope from Morrison. Tell him I'll pay him for it." Stumpy left immediately and Cullen turned to make an announcement to the customers staring at him. "The show's over. You folks get back to what you were doin'."

Short moments later, Harman Gill came in the door from the back hallway, having heard the shot fired. He had cautiously waited to listen for any more shots before he rushed into the barroom to see the cause. Seeing Cullen standing over two bodies lying on the floor, he was not sure what he should do. "Are they dead'?" Gill asked when he walked over to confront Cullen. "I only heard one shot."

"No," Cullen replied. "One of 'em's on the way, looks like. The other one's just tryin' to get his head on straight again. Stumpy Morgan's gone to get Joe Morrison to take care of that one bleedin' out on the floor."

"What are you fixin' to do with the other one?" Gill asked, obviously concerned. "Those are Crooked-T men. Marvin Creed ain't gonna be too happy about this. It might be a good idea if you made yourself scarce and I mean right now."

Ignoring Gill's advice to leave town, Cullen said, "You folks need a jail in this town to lock up troublemakers like these two. Since you ain't got one, I'll have to find some-place to lock this fellow up, so he'll know he's in jail."

"What the hell are you talkin' about?" Gill demanded. His only thoughts were how angry Marvin Creed was going to be when he found out about the shooting. He didn't get an answer right away because Stumpy came back in the saloon at that moment with Joe Morrison right behind him.

Joe went immediately to Skeeter, who was fading rap-idly. "This fellow's a goner," Joe decided right away. "Stumpy, if you'll give me a hand, we'll carry him out to my handcart." He didn't want to waste any time, in case somebody suggested looking through the victim's pock-ets. He preferred to do that chore himself.

"Here's your rope," Stumpy said as he handed it to Cullen. "You didn't say how much you needed, so I brought the whole coil." He quickly grabbed Skeeter's feet then to help carry him out.

"This'll do just fine," Cullen said, and rolled Rob over on his belly. He tied Rob's hands together, then his feet, then he tied hands and feet together to make the gradually reviving man a helpless bundle. "I need a jail," Cullen said, turning to address Harman Gill. "Have you got a store-room or a smokehouse, anywhere I can lock him up?"

"No," Gill sputtered, still confounded by the incident. "I ain't got anyplace like that, nothin' I can lock up. I wouldn't do that, anyway," he added when thinking of how he could explain it to Marvin Creed.

Cullen looked around the gathering of astonished faces but saw no sign of any help from any of them. "We'll just have to have us a make-believe jail, then," he said. "Because that's what happens to men who attempt to attack citizens in a civilized town. They go to jail." He reached down and took hold of the helpless man, hefted him up on his shoulder, and walked out the front door, the rest of the coil of rope on his other shoulder. Everyone in the saloon rushed to the windows to watch, some of the braver ones going out the door to stand on the porch.

He didn't go far before he found a good place for his jail. A huge sycamore tree about a hundred feet from the saloon seemed the perfect thing. With the remainder of his rope, he bound Rob securely around his chest, threw the loose end over a low limb, then hauled Rob up so that his feet were off the ground. Then he tied the rope to another limb, holding Rob in that position, swinging clear of the ground. By this time, he was joined by Stumpy and Joe Morrison, who came to tell him that he had been right. Skeeter died on the way to Joe's barn. "I need to pay you for the rope,"

Cullen said to Joe. "But there's one more thing that's gotta be done. Can you make me a simple sign right away? Something you wouldn't have to go to a lotta fuss to make?" When Joe looked as if he didn't quite understand, Cullen went on. "I'm just talkin' about a couple of words on a flat board, nothin' fancy." Joe figured he could do that if he just settled for black paint. "That'd be perfect," Cullen said, and Joe hurried off to get it.

"Damn," Cullen swore when Rob finally began to come around. "I was beginnin' to wonder about you."

It took a few more minutes before Rob realized he was suspended a couple of feet above the ground. All he was aware of at first was the throbbing in his head and then he gradually remembered the events just before he was crushed under the saloon table. When he tried to move his arm and found that he was bound hand and foot, unable to move, he finally recovered his voice. "What tha . . ." he started, still struggling helplessly. Then he realized where he was and he recognized the dark figure standing before him. "You're a dead man! Cut me down from here," he demanded. "Where's Skeeter?"

"Skeeter made the mistake of puttin' a gun in my face," Cullen answered. "I told him what would happen if he didn't put it away, but I reckon he wanted to see for himself. So I reckon he's about halfway to hell by now. At least, I know for sure he's left here. I expect that's the same trail you'll be ridin', if you keep workin' for outfits like the Crooked-T."

"Mister, you're new around here," Rob replied, "so you don't know it, but you just signed your death warrant tonight. The only chance you've got is if you cut me down from here right now, get on your horse, and ride like hell." He was about to say more, but Joe returned at that moment.

"You can finish threatenin' me later," Cullen interrupted. "I gotta take care of this first."

"Will this do?" Joe asked. "You said it didn't have to be fancy. I had an open can of black paint that was just before dryin' up, but I got enough to write what you said."

Cullen took the board from him. "That's perfect," he said, and turned to hold it up before him while he looked at the tree and the body hanging there. "I wish I'da thought to tell you to bring a hammer and nail."

"I figured you'd need something," Joe said, "so I brought 'em with me."

"Much obliged," Cullen said as he took the hammer and the few nails Joe brought. He picked his spot on the tree trunk and asked, "How's that? Can you see that from over on the street?" Both Stumpy and Joe said it was good, so he nailed the board to the tree. Then he stepped back to look at the sign as if it were a valuable painting. It read, REID'S MILL JAIL.

"Now what?" Stumpy wanted to know.

"Not much more we can do," Cullen said. "Rob's in jail, so we don't have to worry about him anymore. I need to settle up with Joe here on what I owe him. I think we oughta go back to the Whiskey Mill and have one more drink before we call it a night. We could settle up there, Joe. All right?"

"Might as well," Joe said. "Hope thinks I'm workin' in the barn, anyway."

"You just gonna leave him hangin' there in that tree?" Stumpy asked.

"Oh, I doubt he'll be there long before Harman Gill

will have somebody cut him down," Cullen assured him. "Gill has to worry about answering to Marvin Creed. But I'm thinkin' it'll be a whole lot later than this. I don't think Gill will want you town folks to know he cut Rob down."

When the three of them started back toward the saloon, Rob realized they were really going to leave him hanging from the tree limb. "Hey!" he yelled after them. "You ain't gonna leave me hangin' here. Cut me down!"

Cullen paused long enough to answer him. "We can't do that. You're in jail. I can't break you outta jail."

"Jail!" Rob blurted. "I ain't in jail. I'm hangin' in a tree!"

"It'll give you some time to think about changin' your ways."

"You're a dead man. I swear it!"

"Everybody is, I reckon, sooner or later," Cullen replied. As they walked back to the saloon, Cullen asked, "How often does this Marvin Creed fellow come to town?"

Stumpy answered him. "He don't ever come to Reid's Mill. I ain't ever seen him. Have you, Joe?" Morrison answered that he had never seen the man, either.

CHAPTER EIGHT

Everyone retreated back into the saloon when they saw the three men returning. When they walked inside, the room went dead silent. "Archie," Cullen said, "we'll have that quiet drink we came in here for, now that the disturbance has been dealt with." Archie didn't reply—instead, he looked at Harman Gill at the end of the bar, not sure if he should pour them a drink or not. Glaring at Cullen, Gill wasn't sure, himself, but he decided he'd better not risk any more trouble with the obviously capable stranger. So he nodded to Archie and the bartender poured three drinks.

Gill remained at the end of the bar while Cullen paid Joe for the rope. Joe refused the offer of money for painting the sign, however, insisting that his enjoyment upon participating in the sycamore jail was payment enough. He tossed his drink back and said, "I will take my leave now, before Hope finds out where I am. But before I go, I feel like I oughta warn you that you've most likely stirred up a great deal of trouble to head your way. I ain't sure that I ain't gonna catch some hell for my part in it, but I'm afraid you mighta put a target on your back when you shot

Skeeter Shaw. If I was in your shoes, I wouldn't wait for word of this thing tonight to get back to Marvin Creed. I'd wanna be a helluva long way away from here when he does find out."

"I understand what you're tellin' me and I 'preciate your concern," Cullen said. "But I'm the cause of any trouble I'm in and I'm afraid if I skip out on you, Creed's men might take it out on you and Stumpy. And that ain't hardly fair, is it?"

Joe shook his head, slightly perplexed by the man's attitude and his talk about fairness when it came to facing any retaliation from the Crooked-T. The man was a stranger in this town and could not realize the evil code Marvin Creed and the Crooked-T lived by. If McCabe knew that he had struck the first blow against Creed and his outlaws, it was hard to say. But it was obvious he didn't comprehend the fury with which Creed would respond. "All I can say is," Joe said in parting, "if you decide to hang around, you'd damn sure better watch your back."

Stumpy waited until Joe left to go home before commenting, but when he did, it was in agreement with Joe's advice. "I 'preciated you settlin' my account with those two coyotes, but I'm afraid Joe's right. You brung down a whole passel of trouble on yourself and you'd be smart to get on that dun of yours and head him in any direction that leads away from here."

Standing there listening, even Archie saw fit to comment. "You'd be smart to listen to him, McCabe. Them boys that ride for the Crooked-T will turn this town upside down lookin' for you. I don't know what's liable to make them the maddest, you shootin' Skeeter, or hangin' Rob in a tree." He glanced toward the end of the bar to meet

Harman Gill's frown and quickly added, "Course, it don't make no difference to me. Ain't no skin offa my back."

"I 'preciate your concern, Archie," Cullen responded, "especially when I cost you a customer." He gave Gill a quick shake of his head when he said it. Then he turned to Stumpy and declared, "You know, I believe I could use one more shot of that whiskey. How 'bout you? I'm buyin'."

"Why, I don't mind if I do," Stumpy responded. "I could use a little extra help to settle my nerves after tonight's doin's."

Cullen slapped his money down on the bar, then tossed his drink back. He didn't tell Stumpy, but he was drinking a couple more than he normally would have. His main purpose was to stick around the saloon a little longer because he wanted Rob Gillespie to spend some more time hanging. This was just in case he was wrong about Gill being reluctant to have any of the town folks know he ordered Rob to be freed. So he purposefully waited until Stumpy declared he was ready to go back to the boarding-house and go to bed.

When they left the saloon, they walked back to cross the little bridge across the river, which was close to the sycamore tree. With his body swaying slightly, as a result of a brisk breeze sweeping across the river, Rob assumed they were coming to cut him down. When, instead, Cullen and Stumpy turned away to cross the bridge, Rob bellowed his declaration once again. "You're a dead man!"

"I swear, Cullen, I'm afraid you're in a heap of trouble 'cause of me," Stumpy lamented. "It mighta been better if I'da just took the whuppin'."

"You'da regretted it for the rest of your life," Cullen

replied. "You didn't have any other choice. And neither did I, so we'll just take whatever comes of it. All right?"

"I reckon," Stumpy answered, shaking his head.

"Where the hell have you been?" Rob Gillespie demanded. "I've been hangin' up here half the night!"

"It ain't been that long," Archie insisted as he sawed away at the rope holding Rob up. "It just seems a lot longer when you're just hangin' there, I reckon."

"I'll string you up here and see how you like it," Rob threatened, just before Archie's knife sawed through the final strains of the rope. It didn't occur to him to hang on to the rope and lower him slowly. Consequently, Rob dropped like a bag of rocks, releasing a loud oath when he landed on the roots of the tree. "Damn you!" he cursed. "You coulda held on to that rope!" He rolled over to get off an exposed root. "Don't just stand there gawkin' at me. Get me outta these ropes." Archie jumped to the task then. "Where is that dead man?" Rob demanded.

"Skeeter?" Archie responded. "They done carried him off to . . ."

"No, you fool," Rob interrupted. "The dead man that hung me in this tree, where is he? Is he still in the saloon?"

"No, he left a little while ago. Harman sent me to get you down as soon as he left."

"He left?" Rob replied. "Where'd he go? Ain't he stayin' in the saloon?"

"No, he ain't got a room upstairs," Archie replied. "He came in with Stumpy Morgan. Maybe he's stayin' at Stoddards' roomin' house. That's where Stumpy lives."

"Where's my gun? Did he take my gun?"

"No, Harman's holdin' it in the saloon for ya," Archie said as he untied the last of Rob's ropes, freeing his ankles. "I know what you're thinkin', but do you think you oughta go after that stud horse? That cut on the side of your face looks pretty tender."

"I don't care how big he is," Rob boasted. "I'll see how he handles a .44 slug. He got the jump on me this time. That ain't gonna happen again." He got to his feet and headed for the saloon.

Harman Gill looked up from behind the bar when Rob walked into the saloon with Archie following along behind him. "It sure as hell took you long enough to get me outta that tree," Rob complained as he approached the bar. "What were you doin'? Havin' a drink with that drifter? Where's my gun?"

Gill reached under the bar to a shelf, pulled out Rob's .44, and laid it on the bar. "What are you thinkin' about doin' right now? You ain't thinkin' about goin' after that fellow, are you?"

"I sure as hell am," Rob answered. "I ain't lettin' no man get away with what he done to me. When I finish with him, I'm gonna hang his guts on that tree."

"You know, he coulda shot you, but he didn't," Gill pointed out.

"That was his mistake," Rob shot back at once, "and I'm gonna make him pay for it. What are you tryin' to talk me down for, anyway? You got some kinda deal with that jasper?"

"No, I ain't got no deal with him. I never saw him before today. I'm just thinkin' Marvin Creed ain't gonna want you stirrin' up trouble with the people livin' here. You're liable to get 'em to thinkin' about callin' the Texas

Rangers in here. And that wouldn't be good for the Crooked-T, to have them snoopin' around his business."

"This ain't got nothin' to do with the people livin' in this town. He ain't nothin' but a drifter passin' through town. And this ain't got nothin' to do with the Crooked-T's business, either," Rob insisted. "This is a fight between me and him. And it ain't got nothin' to do with your business, either. He just stuck his nose in somethin' between Stumpy Morgan and me, and I aim to see he gets what's comin' to him." He checked his .44 to make sure he had a full cylinder, then shoved the pistol in his holster. "Besides, Harman, you worry too much. Creed ain't even gonna know about this. Me and Skeeter was stayin' in that old line shack with a couple of other men. He don't know what we're doin' and he don't care, just as long as we come runnin' when he calls. Now, how 'bout you tell me where this jasper's sleepin'. Archie says he thinks he's stayin' at that boardin'house on the other side of the church. Is that right?"

"I don't know where he's stayin'," Gill claimed. "I don't ask everybody where they're sleepin'." He shrugged impatiently. "He mighta made him a camp up the river somewhere, or maybe he's sleepin' in the stable with his horse. I don't know."

Rob paused to consider that possibility. *He might be sleeping in a stall with his horse,* he thought. That was not uncommon for drifters passing through a town. And, if a man had a reason to want to get out of town in a hurry in the morning, he could be on his horse and gone before everybody got up. *And he's got a damn good reason to leave town,* Rob told himself. *He knows he's a dead man.* The more he thought about it, the more he was convinced he should check on that possibility at once. If he was wrong, at least he could find out if Cullen's horse was in Moss Pringle's stable, whether Cullen was planning to sleep in the stall or not. That would tell him he was still in town somewhere, so he stormed out of the saloon and got on his horse. He left Skeeter's horse tied at the rail, thinking to come back for it when he was finished with Cullen McCabe.

When he reached the stable, he found it closed for the night. He jumped down from the saddle and started pounding on the door. When there was no response to his knocking, he walked around the stable to the back, where he found a small door that was unlocked. Once inside the dark stable, he started yelling for Moss Pringle. With no response still, he yelled, "I know damn well you're in here! It's so dark I can't see nothin', so I'm fixin' to set some of this hay on fire and light it up in here." He struck a match and picked up a handful of loose hay and set it on fire. It caught up right away, so he reached down and scooped up a large armful and used the small fire to ignite it. Almost at once, a large glow of light was created, enough for him to see the man standing a dozen feet away just before the blast from the double-barrel shotgun knocked him backward. Staggered with fear, Moss pulled the trigger for the other barrel to make sure the job was completed. "Damn you, damn you," he muttered over and over while he stamped out the fire on the floor of the stable. He had heard Rob banging on the front door from his little room in the back of the barn. And he knew it was Clive Dawkins, or some of the Crooked-T gang that had come to his stable the day before, trying to sell him a couple of stolen horses. He knew who one of the horses belonged to, so he knew they were stolen. He told the outlaws that he didn't buy horses and that seemed to make them angry. One of them called him a liar and threatened to burn his stable down before they rode away. And here they were, back to carry out their threat. He was sickened by what had just happened, but he couldn't let him burn his stable down. Almost paralyzed with fear, he forced himself to go to the front door to peek out front to make sure this one was alone.

Once he was assured there was no one else with him, he could manage to breathe again, although he kept berating himself for forgetting to lock the little door in the back of the barn. Maybe this wouldn't have happened. The next thought that struck him was to move the man's horse away from his front door, so he opened the door and led the horse inside, locking the door again after him. Next, he had to get rid of the body, as far away from his stable as possible. Carrying a lantern, he led Rob's horse to the back of the stable, where the body was. A quick inspection with the lantern confirmed that there was no sign of life in the body. It also told him that it was not Clive Dawkins or the man who had threatened him. It made no difference, he told himself, the man was just before setting his place on fire. He had no choice.

After a great deal of strain and struggle, Moss was able to get the body up from the floor and lay it across the saddle. Rob had bled enough to leave a bloody mess on his stable floor. He would have to deal with that later. For now, the important thing was to get this body away from his stable. It struck him as odd that there appeared to be a deep gash right across his temple and it was almost dry. It was not caused by the buckshot from his shotgun and might be cause for speculation later on, but he didn't have time to think about it now. So he put a bridle on the mule he used for hauling, hopped on its back, and led Rob's horse out the rear of the stable. He rode the mule south along the bank of the river, guiding it carefully through the darkness for what he estimated to be a distance of about two miles until he reached a point where a stream emptied into the river. Then he rode the mule up the middle of the stream for about fifty yards before dropping the horse's reins and turning his mule back. He expected the horse to remain there when the reins were dropped on the ground, but the horse started to follow him. "Whoa up there!" He ordered the horse to stop, but the horse, a red roan gelding, continued to follow along behind him. He thought about tying the horse to a tree, but being a man who made his living taking care of horses, he couldn't bring himself to do that. He had just killed a man, his first. He didn't like to think about the horse left tied there to die of thirst and starvation. So he slid off his mule and tied it to a limb. Then he took the roan's reins and led him back to the stream, where the horse started to drink the water. Slipping quietly away, Moss hurried back to his mule and led it away from the stream.

When he had walked about forty yards along the riverbank, he stopped to listen for any sounds that would tell him the roan was following him. When he was satisfied the horse had not come after him, he turned his mule to cross over the river to the other side, in a further effort to discourage the roan. When he got back to his stable, he stopped short of it in order to take a look to see if there were any other visitors before crossing back over the river. There were none, so he cautiously assumed that the man he had just killed had been alone. Still, he knew there was to be no sleep for him on this night, so he didn't even try. Instead, he went to work cleaning up the evidence of the two shotgun blasts, thankful that no one had come to investigate. So he got his shovel and his wheelbarrow and started carrying out the bloody hay from the floor to a fire pit out behind the barn, where he often cooked. Once he had the bloody hay burning, he returned to the stable to scatter fresh hay over the whole area.

When it was all cleaned up, he was left to remain alert for the rest of the night for more visitors. He had to worry that this fellow's friends might begin to wonder where he had gotten off to. Worse, they might know he had gone to the stable and would come to see if he was there. It would prove to be the longest night that Moss could remember.

CHAPTER NINE

When the sun came up the next morning, it was a tired and bleary-eyed Moss Pringle who opened the doors to his stable, walked outside, and looked all around him as if to satisfy himself that he had made it through the night without a visit from anyone on the Crooked-T payroll. Feeling a desperate need for some strong coffee, he picked up his coffeepot and filled it with water at the pump, then set it to boil on the stove he had cranked up earlier. As the sun climbed higher, he felt safe in assuming he had gotten away with the execution of his late visitor of the night just passed. Although tired from the sleepless night, he got busy with his daily chores and the horses in his care.

It was a little later in the morning when Billy Wells, Archie's son, walked down to the stable, leading a horse. "Whatcha got there, Billy?" Moss asked the bartender's fourteen-year-old, who often did chores around the saloon.

"Pa said to bring this horse down here," Billy answered. "He said it belonged to a feller that got shot in the saloon last night. Said it was tied at the hitchin' rail all night long. Thought you better give it some water and maybe some grain. Anyway, said you'd know what to do."

"I'll take care of him," Moss assured him. "I heard what sounded like a pistol shot last evenin'. I figured it musta come from the saloon, but I weren't sure. Who got shot?"

"One of them Crooked-T riders," Billy replied. "Pa said his name was Skeeter."

"And they left his horse out in front of the saloon all night?"

"Yes, sir," Billy replied. "Mr. Morrison carried the dead man off on his handcart and I reckon nobody thought about this horse belongin' to him, so nobody thought they oughta do somethin' with the horse."

"Well, I'll be . . ." Moss started. "I reckon I missed all the excitement, but I generally do, this far away from the Whiskey Mill."

"That ain't all you missed," Billy went on. "That big stranger that rode into town yesterday . . ."

"McCabe?" Moss interrupted.

"Yes, sir, that's the one, McCabe. Well, he's the one who shot the man named Skeeter, but after that, he knocked the feller that was with Skeeter upside his head. Then he tied him up and hung him up in that big tree beside the saloon."

"He hung him?" Moss asked, thinking he had lynched him.

"Not by the neck, just tied him all up, so he couldn't move and hung him up in the tree. Told him he was in jail. That tree was the jail and he just left him there."

Amazed, Moss asked, "Is he still hangin' in the tree?"

"No, sir," Billy said. "Mr. Gill sent my pa to cut him down after McCabe left."

"I swear," Moss responded. "I really did miss all the

excitement, didn't I? It's a wonder that feller didn't go after McCabe, especially after McCabe killed his friend."

"Papa said he did go after him. Leastways, he went lookin' for him. Ain't nobody seen him since last night."

Moss was beginning to get an uneasy feeling after hearing the whole story. "You say McCabe hit this feller upside the head?"

"That's what Pa said. Said he hit him with his pistol right up beside his eye and it knocked him flat-out cold."

"A blow like that would likely leave a big cut or a bruise on a feller's face," Moss remarked. *Like the one I saw on that fellow I shot in my stable,* he thought.

"I reckon," Billy replied. "I weren't there, so I didn't see him, but that's what Pa said."

"Well, tell your pa that I'll take care of the horse till they decide who gets him," Moss said. "I expect that horse belongs to the Crooked-T and they might send somebody after it. Maybe the other feller will come claim it for the Crooked-T." He stood there awhile, holding the reins of Skeeter Shaw's horse, realizing that the man he had killed had come to his stable looking for McCabe. He wondered now if the man had been telling the truth when he said he couldn't see, so he was setting some hay on fire for a light. Then he told himself that it didn't matter. He was out to kill McCabe, so he did the right thing when he shot him. Not only that, but anyone dumb enough to set hay on fire in a stable didn't deserve to live. All that being said, however, he was still burdened with the sin of having killed a man. And he wasn't sure how well his conscience could handle that.

* * *

"That feller ain't in jail this mornin'," Stumpy said to Cullen when he came down to breakfast.

"That so?" Cullen responded, not the least bit surprised.

"Yep," Stumpy replied. "I walked down the street a ways to take a look and your sign's gone, too. Well, it ain't gone, but it's layin' on the ground."

Cullen pulled a chair back and sat down at the table, just as Becca came from the kitchen with the coffeepot. Seeing Cullen at the table, she cast a concerned look in his direction but continued around the table, filling cups for those present. When she got to Cullen, however, she paused a second after filling his cup and quietly stated, "After breakfast, I would like to have a word with you, if you don't mind."

"Yes, ma'am," he replied, already with a pretty good idea what she wanted to talk about. After they had returned from the saloon last night, he went right up to his room. But he knew Stumpy would have to tell anyone who hadn't gone to bed yet everything that happened in the saloon. He knew it was going to create a problem, but he decided he might as well enjoy his breakfast before he dealt with it. He was glad that Becca evidently felt the same.

"Heard you ran into a little trouble at the Whiskey Mill last night," Johnny Mitchell said to Cullen as he passed him the biscuits.

"Yeah, that was an unfortunate thing," Cullen replied. "It's not a good thing when you can't go to a saloon to have a quiet drink after supper. I expect Reid's Mill is gonna have to realize they need a sheriff."

Johnny chuckled softly. "Stumpy said you took on the job of sheriff last night, even had a hangin'."

"I reckon I was just tryin' to make a point," Cullen said.

"But this might not be fittin' talk for Mrs. Stoddard's breakfast table."

Johnny chuckled again, but he could see that Cullen was serious about not wanting to discuss it at this time. So the rest of the breakfast was conspicuously quiet, since the new boarder at the house was still a mystery to them all. When he was finished, Cullen emptied his coffee cup of its last swallow, folded his napkin, and laid it beside his plate. Becca, standing in the kitchen door, met his eye and he nodded. He got up then and followed her into the parlor, where her husband was sitting at the desk.

"I'm very concerned about something," Becca started, "and I feel very uncomfortable telling you this."

"Let me make it easier for you," Cullen interrupted. "You heard about the altercation in the saloon last night and you're concerned about it causin' some trouble in your home, here. Unfortunately, I was left with no option but to shoot a man who was fixin' to shoot me. Then I tied his partner up to keep from havin' to shoot him. These two men were Crooked-T riders, so I expect Marvin Creed ain't gonna be too happy about it. You're worried that when he finds out I've taken a room here, he'll send men here to get me. I don't blame you one bit, so I'm gonna save you the trouble of tellin' me to leave. I'm hopin' that fellow I hung up in the tree won't find out that I took a room here. I think maybe he hasn't because he'da already been here lookin' for me. I've run into this situation before and I don't want you folks to get drawn into any trouble on account of me. I'm sorry to cause you any concern and the best I can do is to tell you I'll try to make it known that

I'm not roomin' here. I'll get my things out of my room and leave right away."

Both Harvey and Becca Stoddard were struck speechless during Cullen's humble statement, since they were not sure what the sober man's reaction might be. Finally, Harvey asked, "You talk like you're still gonna be around town for a while. Why on earth don't you get on your horse and get away from here before that crowd of bandits at the Crooked-T come lookin' for you?"

"Just a little slow-witted, I reckon," was Cullen's reply. "Anyway, that was a fine breakfast. I'll collect my things and be on my way."

"Wait, I owe you some money," Becca said. "You paid for three nights."

"I'll tell you what, you keep the money. Then when things are a little more peaceful around here, I'll come and eat supper one night." He started for the stairs to get his things.

"I'm really so very sorry to ask you to leave," Becca said. "It's just that I . . ."

"I understand," he interrupted her again. "There's no hard feelin's on my part. I was gonna move out, anyway. Like I said, I've had a similar situation like this before and it caused some problems that I don't wanna bring down on you folks." He continued up the stairs to the second floor.

"Good luck to ya, McCabe," Harvey called after him. He exchanged glances of relief with Becca. They had been concerned about a gang of Crooked-T hoodlums showing up to get McCabe and the damage to their home when

McCabe refused to come out. "I don't know what I woulda done, if he had refused to leave," Harvey whispered.

Floyd McCurley pulled his horse to a stop in front of the general store, stepped down from the saddle, and tied his reins and the reins of the horse he had been leading to the hitching rail. The load he was carrying on the second horse had already sparked the curiosity of the few who noticed him when he rode in from the south end of town. One showing a special interest was Moss Pringle and he was walking up from his stable as Floyd went into the store.

"Good mornin', Floyd," Paul Dickson greeted McCurley when he walked in. "I didn't expect to see you back so soon." McCurley had a small farm south of Reid's Mill and he had made his monthly trip into town less than two weeks before.

"Mornin', Mr. Dickson," the slow-talking McCurley responded. "I didn't expect to come to town this mornin', myself. Didn't have no need to," he drawled out. "Thought I'd go deer huntin' instead. There's been a right smart number of deer crossin' the river down near my place ever since that last big rain. They used to cross half a mile south of there. So I told Rena it was about time we had us some fresh venison. I got my shotgun and rode down the river to the new crossin'."

"Did you have any luck?" Dickson asked, in an effort to hurry his slow-talking customer along to the point of his tale.

"Well, there was lots of tracks, fresh ones, so I knew

they was still crossin' the river there. So I pulled my horse back in the serviceberry bushes and sat myself down to wait for some deer to show. Well, sir, I sat a spell without nothin' showin' up. So I decided I'd got thcre too late to catch 'em crossin' over. I was gettin' ready to get back on my horse, but I stopped 'cause I saw somethin' a-wigglin' the branches in some tall laurel bushes. And I warn't sure, but it looked to me like it was headin' to that river crossin' I was watchin'. Well, I cocked the hammers back on my shotgun and drew a bead on the spot I knew that deer had to come out."

"So, you got you a deer," Dickson said, hoping to push him to a conclusion.

"Can't say as I did," McCurley said. "I think I would have 'cause it woulda been an easy shot. I woulda dropped him right there on the riverbank and I woulda butchered him right there by the river."

Dickson looked at him expectantly, but when he didn't go any further, Dickson had to ask, "Why didn't you shoot it?"

"'Cause the first thing that popped outta them laurel bushes was a horse's head." He paused to give Dickson space to be surprised, then with a responsible look, he continued. "And I warn't gonna shoot no horse."

"No, I reckon not. So you went deer huntin' and got a horse instead," Dickson replied, trying to bring his story to an end. "What kinda shape was the horse in?"

"The horse was in good shape," McCurley answered. "A fine-lookin' roan geldin', worth a pretty good price, I figure." He paused again and Dickson waited for him to continue. "Well, the thing that I thought was strange was there was a feller a-layin' across the saddle. So bein' the natural curious type, I walked up to take a look and he didn't look like he was in very good shape. So I decided to bring him on into town and maybe try to get a shot at a deer another day. End of story."

Interested now, Dickson asked, "You've got a dead man out there on a horse?"

"If he ain't, he's got a mighty peculiar way of ridin' his horse," McCurley replied.

"And you brought him to me?" Dickson asked. "Why'd you bring him to me?"

"'Cause you're the mayor. At least, the blacksmith told me you was. So I figured, since there ain't no sheriff, you'd be the man in charge."

"I reckon you did the right thing at that, but I'm beginnin' to think we're gonna have to get us a sheriff." He came out from behind the counter then and headed for the door. McCurley turned and followed in his footsteps.

Outside, they found several gawkers around the body draped across the saddle of the red roan horse. Seeing Moss Pringle and Jim Duncan among them, Dickson asked, "Anybody know who he is?"

"Yeah," Jim answered, "it's Rob somebody. I don't know his last name. He's the fellow Cullen McCabe hung up in the tree last night."

"Crooked-T, right?" Dickson asked. He walked around the horse and took a closer look. "How'd he get shot up like that? Anybody know? Looks like he caught both barrels of a shotgun."

"Maybe McCabe does," Jim said. "Here he comes now. You can ask him." They all turned to see Cullen coming down the main street, carrying his saddlebags and rifle. The one person in the small gathering who asked no questions and offered no opinions was Moss Pringle. But he stared at the body, perhaps harder than anyone, with a feeling like a cold fist in the pit of his stomach.

"He didn't get far before somebody settled his hash for him, did he?" Cullen questioned when he saw who was lying across the saddle. He walked up to take a closer look. "Shotgun. Who did the job on him?"

"We was fixin' to ask you," Jim answered, "since you were the one who put him in jail." There were a couple of chuckles for the sycamore jailhouse.

"Sorry, this ain't my work," Cullen said. "When I left him, he was alive. How'd he get here? That horse just wander into town?"

"No, sir, I brung him," Floyd McCurley volunteered. "I wasn't plannin' to come to town this mornin'. I was fixin' to go deer huntin' . . ."

"He found the horse wanderin' south of here on the river," Dickson quickly interrupted before McCurley impaled them with another long-winded version of his story.

"And nobody wants to own up to blastin' him to hell, huh?" Cullen asked. "Did Gill cut him down outta that tree?"

"He had Archie Wells cut him loose from the tree," Jim volunteered. When Cullen asked what happened to Rob after that, Jim said, "He went off lookin' for you."

"I never saw him," Cullen said. "He mighta gone to the stable, in case I was there. He show up there, Moss?" Moss didn't reply, he just shook his head. "No?" Cullen continued. "Looks like we've got us a secret executioner."

"Maybe we oughta ask Joe Morrison," someone suggested, joking. "He's the only one makin' any money offa these killin's."

That remark brought forth a few more chuckles, causing Dickson to issue an admonishment. "This might not be a laughin' matter when word of these two killings gets back to Marvin Creed. Somebody needs to take that body to Joe Morrison, so he can get it in the ground before they get a chance to see him. Might be best for the town if nobody knows what happened to him."

"I reckon I could take him to the barbershop," McCurley said, "since I'm the one who found him."

"You know, whoever emptied their shotgun on this low-down scum ought not hesitate to admit it to the rest of us," Jim Duncan declared. "Whoever done it just rid our town of one more piece of trash. I'll tell you right now, if the council decides to build a jailhouse for trash like him, I'll volunteer to help build it."

"That's something we'd have to have all the brothers talk about," Dickson said. "Not much good to build a jail, if we don't have a sheriff to use it. And that means payin' a salary to a qualified man. We don't have a budget for that right now."

McCurley led the roan with Rob Gillespie's body to Morrison's and the spectators began to disperse, several of them headed to the Whiskey Mill to tell the folks there about the reappearance of the first and only prisoner in the sycamore jail. "You goin' back to the stable?" Cullen asked Moss Pringle. Moss said that he was, so Cullen said, "I was headed there myself. I'll walk with you." Usually talkative, Moss seemed unusually quiet. Cullen wondered if he was concerned after just having seen the way Rob's body was brutally assaulted. Maybe he needed to get his mind back on business. "I just moved my stuff outta the roomin' house," Cullen told him. "I figured I'd rather sleep in the stall with my horse. That all right with you? Whaddaya usually charge for that?"

Instead of answering Cullen's question, Moss asked, "Ain't you afraid some of that Crooked-T crew will come to the stable lookin' for you? They find out you ain't at Stoddards', they might figure you're stayin' here."

"Maybe," Cullen agreed. "They might think I'm in one of those rooms upstairs in the Whiskey Mill, too. You rather I didn't stay at the stable?"

"I was just thinkin' for your own safety, you'd wanna be as far away from Reid's Mill as you can get."

"I might, or I might not, have stirred up a hornet's nest for your town when I shot Skeeter Shaw, but it couldn't be helped. I didn't see any sense in lettin' that coyote shoot me, if I could help it. But since things happened the way they did, I don't feel right about runnin' away and leaving you and your neighbors to finish what I started. There's another way to look at this. If the Crooked-T comes to your stable, lookin' for me and I'm gone, you'll be by yourself to defend your stable. If I'm here, at least you'll have some help when they come."

"I hadn't thought about that," Moss admitted. "It would be better if there was two of us. We could watch the front and the back."

"That's what I was thinkin'," Cullen said. "We could make it pretty costly for 'em to try to break in the stable."

With new thoughts now of Cullen helping him defend his business, Moss's confidence turned up several notches. "We'd make 'em pay, all right," he boasted. "I ain't much with a six-gun, but I'll give 'em plenty to handle with my shotgun."

"Right, just like you did for ol' Rob back there when he broke in here lookin' for me last night," Cullen said, having reached that conclusion.

Moss blanched, unable to speak for several moments. When he could, he stumbled over his words as he finally said, "Why do you think I shot that man?"

"Couldn't have been anybody else," Cullen said. "Just like Jim said, when Rob was cut down from the tree, he went lookin' for me. And he didn't show up at Stoddards' roomin' house. The only other place he would look would be the stable."

"You got to understand, McCabe," Moss sputtered. "I was all locked up but for one door in the back of the barn and he found it. He was gonna burn the stable down. He set some hay on fire and I had to shoot him or I'da lost my whole place here and might notta been able to save the horses. I had to shoot him. I can show you where he lit the fire."

"Slow down a little, Moss, I ain't got no quarrel with what you did. You oughta be proud of standin' up to one of those outlaws that think they can run over your town. You got a right to protect what's yours. Now, if you don't want anybody else to know it was you that done for Rob Gillespie, I ain't gonna tell a soul. But what you folks in Reid's Mill need is more men like you who won't roll over and play dead for a gang of outlaws."

"When we came to this little valley, we was just lookin' for a place to start our church, so we could build a little community around it. We didn't figure on ever gettin' big enough to attract any of the lawless crowd. And for a while, things looked like they were goin' just like we planned it. Then Harman Gill came along and built that dang saloon and it didn't take long for the trouble to start. We talked about it, the town council, about whether we shoulda gone on into Injun Territory, where they ain't supposed to sell whiskey. But it was too late by then. None of us could afford to pull up roots and move again. Lucien Reid said it right when he told Paul Dickson we shoulda bought this whole strip of land where we built the town, instead of each of us buyin' our lot. If we'da done that, we coulda refused to sell to Harman Gill." He shook his head and released a long sigh in frustration. "Lucien wrote a letter to the governor for us to see if he could help with the outlaw problem. But we ain't got no response from him."

Cullen couldn't help but feel compassion for the man—for the whole town, as far as that was concerned. At this point, he was tempted to tell him that the governor had not ignored the town's request for help. But if he told him the governor had sent one man to "look" at the situation, it would seem the same as no response. Still, he thought he should attempt to explain the seeming lack of concern from Austin. "I reckon the main problem is the state's lack of law enforcement to handle all the state's problems," Cullen offered. "So the men they have, like the Texas Rangers, ain't enough to go around and hit all the brush fires. They're busy trackin' down outlaws that are creatin' hot spots in the bigger towns where more folks are affected. It doesn't seem fair, but the little towns like Reid's Mill are left to work it out for themselves. And Reid's Mill ain't gonna make it unless you folks hire you a sheriff that's gonna be hard on roughnecks and outlaws who make trouble here." He paused then when it appeared to him that Moss was seriously considering what he had just said.

"All that seems to make sense," Moss said, "but we ain't got no money in the budget to hire a sheriff, just like Paul said."

"Well, I reckon you'd best figure out a way to get some," Cullen was very frank in responding. "'Cause, it's like an open invitation to your friends out at the Crooked-T, a wide-open little town with no law enforcement."

"Dang! The more you talk about it, the worse it sounds," Moss remarked. "We ain't even sure how many men Marvin Creed has."

"That's a fact," Cullen replied. "But I know for sure he's got two less than he had."

CHAPTER TEN

"Whaddaya reckon those two hound dogs are up to?" Shorty Taylor wondered aloud. "They said they'd be back yesterday. They musta shacked up with the Molly-Maes."

"I expect they'll be back, broke and hungry, about dinnertime today," Lucky Spence commented. "One thing for sure, the Molly-Maes will love you to death, till your money runs out. Then they treat you like you got the hoof-and-mouth disease and throw you out with the dishwater."

"They better get their sorry butts back here today 'cause we're supposed to ride back to the Crooked-T in the mornin'," Shorty said. "I have to admit, though, it's been a whole lot better in this little ol' shack with Rob Gillespie gone. Skeeter ain't bad. You hardly know he's around, but Rob runs his mouth every second he's awake. And I swear, I think it runs on for a little while after he goes to sleep."

Lucky laughed. "I think I'll tell Rob you said that, then he'll be tellin' you how fast he is with that .44 he wears. Might even give you a chance to find out for yourself."

"Go ahead," Shorty chuckled. "With your reputation as a liar, I doubt he'd believe you." They both laughed at that, then the light conversation died out for a short spell before Shorty became serious for a moment. "You reckon they ran into some trouble in that little ol' town? I mean, they did say they'd be back before now."

"I don't know who could give 'em any trouble," Lucky replied. "They most likely got so drunk, they don't know what day it is." Neither man said anything more for a while, but both were thinking the same thing. When Marvin Creed said to be at the ranch on a certain day, it's best to be there on that day. "Hell, I could use a drink of likker. You wanna ride into Reid's Mill and get one? We can find Rob and Skeeter while we're at it."

"That suits me," Shorty said. "Let's finish up this coffee, then we'll saddle up."

It wasn't up to the standard that Cora set at the rooming house, but it was a supper sufficient to fill the bellies of two widowers. Soup beans that Moss had set out to soak that morning, bacon, and biscuits baked in Moss's iron stove were the bill of fare. Cullen supplied the flour for the biscuits out of his packs, as well as the coffee. He had offered to make the biscuits, but Moss insisted that he should because his late wife, Eleanor, had taught him how to make them just right. Cullen had to admit they were head and shoulders above the rocks he usually turned out. They were eating a little early to accommodate Moss's necessity to attend a meeting of the town council to be held at the church. Mayor Dickson had not called a meeting in several weeks, the last one having resulted in the decision to send the governor a letter requesting help. The topic to be discussed this time would cover the recent killings in town and what, if anything, could be done to prevent more.

Cullen was very much interested in what they would have to say, but at this point, he was considered no more than a drifter who happened to land in their town a couple of days ago. And in some points of view, he was considered the cause of the two recent killings. "Sorry you can't come along to the meetin'," Moss said as he prepared to leave the stable. "They ain't usually very interesting, anyway."

"I think I'll walk up to that sinful saloon you folks are so anxious to get rid of after a while," Cullen told him. "When you get through with your meetin', stop by and I'll buy you a drink."

"I'll take you up on that," Moss replied. "And I'd be willin' to bet I won't be the only member of the council to show up there. Don't forget to lock up when you leave."

In no particular hurry, Cullen took his time to feed his horses some oats before he left the stable and followed the narrow wagon path up to the Whiskey Mill. Since it was right across the river, almost directly facing the saloon, he could see the church and the lights were still on, telling him the meeting was still in progress. Since it appeared that Moss might be sometime yet before he showed up at the saloon, Cullen decided to take a look inside the church with half a mind to walk in on the meeting, even though he wasn't invited. He crossed over the small bridge and walked up to the front door of the church, opened it a few inches, and stood there to listen. After a few minutes of the council's discussion, he decided that it was still too soon to reveal the real reason for his appearance in their town. He had no real solution to their problem at this point, so it was best for them not to know he represented the governor's office. Had he not been listening at the church door, he might have noticed the two riders that crossed over the bridge to the Whiskey Mill.

Lucky and Shorty tied their horses at the hitching rail in front of the Whiskey Mill and went inside. Archie looked up from some glasses he was rinsing in a large pan behind the bar and immediately stopped when he saw the two Crooked-T hands come in. He knew them by name, Lucky Spence and Shorty Taylor. While they were definitely members of the outlaw bunch that rode for Marvin Creed, they were not usually among the troublemakers that gave the gang a bad name. Archie put down the bar rag he had been using to dry the glasses and waited for the two men to approach. "Evenin', boys, what's your fancy?"

"Whatever you got in that bottle there," Lucky said, and pointed to a half-empty bottle on the bar.

"That's corn whiskey," Archie said. "You want the same?" he asked Shorty.

"Nah, I want rye whiskey," Shorty answered. As Archie reached for another bottle behind the bar, Shorty asked, "You seen Skeeter Shaw and Rob Gillespie tonight?"

Archie didn't answer at once while he decided how best to answer the question. He made a deliberate motion of pouring their drinks. Then when Shorty started to repeat the question, he said, "No, ain't seen either one of 'em and I don't expect anybody else has. I reckon you ain't heard, but both of them boys are dead."

His announcement had the effect he expected. Both men were struck speechless for a few moments. "Who?"

Lucky exclaimed finally, still holding the drink in his hand. "How?"

"A drifter passin' through town," Archie answered. "Name of Cullen McCabe, big feller. Least, I know he shot Skeeter 'cause that was right here in the Whiskey Mill. I saw that." Then he went on to tell them of Rob's capture and his hanging in the tree at the corner of the saloon. "Most folks figure McCabe killed Rob, too, but nobody saw him do it. Rob just showed up the next mornin' layin' across his saddle. He was shot twice with a shotgun from a close distance, it looked like." He paused and waited when both men tossed their whiskey down. "I hate to be the one to bring you the bad news. I don't know nothing about Rob's killin', but it was him and Skeeter that pushed McCabe into shootin' Skeeter."

"Damn!" Lucky swore. "I didn't ever expect to hear somethin' like that." He looked at Shorty. "I ain't gonna look forward to tellin' Marvin about this." Back to Archie then. "Pour me another 'un, no, wait, gimme the bottle. I need to set down and think about this. This drifter, where is he? Has he done rode on?"

"As of this afternoon, he was still in town," Archie said. "Didn't seem in no hurry to leave."

"That son of a . . ." Lucky started. "Where does he stay? It ain't here, is it?"

"No, he don't stay here," Archie replied. "I don't know where he's stayin'."

"Does he come in here?" Shorty asked.

"Oh yeah, he'll come in here to get a drink. That's how Skeeter got shot. McCabe was in here havin' a drink with Stumpy Morgan. Skeeter and Rob came in and started into doggin' Stumpy. McCabe didn't like it and told 'em so. Well, that riled 'em up and Skeeter drew his gun on him. He was holdin' it in McCabe's face when McCabe shot him."

"Is McCabe that fast?" Lucky asked. "Or was Skeeter that drunk?"

"Mighta been a little bit of both," Archie replied, "but McCabe moves pretty fast for a man his size."

"Sounds like it might be a good idea to dry-gulch him. Come on, Shorty, let's set down at a table and wait awhile to see if he comes in tonight. It'll be a whole lot easier to tell Marvin about Rob and Skeeter, if we can tell him we shot the sidewinder that done for 'em." He took the bottle and picked out a table near the back of the room, against a side wall.

As soon as they sat down, Mae Davis sauntered over and plopped down in one of the chairs at their table. "You sure look like two lonesome boys," was her opening line. "You're gonna need some help emptyin' that bottle."

"Any other time, darlin'," Lucky told her. "Right now, we got some important business goin' on. Expectin' some company and I wouldn't want you to get in the way of a stray bullet."

She made a little pout and started to get up, but Shorty stopped her with a hand on her arm. "Might not be a bad idea to let her visit awhile. With her settin' in that chair, it makes it a little harder for somebody comin' in the door to notice us."

"I'll be damned," Mae responded. "What was that you said about stray bullets? I don't know what you boys are up to, but I ain't gonna set here so you can use me for cover."

"Ah, he was just japin' you, Mae," Shorty assured her.

"We ain't got no business that'll cause you no harm. I'd just like to have some company besides Lucky. I get tired of him all the time."

Realizing what Shorty said was not a bad idea, Lucky gave her a big smile. "He's right, darlin', I was just japin' ya. Here, have a drink."

She produced a shot glass she brought with her and poured a drink. "You better not be japin' me now," she threatened, and tossed her whiskey back.

"Atta girl," Lucky said. "If things go right tonight, I might take a little trip upstairs with ya." He was grinning ear to ear when he thought about it, then became puzzled by the frozen look on Shorty's face. "What's wrong with you? You look like you've seen a . . ." He stopped in midsentence and turned to follow Shorty's stare toward the door.

"It's him!" Shorty finally managed to blurt out. "It's that devil that broke Clive Dawkins's nose!" In the span of a moment, the feeling that had gripped him in the Smith House in Waco, when he looked into the eyes of a mountain lion about to attack, returned to paralyze him. He remembered the feeling that he didn't want any part of this man. Then he suddenly realized that Lucky was shaking him.

"Is that him?" Lucky pressed frantically . He grabbed Mae and shook her. "Is that the one called McCabe?" He pushed his chair back to give himself room. She took the opportunity to jerk her arm away from him and run to the other side of the room, trailing a list of obscene names for him behind her for endangering her life. Lucky drew his pistol.

Immediately alerted when Mae suddenly bolted across

the room, Cullen dropped to one knee, drawing his six-gun in the process. The bullet from Lucky's .44 passed directly over his shoulder. He answered the shot with a round that embedded in the table, now on its edge and being used for protection. It was enough to cause Lucky to duck down behind the cover of the table while he cocked his pistol. When he popped up again to take another shot, Cullen was no longer there, but Lucky was quick enough to see the batwing doors still moving gently back and forth. "He's runnin'!" Lucky yelled to Shorty, who was still hugging the floor behind the overturned table. "Come on!" Lucky yelled again, and charged toward the door. "Don't let him get away!" But Shorty failed to rally to the charge. Lucky was halfway to the door when Cullen suddenly stepped back inside and opened fire, placing two rounds in Lucky's chest. He crashed heavily to the floor right in the doorway. Already with a third cartridge in the chamber, Cullen stepped around Lucky's body and advanced toward the overturned table, ready for the first sign of the man still behind the table.

"I give up," Shorty called out from behind the table. "I ain't fired a shot. It was all Lucky's idea. I didn't have no part in it."

It struck Cullen that the voice sounded familiar and he had been in a similar situation before. "Let me see your empty hands above the table," he ordered. When Shorty raised both of his hands above the edge of the table, Cullen told him to get on his feet. "I've seen you before," Cullen said when Shorty got to his feet. "Smith House dinin' room, right?"

"Yes, sir, that's right," Shorty replied. "I didn't draw my weapon on you then and I didn't draw it now."

"Why did your friend shoot at me?" Cullen asked.

"You killed Rob Gillespie and Skeeter Shaw," Shorty answered simply.

"So you and your partner, here, ride for the Crooked-T. Right?" When Shorty didn't answer, Cullen asked, "Why didn't you shoot at me, if you thought I killed two of your men?"

"'Cause I didn't wanna end up like him," Shorty said, and nodded toward the body lying in the doorway. He was totally convinced that Cullen would kill him if he ever raised his hand against him. He was not a coward. He was sure of that. But he felt that the big, broad-shouldered man had his number, the same as he had Lucky's, so it didn't make any sense to give him the opportunity to punch it.

The man's attitude was enough to baffle Cullen, but he recalled that it was the same in Waco when he had knocked his friend Clive senseless. And he frankly didn't know what to do with him. If there was a sheriff in Reid's Mill, he might consider throwing him in jail, if there was a jail. "Mister," he finally said, "you need to find you a better class of friends. Since you didn't try to shoot me, I reckon I ain't got any quarrel with you. So, as far as I'm concerned, this little misunderstandin' was between me and your friend and it's done. That don't mean I won't kill you, if I see the first sign that you changed your mind. I'll leave it up to you, whether or not you wanna take your friend's body back to the Crooked-T. But we'll need to get him outta the door, so folks won't have to step over him."

"I'd appreciate that," Harman Gill spoke up then. Having been summoned from his office once again by the sound of gunshots in his saloon, he had joined the few spectators to gather around the corpse. "At least, pull him out on the porch while you're deciding what you're gonna do with him."

One of the gawkers, Mae Davis, took a closer look at the body, then leaned down and asked, "Why the hell do they call you Lucky?" She snorted once and returned to the table on the far side of the room, where she had fled just before the shooting started.

While Cullen stood there watching him, Shorty decided what he would do, so he grabbed Lucky's arms and started dragging him out the door. When Cullen saw that he was going to try to load the body on Lucky's horse, he reached down and got Lucky's boots. They carried him out to his horse and laid him across the saddle. "You owe me for a bottle of whiskey," Archie reminded Shorty.

"Right," Shorty said, and walked back to the overturned table to pick up the bottle that had not spilled all of its whiskey out. "I'll take it with me," he told Archie, and paid him for it. He looked around him then, from Archie, to Cullen, to Gill, as if looking to see if there was any objection. When no one said anything more to him, he climbed up into the saddle and turned his horse away from the rail, fully expecting a shot in the back. When there was none, he led Lucky's horse toward the bridge to the main street, crossing it just as the men of the town council filed out of the church, their meeting finished. Apparently, the sound of the gunshots had something to do with it. The body lying across the saddle of the horse being led was explanation enough for the shots they had heard. As far as the man leading the dead man's horse, not one of them knew who he was, so most of them went straight to the Whiskey Mill to find out.

Moss Pringle was among the first to go in the door,

where he met Archie using his foot to wipe up a splatter of blood with a large rag. "Cullen?" Moss asked.

"Yep," Archie answered, and continued mopping. Moss looked around the saloon and spotted Cullen sitting at a table near the back. He went straight for it.

"Crooked-T?" Moss asked before he was even settled in a chair.

"That's a fact," Cullen answered. "Archie knew 'em. The one that left here layin' on his belly was a fellow named Lucky Spence, fellow ridin' the horse was Shorty Taylor."

"What started the shootin'?"

"The dead one took a shot at me when I walked in the door," Cullen answered. "Archie said it was because I killed Rob and Skeeter."

"You shoulda told 'em it was me that killed Rob," Moss said.

"They didn't take time for any discussion," Cullen said. "Just started shootin'. At least, one of 'em did, the other 'un just came along to watch, I reckon. Anyway, it doesn't make much difference. I reckon they'd try just as hard to shoot me for one as they would for two. No sense in puttin' your name on their list." He looked around to see where Archie was. "I believe I owe you a drink, then you can tell me what you and your neighbors decided to do at your meetin'."

Before Moss had time to respond to that matter, he was interrupted when Paul Dickson walked over, pulled a chair out, and sat down at the table. "Mind if I join you fellows?" Dickson asked after he was seated. "I'll buy you a drink, McCabe. What are you drinkin'?"

The offer was quite a surprise to Cullen. His natural

instinct told him something was wrong. "I was just about to buy Moss a drink," he replied. "I owe him one."

"In that case, I'll buy us all one," Dickson declared, and signaled Archie, who was busy pouring whiskey and relating the latest shooting details at the bar. "I might have to go pick 'em up," Dickson decided.

"I'll pick 'em up," Moss volunteered. "Archie looks pretty busy. If you're doin' the buyin', I can do the fetchin'."

To Cullen, Moss looked like he was glad to find an excuse to leave the table. He had a feeling, so he turned to Dickson and asked, "What can I do for you, Mr. Mayor? You look like you've got something on your mind."

Dickson looked a little surprised, but he responded casually. "Oh, nothin', really. I would like to say how sorry I am that you've run into so much bad luck in our little town. And Archie just told me that fellow you had to kill just now came in the door gunnin' for you. Did you know him?"

"Nope," Cullen replied. "This was the first time I ever saw him."

"Do you mind if I ask you a question that I'm just curious about? I don't want to ask you anything you think ain't any of my business. I'm just curious."

Cullen couldn't help but smile at the mayor's fumbling attempt to get information. "No, Mr. Mayor, you can ask me anything you want."

"How long are you plannin' to stay in our little town?"

"Are you askin' me to leave?" Cullen responded.

"No, no, nothing of the sort," Dickson quickly responded, interrupted then when Moss returned with the whiskey. "Of course, you're welcome here. It's just hard to understand why you would linger here when, like this very night, the Crooked-T keeps sending men to kill you. Do you have an old score to settle with Marvin Creed?"

"Never met the man," Cullen said.

"We here in Reid's Mill are concerned for your safety just as much as we are for our own citizens. We've been having more than our share of trouble with the Crooked-T hands. But it's been mostly destroyed property, loud and improper behavior with our women and children, drunken brawls, and such. Now, since you've arrived in town, it's gunfights and loss of life, even though I have to admit most of it has been aimed at you. But I'm afraid some of our citizens might get in the way and lose their lives as a result—Moss, here, for example. Moss confessed in the church tonight that he was the one who shot Rob Gillespie when he was actually looking for you."

Cullen looked at once toward Moss and Moss tried to explain. "I couldn't let you go on and take the blame for that, Cullen. I was settin' right there in the church with the reverend and the brothers. I just couldn't stand hidin' that any longer."

Well, damned if this isn't going really well, Cullen thought, as he looked from the mayor to Moss and back again. *I wonder what Governor Hubbard would think of his special problem solver right about now. Sent me up here to solve their problem and I made it worse than it was before I got here. Some special agent.* At this point, he really didn't know what he should do. But he supposed it might be better for the town if he wasn't there. *I should have gone back after the first day with the recommendation that the town hire a sheriff.* It seemed the only thing to help the town's immediate problem and he couldn't understand why Dickson and the rest of the council didn't see that.

The look on Cullen's face must have revealed some concern for Moss, so Dickson was quick to assure him. "Brother Moss has in no way been shunned by the church for the killing of that man."

"Well, I hope to hell not," Cullen responded. "He broke into the stable and set fire to the hay, fixin' to burn the place down. I don't see that Moss had any other choice."

"That's right," Dickson said, "and every member of the church thinks the same. But it's also good that he confessed to the act, instead of keepin' it secret."

"I don't know about that, one way or the other. I reckon that's between a man and his conscience, but in this particular case, I don't think it'd be such a good idea to let the Crooked-T know Moss confessed to killin' one of their hands."

"Of course not," Dickson replied. "That would, in all likelihood, invite the Crooked-T to send assassins to seek out Moss." He paused to make sure Cullen was following him, then continued. "Which brings us back to you, Mr. McCabe. It seems that you have been unfortunate to attract assassins on a regular basis ever since you got here. How long are you plannin' to stay?"

"Like I said when I first got here, I just planned to look around at the open land around here for a few days, however long it takes me. Is this your way of tellin' me to hurry it up a little? You figure you won't have any more trouble after I leave town?"

Dickson shrugged and said, "It's an even bet." Then he favored Cullen with a friendly smile.

"You know what you need, don't you?" Cullen asked.

"Like I told you before, you need to find you a good man to hire as sheriff. Build you a jailhouse and let the wild ones know they'll go to jail if they raise hell in Reid's Mill."

"You talk like you're lookin' for the job," Dickson said, the thought just occurring to him. He had thought, if anything, McCabe rode on the other side of the line. He and Jim Duncan had speculated on the possibility that he might have a well-known name in the fast-gun circles. And that fact accounted for the sudden rise in deaths soon after he arrived in town.

"Nope," Cullen informed him at once. "Like I said before, I'm just in town for a few days and then I'll be movin' on. How about Jim Duncan? He's young enough and strong enough. Maybe he'd be interested in takin' on the job part-time. He'd have to know for sure that you and the other men in town would back him up." He paused to gauge Dickson's reaction and decided he showed some interest in the possibility. "You might have you a good man right here in your little community and maybe you could afford him on a part-time basis. As far as I'm concerned, I'll move on outta town a little sooner than I had planned, if you think that would be best."

"I don't want to seem inhospitable," Dickson was quick to reply. "I was really just discussing possibilities with you. As long as Moss welcomes you to stay in his stable, there's no need to feel the town wants you to move on. Maybe the Crooked-T has already learned its lesson and they'll find it too costly to send gunslingers over here looking for you."

Dickson's opinion was fairly obvious and Cullen could understand how the mayor arrived at such an assumption. "The fact of the matter," Cullen said, "is the town was havin' problems with troublemakers drawn in by the saloon. Then I showed up and defended myself against some of those causin' the problems. Because I did, the feelin' in town is that I'm the cause of your problems. Right?" He paused, but Dickson did not respond, so he continued. "Now, if I move on outta town, what makes you think you won't have the same problems you had before I showed up?"

Dickson hesitated. "Well, we might, but we won't have the killin'."

"I guarantee you the killin' will come," Cullen stated. "It always does when a drunken gang of saddle bums realize there ain't no punishment for murder. And the quickest way to settle an argument is one squeeze of a trigger." Dickson didn't reply, but the way he raised his eyebrows and shrugged told Cullen that the mayor was inclined not to go to the expense of establishing a sheriff's office at this time. He was obviously counting on things getting better as soon as Cullen left town and evidently ignoring the trouble written about to the governor. *Looks like I'm gonna have to push a little harder,* Cullen thought.

CHAPTER ELEVEN

While Cullen was debating the town's problem in the Whiskey Mill with Paul Dickson, Shorty Taylor was on his way back to the old line shack. Of the four men who were camping at the shack, he was now the only survivor, the other three having been done in by Cullen McCabe. To Shorty, it was akin to being exposed to smallpox or any other deadly disease and usually fatal. Clive Dawkins was the only man he could name who had gone up against McCabe and lived. And Shorty was convinced that was because McCabe had some reason for sparing Clive. But to brand him, he left him with a permanently crooked nose. Riding now over a faint trail under a rising new moon, Shorty imagined he could see that steely face of the mountain lion, just after putting two slugs into Lucky's chest. He had looked up at once toward him, waiting for him to come out from behind the table. Remembering the feeling, Shorty became sick inside from a feeling of cowardice and he had a sudden desire to rid his body of its contents. He stopped the horses and slid off to land in a gully beside the trail, barely making it in time to keep from soiling his clothes.

When he felt he could stand again, he got to his feet and prepared to climb back into the saddle. He hesitated and looked at Lucky's body draped across his saddle. Suddenly consumed in a fit of disgust, he walked back to Lucky's horse, took hold of the dead man's boots, and pulled his body off to land on the ground so hard that it caused the horse to jump sideways. "You can stay here and rot," he declared. "It ain't my responsibility to have to bury you!" He started to get on his horse, but once again, he hesitated. Then he went back to the body to strip it of anything of value. In the saddle finally, he kicked his horse into a gallop for a couple hundred yards before reining him back to a walk. He was already thinking about what he was going to tell Marvin Creed. His first question was bound to be, *How come he ain't dead? You're still alive.* It wasn't going to be easy to explain the loss of three men to Creed, but he was going to have to do it. And when he asked for the reason McCabe was still alive, Shorty was going to have to lie about it. He couldn't admit the real reason why he found himself incapable of challenging the stone-faced killer. He would have turned and ridden in the opposite direction from the Crooked-T, but he feared Marvin Creed almost as much as he feared Cullen McCabe. By the time he reached the line shack, he had convinced himself that a good night's sleep would clear his head enough to account for his lack of action in the confrontation with McCabe that cost Lucky his life.

Morning found Shorty Taylor bleary-eyed and headachy after a nearly sleepless night. He had finished a good portion of the bottle of whiskey he bought in the Whiskey

Mill when he got back to the line shack. That, alone, would normally have insured unconsciousness, but on this occasion, it served only to suspend him halfway between sleep and wakefulness. Consequently, he found it necessary to build a pot of strong coffee to try to rid his head of the fuzziness of the night just passed. It was not until he had consumed almost the whole pot that he felt he could undertake the job of packing up for the short ride to the Crooked-T. There was not that much to pack, but in his condition, it seemed a lot. He saddled his horse and Lucky's horse. And there was the one packhorse the four of them had used to handle the supplies they had carried down to the shack. That was it. He tied the packhorse on a line tied to Lucky's saddle, then he led Lucky's horse and left the shack for the seven-mile ride to the Crooked-T.

Blackie Welch was the first to spot him when he rode into the barnyard at the ranch. On his way back from the outhouse, Blackie called out to him. "Hey, Shorty. We was wonderin' when you was gonna show up. Where's the other boys?"

"They ain't comin'," Shorty replied. "They're dead."

"Dead? Whaddaya mean, they're dead?" Blackie asked, confused. "What happened to 'em?"

"They run into trouble in Reid's Mill," Shorty replied. "Where is everybody?"

"Still in the bunkhouse," Blackie said, "waitin' for Creed to come tell us how we're gonna work the next job comin' up."

"Well, let's just go there and I'll tell you about what happened to Rob and Lucky and Skeeter. I just wanna tell it once," Shorty said. "I'll be there in a minute after I take care of my horses." He guided his horse to the barn and Blackie hustled back to the bunkhouse to tell the others.

When Shorty walked into the bunkhouse, the men sitting around on their beds were waiting to hear his story and the questions started flying before he could get himself a cup of coffee to put on top of what he had already consumed. "Blackie said you told him that Rob and Skeeter and Lucky are dead," Clive Dawkins said. "What was you talkin' about?"

"I'm talkin' about they're dead," Shorty answered him. "One night, Rob and Skeeter rode into Reid's Mill to do a little drinkin'. Me and Lucky didn't go with 'em. They never came back, so me and Lucky went into Reid's Mill the next day to see if they was all right. You know Archie, the bartender? Well, he told us Rob got to hasslin' some little jasper that he had run outta the saloon the last time he was in town. He had a feller with him, a drifter just passin' through town, Archie said. And that drifter shot Skeeter down." Shorty went on to tell them about the drifter hanging Rob in the tree and Rob showing up dead the next morning. "Archie figured it was the same jasper that shot Skeeter. So we was settin' there at a table and this jasper walks in. Lucky didn't wait for no howdy-do, he pulled his .44 and threw a shot at him, but he missed." He told them how Cullen had stepped back out the door, only to step back in again and shoot Lucky twice in the chest.

"What were you doin' while all this was goin' on?" Marvin Creed asked, surprising Shorty. Creed had stepped inside the door of the bunkhouse, unnoticed, in time to hear Shorty relating the events that took the lives of three of Creed's men. His foreman, Shane Roper, was with him.

"They had me in a fix," Shorty claimed. "I was on the

floor after the table got turned upside down and there was too many people that had me covered, so that I couldn't do nothin'."

"Hmm . . ." Creed responded. "Had you covered, eh? Do you know who this big killer is?"

"Nope, I don't know nothin' about him, but I've seen him before and I know his name now. Clive knows as much about him as I do." His comment caused Clive Dawkins to jerk his head back in surprise. "He's the feller that busted your nose in the Smith House," Shorty said.

Clive jumped to his feet. "That son of a . . ." he roared, then interrupted himself to demand, "Why didn't you shoot him?"

"I told you, they had me boxed up there. I couldn't pull my gun."

Clive's whole face turned a violent red with anger, except for his crooked nose, which stood out like a blanched white light. "What's his name?"

"Archie said his name's Cullen McCabe," Shorty said.

"Cullen McCabe," Roper repeated, searching his memory. "That's not a name I've ever heard of. If he's got a reputation, it must be somewhere a long way away from Texas or Mexico."

With his anger approaching the boiling point, Clive began snorting through his battered nose, sounding like a wild boar preparing to attack. Memories of the encounter that knocked him senseless were creating sharp pangs of pain in his imagination, until he could stand it no longer. "I'm headin' to Reid's Mill right now."

Tater Owen, who was seated on a corner of the bunk-house table and closest to Clive, thought to remind the angry man. "You can't go to Reid's Mill today. Boss is gettin' ready to tell us about a job."

Overhearing Tater's comment, Creed said, "That's right, Clive, I'm lookin' at a little job up toward Palo Pinto County. And I come in here this mornin' to find out that I'm already three men short. I've got my eye on a big herd Herman has been scoutin' for the last week or so and he says they're ready." Herman Thompson had been scouting herds to rustle for a long time for Creed. And the men knew that if Herman said they were ready to move, Creed wouldn't hesitate because that meant the cattle were probably grazing a long way from the ranch headquarters.

"I've got to get this scum-suckin' dog," Clive roared painfully. "I've got to go today, right now. He might not hang around that town much longer. He's got to pay for this!" He pointed toward his battered nose. As an afterthought, he said, "And how about the three men he killed?" He looked at Creed to emphasize. "Three good men, he needs to answer for that."

Creed could see that Clive wasn't going to have his focus on the business of rustling cattle as long as killing Cullen McCabe was the only thing on his mind. So he made a compromise for him. "Roper and the rest of the men are moving out this afternoon to Palo Pinto. It'll take two full days to make that ride up there. So, if you can get your business done in Reid's Mill and get up to Willow Creek, where you camped the last time you were up that way, two nights from now, that's where Roper and the men will be. But you keep it in mind, if you ain't there to work those cattle, you get no share of the money when I sell 'em. You understand that?"

"I understand," Clive said at once. "I'll be at that creek

two nights from now. Where we took that herd of horses, right?"

"That's the place," Roper said. "Now, you'd best get goin', if you're gonna have any time to hunt that drifter down."

"Yes, sir!" Clive said, and headed for the bunkhouse door.

Shorty headed him off to meet him at the door. "You best not get careless, if you do run into that devil. I'm tellin' you, that man's dangerous." He never particularly liked Clive Dawkins very much, but he felt he should warn him, since they both rode for Marvin Creed.

"Hell," Clive responded in his usual manner. "You'd do better to go warn Mr. Cullen McCabe that thunder and lightnin' is fixin' to blow his sorry ass into hell."

"Just remember I told you," Shorty said.

"Yeah, I'll remember," Clive told him. "I remember that you've been with two of us when we had a run-in with that devil, but you never got hurt. And you never had a chance to get a shot at him. I've been thinkin' about that."

"You got no call to say somethin' like that," Shorty said, "specially when he drove his shoulder through you and took your gun away from you and rapped you across your nose with it. And he had your gun on me just hopin' I'd reach for mine. You just remember that part of it. He's dangerous and you'd do well to keep that in mind is all I'm sayin'."

"Huh," Clive snorted in contempt for Shorty's warning. "He caught a lucky break that night. His luck's run out now. I'll see you at Willow Creek."

* * *

Pretty much of the opinion that his mission to Reid's Mill was a failure, Cullen was thinking that maybe the mayor was right and things would be better if he left town. The only accomplishment he could count was the elimination of three worthless souls the world was better off without. As one last shot, he considered sounding out Jim Duncan about any interest the blacksmith might have in taking on the duties of a sheriff. Since he had already told Jim that he wanted him to shoe Orphan and his packhorse, he decided he might as well take them to be shod this morning. So he took both horses out of the stable and led them a hundred feet up the river to the blacksmith shop.

"Mornin', Jim. Did I catch you at a good time to take care of my horses?"

"Sure did," Jim replied, "as good a time as any. Lead 'em on in here." Cullen tied Orphan to a post at the back of the shop and handed the packhorse's reins to Jim. He figured it'd be a good idea to see what kind of job Jim did on the sorrel before he decided to let him work on Orphan. He was satisfied to see that Jim knew his trade right away, so they were soon discussing the meeting of the town council on the night before.

"Talkin' to Paul Dickson afterward, I got the idea that the council was of the opinion that I was drawin' gunslingers to Reid's Mill," Cullen commented.

"That was brought up," Jim admitted. "But I don't know that everybody thinks you're drawin' 'em. I, for one, don't think that way a-tall and I told 'em that. If you was attractin' gunslingers, lookin' to make a name as a fast gun, they'd be strangers from all over. But these fellows you shot were all from the Crooked-T. They didn't come to town lookin' for you. The only difference is when they pushed you, you pushed back. And they weren't used to that. I told 'em that! Stumpy Morgan got hot about it. He said you saved his life that night in the Whiskey Mill."

"I reckon I can see, with what's happened, that I'm the bait that's drawin' some of those Crooked-T hands to town, lookin' to settle up for their friends. So I can't say as I blame the mayor and some of the others for wantin' to get rid of me. And I'll move on outta town." He smiled then and said, "I might stay around long enough to go up to the Stoddard House to get me a real good dinner and then leave town."

"If you ain't particular about your company, I might go with you," Jim said.

"Sounds like a good idea," Cullen responded. He paused a few seconds as if it just occurred to him. "That's right, you ain't got a wife at home, cookin' for you, have you?"

"No, I reckon I never got around to hookin' up with the right woman," Jim said as he worked on the sorrel's hoof. "And Reid's Mill ain't the best place to find a decent woman who ain't already spoken for." He looked up at Cullen and grinned. "But I ain't gonna give up yet."

"Your business here keep you busy?" Cullen asked.

"Well, not as busy as I'd like to be," Jim allowed, "but there just ain't that much call for a blacksmith in a town this small."

"You ever think you'd like to be a peace officer?"

"Why, no. That's one thing I don't reckon I've ever given any thought to. Why?"

"Because Reid's Mill needs a sheriff," Cullen told him frankly. "And if it was up to me to pick somebody for the job, I'd pick you. You're young enough to handle the job and old enough to have good judgment. And there ain't no doubt you're strong enough to handle the typical drunk. You could even take it on part-time and keep your smithin' business." He could see that Jim was giving his words some consideration, so he waited for his response.

"You think that, do ya?" Jim asked. "I don't know the first thing about bein' a sheriff. Like I said, I never thought about it."

"There's not a great deal to learn. You just need a basic sense of what's right and what's wrong. When you catch somebody doin' something wrong, you stop 'em from doin' it. I'd be glad to help you get started. I used to be the sheriff in a little town called Sundown. Wouldn't take you no time a-tall to get the hang of it." He could see that the idea was turning over and over in Jim's mind now. So he grinned and said, "You need a jailhouse, though. I already tried a tree and that didn't work out too well. You think about it."

During the balance of the time that Duncan was working on Cullen's two horses, there were a lot of questions from him about the workings of a typical sheriff's office. Cullen could see that there was a definite interest on Jim's part about the possibility of his actually taking on the role. By the time Jim was finished with the shoeing, Cullen was convinced that he had a bona fide candidate for the sheriff's job. The only qualification he could not be sure of was Jim's courage under fire and that was something that could be determined only in an actual confrontation.

Jim had one last question on his mind that he wondered about before they returned Cullen's horses to the stable and went to dinner. "I'm a pretty good shot with a rifle and a shotgun," he told Cullen as they walked the horses back. "But I've never spent a lot of time practicin' drawin' my pistol. I don't know how fast I am, if I was to come up against a real fast gunslinger."

"I'm glad you brought that up," Cullen declared. "'Cause one rule you shouldn't ever forget, you're a lawman. You ain't in a fast-draw competition—ever. You don't fight duels with lawbreakers, you arrest 'em, and if they resist arrest, you shoot 'em. If you feel more comfortable with a shotgun, carry a shotgun." By the time they reached the rooming house, Cullen felt like he'd just hired a sheriff. All that was needed now was an available position and a jailhouse. That part was going to take some persuading by the other members of the town council.

"Well, welcome back," Becca Stoddard greeted Cullen cheerfully when he and Jim walked in the door. "And you brought someone with you. How are you, Jim?" she greeted him.

"I hope Cora cooked up plenty of food," Stumpy joked. "That looks like two pretty big eaters to me." He waved Cullen and Jim over to sit beside him. "How you likin' your new sleepin' arrangements down at the stable with Moss?"

"I've had worse," Cullen answered, "but the cookin' ain't quite as good as Cora's."

"That right? What's the matter, is ol' Moss gettin' too stingy with the oats?" Stumpy was clearly happy to see Cullen again. He got serious for a moment. "That was bad business about that shootin' at the Whiskey Mill last night. I know it wasn't nothin' you coulda helped doin'." He paused then added, "Specially after what most of the meetin' in the church was about."

"Askin' me to get outta town?" Cullen responded. "I have to say, Paul Dickson tried to be as nice about it as he could. So I told him I'd be movin' on."

"All of us wasn't thinkin' that way," Stumpy insisted. "Tell him, Jim. We tried to tell Dickson that you didn't start none of the trouble with those Crooked-T fellers. They just decided to commit suicide."

"I 'preciate it, Stumpy," Cullen said. "You folks will stop most of your trouble with the Crooked-T hands when you decide to hire a sheriff and build a jail. I told Dickson that, but he doesn't wanna pay for it. It's gonna take the rest of the town council to push for it."

"Even if we did," Harvey Stoddard asked, "and I think that's a damn good idea, where we gonna find a man to fill the job?"

"Fellow sittin' right next to me," Cullen said.

"Stumpy?" Harvey blurted.

"He's talkin' about me, Harvey," Jim Duncan spoke up. "I'm thinkin' about takin' on the job, if the town's okay with it."

"That's a great idea," Becca Stoddard declared, having stopped at the end of the table to listen to the discussion. "I don't know why somebody didn't think of that before." By the time the beef stew was finished, Johnny Mitchell was proposing the formation of a committee to push the merchants to come up with the funds to establish a sheriff's department. Cullen figured it was a good start toward the town solving their problem themselves, but he was unaware of a problem of a more urgent nature awaiting him.

CHAPTER TWELVE

"Uh-oh, here comes trouble," Archie Wells muttered to Molly Dugan when he saw Clive Dawkins walk in the front door. The ruthless brute stood in the doorway for a long moment while he looked the room over. His last visit to the saloon had resulted in a broken front window, the result of Clive's heaving a young cowhand through it.

"He looks meaner than ever," Molly said.

"It's his nose," Archie said. "Looks like somebody hit him with an ax. I was hopin' he wouldn't be back here in a while."

When he finished searching the room, Clive started toward the bar. "I'm gettin' the hell outta here," Molly announced at once, and headed briskly toward the other side of the saloon.

"You better run!" Clive yelled, delighting in her obvious fright. "Pour me a drink," he directed Archie then. He waited for Archie to pour it, then tossed it down immediately. "I'm lookin' for one Mr. Cullen McCabe. You seen him today?"

"You're lookin' for McCabe?" Archie replied, finding it surprising.

"Ain't that what I just said?" Clive responded. "What's the matter with you? Are you hard of hearin'?"

"McCabe don't usually come in here this early in the day," Archie answered. "Matter of fact, he don't come in here very often at night. Anyway, I ain't seen him today."

"He's still in town, ain't he?"

"I ain't got no idea whether he is or not," Archie tried to explain. "All I can tell you is I ain't seen him today." He could see that his answers to Clive's questions were serving to make him angry, so he offered a suggestion. "Maybe he's down at the stable. That's where he's been sleepin'."

Clive thought that over for a moment, thinking that Archie just might be trying to get rid of him. "You know it ain't gonna be too good for you if I go down to the stable and find out McCabe ain't been there."

"I ain't lyin'," Archie insisted. "That's where he's stayin', there with his horse. I don't know if he's there now or not. That's all I'm sayin'."

"Pour me another 'un," Clive ordered. After he tossed it down, he turned and headed for the door.

"Hey, you forgot to pay me for two drinks," Archie called after him.

"Start me a bill and I'll pay you when I come back," Clive yelled back over his shoulder.

"That no-account cattle rustler," Archie mumbled when Molly came back to the bar to see why Clive left right away.

"I can't say I'm sorry to see him walk right back outta here," Molly said. "What did you say to him?"

"I told him to get his big behind outta here before I had to throw him out," Archie couldn't resist japing. Before she could call him a liar, he quickly told her the truth. "He's lookin' for Cullen McCabe, wanted to know if he'd been in here. I told him I ain't seen him."

"He left in a hurry," Molly said. "Where's he goin' now?"

"Well"—Archie hesitated—"maybe I shouldn't have told him, but I said McCabe was bunkin' in with his horse at the stable."

"McCabe best be ready when Clive comes to call," Molly said, thinking of a contest between the two big men and the sport it would be to watch it. "Knowin' Clive's style, he'll just shoot McCabe in the back if he gets the chance." She walked out to the front porch then and peered down the narrow wagon track that led to Moss Pringle's stable. She was joined shortly by Mae Davis.

"Archie said Clive Dawkins went lookin' for Cullen McCabe," Mae said. "You see anything?"

"No," Molly answered, "and I ain't heard no gunshots. McCabe must not be at the stable."

Molly's guess was right, McCabe wasn't at the stable. He was at the opposite end of town at Stoddards' rooming house when Clive stepped down from the saddle and walked in the stable to startle Moss Pringle. "Where's McCabe?" Clive demanded.

"I don't know," Moss answered when he found his voice again. "He ain't here right now. He took his horses this mornin' to get shod." He didn't volunteer the information that Cullen and Jim Duncan had brought his horses back to the stable, then went up the street to eat dinner. Cullen had invited Moss to go with them, but he had declined.

"Don't you lie to me," Clive threatened. "I just passed

by the blacksmith and there ain't a soul there. I ain't got time to waste on you." He drew his .44 and cocked it as he brought it up to aim in Moss's face. "Now, I'll ask you again, where's Cullen McCabe?"

Moss's knees almost buckled under him. "I swear, I don't know where he is! I ain't lyin', he took his horses to get shod, but he's already brought 'em back. I think him and the blacksmith went to eat some dinner up at the boardin'house."

"You coulda told me that at first," Clive said. "I've got a mind to shoot your sorry ass for wastin' my time." He continued to hold his pistol on the frightened man for what seemed an eternity to Moss, while he decided whether or not to shoot him. Finally, he eased the hammer back and holstered the weapon. Then he turned and walked out of the stable, having reluctantly decided he couldn't afford to warn McCabe with the sound of the gunshot.

Back in the saddle, Clive guided his horse across the bridge to the main street and headed up toward Stoddards' rooming house. If he was in luck, he might be in time to catch McCabe sitting at a table, eating dinner. He formed a picture in his mind of the solemn man facedown with his brains spilling out on his plate. Although a gratifying picture, it was not to be, however, for he met Cullen and Jim in the street as they were leaving Stoddards'.

The two men recognized each other at the same time. Clive reined his horse back to a hard stop and slid off the saddle to find Cullen with his six-gun already in hand and aimed at him. "Stand away from me, Jim," Cullen cautioned softly, and Jim took a few steps to his left. "What do you want, Clive?"

"Cullen McCabe," Clive replied, his lips curling into a

sneer. "And you remember my name. I'm glad you do 'cause I remember you. Every time I shave, I remember you. You got the jump on me that night in Waco and here we are now with you already holdin' a gun on me. And you ain't got no cause to hold a gun on me. I didn't do you no harm that night. I'm the one with the busted nose."

"You made the mistake of tellin' me what you were plannin' to do. Something about breakin' my back, if I remember correctly. Right now, the best thing for you is to get back on your horse and get on outta town," Cullen said. "I could have shot you in the head that night instead of breakin' your nose. So you've got no reason to come after me."

"See, now that's where we disagree," Clive replied. "I don't like the way my face looks after you smashed my nose."

"I didn't like the way it looked before I smashed your nose. Now get on that horse and get outta here while you still can."

"That sounded like a threat to me, so I'm callin' you out, McCabe, man-to-man, guns or knives. We'll settle this thing between us once and for all. Whaddle it be?"

"How 'bout cannonballs at thirty paces?" Cullen replied sarcastically. "You damn fool. I'm standin' here holdin' a gun on you. You're done for, if you don't get back on that horse and get outta here."

Clive stood there, glaring at the man who had beaten him again. Finally, he said, "All right, McCabe, I tried to give you a chance to face me fair and square, but the time will come when you have to answer to me."

"Just get on your horse before I shoot you down right here in the street," Cullen told him.

"I'm goin'," Clive said, and turned to step up in the saddle, but he paused a moment, standing there with his left hand on the saddle horn, ready to pull himself up. Then suddenly, he spun back around, gun in hand, only to catch a .44 slug in his throat and another in his chest from Cullen's six-gun.

Cullen looked at Jim and was satisfied to see Jim's weapon in hand as well. "How'd you know he was gonna try it?" Jim asked.

"I didn't know," Cullen answered, "but I figured he probably would 'cause he came here to kill me and he agreed to get back on his horse without much fuss a-tall. He did me a favor when he reached for that gun. If we hadn't got it done right here, I woulda had to worry about takin' a round in the back sometime later on."

When the first of the curious started to gather in the street, Jim suggested that he should fetch Joe Morrison. "Yeah, I expect so," Cullen said, then stopped him. "No, wait a minute. I think I'll keep this one. Help me load him on his horse. I think I'll return this one to his owner." He decided it was time to have a meeting with the enemy, since the present way of operating wasn't working. Maybe there was a chance that Marvin Creed was weary of losing his men and was ready to find a peace between his ranch and the town of Reid's Mill.

Jim was not sure he understood. "You tellin' me you're fixin' to take this fellow's body back to the Crooked-T? Ain't that the same as committin' suicide?"

"Maybe. I don't know for sure, but talkin' to Marvin Creed is something you folks ain't ever tried to do. Am I right?" Jim conceded that point, so Cullen continued. "If Creed ain't ever been here before, he might think it's the town that's so hard on his men and not the other way around."

"You're talkin' like you expect to meet a man who's willin' to get along with other folks," Jim protested. "Marvin Creed takes what ain't his and sells it to anybody who'll buy it. Ain't nobody been able to prove it yet, but there are some of us who think Creed is the money backin' Harman Gill. And the Whiskey Mill ain't nothin' but a place for his men to let off some steam. When he's ready, I figure Creed will take over this town and he'll put his own man in the sheriff's office."

"Has Creed ever actually been to Reid's Mill?" Cullen asked a question that he had asked before.

"Not that I ever heard of," Jim replied, giving him the same answer he had gotten before.

"All the more reason to get some backbone in this town and a strong sheriff's department before he makes his first visit here. I expect all he hears about from his men is the Whiskey Mill." With Jim's help, he placed Clive Dawkins's body on his horse. "Now, can you tell me how I can find the Crooked-T?"

"Ain't nobody here that's ever gone there," Jim said, "but it ought not be too hard to find. Creed's men ride back and forth so often that there oughta be a pretty clear trail wore over the prairie by now. I can show you where it starts. You'll see it. Between Dickson's store and the barbershop." He paused to give Cullen a doubtful look. "You sure you know what you're doin'?"

Cullen reached in his pocket and pulled out some money. "I'll pay you for shoein' my horses, in case I don't. Now, I gotta get goin' before I use up all my daylight." He left Jim standing there shaking his head while he led Clive's horse to the stable to get Orphan.

He found Jim's speculation to be right. There was a distinct trail leading away from the town and heading almost straight east. Orphan was ready to get away from the stable apparently, for he maintained a spirited gait to try out his new shoes. Cullen knew it couldn't be a long ride, for he had been told that the Crooked-T was on the west bank of the Brazos and that river wasn't much more than fifteen miles from the Bosque River. So he followed the trail until he reached what appeared to be an old line shack. There was no sign of anyone there, but he gave it a "Hello, the shack," just in case. There was a good creek there, so he stopped long enough to let the horses have water before going on. He estimated that he was about halfway to the Crooked-T at that point. As he rode on, he occasionally passed small groups of cattle that appeared to be strays, causing him to wonder where the main herd was. Maybe the people in Reid's Mill were right and Marvin Creed did not actually raise cattle.

He followed the trail through a notch in a low line of hills that led him to a flat grassy plain and a line of trees in the distance that had to outline the Brazos River. Just short of the thickest growth of trees, he saw the barn and corral, and beyond that a bunkhouse and kitchen. Still farther and closer to the river's edge, he saw the ranch house, the headquarters of the Crooked-T. He pulled Orphan up to a stop and watched the ranch for a little while, looking for some activity. But there appeared to be no one around the barn or bunkhouse. There were a dozen or so horses in the corral, but no sign of any ranch hands. "The place looks deserted," he told Orphan, and gave the dun a nudge with his heels.

Entering the barnyard at a fast walk, he tried to get a look into the barn as he went by, but it was not until he rode by the bunkhouse that he saw someone. He reined Orphan to a full stop and waited while the man walked toward him, holding a rifle across his body. It was Cullen's guess that the man was Mexican and it was obvious that it was a rare occasion when a stranger approached the ranch. "What is your business here?" Juan Lopez asked while craning his neck to see the body lying across the saddle of the horse behind Cullen.

"I'm returnin' something that belongs here," Cullen answered. "That is, if this is the Crooked-T Ranch."

Suspicious, Juan took a wide arc around the big man on the dun horse in order to get a closer look at the body on the gray gelding, a horse he was sure he recognized. "Señor Dawkins!" He looked back at Cullen. "He is dead?"

"I'm afraid so," Cullen answered. "Maybe I'd better talk to the boss. He'll most likely wanna find out what happened to him. Is the boss here?"

"*Sí*, Señor Creed is here," Juan answered. "You wait here. I will tell him." He paused a moment to make sure Cullen understood, then turned and trotted to the ranch house. Cullen sat there for a few moments, looking all around him and still puzzled that there seemed to be no one there but the Mexican. Suddenly feeling like an easy target sitting there on Orphan, he stepped down and stood beside his horse. He watched Juan until he disappeared into the back door of the house.

Lola Lopez looked up in surprise when her husband

came into the kitchen. "There is a man out there with Clive Dawkins's body on his horse. He needs to talk to Señor Creed."

"I'll tell him," Lola said. "You wait here." She started toward the door. "And don't stick your fingers in that pot of stew. Supper's not ready yet." She went out the door then, and in a few minutes, she was back again. "Señor Creed said to bring the man to the front porch. He will speak to him there." She gave Juan a little push toward the back door to get him started.

"Follow me," Juan said to Cullen when he returned. Using his rifle to motion him on, he turned and led him to the front of the house. Cullen dropped Orphan's reins to the ground and tied Clive's reins to a porch post.

In a few minutes, Creed walked out on the porch, gave Cullen a brief nod, then looked at the body on the horse. Looking back at Cullen, he studied him for a few seconds before asking, "Why did you bring his body here?"

"I figured he worked for you," Cullen answered. "So I figured you might wanna know what happened to him."

"What did happen to him?" Creed asked almost casually.

"He got shot," Cullen replied, equally calm.

The two men eyed each other intensely for a long moment before Creed asked, "Who shot him?"

"I did," Cullen answered.

Creed continued to study him for a couple of moments more before stating, "You're Cullen McCabe."

"That's right," Cullen said, somewhat surprised that he guessed, "and you'd be Marvin Creed. I've heard a lot about you."

"So, did you ride all the way from Reid's Mill just to

bring Clive Dawkins's corpse back here? Don't you have a graveyard in Reid's Mill?"

"Well, I reckon I really rode all the way over here to let you know you've lost another one of your hands that mistakenly came to town thinkin' the rules of civilization didn't apply to him. As far as the graveyard is concerned, it's startin' to fill up with Crooked-T hands, so I thought I'd bring this one home to rest in peace with his friends. It looks like the town is gonna have to expand the little graveyard, if things keep goin' the way they have been. Your men have already taken up a good-sized corner of it. So it would help in our plannin' if you would tell me how many men you've got left and we can reserve that much space for 'em." He paused then to take a look back toward the barn. "Where are all your hands? I don't see anybody workin' but this fellow." He nodded toward Juan.

"This is a cattle ranch, Mr. McCabe," Creed replied, a wry smile on his face. "They're all out working the cattle. That's where Clive Dawkins was supposed to be. I'm sure my foreman is wondering where he is. Where was he when you shot him? I'm assuming you had good reason to shoot him, or you wouldn't have brought his body here."

"He was in the middle of the street in Reid's Mill and the only reason I shot him was because he was fixin' to shoot me. I brought him back to you because it seems like your men all come to town with a notion to shoot me. I don't have much choice in the matter. Seems to me you would get tired of losin' men every time they came to town. I was hopin' you were a reasonable man and you'd wanna put a stop to all your men's hell-raisin', so they'd be welcome in Reid's Mill. I think the town council is already takin' steps to start a sheriff's department and that'll help you keep your men under control."

With a patient smile on his face Creed listened to Cullen's presentation, and when Cullen finished, Creed asked one question. "Who the hell are you, McCabe? The word I got on you is that you're just a drifter who happened to ride into town the other day. Why would the town council send a drifter, a stranger, out here to talk to me about a peace agreement?"

"Did I say the town council sent me out to talk to you?" Cullen was quick to respond. "If I did, I didn't mean to. No, it just seemed to me it was something that needed doin'. When a fellow over there told me that ain't nobody in town ever rode over here to meet you, I thought it'd be a good idea if somebody did. And I didn't have any plans for today, so when Clive decided he was gonna shoot me, it just seemed like a good time to find out what kinda man you are. And come to find out, you're a pretty straight-talkin' fellow."

Ignoring the compliment, Creed continued to question this unlikely visitor to his outlaw compound. "Shorty Taylor said he and Clive ran into you first in Waco, in the Smith House. And that's where you broke Clive's nose. It seems kinda strange to me that you'd cross paths with my men again in Reid's Mill, if you were just a drifter."

"It seemed kinda strange to me, too. I was just unlucky, I reckon. It just happened to be the direction I was driftin' in," he said, shrugging.

"I got a feeling you're not just a drifter," Creed decided, finding himself intrigued by the soft-talking man, brazen enough to ride into his headquarters hauling the corpse of one of the Crooked-T's most dangerous men. He was tempted to try to find out who he really was. "I was just getting ready to have my supper, so why don't you join me?" Before Cullen had time to respond to the invitation, Creed motioned toward the gray horse tied to the porch post. "Juan, take Clive and his horse back behind the barn. Take care of his horse and you can dig a hole to bury Clive after you've had your supper." Back to Cullen then, he asked, "Are you going back to Reid's Mill tonight?" Cullen said that he was, so Creed told Juan to take Cullen's horse to the corral so the horse could drink.

"That's mighty neighborly of you, Mr. Creed," Cullen said, "but I wouldn't wanna surprise your family with another mouth to feed."

"You don't have to worry about that," Creed said, laughing. "There's nobody here tonight. I don't have any family. Juan's wife, Lola, works as my cook and house-keeper and she always cooks more than we can eat. You'll be welcome." He walked across the wide porch, opened the front door, and called, "Lola, we'll have a guest for supper."

"Well, I brought some beef jerky in my saddlebags that I planned to have for supper on my way back to Reid's Mill, but I'll try to make do with whatever your woman cooked." His attempt at humor brought a hardy laugh from Creed.

The woman, Lola, proved to be an excellent cook, and Creed had been correct when he said that she would cook more than they could eat. She was polite and very atten-tive, watching both men while they ate to be sure they didn't want for anything. Afterward, Creed called for brandy and cigars, which was a new experience for Cullen. He enjoyed the cigar, but he decided rye whiskey was still his drink of choice. After much discussion about cattle and horses, and questions about various subjects, Cullen came to the conclusion that Creed was interested in knowing exactly how he was wound inside. It must have been favorable because before the cigars were out, Creed proposed that it would be a good idea if Cullen came to work for him.

"That's a mighty interestin' idea," Cullen responded, "and I'd say a man would be a fool to turn down that offer. But I've been accused of bein' a fool enough times that I'm wonderin' if there might be something to it. So I'll thank you for the offer, but like they told you, I'm just driftin' right now. And pretty soon, I'm gonna be movin' on outta town."

"You sure you don't want to take the opportunity I'm offering?" Creed asked. "It could mean a good bit of money for you. Besides, you should fill the vacancy you just created in my crew. Clive Dawkins will be hard to replace."

Cullen gave him a faint smile for his attempt at humor before refusing the job offer. "Thank you again, but I reckon not." He turned to smile at Lola, standing near the kitchen door. "And thank you for that fine supper, ma'am. I believe Mr. Creed has got himself the best cook in the territory." She blushed appropriately.

Cullen took his leave from the owner of the Crooked-T after a final word of hope that there would be peace between the ranch and the town. Then he walked across the barnyard to the corral in the fading light to find his horse waiting outside the corral. He climbed up into the saddle, and after one more look around him, he headed back toward Reid's Mill. Behind him, Marvin Creed walked into the kitchen, where Juan was eating his supper. "Get finished up here pretty quick, follow him off the ranch, and kill him." He had been serious when he offered Cullen the chance to work for him. But he had a strong feeling that he couldn't afford to have Cullen working against him. *It's a shame to waste good potential like that,* he thought, disappointed that Cullen had refused.

"Sí, señor," Juan replied, and got up at once. He took the last gulp from his coffee cup and put a biscuit in his pocket. With the exchange of a worried look with his wife, he went out the back door.

"Well, Orphan, I reckon I just passed up a job that'll pay a good bit more than I'm gettin' from the state of Texas," he informed the dun gelding as he rode back through the notch in the low line of hills. Even in the fading light, it was an easy trail to follow. "Had me a damn good supper, though. Even though I had to ride a long way to get it." He decided to see how he and his horse felt by the time they reached the old line shack he had passed on the way to Crooked-T. He figured he might decide to camp there and go on into town in the morning. But first, there was another matter to take care of. He rode on another mile when he came to a small stream that cut across the trail. He turned Orphan up the stream for a couple dozen yards before pulling him up to a tree and dismounting. After looping the reins around some branches to be sure Orphan didn't try to follow him, he walked back to find himself a place beside the trail.

Thinking about Lola's beef stew, he decided that if he ate that much every night at supper, it wouldn't be long before Orphan wouldn't be able to tote him. He knelt there beside a laurel bush for a long while, listening to a bullfrog greeting a rising moon until finally he heard the soft padding of a horse's hooves on the sandy soil. He braced himself then, ready to act, waiting for the horse to approach the stream. In a few seconds, the horse was beside him. He sprang up from the bush, grabbed Juan by his shoulders, and jerked him off his horse.

Totally surprised, Juan yelped as he was thrown roughly to the ground, the rifle he had been carrying went spinning in the opposite direction as Cullen pinned the smaller man to the ground. Juan struggled to free himself but was helpless against Cullen's superior strength. Finally, he gave up the struggle when he felt the muzzle of Cullen's six-gun against the back of his head and he lay still. "I want you to listen to me now, Juan," Cullen told him, speaking in a calm but authoritative voice. "I know Creed sent you to kill me . . ." He had to pause when Juan, in his fright, reverted back to his Spanish tongue to pray for his life. "Hush!" Cullen blurted. "Just shut up and listen to me and you'll be all right. You understand?"

"*Sí*, I understand," Juan cried, although he was still totally confused.

"I've got no reason to want to kill you," Cullen told him. And I know you don't want to kill me. Am I right?"

"*Sí*, that's right. I no wanna kill you. Señor Creed say to kill you and I afraid to say I don't do it."

"Right," Cullen said, and released his hold on him, letting him sit up. "Now, here's what you do. You tell Creed you shot me in the back, but I stayed on my horse. You followed until your horse stumbled in the dark and threw you and knocked you out. When you woke up, I was gone, but you think I'm likely dead from your shot. Whaddaya think? Can you pull that off?"

"*Sí*, I pull it off," Juan said, gratefully.

"All right, go on and chase your horse down, then go on back to that little wife of yours." Juan didn't say any more, he just nodded his head up and down, happy to be alive. "And, Juan," Cullen said in parting, "if you change your mind and decide to come after me, I'll kill you next time. Understand?"

"*Sí, señor,* I understand. I don't change my mind."

CHAPTER THIRTEEN

Rather than make a breakfast of coffee and jerky, Cullen decided to saddle up and ride on into Reid's Mill for breakfast at Becca Stoddard's dining room. He had spent some time the night before to make sure Juan Lopez didn't have a change of heart out of fear of disobeying Marvin Creed's orders. He followed the reluctant Mexican halfway back to the notch in the hills before deciding he didn't have to worry about him anymore. When he started back again toward Reid's Mill, he decided he might as well camp in the line shack for the night. There was a fireplace and wood already stacked inside, so he figured he would take advantage of the Crooked-T's hospitality. He wasn't worried about unexpected company because of the absence of hands at the ranch. His guess was that somebody's cattle were being rustled that night.

When he got to Reid's Mill the next morning, he decided to go straight to the dining room and take Orphan back to the stable afterward. He was craving a fresh cup of coffee and his horse was not tired after the short ride from the line shack, so he figured Orphan wouldn't complain. "Well, good mornin', Mr. McCabe," Becca Stoddard greeted him when he paused at the door to rid himself of his hat and his gun belt. Holding a coffeepot in her hand, she waited while he selected a place to sit down. She turned the empty cup right-side up and filled it before commenting. "I'm glad to see you this morning. Have you seen Moss Pringle or Jim Duncan since you got back? They both came here to see if you had come in for supper last night." She looked at him and shook her head slowly. "They told me where you went yesterday." She shook her head again in pretended impatience. "We heard the gunshots in the street after you left here. Shoulda guessed they had something to do with you. When we found out where you had gone, we figured that was the last we'd ever see of you."

"Sorry to disappoint you," Cullen replied. "What's for breakfast?"

"Same as every day," Becca replied, "but this mornin' Cora mixed up some batter for flapjacks. She musta thought we needed something special to celebrate you comin' back." She paused then when she glanced toward the window. "Uh-oh, here comes Jim Duncan. He musta seen you ride in. I'll go tell Cora to cook you some flapjacks." She headed for the kitchen, just as Jim walked in the door.

"Hot damn," Jim declared when he walked up to the table. "I see you made it back. I wouldn'ta give you two cents for your chances of takin' that body back to the Crooked-T and comin' back alive." He looked around for Becca and turned the coffee cup over before sitting down. She nodded to him from the kitchen door. Back to the subject at hand, he asked, "Did you take Clive all the way back to the Crooked-T?"

"I left him at Marvin Creed's front steps," Cullen said, "and told him it was time to make peace with you folks here in Reid's Mill."

"You're joshin' me now," Jim came back. "What did he say to that?"

"He invited me to supper and after it was over, he sent his hired hand to follow me and shoot me. Interestin' fellow, got a fine cook, though."

"You wantin' breakfast?" Becca asked when she came from the kitchen.

"No, ma'am," Jim said. "I just want some coffee." Back to Cullen then, he asked, "He just let you ride in, totin' the body of one of his men?" Cullen shrugged. "What did Creed have to say about Clive and the rest of 'em that got shot here in town?"

Before Cullen could answer, Moss came in the door and Cullen had to start over. So they sat while he ate Cora's flapjacks and bacon, with three scrambled eggs on the side, and described the Crooked-T headquarters for them. "You were mighty damn lucky there weren't nobody there," Moss said. "Else, I doubt you'd be settin' here in Becca's dinin' room this mornin'."

"You might be right," Cullen said. "You're dealin' with a man with no conscience a-tall. He offered me a job after I came to tell him you folks in Reid's Mill were fixin' to build a jail and hire a sheriff. I told him you were tired of his wild hands tearin' up the town."

"You told him that?" Moss exclaimed, almost in a panic. "Nobody's talked to Paul Dickson about gettin' a sheriff."

Cullen casually took his knife and cut up his pancakes in bite-sized pieces, picked up a couple with his fork, and smeared them around in the syrup on his plate. Then he paused to say, "I reckon you'd best get around to talkin' about it," and stuck the forkful in his mouth.

"Cullen's right," Jim said. "We ain't got no choice. If we don't protect our town, we're not gonna have a town. It's gonna be like Dodge City or Tombstone. It's halfway there already. Before long, it won't be safe for a woman or child to be out on the street a-tall. It ain't a good idea to be out after sunset now. And we just accept it. The sun goes down and most nights you can count on some of that bunch of drunks to be racin' up and down the main street, shootin' off their guns."

"I'll say amen to that," Becca commented, having stopped to hear Jim's inspired oration. "The trouble is you men don't really have a town council. You've got a one-man council. Paul Dickson makes all the decisions."

All three men turned to look at her. Cullen nodded his head in agreement and Moss said, "You know, that ain't no lie."

"Is Paul Dickson the only one who can call a council meetin'?" Cullen asked, between bites.

Jim and Moss looked at each other apologetically. Moss was the first to answer. "Well, Dickson is the mayor and I reckon it's always the mayor who calls the meetin's."

"Why can't any member of the council call a meetin', if he thinks there's something to discuss that affects all the other members?" Cullen asked.

"That's a good question," Becca commented, being strongly interested in the future of her and her husband's business. "You didn't elect him to be king, did you?"

Ignoring Becca's interruption, Jim responded to the question. "I reckon, if we was to have any rules, they'd say we all got equal rights. I don't remember ever seein' any rules. It just seems like Dickson has always been the one knowin' what's best for the town. And when he wants to make some rules or something, he calls a meetin'."

"Hell, I don't see no reason why any one of us can't ask for a meetin'," Moss declared. "The thing to do is to go talk to the other members and tell them we want to come together for a meetin'. We could wait till we got enough of 'em to say they'll come. Then we tell Dickson there's a whole bunch of us that wanna have a meetin' and ask him if he's comin'."

"That's a good idea," Jim said. "He ain't likely to say he ain't comin' if we tell him everybody else is. And we'll be callin' some decisions to a vote," he added with a grin.

"Sounds to me like you fellows have got it all figured out," Cullen commented.

"The sooner the better," Becca encouraged. "Speaking for my husband, Harvey Stoddard will definitely be there. And if you don't wanna hold it in the church, you're welcome to hold it here in my dinin' room. Like the church, there won't be any whiskey sold, but there will be coffee." *And if you hold it here,* she thought, *I'll stick my two cents in, if I feel it's necessary.*

"That's three of the council already," Jim said, "and Stumpy will come. Ain't no doubt about that."

"Lucien Reid always comes," Moss said. "He wants to make sure the town ain't gonna do somethin' that don't include him. When you wanna have it? We might as well get out and tell everybody this mornin'."

"Hell, have it tonight," Becca said. "Our situation ain't gettin' no better if we keep puttin' it off." She looked at each one of the three in turn, then snorted, "Shoulda built us a jail a long time ago." She turned to leave them when she heard Cora calling her from the kitchen, but she tossed one last remark over her shoulder as she walked away. "The dinin' room will be cleared away and ready at seven o'clock, if you decide to have the meetin' here."

Marvin Creed walked into the kitchen where Juan Lopez was seated at the table eating his breakfast. Juan normally ate all his meals with the rest of the hands in the bunkhouse, but since everyone was gone, including Tater Owen, the cook, Juan ate in the kitchen. On this particular morning, he would have preferred to eat somewhere else. Lola cast a worried glance in her husband's direction when Creed, carrying his coffee cup, came in the kitchen. He would have normally called from the dining room when he wanted more coffee. But Lola knew he was still perturbed with Juan. "How long did you lie there on the ground?" Creed asked.

"I don't know, Señor Creed," Juan answered, and reached up to feel the cloth bandage wrapped around his head. "It was a long time."

"And he didn't come back looking for you?" Creed asked, repeating the questioning he had administered earlier in the middle of the night.

"No, señor," Juan lied. "I think maybe I hit him with my first shot. I think maybe he kept going." At Cullen's suggestion, Juan had waited a long time before returning to the little room off the back of the kitchen where he slept with his wife. She had been extremely alarmed when she saw the blood running down his neck from a wound on the side of his head. Then he told her that it was self-inflicted and explained, telling her about trailing Cullen McCabe from the ranch, as Marvin Creed had instructed. "I did not want to shoot McCabe. I don't want to shoot anyone. He was too clever, anyway." He went on to tell her how Cullen had ambushed him but did not want to harm him. Then he suggested the story about his horse stumbling. Out of his fear of a reprisal from Creed, he had taken a rock and hit himself hard enough to make his head bleed. He had hoped this would make his story seem believable. His wife watched for Creed's reaction to Juan's story, afraid he would see that he was lying. She was relieved when Creed finally spoke again.

"Bumbling idiot," Creed muttered, and held out his cup to Lola. "Pour me some more coffee. Maybe his shot hit McCabe." Turning back to address Juan, he said, "Since you can't hit a man with a rifle and you can't stay on a horse, why don't you see if you can walk out to the barn and take care of the stock that was left behind? Then saddle my horse. I have to ride to Fort Worth to meet the men with the herd."

"*Sí, señor,* I take care of." He got up from the table immediately and started for the door, exchanging smiles with Lola when he passed her and she pressed a biscuit into his hand.

Creed picked up his fresh cup of coffee and returned to the dining room. He was convinced that McCabe was a genuine problem. And he was sure that he was more than a common drifter who had just stumbled into the little town of Reid's Mill. He was staking it out as his territory. When the deaths of three Crooked-T men didn't send the message he wanted sent, McCabe brought Clive's body to the ranch as his calling card. Did he actually have the guts it took to ride into his ranch carrying the body of one of his men? Or did he know all his men were gone? Two could play that game. It was not the first time Creed had been challenged. He could not deny his frustration, however, for the opportunity he had failed to take advantage of. He could have answered McCabe's challenge yesterday, and would have, had it not been for Juan's inadequacies. He should have shot McCabe down, himself, before he left his ranch. Now he had to wait until he could answer in force, so he would have to hold off until after his men were back. And it would no doubt be all he could think of on his trip to Fort Worth.

It was a day and a half's ride to the stockyard of the man who bought his cattle. Ford Wyatt was a man never obsessed with brands and Creed had dealt with him for a long time. It would take his men almost four days to drive that herd to the stockyard. Any faster would drive the weight off the cattle. Creed would arrive early enough to enjoy a couple of nights in a hotel and visit a brothel that Ford Wyatt also owned, all at special rates. After the cattle were sold, he would ride back with the men. Then the matter of Mr. Cullen McCabe would be dealt with.

Paul Dickson didn't know what to say when Stumpy Morgan informed him of a special meeting of the town council at the Stoddard House dining room at seven that night. After a few moments while he tried to be sure he was hearing correctly, he replied, "What are you talkin' about, Stumpy? I didn't call for any meeting."

"I never said you did," Stumpy replied with a grin that threatened to pull one end of his drooping mustache into his mouth. He had volunteered to be the messenger to inform Dickson of the meeting, eager to see the mayor's reaction. "Different ones of us has been talkin' about a problem here in town, so we've called for a meetin' to see what we can come up with."

"What problem? No one has said anything to me about a problem," Dickson replied. "We just had a meeting and we talked about everything then. I usually call a meeting if one is necessary. We need to go through proper procedure. Who is it that wants a meeting, besides yourself?"

"Oh, it ain't just a couple of us. So far, it's everybody on the council but Doc Stevens and he don't ever come to the meetin's, anyway. You're just the last one I got around to tellin'. I wasn't in no hurry to get to you 'cause I was pretty sure you'd wanna come."

"I'm not sure it's proper parliamentary procedure for just anybody to call for a meeting," Dickson said.

"Well, I reckon we can talk about that at the meetin'," Stumpy said. "We'll see you at seven o'clock." Without waiting for further discussion, he turned and walked out, leaving the mayor to sputter in disbelief to his wife.

"That doesn't leave you much time after supper, does it?" Sarah Dickson asked.

"They can't just call a meeting anytime they feel like havin' one," her husband complained.

She shrugged. "Sounds like they did. Are you goin'?"

"I most certainly am," Dickson replied. "I'm still the mayor of this town."

* * *

At seven sharp, every one of the members of the Reid's Mill town council was present at the Stoddard House dining room, except Doc Stevens and the Reverend Eugene White, who showed up ten minutes later. Becca Stoddard had two big pots of coffee on the stove and a platter of molasses cookies at each end of the big table. Mayor Dickson took a seat at one end of the table and called the meeting to order. "I'm not sure this sudden meeting has been called under the proper procedures," he started right away. "But we're all here"—he paused to cast an eye in the direction of Cullen, standing with a cup of coffee near the kitchen door—"and a few visitors." He nodded politely to Becca then. "So, will someone care to tell us why this meeting was called ?"

"Yes, sir, Mr. Mayor," Lucien Reid said, standing up, "I'll be glad to do it." He gestured with his hand, indicating everyone at the table. "The majority of us feel like it's time to have some means of protection for the merchants and citizens of our town. And we think the first thing to do is to elect a sheriff and build a jail." He sat down again.

"I don't understand," Dickson said. "We talked about this at the meeting the other night."

"That's a fact, Mr. Mayor," Stumpy said, "but we didn't do nothin' about it. This here meetin' is to vote on whether or not we do somethin' about it."

Feeling as if he was being impeached, Dickson could only ask, "Is this the way you all feel about this?" When his question was met with a chorus of yeses, he said, "We haven't allowed any funds for a jail building in our budget or a sheriff's salary. How are we gonna pay for it?"

"The same way we're payin' for everything else," Joe Morrison said. "We figured it out and a small contribution from every business would be enough to start. Fred Sowers has agreed to supply the lumber from his mill and we have several volunteers to help with the construction. Temporarily, we can use my back storage room as a jail, till the real jail is built."

"If that gets too full, we can hang 'em in the sycamore tree by the saloon," Stumpy japed.

After the tide of laughter subsided, Dickson glanced at Cullen, then asked, "What are we gonna do for a sheriff?"

"Jim Duncan is runnin' for sheriff," Harvey Stoddard said. "I make a motion we vote on it now."

"I second it," Moss Pringle announced.

Feeling he had lost control of the meeting but seeing that there was nothing he could do about it, Dickson surrendered. "All right, we'll put it to a vote. All in favor of electing Jim Duncan sheriff say *aye*. Well, that's almost unanimous," he announced after the vote. "I'll add mine and I reckon it's unanimous, Sheriff Duncan."

"You're under arrest," Jim came back at him, bringing forth another wave of chortles.

"I'll print some notices we can nail up telling folks we got a sheriff," Johnny Mitchell offered. "Let 'em know we've got law and order."

By this time, it was fairly obvious to the mayor that this project had already been worked out among a core of several council members. Still he had questions. "We've got ourselves a sheriff. Now, I'd like to know what kind of experience Jim has as a law officer." He directed his question directly at Jim.

"You know the answer to that, Paul," Jim replied. "I've got none. But Cullen McCabe has agreed to stay in town a little while longer to help me settle into the job. He was the sheriff in the town of Sundown for a number of years." He didn't express it, but he was grateful to have Cullen to back him at present, when they could expect big trouble with the Crooked-T crew.

"I see," Dickson commented. "I figured McCabe was attending our council meeting for some reason. Thank you, McCabe." In his mind, he still had to wonder if the grim gunman would hang around if things got too rough with Creed's gang of outlaws. This, even though he had shown no sign of fearing anyone. "Well, good luck to us all," he announced. "Meeting adjourned."

Everyone gathered around Jim Duncan to congratulate him and wish him luck. Cullen felt it necessary to tell them that Jim's success was going to depend a lot on the support he got from the merchants who elected him. "In the beginning, that's especially true," he told them. "He's gonna be tested by every saddle tramp that drifts through town until all the drifters find out that Reid's Mill is a lawful town and the sheriff has the backing of every citizen here." There were immediate vows of support, but Cullen knew Jim couldn't count on a gun in the hand of every shopkeeper in the event of a gang shootout. He had faith, however, that Jim Duncan was made of good stock and he had a chance to make it.

CHAPTER FOURTEEN

The days immediately following the council meeting at Stoddard House were quiet days in the town of Reid's Mill, with no sign of any trouble in the form of Crooked-T riders. This was no surprise to Cullen. He had no idea how long this peace would last, but he was secure in the knowledge that all Marvin Creed's outlaws were driving a herd of stolen cattle to some market somewhere. It gave Jim a chance to make himself known as the sheriff. It was a well-received notification with every business in town, with the exception of the Whiskey Mill. The notices that Johnny Mitchell printed were posted all over town, so anyone new to town was made aware that there was law enforcement here. The only thing missing was an official sheriff's badge. Cullen figured that would have to come later. He could take a short ride up to Clifton and wire Austin to send him a badge. But he was not willing to expose his real reason for being in the little town. By the end of the week, Jim was already comfortable in his position. A temporary lockup was being secured, using the barn Joe Morrison used for his undertaking business. There was no sheriff's office and jail as yet, but construction was already under way.

* * *

Also at the end of the week, Marvin Creed and his gang of cattle rustlers returned to the Crooked-T Ranch. It was a tired but happy crew that rode back into the barnyard of the Crooked-T. It had been a relatively easy drive of the herd of cattle, that foreman, Shane Roper, reported to Marvin Creed. There had been only three men watching the herd and all three were killed with no one escaping to report the theft of the cattle. Creed's sale with his friend Ford Wyatt went quickly and to Creed's satisfaction. So he handed his horse to Juan when they rode in and went in the house while his men unsaddled their horses and turned them out to graze. While Tater Owen unloaded his chuck wagon, Juan built a fire for him in the bunkhouse kitchen. The men would be paid in the morning, so any celebrating would have to wait until the next day. But there was no complaining because they were tired and their horses were too tired to ride an additional fifteen miles to the saloon at Reid's Mill. It was Creed's usual policy to keep half of the men at the ranch every night, so there would be much haggling and deals made the next day to be one of the ones to hit the saloon first. Those remaining would most likely risk their cut of the cattle money in a bunkhouse card game.

Curious to hear more about Clive Dawkins, Shane Roper walked over by the woodpile where Juan Lopez was chopping more wood to stack in the bunkhouse. Seeing the foreman approach, Juan let his ax drop to the ground while he waited. "The boss told us you had a little visit from Cullen McCabe while all of us were gone," Roper began.

"*Sí*, Señor Roper. McCabe bring Clive Dawkins's body here. I bury him behind the barn."

"Where was he shot?" When Juan said he didn't know, Roper explained that he meant where on his body and Juan told him Clive was shot in the neck and chest. "Face on?" Juan nodded. "Not in the back?" Juan shook his head. That could be bad news, Roper thought. He would have rather heard that Clive was shot in the back because this indicated that Clive had called him out. And McCabe was evidently the faster man. "I heard Boss sent you after McCabe when he left here that night. I see you've still got a rag tied around your head. Boss said you mighta got a round in McCabe. Is that so?"

Juan was not at all comfortable with the lie he was living, but he felt he had no choice but to perpetuate it. "I not sure," he said. "I shoot and he dropped down, but I no see. My horse stumble then. I not see McCabe no more."

Roper studied Juan's expressions as he talked. He saw a definite reluctance in Juan's retelling of the incident. "How bad is your head hurt?" Roper asked.

Juan quickly put his hand up to feel the rag around his head. "Not bad, hurt a little, get well quick."

Roper nodded. "You were lucky, I reckon." He turned and went back to the bunkhouse with a pretty good idea that Cullen McCabe was alive and well and had no idea Creed had sent Juan after him. He also knew that McCabe had earned himself a ticket to hell. He had already done more damage than Creed could afford. Like Creed, Roper suspected that McCabe was more than a footloose drifter who just happened upon Reid's Mill. What puzzled him was the fact that McCabe appeared to have no backing, other than his own six-gun. Creed would expect answers to these questions within the next couple of days.

Saturday morning broke clear and warm and Marvin Creed appeared in the bunkhouse right after breakfast, carrying a canvas bag of cash money. He sat himself down at the end of the long table at the head of the bunkhouse and announced the payday. Just as any careful employer would do, Creed kept a payroll ledger with a list of names, which he checked off as each man lined up to get his cut of the sale of the stolen cattle.

When the payday was completed, Creed returned to the house while Roper talked to the men who won the privilege of going into town the first day. Roper was going to be one of the first four, an occurrence that was unusual, for normally, Roper didn't go into town at all. That contributed to the solitary image the men had of him and allowed him to remain somewhat of a mystery to them. He would not have been going to Reid's Mill on this occasion had it not been Marvin Creed's directive. The riddle that was Cullen McCabe had been discussed at length between Creed and Roper, with Creed dictating the way it would be handled. Unsure of Juan Lopez's account of his attempt to kill McCabe, Creed wanted to find out if there was any chance Juan had actually hit him. As far as the three men who went in with Roper, they were to know nothing other than it was a chance for them to enjoy themselves.

Only Shane Roper knew of Marvin Creed's grand plan to become the king of Reid's Mill. It was a simple plan actually, with the crew of the Crooked-T unwittingly acting as the pawns in Creed's plan to take over the town. His strategy had been working to his satisfaction up until Cullen McCabe arrived on the scene. And while he was confident that McCabe alone could not stop his plan, he had made himself a nuisance to the point where Creed wondered if he was, in fact, competition thinking to take control of the town. Too much had been spent to risk it all on a common gunslinger.

So, instead of Roper's customary drink in the solitude of his room on the end of the bunkhouse, he would have a drink in the Whiskey Mill, the saloon bankrolled by Marvin Creed, to be managed by Harman Gill. That saloon was to be the honey that drew the bees to the hive and Creed supplied the bees in the form of his "cowhands" who flocked to the town. When the time was right, Creed was prepared to move in to save the town from the wild and reckless cowhands. And Shane Roper was to be his sheriff, who enforced his laws.

The four riders entered the town on the eastern side on the trail cut by Crooked-T hands, a trail that many in the little community wished they could fence off. "You boys go on and start drinkin'," Roper said as they rode out into the street. "I'm gonna take a little look around, since it's been a spell since I was here. I'll join you later at the saloon."

"You're liable to get too far behind to ever catch up," Blackie Welch replied. He wheeled his horse toward the Whiskey Mill. Herman Thompson and Sam Culver were right behind him, already whooping about visiting the Molly-Maes.

Roper wheeled his horse in the opposite direction, heading toward the upper end of the street and the Stoddard House. He was already hungry and had no desire to go with the other three to drink whiskey on an empty stomach. So he decided to see if the dining room in the rooming house was as good as he had been told. He looked at the stores and businesses he passed, most of them built since he had last been in town. He had to agree with his boss, it looked like the time was right to make the move. There were more people on the street than he had expected to see, even allowing for the day to be Saturday.

He pulled his horse up to the hitching rail in front of Stoddards' and dismounted. Walking up to the door, he noticed a printed flyer tacked beside the door, but started to ignore it until his eye caught the word *Sheriff*. He took a half step back to read it.

WELCOME TO REID'S MILL

*The Town Council is pleased you've chosen
to visit our town.
We welcome all peaceful visitors
who choose to obey our laws.
All others will be prosecuted
by the Reid's Mill Sheriff's Department.*
—JAMES B. DUNCAN, *Sheriff*

"What tha . . ." Roper muttered. "Sheriff's department?" This must have happened overnight, he thought, for surely some of the men would have noticed it when they were here.

"You goin' in?"

He was startled by the voice behind him, unaware for

the moment of anything but the sign by the door. "Sorry," he said to the little man with the droopy mustache, "didn't hear you behind me." He reached for the knob then and went on inside.

"Evenin'," Becca Stoddard said. "This your first time in our dinin' room?" Before he answered, Becca looked beyond him and said, "Evenin', Stumpy." Stumpy returned her greeting and proceeded to the big table. Becca returned her attention to the stranger. "We ask you to remove your gun belt and weapon and place them on the table. That's just in case you don't like the food. It gives the cook a head start." She smiled in appreciation of her humor, but he showed no indication of realizing it as such. He nevertheless unbuckled his gun belt and deposited his weapon on the table set there for the purpose. "Seat yourself anywhere you like," she said.

He seemed undecided, so Stumpy invited him to sit at the big table. "You must be a stranger in town," he said. "Set yourself down over here and you'll be closer to the kitchen and you'll get to the bowls as soon as they hit the table."

"Thanks, that sounds like a good idea," Roper said, and took a seat right across from Stumpy. He said yes when Becca asked if he wanted coffee, then he turned back to talk to Stumpy. "I didn't mean to hold you up outside the door just now. I was readin' that sign posted by the door about the sheriff's department."

"That *welcome to town, but you'd best behave yourself* sign?" Stumpy asked with a chuckle.

"Yeah," Roper replied. "I didn't think Reid's Mill even had a sheriff."

"We didn't till a couple of days ago," Stumpy said. "Got

one now, though, and a good 'un. Jim Duncan, he's a blacksmith, too. He can throw you in jail and put new shoes on your horse while you're in there." He grinned at the tall, somber man, thinking him devoid of a sense of humor. "I'm Stumpy Morgan, I own the harness shop next to the general store. We just elected Jim to be the sheriff the other day and we shoulda had one sooner to keep some of the saddle trash from tearin' the town up."

"Is that a fact?" Roper responded as Becca placed a plate of biscuits on the table. She was followed by Cora, carrying a platter of pork chops on the table between them.

Stumpy gave Roper a wink. "See what I mean? This end of the table gets the meat platter first." He helped himself to a big one, then pushed the platter over toward Roper, who took the next biggest chop.

"Let's keep that platter movin'," Johnny Mitchell grumbled.

"Don't be impatient," Becca scolded. "There are plenty of pork chops, enough for everybody. You're embarrassin' us in front of a new visitor to the table."

"My apologies, sir," Johnny offered grandly. "But I wasn't talkin' about you. I was aiming my remarks at Stumpy."

Just a hint of a smile creased the solemn face of the stranger as he replied. "I'm used to a lot worse than this," he said, thinking of the bunkhouse back at the ranch.

"You just passin' through town?" Stumpy asked.

"No, I live close by. I just don't come to town very often."

"How do you make your livin', if you don't mind me askin'?" Stumpy inquired.

"I'm the foreman on a cattle ranch about fifteen miles

from here. I just decided to come into town for supper and maybe a drink before I go home."

"Must be west of Reid's Mill," Johnny speculated, trying to recall the names of some of the small ranches in that vicinity.

"No, east of Reid's Mill," Roper replied, enjoying the game now.

"Fifteen miles east of Reid's Mill," Stumpy questioned. "Have you got your directions mixed up? 'Cause the only ranch fifteen miles east is . . ."

"That's right, the Crooked-T," Roper finished for him. "Pass me that bowl of beans, please." The bowl filled with beans was passed down the table in a deadly silence. He dipped out a couple of spoonfuls and said to Becca, "They were right about the food in this place. I might get over this way more often."

Becca stood there in shock for a few moments, not sure what to say. Finally, she mumbled, "Thank you," turned, and fled to the kitchen where she encountered Cora staring at her, her mouth and eyes wide open. She didn't have to ask if she had heard.

The rest of the meal was eaten in near silence, save for the occasional request to pass a plate or a bowl. That is, at least until Shane Roper finished, paid Becca, and walked out the door while strapping on his gun belt. As soon as the door closed tightly, it acted as a switch that turned the stunned diners' vocal cords on. "I ain't believin' that," Johnny Mitchell exclaimed. "The foreman of the Crooked-T, you suppose he was just funnin' us? Somebody mighta put him up to it."

"I don't know," Harvey Stoddard replied. "If he was, he did a mighty good job of it."

"He seemed like a pretty reasonable man," Becca remarked. "You think when he goes to get that drink of whiskey he said he wanted, he'll turn into a wild drunk, like the rest of his men?"

As for Shane Roper, he had thoroughly enjoyed the supper with the people at Stoddard House. The food was excellent and the obvious show of fear he thought he detected when he told them who he was, was the respect he intended to demand from the people of the town. He congratulated himself for his professional manner. They would remember him that way when he was their sheriff and show him that respect. Now, he was ready to see how the men were doing at the Whiskey Mill.

As he rode back down the street, he now noticed the sign about the sheriff's department was tacked by every door. And when he arrived at the saloon, he saw one posted on both sides of the door. *They're in for a hell of an awakening,* he thought as he stepped inside. Without hesitating, he walked straight through the small crowd of drinkers and went to the bar. Having never seen Roper before, Archie greeted him indifferently. "Howdy, stranger, whaddle it be?"

"Rye whiskey," Roper replied, "uncut."

"Mister, we don't sell no watered-down whiskey. It all comes straight out of the bottle right from the distiller."

"In that case, pop a cork on a new bottle and pour my drink out of that one," Roper calmly directed.

Archie was just before refusing to do so when he was interrupted by Harman Gill. "I'll swear," Gill exclaimed,

"Shane Roper. What in the hell got you to come to Reid's Mill?" He turned to his bartender then and said, "Archie, this is Shane Roper. You've heard me talk about him." He shielded his mouth with his hand so no one could hear him say, "This is the real new sheriff come to town."

"Howdy, Harman," Roper said, shaking his hand. "I wouldn't be here tonight if the boss hadn't told me to come."

Archie, more than a little flustered, for he had been told about the mysterious gunman who was Marvin Creed's foreman, reached under the bar for an unopened bottle of rye whiskey. "I didn't have no way of knowin' who you were," he said.

"No harm done," Roper told him.

"What does bring you into town, Shane?" Gill asked. "I saw the other boys. They've been goin' at it pretty strong."

"There are a couple of things the boss will wanna hear about," Roper replied. "One of 'em will be this new sheriff business. We ain't heard nothin' about this town gettin' a sheriff until I walked into it today. That McCabe jasper brought Clive Dawkins's body back to the ranch while all the rest of us were gone. He told the boss the town was talkin' about gettin' a sheriff, but Creed didn't put any stock in that. So I need for you to tell me everything you know about that business. The other thing is Cullen McCabe. We think he mighta been shot when he left the Crooked-T that night, but we ain't sure."

"Well, I can tell you the answer to that right away," Gill said. "If he was shot, he sure don't show it. He was in here last night, had a couple of drinks, and left. That's all he usually does. Here, take that bottle and we'll sit down at a table and I'll tell you all I know about the new sheriff."

When they sat down at a table in the back of the saloon, Gill said, "This town hadn't said word one about hiring a sheriff until this Cullen McCabe character rode in one day. But I'll guarantee you, he's the one who got the rest of the town council all worked up about havin' to have a sheriff to put a stop to all the trouble your boys have been stirrin' up. I'm tellin' you, Shane, you tell Creed that his plan was workin'. The only trouble is McCabe rode in here and made the move to set up a sheriff and cut down the trouble-makers and take the town over. And he don't mind gettin' his hands dirty. We could ask Skeeter Shaw, Rob Gillespie, Lucky Spence, and Clive Dawkins about that."

"Who is Cullen McCabe?" Roper asked. "Where did he come from? I ain't never heard of him, and a gunslinger like that, we should have."

"Nobody knows," Gill insisted. "Nobody. Like I said, he just drifted into town and started killin' people. And the only ones he was killin' was your men from the Crooked-T."

"You say he ain't been in tonight?"

"Not so far," Gill said with a shrug. They sat up suddenly when they heard one of the Molly-Maes squeal. "It ain't nothin' but your boys gettin' rough with Molly. She'll get him a little bit drunker, then she'll give him a whuppin' like he ain't had since he was a young 'un."

The sight of his three men making absolute fools out of themselves was enough to make Roper want to go knock some heads together. He realized, however, it was not really the men's behavior that had him riled. "I need to see this Cullen McCabe," he stated emphatically. Frustrated, he said then, "Tell me about this new sheriff."

"Jim Duncan," Gill stated. "Until they decided to elect him sheriff, he was the blacksmith."

"He never had any experience as a lawman?"

"Not the first day," Gill replied. "But he's a big, strong man, and a better choice than anybody else in town."

"He shouldn't be any real problem," Roper reckoned. "We'll arrange to have him catch a bullet right away." He paused for a second when the thought struck him. "I'da thought this McCabe stranger woulda had his eye on the sheriff's job for himself. From the way he cut down some of our men, it looked like he was takin' on the job of sheriff, right from the start."

"It does look that way, don't it?" Gill replied. "But he said the first day he walked in that he was just passin' through and he ain't changed his tune yet. Matter of fact, from what I hear, McCabe was the one that started the talk about makin' Jim Duncan sheriff." He watched Roper as he seemed to consider what he told him. "The fact of the matter is," Gill continued, "McCabe didn't go after any of those men he killed. They came after him."

That fact caused Roper a deeper concern about the mysterious stranger. "I need to meet this jasper," he stated. "Have you got a vacant room upstairs?" Gill said that he did. "Then I think I'll stay here tonight. So I think I'd better take my horse down to the stable before it's locked up for the night."

CHAPTER FIFTEEN

The front door of the stable was still open when Roper reined the black Morgan gelding to a halt and dismounted. He walked inside the stable, and seeing a man standing outside a stall near the end of the building, he walked back toward him. In the darkness of the stable, Roper could see it was a sizable man standing by the stall, but the light was too dim to see sharply. "Glad I caught you still open," Roper said. "I need to leave my horse with you tonight."

"I'm not the owner," Cullen replied, "but I'm pretty sure Moss will be happy to take care of your horse. He's in the barn right now, but he'll be back in a minute."

"My mistake," Roper said.

"Not a-tall," Cullen responded. "The light is kinda dim back between these stalls this time of day. You new in town?"

"I might as well be," Roper answered. "It's been a helluva long time since I was in Reid's Mill."

"Well, the fellow that owns this stable is Moss Pringle and I can tell you he takes good care of the horses. I know he takes good care of mine."

"Good, glad to hear it," Roper replied. Now that he was

standing close to Cullen, he made a point to study him more intensely. The man was even bigger than he had appeared from the distance between the front door and the back stall. Roper couldn't help wondering if by chance he was talking to the new sheriff. Harman Gill said the sheriff was actually a blacksmith and Roper could see a set of powerful-looking shoulders on this soft-spoken fellow. He decided to ask him if his name was Jim Duncan, but Moss came in from the barn at that moment, so he turned to address him.

"Here's a fellow that needs to leave his horse with you, Moss," Cullen said.

"Yes, sir," Moss responded. "My name's Moss Pringle. I'd be proud to take care of that horse for ya. You gonna be in town awhile, or just overnight?"

"Just overnight, Moss," Roper answered. "I expect I'll be leavin' sometime, maybe right after dinnertime. He ain't been worked hard today, but give him a portion of oats, anyway."

"I'll do it," Moss responded cheerfully. "I just got done puttin' fresh hay in the stalls on this side. I'll put your horse in one of them, Mr. . . . . I didn't catch your name."

"Roper," he said, and reached out to take the hand Moss extended, "Shane Roper."

"Yes, sir, Mr. Roper, I'll take good care of your horse for ya. Cullen will tell you that. Right, Cullen?"

"I already told him you would," Cullen answered.

In the dim light of the stable, the startled expression etched across Roper's face went unnoticed. He was not an easy man to take by surprise, but he had not been prepared to have a close confrontation with Cullen McCabe in this unlikely place. Thoughts of taking care of the Cullen McCabe problem, here and now without warning, instantly came to mind. Several things told him to wait, however. He wasn't sure how fast McCabe was. Also of importance, was the fact that he intended to be the sheriff here when Creed made his move. There was also the danger of a shot from Moss in retaliation. *Best not rush into a fight on the spur of the moment,* he told himself. *I want to get McCabe, but I don't want a bullet in my back from Pringle.* He decided then that he would definitely stay in town long enough to engage McCabe in conversation. Maybe he could find out if he was working strictly on his own, or if he was just working for a higher boss— like Roper was, himself. Fear for his life didn't enter the equation, for Roper feared no man. But the more he thought about it, the more he was intrigued by the somber man facing him in the stable. "Well," he declared, "I feel like I'm leavin' my horse in good hands. And I'm pleased to meet you, Mr. Cullen McCabe"—he turned toward Moss—"and you, too, Mr. Pringle. As soon as I pull my saddle off my horse and we put him away, I'm headin' for that saloon up the street. It would be my pleasure to buy you both a drink."

Cullen didn't respond immediately, but Moss said, "Well, now, that's mighty sportin' of you, Mr. Roper. I gladly accept the invitation, but let me do the unsaddlin' for you and get your horse some water and those oats you wanted. Then I'll join you at the saloon."

"Fair enough," Roper said. "How 'bout you, Mr. McCabe?"

Cullen's initial feeling was that he was not interested

in spending any time in the Whiskey Mill, but he changed his mind. The spark that caused him to reconsider the invitation was the simple fact that Roper had referred to him as Cullen McCabe. And it occurred to him that he had not introduced himself to Roper, and Moss had called him Cullen. He never said *McCabe*. He found it interesting that this stranger who just bumped into him in a dark stable for the first time, knew his name was McCabe. He was curious enough to find out the reason. "That's mighty neighborly of you, Mr. Roper. I'd be right interested in having a drink of whiskey with you, interested to know what brings you to Reid's Mill."

They left the stable and walked up the narrow wagon track that ran between the two bridges to the main street. Both men attempted to walk evenly, shoulder to shoulder, so as not to let the other man drop even a step behind. Not even aware of it, they acted from a natural sense of survival. When they passed Jim Duncan's darkened shop, Roper commented, "I reckon that's the blacksmith shop, right?"

"That's right," Cullen responded, but elected not to mention the owner's name.

When they walked into the Whiskey Mill together, it caused an instant halt to the idle banter and laughter in the saloon. Archie Wells stopped filling a shot glass in midstream and stood gaping at the unlikely pair. When he started pouring again, he was still unable to take his eyes off the two until the customer for whom he was filling the glass told him he was pouring whiskey all over the counter. Archie corked the bottle and hurried to the office door to summon Harman Gill, leaving the customer to soak up the spilled booze and squeeze the rag's contents into his mouth. After squeezing the last few drops out of the rag, the customer wiped his chin and whiskers with the rag and dropped it back on the bar. "Archie oughta be right back," he informed Cullen and Roper.

The only one of his men he saw in the saloon was Herman Thompson, and Roper was satisfied to see Herman sitting at a table across the room. His feet were stretched straight out in front of him and his arms were hanging down over the arms of the chair. It was obvious that he had passed out. One of his friends had evidently propped his hat over his face while both of them went upstairs with the Molly-Maes, for he didn't see Blackie Welch or Sam Culver anywhere in the room. This suited Roper just fine, since he preferred to hide his position as foreman of the Crooked-T until after he had a chance to get a clue as to McCabe's real purpose for coming to Reid's Mill.

Cullen thought it strange that Archie rushed from the bar when he and Roper walked in, but the bartender came out of the office door almost immediately to return to the bar. Behind him, Harman Gill stood in the office doorway, seeming to look over the customers, not an unusual occurrence for the owner of a saloon at any time. "Whaddle it be, gents?" Archie sang out as he rounded the end of the bar.

"Better give me a bottle and three glasses," Roper said. "We'll have Mr. Pringle joining us in a few minutes." He reached in his vest pocket for a roll of bills.

"I'll help with that," Cullen said, and reached for some money, too.

Roper stopped him. "This is on me," he insisted, and waved Cullen's money away. "You can bring the glasses."

He picked up the bottle and walked toward a table in a back corner. When they were seated and whiskey poured, Roper started the questions. "How long have you been here in Reid's Mill, McCabe?"

"Not long," Cullen answered.

"Oh, so you're not a local resident," Roper responded, playing the part. "Well, if you don't mind me askin', what brings you to this dead little town?"

"Nothing, really, I just happened on it. Never been here before and I thought it looked like a right nice little town they've got goin'. So I thought I'd stay a few days to get the feel of it. How 'bout yourself? What brings you to Reid's Mill?" He knew that Roper was playing some kind of game and he decided to play along to see if he could figure it out.

"I'll just be here overnight," Roper responded. "Just passin' through on my way to Waco and decided I'd stop for some supper and a drink of whiskey. But you don't strike me as a drifter. If I had to guess, I'd figure you were on the payroll of somebody who's lookin' to take over a town this size. That's kind of a hobby of mine, sizin' people up and figurin' out what they've got on their minds." He had decided he'd take a shot and see how Cullen reacted.

"You've got a helluvan imagination," Cullen said. "I'll give you that. But you missed on this one. I don't work for anybody like that and I sure as hell don't wanna own a town."

Roper smiled and shrugged. He was not convinced and was about to say as much when they were interrupted by Moss Pringle. He walked up to the table, hesitated for a moment, then sat down. Roper poured him a drink and slid it over toward him, but he didn't take it right away.

Instead, he announced, "I just ran into Stumpy at the front door. You know what he told me? He said you're settin' here havin' a drink of likker with Marvin Creed's foreman of the Crooked-T."

His statement was enough to startle Cullen for a moment. He had been sure that Roper was up to something, but for him to be Creed's man was something that had not entered his mind. Many questions and thoughts were turning over in Cullen's mind now that Roper's identity was exposed, but there was no change in the usual stoic expression on his face. "Is that a fact?" He responded to Moss's announcement. "That makes this a lot more interestin', doesn't it? His whiskey tastes pretty good. Might as well drink it." He looked back at Roper, who was smiling smugly, watching his reaction. "I reckon this is the longest I've ever talked to a hand from the Crooked-T without him tryin' to shoot somebody."

"Well, now, that's a harsh impression you've got of our men," Roper countered. "I'll admit that sometimes a young cowhand will get liquored up and do some things he wouldn't do when he's sober. But that's the case on every cattle ranch, don't you think?"

"I expect I'd have to agree," Cullen answered. "But what you just described hasn't got anything to do with that gang of outlaws ridin' for the Crooked-T. You talk like you've got a decent amount of good sense, so don't waste my time talkin' to me like I ain't. I delivered the last assassin you sent in here after me and I told that devil you work for that this town wasn't available for any cattle rustler that had a mind to take it over. I told him then that the town was fixin' to hire a sheriff and they weren't gonna stand for any more of that Crooked-T hell-raisin'.

And you know what? He invited me to supper. Then the son of a buck sent a man after me to kill me when I left there. These folks here ain't gonna put up with a man like that. They're gonna fight for their town. You tell your boss that when you go back home."

"You've got it all wrong," Roper responded. "Marvin Creed is an honorable man. He wouldn't have sent anybody after you when you left there. What happened was that one man went after you on his own accord. The men are so loyal to Mr. Creed that they fly off the handle if they think somebody might be threatening him. When he found out that Juan Lopez took a shot at you, he came down hard on him."

Cullen smiled, thinking of that night and how a terrified Juan Lopez had been ordered to follow him and kill him, and was too afraid to tell Creed he couldn't do it. Creed had evidently believed Juan's story about taking a shot at him, and Cullen was glad about that. The poor man had been frightened to return home. "Why don't you tell Creed that his plan to take over Reid's Mill won't work? It's best to start lookin' someplace else for his little kingdom."

Roper didn't respond to the suggestion right away. He carefully poured himself another drink while he studied the granitelike features of the big man called Cullen McCabe. He was not at all like the picture he had carried in his mind of a swarthy gunslinging monster. "You know what I find mighty strange? You just come driftin' through town, total stranger, and the town people send you out to the ranch to talk peace with Marvin Creed. That seems mighty unlikely to happen, by my way of thinkin'."

"The town council didn't send me out to talk to Creed,"

Cullen answered. "I went out there on my own 'cause I was the one your men kept tryin' to shoot."

"Why didn't you just move on outta town, since you said you were just passin' through in the first place?"

Cullen smiled. "'Cause I never have liked to be run outta any town."

"It's been right interestin' talkin' to you, McCabe. I think your style is a lot like my own. I hope this business between Reid's Mill and Crooked-T doesn't come down to you and me havin' to settle it in the middle of the street." He favored Cullen with a generous smile. "I swear, I ain't got no idea which one of us would walk away, but it'd be interestin' to find out."

"I don't participate in duels, Roper, so if you decide to come after me, you'd best do it with guns blazin' 'cause I'll shoot you down while you're talkin' about the rules."

"Fair warnin'," Roper said.

"Thanks for the whiskey," Cullen replied, and got to his feet. Moss jumped up as well and followed Cullen out of the saloon.

Behind him, Harman Gill came out of his office before Cullen and Moss reached the front door. "What the hell were you two talkin' about all that time? You know that was Cullen McCabe, don't you?"

"Ha," Roper responded with half a chuckle. "We were just havin' a friendly little drink to talk over a few problems standin' between the Crooked-T and him. He was just givin' me all the reasons I need to kill a man. He's the big problem here right now. I don't think he's workin' for anybody but himself. And that's not a hard problem to solve." His last few words were almost drowned out by the sudden rumble of snoring from Herman Thompson, who was still in the embrace of his drunken sprawl. It seemed to irritate Roper. He got up from his chair, and to Gill's surprise, walked over to the other side of the room where Herman was in full chorus now. He lifted his boot and kicked the side of the chair hard enough to turn Herman out on the floor, cursing and sputtering. He managed to pull his .44 out of his holster, only to have his wrist pinned to the floor by Roper's foot. Roper reached down and wrestled the gun out of Herman's hand. "Get up from there," he ordered.

"Roper! What the hell?" Herman blurted, when he made out his foreman's face through his whiskey haze.

"Where's Blackie and Sam?" Roper demanded.

Totally confused by Roper's manner, Herman said, "Hell, I don't know. They went upstairs with the Molly-Maes. I reckon they're still up there." He had progressed only so far as his knees, so Roper grabbed the back of his shirt and jerked him up to his feet, where he teetered back and forth for a few minutes.

"Can you walk?" Roper demanded. Herman, still mystified as to what he had done to anger him so much, said that he thought he could. "All right, go upstairs and find Blackie and Sam. Tell 'em it's time they started back to the ranch. Tell 'em I said so."

"Right," Herman replied, and began an unsteady walk toward the stairs to the second floor.

Roper stood watching him as he slowly ascended the steps, holding tightly to the banister. Satisfied that he was going to make it, he turned back toward Gill, who was watching, astonished by Roper's behavior. His men were acting pretty much as they always did when they came to town. He could believe only that the formidable foreman did not endorse his men's typical behavior. It was, after all, the first time Roper had been in town since he could remember. Either that, or it was his surprise meeting with Cullen McCabe. He decided it was that, the meeting with McCabe, so he commented, "That was a bad-luck day when Cullen McCabe rode into town. There ain't no doubt about that." His remark brought an instant narrowing of Roper's eyes.

"It was a bad-luck day for Cullen McCabe," Roper said. He remained standing at the foot of the stairs, waiting for the three men to come down.

Finally, Blackie Welch appeared at the top of the stairs, his boots in his hand. "Roper?" he asked, uncertain, since Herman had been so drunk. "Did you send Herman up here to get us?"

"I did," Roper answered him.

"What for?" Blackie asked. "What's up? I'm kinda in the middle of somethin'. So's Sam."

"It's time for you three men to climb on your horses and head back to the Crooked-T. So get the others and get your sorry asses down here."

Blackie couldn't understand the reason for the order. "What's goin' on? Whadda we gotta get back to the Crooked-T for? We ain't got nothin' we gotta do in the mornin'."

"If I have to go up those stairs and kick you down here, I promise you, you ain't gonna find it a pleasure," Roper threatened.

Herman appeared at Blackie's side then and whispered to him. "I told you. He's gone mad as a hyena eatin' locoweed. You can argue with him, if you want to, I'm gettin' myself downstairs."

"All right, Roper," Blackie said. "I'll go get Sam and we'll be right down." He left to fetch Sam while Herman made a shaky descent down the steps. They would talk about it all the way back to the ranch, but none of them would ever understand that Roper had felt he had not planted any fear in Cullen McCabe and he didn't like the feel of it. Then to suffer the weak, ineffective appearance of his men, he thought that McCabe held no respect for him as a fighter. There was going to be a war and he came away from his meeting with the enemy as the leader of a ragtag bunch of drunks.

It didn't help matters when Gill, seeing him upset, told him that these men tonight were more or less typical of all the Crooked-T hands. So he hoped he wouldn't come down too hard on them. "Are you goin' back with them? Or do you still want your room upstairs?"

"No, I'm not goin' back with 'em. I'll need that room." He didn't want there to be any chance that Cullen McCabe might think he left town because of their conversation.

In a little while the other two men made it downstairs, Sam with the help of Mae Davis, who was carrying some of his clothes for him. It was the sight of Molly Dugan following behind them carrying both gun belts and weapons that fed the flame of contempt already burning in Shane Roper. He walked outside with the three men and stood there while they managed to get in their saddles. "We'll see you back at the ranch," Blackie said as they headed toward the tiny bridge that took them back to the main street. Once they crossed the bridge, Roper turned around and went back in the saloon. He was still on the porch when he heard the sound of pistols going off and drunken whoops from the street across the river. It served only to cause him to clench his teeth.

The sound of gunfire and hollering was a customary signal to the people of Reid's Mill that cowhands from the Crooked-T were either coming to town or leaving. It seemed they always felt a necessity to inform the whole town on both events. With a sense of new responsibility, Jim Duncan came out of the little shack he lived in behind the blacksmith shop to see if it was the usual annoyance, or something more serious. He was in time to see the three riders turning their horses onto the trail between the barbershop and the general store, which led straight east. *Good,* he thought, *they're going.* He turned around, but before he went back to his shack, he decided to check the stable next door to see if Cullen and Moss were still up. He found them sitting by a fire in a pit dug for that purpose outside the front door of the barn. "I heard the Crooked-T boys leavin' town," Moss said to Jim when he walked up.

"Yep, I was back in my shack, but I'm gettin' ready to take a little walk up the street to see if everything's all right," Jim said. "I saw 'em hit the trail back to the ranch." Looking at Cullen, he continued, "Understand we're honored by a special guest in town tonight."

"Hell," Moss spoke up right away, "me and Cullen went to the saloon with him. He bought us a drink. Didn't he, Cullen?" Cullen nodded. "He didn't go back with those other men, though, unless he walked, 'cause I got his horse here in the stable, second stall from the back, right next to Cullen's horse." He laughed at the thought.

"I thought if their horses got to know each other, maybe him and Cullen could get to be friends, too." His joke brought a healthy chuckle from Jim, but only a thin smile from Cullen. It caused Moss to wonder, as he had several times before, about the mysterious drifter who had been the driving force behind the town council's resolution to defend their community. He had no intention of remaining in Reid's Mill. He said as much from the start, so why was he still here?

Sitting by the fire pit, Cullen found himself staring into the flickering flames, wondering about the same thing. He had decided early on that the only solution he could offer the governor for Reid's Mill's problem was to hire a strong sheriff. Now that it had been accomplished, he told himself that his job was done. Yet he was reluctant to move on, with Jim Duncan still breaking in his sheriff's spurs. He was afraid it was going to take more than the act of having a sheriff in place, especially after having met with Shane Roper. The foreman for Marvin Creed's Crooked-T Ranch was not typical, as a gunslinger, or a cattleman. He displayed the confident air of a man who knew he was fast with a weapon. The tied-down, quick-draw holster he wore would testify that he had been tested more than once. But in contrast to that image, he was capable of intelligent discussion. Cullen decided that Shane Roper had reason to be confident. And that was the reason Cullen decided to linger in Reid's Mill.

CHAPTER SIXTEEN

"You fellers came back pretty early this mornin'," Tater Owen commented when Blackie and Sam showed up for breakfast. "Where's Herman? Did you leave him in town?"

"Nah," Blackie replied. "He's back there in his bunk. He got so dang drunk he can't see straight this mornin'."

"How come you boys got back so early? Run outta money?"

"Nope, I still got a little bit left. I don't know about Sam, but I expect he's in about the same boat. I'll tell you the truth, I'da still been in the Whiskey Mill, if it hadn'ta been for Roper. I had me a little somethin' goin' with Mae Davis that I know woulda lasted all night. But Roper called me outta her room, called Sam out, too, and told us to get on our horses and get back here."

"Why?" Tater asked.

"Danged if I know, but he acted like he was mad about somethin' and I sure as hell wasn't gonna cross him."

Tater nodded his head thoughtfully. "Yeah, that's right. You never know what Roper's thinkin'. Maybe he was thinkin' you boys shouldn't spend all the money you made on them cows in one night at the Whiskey Mill."

"You mean, like your daddy would?" Blackie asked with a laugh. "I don't think so. He acted like he was mad at us. And, hell, he didn't even come back with us."

Jake Williams walked up to join them. "I hope you boys didn't drink up all the whiskey last night," he said. "Hope you saved a little bit for the rest of us."

"'Cause I'm gonna need a lot of it to catch up with some of you drunks," Lem Trask bellowed as he joined them. "I ain't like ol' Shorty and go to town every other day. I was broke as the Ten Commandants until we hit that herd the other night."

Blackie looked over at Shorty Taylor and chuckled. "You boys best watch yourself, since you're goin' in with him. Seems like every time Shorty goes to town with anybody, they end up gettin' crossways with Cullen McCabe."

"Damn," Lem swore, "maybe we best make Shorty ride in by hisself."

"Maybe so," Jake said, "but if McCabe starts to get crossways with me, he'd best be ready 'cause I ain't gonna waste no time on talk."

"I'll tell you somethin' you don't know," Blackie said. "They got a sheriff in Reid's Mill now."

That remark caught everyone's immediate attention. "McCabe?" Jake asked, that being the name that naturally popped up in their minds.

"Nope," Blackie answered. "It ain't McCabe. It's Jim Duncan."

"Ain't that the blacksmith?" Shorty asked.

"Sure is," Blackie drawled. "They got signs tacked up all over town tellin' you to behave yourself, or Sheriff Jim Duncan will throw you in the jail that they ain't got."

"That sounds like a good chance to have some fun,"

Jake declared. "Welcome him to his new job as sheriff." He grinned at Blackie. "Did he say anything to you boys?"

"Didn't say nothin' to me," Blackie responded. "'Course, he'da had to be upstairs in Mae Davis's room to talk to me. That's where I was nearabout the whole time I was in town."

"I hope you was on your best behavior," Lem said. "'Cause I'm fixin' to ask her to marry me tonight."

"Ha! She'd sooner marry that flea-bitten gray you ride," Blackie japed.

"Well, I'm goin' to town," Jake declared. "You fellers can stand around here and shoot the breeze with Tater."

Morning found Shane Roper with less than a cheerful disposition after a night upstairs over the noisy saloon. At one point, during the middle of the night, he was prompted to grab his six-gun and kick the door open to the room next door to his to put an end to a fight between Molly Dugan and one of her customers. Apparently, he objected to her lifting his money from his pants while he had been passed out. She, of course, denied it, saying she went downstairs while he was sleeping it off. It proceeded into a loud fight when she returned, so loud that it awakened Roper. The young cowhand attempted to prevent his eviction, which earned him a rap over the head with Roper's six-gun and a bumpy ride on his back down the stairs.

After a cup of coffee with Harman Gill and Archie Wells, Roper felt calm enough to go to the Stoddard House for breakfast. He was ready to go back to the Crooked-T, but he wanted to be seen in town this morning. He wanted

Cullen McCabe to know he had not left with his men the night before.

"Well, good mornin', Mr. Roper," Becca managed when he walked in the dining room. "I see you're still in town."

"Good mornin' to you," he returned. "Why did you think I wouldn't be?" In his mind, he was beginning to believe that everyone thought he would flee after meeting McCabe.

"Oh, I don't know," she replied as he unbuckled his gun belt. "I just thought you were in town for the day only. Sit wherever you like and we'll be glad to feed you." She started to turn away, but he stopped her.

"I'm takin' my gun off, but I'm lookin' at a man sittin' at that little table back there and he's wearin' a gun. Why the double standard?"

Becca took a glance toward the table. "That's because he's the sheriff," she said. "Lawmen don't have to take their weapons off."

"Oh . . . Jim Duncan, right?"

"Right, Jim Duncan," she said.

Remembering what Stumpy had told him the day before, Roper went to the end of the long table where the meat platters started out. He propped his hat on his chair to claim it, then went over to the individual table where Jim Duncan was eating. "Beg pardon, Sheriff," he said, "just thought I'd say howdy and congratulations on bein' elected sheriff."

Surprised, Jim looked up at the dark, burly stranger standing over his table. "Howdy, and thanks," Jim replied. "Sorry, I can't remember your name."

"I doubt you ever knew it," Roper said. "I don't get into

town very often. My name's Shane Roper." He paused a moment and waited while Jim was obviously trying to place it. "I'm the foreman out at the Crooked-T Ranch." He paused again to study Jim's reaction to hearing that. He was gratified to see the sudden raising of the sheriff's eyebrows in response.

Jim recovered quickly, however. "Foreman for the Crooked-T," he said. "Well, I'm right glad to get the chance to meet you. You can sit down at this table with me, if you want to."

"Thanks, I will," Roper said, and pulled the other chair out. He signaled Becca for a cup of coffee.

"What brings you into town, Mr. Roper? I didn't think you ever came into Reid's Mill. Figured you must do all your business in Clifton or Waco."

"That's pretty nigh the story," Roper said. "But I know a lot of Crooked-T hands like to come here to town and I've been gettin' reports that some of them have caused problems. So I thought I'd best ride on over here and take a look. Of course, that gate swings both ways. Crooked-T has suffered the loss of four of our best hands, shot down on the streets of Reid's Mill. And from what I hear, the killer turns out to be the same gunman, fellow named Cullen McCabe. So, I figure now that there's a sheriff here in town, maybe you'll do something about this gunslinger that's feedin' offa my men."

Duncan was at a loss for a response at first. The implication was so ridiculous he thought the man might be crude enough to be making a joke of it. Roper's expression was quite serious, however, so Jim made an effort to treat the remark seriously. "I think maybe your men haven't told you the straight of these killin's you're talkin' about.

Mr. McCabe was the victim in every single case of a Crooked-T death. In every one of 'em, he was the one threatened and the one who had to act to save his life."

"Is that what he says?" Roper asked.

"He didn't have to say it," Jim insisted. "There were plenty of witnesses who saw it. I hate to say it, Mr. Roper, but it looks like you ain't got any idea of the wild and reckless crew you've got ridin' for the Crooked-T."

Roper didn't respond for a few moments. He had thought to approach the sheriff from the standpoint that he had an uncontrollable gunslinger on his hands. But the sheriff knew better, so it brought Roper back to the only course of action to rid the town of McCabe. He had to do it, himself. He smiled at Jim Duncan while he thought to himself, *It'll be a pleasure*. "Well," he said, "I've interrupted your breakfast enough as it is, talkin' business. I reckon we've both got our work cut out for us." He held his hand up to catch Becca's attention. "Set my plate there on the big table. We're both pretty good-sized men. We need a little more room. Right, Sheriff?"

"Reckon so," Jim replied. He was thinking that Roper was hoping to accomplish something by that cock-and-bull story, but he couldn't guess what it was. He didn't mention it, but Jim knew Roper had bought Cullen a drink the night before. *Cullen oughta be interested to hear that I almost had breakfast with him.*

After he finished eating breakfast, Roper walked down to the stable to get his horse. He looked to see McCabe as he walked the street, but Cullen was nowhere in sight. *Where the hell is he?* he wondered, for the town wasn't big enough to hide a man that size. Had he looked behind the barbershop, he might have spotted Cullen working with Harvey Stoddard and Joe Morrison to strengthen the doors in Joe's barn. They were preparing it to be the temporary jail until the real one was constructed. At least Roper was able to get a good idea of the man who had taken the sheriff's job. There would be a great deal to talk about with Marvin Creed.

Thinking McCabe must be at the stable, Roper walked in to find no one there but Moss Pringle. "Ya leavin' us, Mr. Roper?" Moss greeted him. "I'll get him ready for ya." Roper didn't have much conversation to waste on Moss. He paid him, checked his cinch, and climbed aboard. Then with a tip of his hat, he crossed the little bridge and went up the street at a trot to take the trail to the Crooked-T.

He was approaching the old line shack when he met the three riders from the ranch on their way into Reid's Mill. He pulled up and waited for them to come up to him. "You're headin' the wrong way, Boss," Lem Trask japed. "All the likker's thisaway."

"You boys better watch yourselves," Roper said. "The town's got a brand-new sheriff."

"Yeah, that's what we heard from Blackie and them," Jake said. "But they said they didn't see no sign of him."

"Is that so? Well, I had breakfast with him this mornin'," Roper told them. "I expect he'll be sheriff until he tries to arrest a fast gunhand and then they'll be lookin' for another one."

"What about McCabe?" Shorty asked. "You see him?"

"Not this mornin'. Saw him last night in the Whiskey Mill. Had a drink with him. He's another one with a bullet with his name on it. You boys go on in town. You got money, so the whole damn town is yours to have a good time." He reached over and gave Jake's horse a slap on its croup and they were off at a lope. *Tear that damn town up,* Roper thought.

"Reckon what Blackie and them were talkin' about?" Lem Trask said when they reined their horses back to a walk again. "Roper seemed all right to me."

"Yeah, he did," Jake agreed. "Blackie said he was actin' like he had a briar up his behind last night. But he sure seems to be in a good mood today."

"I am, too," Lem boasted. "Maybe we can get the new sheriff and McCabe to set down and have a drink with us, both of 'em at the same time. Wouldn't that be somethin'?"

Shorty Taylor listened to their boastful chatter. He had nothing to say, satisfied to let the two of them brag about what they would do. He had been in close contact with Cullen McCabe and he wanted no part in any meeting with him again. There were things in this world you couldn't explain and that goes for people, too. He had never been able to forget the night in Waco when Clive Dawkins's nose was broken. He had looked directly into Cullen McCabe's eyes and he knew he was looking into the eyes of death. He saw it again when Lucky chased after McCabe when he thought McCabe was running.

It was still early in the day when the three Crooked-T riders rode out on the main street of Reid's Mill. As a matter of ritual, Jake and Lem pulled their pistols out. "Let's let 'em know we're here," Jake said, so Shorty reluctantly drew his gun as well. "Whoo-eeee!" Jake whooped, and the three of them shot their guns in the air as they galloped the length of the street, turned about, and charged back as far as the little bridge across to the saloon. There, they encountered Jim Duncan standing at the east end of the bridge, his feet spread wide and solid, his double-barrel shotgun held in both hands in front of him. "Whoa!" Jake exclaimed. "Who the hell are you?"

"I'm the sheriff," Jim answered, "and you'll keep those weapons holstered when you come in this town. I know ain't nobody ever told you that before, so I'm gonna let you go with a warnin' this time. The next time it happens, I'll arrest you for disturbin' the peace and endangerin' people's lives and I'll lock you up."

Lem spoke up quickly, knowing Jake's tendency to challenge any threat with one of his own. "We was just havin' fun, Sheriff. We didn't mean nobody no harm. It's a waste of cartridges, anyway. Ain't it, boys? No more shootin' in the air and we'll go on about our business. Ain't that right, Jake?"

"Yeah, I reckon," Jake finally answered, his eyes still locked on Jim's. "Are we done now? 'Cause I'd like to get a little food in my belly before I start drinkin'." As soon as Jim stepped to the side, Jake rode across the bridge and headed to the Whiskey Mill. Jim studied their faces as they passed by him. The first two, Jake and Lem, he had seen in town before, but remembered nothing in particular about them. Shorty, on the other hand, had been in town recently and was present during the gunfights involving Cullen McCabe. Jim could only hope that his warning carried enough clout to influence their behavior while they were in town. He remained at the bridge to watch them all the way to the saloon, before crossing the bridge, himself, and walking down to his blacksmith shop.

"Howdy, boys," Archie greeted them. "Gettin' an early start, ain'tcha?" It was unusual to see the men from the Crooked-T in town before dinnertime.

"I don't want nothin' before I put some food in my belly," Jake informed him. "What's ol' Cow Bell got cooked up back there?" The saloon employed a cook who fixed something to eat every day for customers who were not particular about what they put in their bellies. A sad-faced, plodding woman of uncertain age, her name was Callie Belle Sykes. Regular customers of the Whiskey Mill called her Cow Bell, but not to her face. No one could say who the originator of the nickname actually was, but it seemed to fit her bovinelike manner.

"She cooked up a big pot of hash," Archie replied. "It's got two or three different kinds of meat in it—beef for sure and some squirrel—I don't know what the other one is. I was afraid to ask." He laughed in appreciation of his humor. "I ate some of it for breakfast and it wasn't bad. Harman ate some of it, too." He chuckled again. "He ain't come outta his office since, but I'm still standin'."

"That sounds like just what I need," Lem declared. "Tell her to dip me up a bowl of it with some crackers, if she's got any." He looked at Shorty and got a nod in return. "Make it three bowls." They walked over and sat down at a table while Archie went to the kitchen to deliver the order.

When he returned from the kitchen, Archie asked if they wanted coffee. Shorty and Lem both said they'd like some, but Jake said, "Just bring me a glass and a bottle of that whiskey. That'll kill whatever Cow Bell didn't get."

That was good for a chuckle, then Lem asked, "Where's the Molly-Maes? They didn't eat none of that hash, did they?"

"Nah," Archie replied. "Ain't seen hide nor hair of either one of 'em so far this mornin'. I think they must be restin' up. They had a pretty hard night's work with a couple more of your boys last night. Blackie and Sam, I swear, I believe they'd still be here this mornin' if Shane Roper hadn'ta run 'em outta here. The women will be comin' down pretty soon."

"We appreciate you havin' the new sheriff meet us at the bridge to welcome us to town," Jake said while he poured himself a drink from the bottle Archie set down on the table. "Kinda made us feel special."

"I heard the gunshots when you hit town, so I walked out on the porch to take a look. And I saw Jim Duncan talkin' to ya at the bridge," Archie said.

"He said he'd throw us in jail, if we shot our guns off again," Shorty said. "There ain't no jail here in Reid's Mill, is there?"

"No, but they've already started buildin' one on the other side of the river, across from the stable. But he's got a barn he's usin' for a jail till the real one gets built."

"He'll play hell tryin' to throw me in a barn," Jake predicted flatly. "I ain't no damn mule." Discussion about the new sheriff was interrupted then when Callie Belle came from the kitchen carrying a tray with three bowls of hash on it. She put the tray down on the corner of the table while she placed a bowl before each one of them. "Dang, that stuff's givin' off a funny odor," Jake japed. "Or is that comin' offa you, Cow Bell?" He reached over to pat her behind and she rapped his knuckles hard with a large wooden spoon she carried on the tray. "Yowl!" Jake exclaimed, and drew his hand back quickly. She picked up her tray and returned to the kitchen.

"I swear, Jake," Archie said, shaking his head and laughing. "I thought you've been comin' in here long enough to know better'n that. You're dang lucky she was carryin' a wooden spoon instead of a butcher knife."

"Damn crazy ol' cow," Jake grumbled, still rubbing his knuckles. He held his hand up, opened and closed his fist a couple of times, then declared, "She's lucky it weren't my gun hand."

CHAPTER SEVENTEEN

Hope Morrison insisted that Cullen and her husband should lay their tools aside long enough to eat some bean soup and fresh-baked bread. It was a welcome break, since they had been hard at work to transform Joe's barn into the temporary jail. The two would-be carpenters were almost finished, having been spurred on by the sound of the arrival of the Crooked-T cowhands earlier. When they heard the gunshots, Cullen was tempted to respond to see if Jim needed any backup. But he told himself, Jim was ready to handle it. Still it was a great relief when the shooting was stopped and did not occur again.

Back at it after the soup and fresh bread, they were finishing up the hanging of the reinforced door when Jim Duncan stopped by to see their progress. "Another hour at most," Cullen speculated, "and you can throw your first prisoner in, and I don't think he'll be able to get out." Jim told them about his stopping the three Crooked-T men at the bridge. "They didn't give me any trouble," he told them. "Said they didn't mean any harm, so I gave 'em a warnin' and let 'em go. Told 'em I'd put 'em in jail if they shot those guns off again." He laughed and added, "I'm glad they didn't ask me where the jail was."

"Like Cullen said, we oughta be through here in about an hour," Joe announced. "And I'm plannin' on celebratin' it with a drink of likker. How 'bout you, Cullen?"

Cullen smiled and nodded. "I reckon it does call for a drink. It turned out to be more work than I figured before we got into it." He motioned toward Jim. "You can join us and we'll drink to your new jailhouse."

"I just might do that," Jim said.

"Looks like they're doin' a good business tonight," Joe Morrison commented when he and Cullen walked across the bridge in front of the Whiskey Mill. There were half a dozen horses tied at the rail. "Harman Gill oughta be happy." They walked inside, their intention to have a drink or two, then leave, Joe home to supper and Cullen to the Stoddard House, where he had taken to having breakfast and supper every day. So they made their way through a better-than-average-sized crowd of customers. The saloon had seen an increase in local residents during the last week when there was an absence of most of the wild drunken antics of the Crooked-T. Cullen suspected the lull in trouble was attributed to nothing more than the fact that the entire Crooked-T crew was away rustling cattle. He was not encouraged by their sudden absence and expected to see the trouble return. The appearance of Shane Roper and three of his men the night before was evidence enough. And now, to support that evidence, was the appearance of three more Crooked-T men today, so they were evidently through with their rustling.

"Evenin'," Archie greeted them when they found a spot at the bar. He looked at Cullen and asked, "Rye?"

When Cullen answered with a nod, Archie asked, "How 'bout you, Joe?"

"That'll do," Joe answered. "Lookin' pretty busy tonight," he commented then. "Your Crooked-T customers behavin' themselves, or am I gonna need my handcart tonight?"

"Everything's quiet so far," Archie allowed. "They're buyin' plenty of whiskey and Jake Williams has been spendin' most of his time goin' up and down the stairs with Mae. Shorty and Lem are mostly just drinkin'." He smiled. "And that's good for business."

"Well, that's good news," Cullen said. "I'll have another and that's gonna be it for me. I wanna get some supper before Becca closes up."

His simple plan was interrupted, however, because Shorty Taylor suddenly blurted, "It's him!"

"Who?" Lem asked, trying to see in which direction Shorty was looking.

"At the bar," Shorty said, not really talking to Lem, instead, simply speaking his thoughts as they occurred to him. "Cullen McCabe."

Hearing him, Jake looked at once toward the bar. "The big feller talkin' to Archie?" Lem said that was McCabe. "So he's the big gun that's cuttin' down half our crew," Jake continued to rant. "What the hell is he doin' in here? This saloon is owned by Harman Gill and Harman's partner is Marvin Creed. McCabe ain't got no business in here."

"Hell, it's a saloon, open for business," Shorty said, not anxious to see Jake get worked up enough to mess with McCabe.

"If you own a business, you got the right to refuse to serve anybody you don't wanna serve," Jake insisted.

"Maybe Archie don't know that." He continued to stare at the bar until the fire built up inside him. "I think I best go tell him."

"Good idea," Lem said. "Go tell him, Jake. I'll entertain Mae while you're gone."

"I'm tellin' ya," Shorty insisted, "it ain't a good idea to mess with McCabe. It's best you just leave him be."

"Shorty's right," Mae Davis, who was sitting on Jake's knee, implored, "it's best to leave him be."

"That'll be the day," Jake mumbled, and picked her up as he got to his feet. "You set right there. I'll be back in a minute." He strode directly to the bar, shoving customers aside who got in his path. He stepped up to the bar about six feet from Cullen and Joe and slapped the top of the bar hard enough to get everybody's attention. Cullen turned to face him when he heard the blow on the bar. "This is a privately owned saloon," Jake announced loudly. "And the owner is particular about who can walk in here and buy whiskey. He don't allow no scum-suckin' back-shooters in here. And I'm the one that lets 'em know." There was one customer standing at the bar between them and he immediately moved out of the way.

Cullen didn't respond immediately. He turned halfway around to face Jake, far enough to have free movement to draw his weapon in case he was given a reason to. He looked at his antagonist, slightly slump shouldered, almost as if already reaching down for the weapon he wore. A foolish grin upon his unshaven face spoke of certain self-confidence. "You're askin' me to leave?" Cullen finally responded.

"No, you dumb clod, I'm tellin' you to leave."

"All right, I'll leave, but not until I have another drink,"

Cullen said. "I came in to get a couple of drinks and I ain't had but one. So after I have my second drink, I'm gonna leave, anyway. So that oughta satisfy you, right?" He motioned for Archie to pour the drink, then he picked it up and said to Joe, "Here's hopin' we don't have to fill your barn up with people like this fellow."

"What the hell's the matter with you?" Jake erupted. "I told you to get outta here! Are you deaf, or just dumb as a stump?"

"No, I heard you," Cullen replied. "Everybody heard you, so now everybody in here thinks you're meaner than barbed wire. When I finish this drink, I'll be walkin' outta here 'cause I don't feel like foolin' with a half-drunk cattle rustler right now. And you can tell your friends over there that you ran me out. All right?" Confused by Cullen's response, Jake wasn't sure what his next move should be, so he stood dumbfounded and watched Cullen down his shot of whiskey. Then Cullen tossed a couple of coins on the bar to pay for his drinks, tipped his hat to Jake, turned, and walked away. Every bit as dumbfounded as Jake, Joe Morrison followed him out the door.

When they got outside, Joe asked, "That coulda gone real bad back there. You took a helluva chance, turnin' your back and walkin' out. How'd you know he wouldn't shoot you in the back?"

"I didn't," Cullen said. "It crossed my mind, but when you followed me out, I figured you had me covered."

"I swear," Joe exclaimed, "I didn't think about that." Cullen couldn't help laughing.

They parted company then when Joe went home and Cullen decided he'd check on his horse before going to supper, so he headed for the stable. Behind him, a confused

Jake Williams stood, trying to decide if he had bluffed the big man, or if he had been made a fool of. He looked at Archie, who was grinning at him, and said, "I reckon the big gunslinger turned tail and ran."

"Yeah, he ran, all right," Archie replied. "You'd best thank your lucky stars he did. I've seen that man work."

"Hell, you ain't ever seen me work," Jake boasted. "I'da enjoyed cuttin' that jasper down to size."

"If you say so," Archie commented, thinking he'd best not push his luck. Jake remained standing at the bar for a while longer, still watching the door. Then he suddenly turned and went back to the table.

Mae got up from the chair, so he could sit down. "Just stay set," Jake told her. "I've got somethin' I gotta take care of. I'll be back in a few minutes."

"Where you goin'?" Mae whined.

"Yeah, Jake, where you goin'?" Lem asked. "Me and Mae are fixin' to go upstairs."

"I ain't gonna be gone long," Jake answered. "I'm fixin' to go pull a rattlesnake's teeth."

"You ain't fixin' to go after McCabe, are you?" Shorty asked. Jake just grinned. "You'd best set down here and have another drink and forget about him. That's just what he's wantin' you to do."

"Then I reckon I'd best not keep him waitin'," Jake said. The more he thought about it, the more he convinced himself that McCabe was afraid to face him. "Ain't no man gonna turn his back and walk out on me," he boasted. "It's time somebody evened up the score with that killer."

"You're makin' a mistake, Jake," Shorty tried to warn him. "Most likely, he's countin' on you followin' him."

"Well, I don't wanna disappoint him," Jake said, and

turned at once toward the door. It occurred to him that Shorty might be right, so he hurried outside, hoping to see where McCabe had gone. He was in luck, for he saw McCabe walking down the narrow trail that led to the stable. So he started out along the track after him, hurrying to close the distance a little, but not close enough that McCabe might become aware of the fact that he was being followed. Past the blacksmith shop, McCabe kept walking, so it was obvious he was going to the stable. To be sure, Jake paused to linger in front of the empty blacksmith shop until he saw McCabe walk in the door to the stable. Then he hurried around to the back of the stable, where he found a small window. A quick peek through the window told him he could look down the alley between the stalls. He took his hat off, so he could sneak one eye past the edge of the window without giving himself away. There was no one in the alley. McCabe had to be in one of the stalls, he thought, for he had seen him walk into that alleyway. *He's got to come out of there sooner or later,* he thought. He decided to wait him out.

What the hell is he doing? he thought, after a long period with no sign of anyone in the stalls. The horses were in the corral, since it was too early to put them in the stalls. He pulled himself up higher on the windowsill, his .44 in hand. Then a door opened midway down the alley and a man came in from the barn. Jake raised his pistol but recognized Moss Pringle. *Damn*, he thought, and quickly dropped back down on the ground.

"Lookin' for me?"

Startled, Jake turned and raised his weapon too late to stop the .44 slug that tore into his gut. He dropped his pistol on the ground and grasped the windowsill to try to support himself, but he doubled over with the pain and sank down beside his pistol. When he grasped the weapon again, Cullen stopped him with a shot in his forehead. He walked up to look down at the body, sitting in a twisted position under the window. A few moments later, Moss appeared at the window. "Cullen, what the hell?" Moss asked, no longer wondering why Cullen had walked into the stable and pulled him through the side door to the barn, then told him to stay there. After that, he had left him while he went out the back door of the barn.

"I had a feelin' I was gonna end up havin' to shoot him," Cullen said. "He started in on me when Joe and I had a drink at the saloon and I tried to back away. But he just wasn't gonna let it go."

"Looks like he was plannin' to shoot you through the window," Moss commented. "He weren't lookin' for a face-off."

"No, I reckon not and I was hopin' to avoid another shootin' here in town, since it has been pretty quiet for a few days. I'll go see if I can find Jim." He had no sooner said it when they heard the sheriff enter the stable behind Moss.

"You all right, Moss?" Jim Duncan called out.

Moss turned away from the window and answered, "Yeah, I'm all right, but there's another Crooked-T hand that ain't gonna make it back tonight."

"I heard the shots. Who was it?"

Moss looked out the window again and asked Cullen, "You know who he was?"

"I don't know his name," Cullen answered. "But he's Crooked-T, all right. He was one of those three fellows you stopped at the bridge."

Recognizing Cullen's voice, Jim said, "I was gonna ask who shot him, but I reckon I shoulda guessed."

"He didn't give me a choice," Cullen said. "He tried to get me to fight him in the saloon. When I wouldn't do it, he followed me down here to the stable, sneaked around behind to try to get a shot at me through the window. I reckon I'll have to haul his body up to Joe's barn. I'll throw it on Orphan's back and take it right now, so I can get to Becca's before she closes. I shoulda gone to supper first and maybe he wouldn't have tried it where there were witnesses around. But I wanted to see how Orphan was doin'. I haven't paid much attention to him in the last day or so."

"I reckon I can take the body to Joe's for you," Jim said, and Moss volunteered to help in addition to supplying his mule to carry the corpse. So all three loaded Jake's body on the mule and walked up the street as far as the barbershop, where Cullen left them and continued on to the dining room. "Well, that little piece of business behind the stable didn't seem to affect his appetite, did it?" Jim remarked as they watched Cullen walking away. "I ain't sure I can ever get that used to killin', no matter how long I make it as a sheriff."

"You ain't cut outta the same cloth as Cullen McCabe," Moss was quick to point out. "And neither is anybody else. By my count, he's killed four men since he landed in our town. We don't know nothin' about him, who he is, or where he came from. But lookin' at what he's done since he came here, there ain't no tellin' how many men he's killed before. So far, everything he's done seems to be in our favor. He's sure as hell thinnin' out the Crooked-T for us, but I keep waitin' to see if he's thinkin' about runnin' this town after he cuts Marvin Creed down."

"I'd be surprised if that ever happened," Jim replied. "I don't see any sign of that in Cullen. I think any day now, he's gonna decide he's ready to move on to someplace else, and he'll just climb on that dun and ride on outta Reid's Mill."

"Am I too late?" Cullen asked when he walked in the door of the dining room and saw Becca and Cora clearing the dirty dishes off the tables.

"No, but you didn't miss it by much," Becca answered. "We ain't thown everything out yet. Cora can fix you up a plate." Cora went at once to the kitchen while Becca handed Cullen a cup. "Here, pour yourself some coffee. There's still some in that pot." She pointed toward a large pot sitting on the edge of the fireplace. "I just set it there a minute ago."

"I 'preciate it," Cullen said, and went to the fireplace. "I'da been here sooner, but I got held up at the stable." He grabbed the handle of the big pot and yelped, "Yowl!" And he immediately released it.

Becca glanced his way and commented casually, "I didn't think I'd have to tell you to use that rag to pick it up."

Cora came back with a plate piled high with food and set it down at a small table by the kitchen door. "If you don't mind, I'm gonna set you down at this little table, so we can go ahead and clean up the big table." She glanced at Becca then and said, "You might as well turn the closed sign around 'cause there ain't much left except what's fit for the hogs."

"I 'preciate you lettin' me eat," Cullen thanked them again. "I wasn't in the mood to eat sowbelly and hardtack, and that's about all I've got in my packs now. This is a mighty generous servin', too. Might be you oughta charge me double."

"It'll just be the regular price, as long as you don't say nothin' to the hogs about it," Becca said with a chuckle.

He finished his supper while the two women cleaned the dining room up to the little table he occupied. When Becca took his empty plate, he asked, "Mind if I pour one more cup of coffee? I'll stand up to drink it, so you can clean up around the table." Becca told him to help himself, so he poured himself another cup, using the rag to wrap around the handle of the pot. Then he stood by the fireplace while he drank it. That was where he was when Jim Duncan knocked on the outside door.

"I know you're closed," Jim said. "I'm lookin' for Cullen." And then he noticed Cullen standing back by the fireplace. "Cullen, I figured you'd still be here. I thought I'd best let you know what's goin' on with those other two Crooked-T hands." He interrupted himself to ask, "Any more coffee left in that pot?"

"Yeah, there's another cup, I reckon," Cullen said. Jim turned around to find Becca holding out a cup for him, one she picked up from the table already set for breakfast. "Use the rag to pick it up," Cullen said.

"I went back to the Whiskey Mill to tell those two fellows that their friend was dead and they weren't too happy to hear about it. At least one of 'em wasn't, but the other one, that one named Shorty, he didn't make no fuss a-tall. He even admitted that he tried to tell the dead one not to go after you. But his friend, he wouldn't tell me his name, he acted like he was pretty hot under the collar about it. Wanted to know what I was gonna do about it. I told him I reckoned we'd dig a hole and stick him in the ground, unless he wanted to take him back to the Crooked-T to bury him. He said he meant what was I gonna do about you shootin' his friend. He said his friend's name was Jake Williams. I told him I'd most likely tell you it's a good thing you caught Jake tryin' to sneak up on you. From the way he acted, I don't think that was what he was lookin' for." He paused to take a sip of the strong coffee. "I told him I wasn't gonna arrest a man for defendin' himself against a yellow back-shooter. It didn't look like he liked that, but Shorty tried to calm him down. So I came to tell you to be careful and keep a sharp eye till those two fellows leave town."

"Thanks, Jim," Cullen said. "I'll keep an eye out."

Becca and Cora were dumbfounded to hear about the shooting. In addition, they both found it fascinating that Cullen had come directly to the dining room after killing a man. As Cora put it, "Who could eat at all, after just shooting a man to death, especially a plate of food the size of the one he polished off?"

CHAPTER EIGHTEEN

"What are we gonna do about that killer?" Lem Trask fumed. "It's up to me and you to do somethin'."

"I tried to tell Jake he was makin' a big mistake goin' after McCabe," Shorty said. "He wouldn't listen. I tried to tell him McCabe is just bad news. I was hopin' Jake wouldn't find him, but he did."

"Shorty's right, honey," Mae Davis said to Lem. "It's best you leave Cullen McCabe be. Look at what's happened to everyone who's tried him."

"He's cuttin' down the Crooked-T crew one by one. If he ain't stopped pretty soon, there ain't gonna be enough of us to move a small herd of cattle."

"That's because it's Crooked-T riders that keep comin' after him," Mae said. "He ain't killin' nobody else, honey."

Ignoring Mae's pleas, Lem continued to struggle with his conscience. "Whadda we gonna tell Roper when he wants to know what we did about it?"

"We'll tell him we couldn't find McCabe, or we ain't sure who shot Jake," Shorty suggested. He had been in this position before. And rather than take any more questions regarding his bravery, he wouldn't hesitate to lie to

Roper—or Mr. Creed, either. The fact of the matter was, in his mind, if you went after McCabe, you were bound to die. He believed that and he told Lem, "I'm not goin' after McCabe. If you do, you'll be by yourself. I've seen that man under threat too many times to put myself in his path."

"It'd be a lot easier, if we was to both go after him," Lem argued. "Come at him from two different directions. He can't see in opposite directions at the same time, I don't care how sharp his eyesight is. Ain't that right?"

"I don't know if it is or not," Shorty replied. "He ain't like any other man I ever saw in a fight." He made up his mind. "I ain't goin' lookin' for him and I'd just as soon he didn't find me. Matter of fact, I'm done drinkin' for the day. I'm ready to go back right now. I'll tell Roper about Jake and let him decide what to do about McCabe."

"Maybe you're right," Lem said. "Maybe we'd best go on back and tell Roper and let him and Creed decide what they wanna do."

"Ah, honey," Mae protested at once. "It's too early to leave here now. We ain't even got started good. I was plannin' on showing you a real good time tonight."

"I hate to miss it, Mae, but I think Shorty's right. We need to let Mr. Creed know about Jake right away. I'll be back to see you before long."

"Maybe you ought not to bother," she said, pouting. "I've got a lot of boys waitin' for me to have some free time for them." She promptly got up and walked over to another table where Molly Dugan was drinking with two customers.

* * *

"What are you boys doin' back this early?" Tater Owen asked when Shorty and Lem came into the bunkhouse. "Where's Jake?"

"Jake's still in Reid's Mill," Lem answered him.

"When's he comin' back?" Blackie asked.

"He ain't," Lem answered. "He's stayin' there." That got everyone's attention.

"What are you talkin' about, Lem?" Tater asked. "Spit it out. The new sheriff?"

"McCabe," Lem said. "Jake tried to call him out in the saloon, but McCabe wouldn't have none of it and walked out. Turned his back on Jake and walked out. We said let him go. Hell, he called him a coward and McCabe still walked away. But Jake weren't satisfied. He went after him. Me and Shorty figured McCabe was thinkin' about settin' up an ambush and tried to tell Jake he might be walkin' into it. He went, anyway. A little while later, that new sheriff came in the saloon to tell us Jake was dead, said McCabe did the shootin'."

"Did you and Shorty go after McCabe?" Sam Culver asked.

"We looked for him, but we couldn't find him," Lem said, and looked at Shorty. "Then we decided we'd best get back here and tell Roper right away." He looked at Shorty again, who nodded slowly. "Has he gone to bed yet?"

"I don't think so," Tater said. "He was in here a few minutes before you two came in and got a cup of coffee to take back to his room. Knock on the door. He'll let you know soon enough if he's still up."

The two of them walked to the other end of the bunk-house and Lem knocked on the door to Roper's room. "Come on in," Roper called out. They filed into his private room like two boys filing into the principal's office. "What are you two doin' back so soon? I didn't expect to see you until breakfast."

"There's somethin' happened we figured you'd wanna know right away," Shorty said. Then the two of them went on to relate the happenings of the evening, their make-believe search for Jake, and their decision to get the story back to him.

"McCabe," Roper spat. "In that little town, how could you not find him?"

"That's what we was sayin'," Shorty answered. "He musta took to hidin' after he killed Jake. We finally gave up and got back here so you could tell Mr. Creed about it."

"It's too late to tell Mr. Creed tonight," Roper said. "He goes to bed earlier than this. And if there was some good news to tell him, I'd wake him up for that. But I ain't gonna wake him up to give him some bad news. I'll talk to him in the mornin', after he's had his breakfast." They started to leave his room, but he stopped them with one more question. "You said the sheriff told you about this. What did he say about McCabe? What was his version of the shooting?"

"He said they wouldn't do nothin' to McCabe," Lem answered. "They said it was self-defense, that Jake came after him."

"That figures," Roper said. "McCabe's got that sheriff in his pocket."

As he had said the evening before, Roper waited until he was sure Marvin Creed had eaten his breakfast and finished his daily after-breakfast session on his chamber pot before he knocked on the kitchen door of the ranch house. When Lola Lopez came to the door, Roper told her he needed to talk to Mr. Creed. "*Sí*, Señor Roper, I go tell him," she said, and went at once to Creed's study. In a few minutes, she returned to the kitchen, carrying a brass chamber pot. "Señor Creed wait for you in his study." Roper nodded and went to the study while Lola carried the chamber pot out the back door.

"What is it, Roper?" Creed asked when his foreman walked in the room.

"Mornin', Mr. Creed," Roper replied respectfully. "I just learned we lost another man yesterday. Jake Williams, he was in town with Shorty Taylor and Lem Trask. They came back after you'd gone to bed and told me Jake was shot down by Cullen McCabe."

Creed grimaced and clenched his teeth. "What about that new sheriff you told me about yesterday? Did he arrest McCabe?"

"No, sir, the sheriff told Shorty and Lem that it was self-defense, that Jake attacked McCabe." He waited for Creed's explosive reaction and in a few seconds it came.

Laced with a long string of profanity, Creed expressed his anger and frustration over his plan to capture the town of Reid's Mill. "Correct me if I'm wrong," he ranted. "By my count, we have lost five men to Cullen McCabe. Five men," he repeated, and slammed his fist on his desk. "Five men who were recruited to ride for me because of their reputations for toughness and skill with their firearms! And yet, every time any of my men go up against McCabe, they lose. In the battle for control of Reid's Mill, the score is McCabe five and Crooked-T zero. Is there not one of my men who can call McCabe out and beat him in a fair fight?"

"There's only one that I know of for sure," Roper answered. His confident reply was enough to cause Creed to pause and settle down.

"I know," Creed said, speaking calmly now. "And this might be the right time to use your skills to further our plans." The first time he ever saw Shane Roper came to his mind. It was outside a saloon in San Antonio. Roper had been called out by a local gunslinger with a reputation as a fast-draw killer. Creed had been amazed by the light-ninglike reflexes of the somber stranger as he cut the local champion down before he cleared leather. Creed had hired Roper on the spot, determined to have the fastest gun in Texas on his payroll. "Are you ready?" Creed asked then.

"I'm always ready, Boss. Just waiting for your signal."

"Good, then we might as well go ahead and start this takeover now," Creed said, his eyes focused on something outside the window as if looking into the future. "It will be a little different from the peaceful takeover I had planned when they had no sheriff. But the arrival of one Cullen McCabe has forced our hand a little early. As I see it now, there are only two roadblocks in our path, Cullen McCabe and Sheriff Jim Duncan. If you are ready, as you say, you can take care of McCabe. But it must be an open challenge, so there will be no objections when I name you sheriff. As far as the present sheriff, you can arrange a simple assassination to get rid of him. Use the men for that, if you wish. They should be able to carry out an assignment that simple."

"How soon do you want me to start on the first road-block?" Roper asked.

"Whenever you think you're ready," Creed replied. "The sooner, the better. I'm tired of waiting for just the right time."

"Then I'll ride into Reid's Mill today," Roper stated. He smiled. "I had a feeling it was going to be a good day when I woke up this morning." He got to his feet, as did Creed.

"Good hunting," Creed said, and extended his hand. When they shook hands, Creed said, "I think this will be the start of a great adventure and the seed for both our fortunes."

"Thank you, sir," Roper said humbly, and walked out the door. Out through the kitchen he went and as he descended the back steps, he nodded politely to Lola, who was washing the master's chamber pot at the pump. On his way to the bunkhouse, he stopped by the barn to tell Juan to saddle his horse. Then he went to his room at the end of the bunkhouse to dress for his trip to Reid's Mill. On this special occasion, he chose to wear his black boots with the silver inlay trimming, his black suit with the leather vest, and his favorite flat-crowned, wide-brimmed hat. This was his funeral suit and the funerals he wore it to were always those that he caused. When he was ready, he went out to the corral, where his horse was now saddled and waiting. He threw his saddlebags, containing extra underwear and a shirt, on the horse. These were just in case it took a day or two to set up his meeting with Cullen McCabe. Everything in order then, he climbed up into the saddle and left the Crooked-T headquarters at a comfortable lope. Guiding his horse onto a well-worn trail that led through a notch in the line of hills directly to his west, he set out once again to visit Reid's Mill.

* * *

Sheriff Jim Duncan stepped forward to lend a hand to the carpenters unloading a wagon of lumber from the sawmill. He had stopped by to see the progress of the new sheriff's office, and as usual, he offered a hand. "That oughta be enough for that outside wall," Fred Sowers said when he walked over to talk to Jim. "At the rate these boys are workin', you're gonna be needin' some furniture in a few days."

"At least I hope I can set my cot up inside before too long," Jim replied. He started to tell Sowers about a little wood stove he had ordered for his office when his eye caught sight of an approaching horse. "I thought he left town," Jim murmured.

"Maybe he's comin' to turn himself in," Sowers joked when he looked to see whom Jim was referring to. "You have to tell him he'll have to wait a few more days. We ain't even started on the cell room yet." He was still chuckling when Roper turned his horse in their direction.

"Howdy, Sheriff," Roper started off as soon as he pulled his horse up beside them. "Mr. Creed sent me into town to talk to you."

"Oh, is that so?" Jim replied. "How can I help you?"

"We're wonderin' when you're gonna take care of the problem of Cullen McCabe," Roper answered.

"What problem is that?" Duncan responded, knowing full well what was coming.

"I'm sure I don't have to point it out to you, Sheriff, but it seems like Mr. McCabe has taken it upon himself to kill every cowhand who rides for the Crooked-T. We've lost five good men, all since McCabe came to town. Don't that seem just a little bit odd to you?" He paused to wait for Jim's response and when it didn't come right away, he said, "We think you need to arrest Cullen McCabe for murder. Might be good for the people of Reid's Mill to see a trial and a hangin'."

His statement brought a startled reaction from both Duncan and Sowers. "A hangin'?" Jim responded. "That's a little harsh treatment for a man who's forced to defend himself, ain't it? Every one of those men McCabe shot pulled a weapon on him first and he didn't do nothin' but react to save his life. And that ain't just his word. There've been plenty of witnesses that'll tell you the same thing."

"How about the murder of Jake Williams last night? Were there any witnesses to that one?" Roper insisted.

"None that saw the shots," Jim said impatiently, "but Moss Pringle was there right after he got shot. And my question to you is what was Jake Williams doin' down there back of the stable? His two friends were still back in the saloon drinkin' while he was followin' McCabe to the stable. I can understand you gettin' riled about losin' your men, but all the advice I can give you is to keep 'em to hell outta Reid's Mill. And that'll take care of your problem."

Roper said nothing more for a few moments, while he studied the defiant face of Jim Duncan. The sheriff's response had been exactly what Roper had anticipated. The only reason he had confronted him was to make it appear he had asked for help from the law before he took matters into his own hands. "I reckon, if I'm gonna get any justice outta this problem," he finally declared, "I'm gonna have to see if I can reason with Mr. McCabe."

Somewhat concerned by that, the sheriff was quick to

issue a warning. "I think I oughta make it clear that you, or anybody else, that decides to take somebody's life in this town will be arrested and tried for murder. You'd best keep that in mind."

"You don't have to warn me, Sheriff." Roper said. "If it comes to that, it'll be man-to-man with both of us ready to settle our quarrel in a fair contest. You got any problem with that?"

Duncan didn't know how to answer that at first. After a moment's hesitation, he said, "I reckon that would be between you and him. And as long as it ain't in town where a stray bullet could hurt an innocent bystander and there's a second for each of you to make sure everything's fair and square."

"You have my word on that, Sheriff," Roper assured him. "I'll have a word with Mr. McCabe. Maybe it won't lead to bloodshed." He wheeled his horse away from the partially built jail and went to look for Cullen, leaving two concerned citizens of Reid's Mill behind him.

"Where is Cullen?" Fred Sowers asked.

"I don't know," Jim answered. "I ain't seen him this mornin' since breakfast at Stoddards'. He might be at the stable. He said somethin' about his horse not gettin' rode enough."

"That son of a gun looked like a real gunslinger to me," Sowers stated, referring to Roper. "Cullen needs to be warned that he's lookin' for him."

"You're right about that," Jim said. "I'm goin' down to the stable to see if he's there. If he ain't, Moss might know where he went. There ain't many other places he goes here in town. It's close to dinnertime and he's taken to eatin' a lot of his meals at the roomin' house the last few days."

"I'll take a look in the saloon, just in case he decided to have a drink," Sowers volunteered. "Then I'd best get back to the sawmill."

"Yeah, you do that," Jim said, thinking it highly unlikely Cullen was at the Whiskey Mill at this time of day. He had an idea that Sowers would have a drink or two while he was looking for McCabe.

CHAPTER NINETEEN

Cullen glanced up from his plate of stew when Jim Duncan walked into the dining room and seated himself across from him at the end of the long table. "Jim," Cullen greeted him simply, then waited, since the expression on the sheriff's face conveyed a deep concern about something.

Before Jim could speak, he was interrupted by Becca. "Howdy, Jim. You eatin' dinner?"

"No," Jim answered hurriedly, "just give me some coffee." She turned to leave and he stopped her. "Wait. Yeah, bring me a plate."

She raised her eyebrows, amused. "Make up your mind. You wanna eat, or don't you?"

"Yeah, bring me a plate."

"What's on your mind, Jim?" Cullen asked. "You're actin' like you've got a burr under your saddle."

"I'm just glad I found you first," Duncan replied. "I need to warn you about some trouble. That damn gunslinger Marvin Creed hired as his foreman just rode into town and he's lookin' for you."

"Well, I ain't that hard to find," Cullen said, but he figured there was more to it than that, since Jim seemed so concerned.

"You nccd to bc rcady for troublc," Jim said. "Hc came to me, askin' me what I intended to do about you killin' Crooked-T men. He was talkin' about a trial and a hangin'. I told him how those killin's happened, that his men came after you, and they all drew their weapons first. But it didn't give him no satisfaction, so he said he was goin' to look for you to settle it."

"I 'preciate the warnin'," Cullen said. "I'll make myself available, so he won't have any trouble findin' me. Maybe he just wants to talk about how to keep trouble from happenin' between his men and me." He knew that was merely wishful thinking, even as he said it. There was no doubt in his mind that Shane Roper was a fast-gun artist. He decided that the first time he met him, not only by his holster and the way he wore it, but also by the way he carried himself. Confident to the point of being smug about his person, he gave off an air of superiority. From what Jim was telling him, he had to surmise that Creed had been pushed into taking strong action. And he had decided to send his executioner to eliminate the source of his current problem, one Cullen McCabe. Cullen figured this would be in the form of a formal challenge to a face-off, a duel to determine who had control over the town. A formal duel would provide a sense of honor, in which Roper and Creed would not be looked upon as assassins. Cullen knew that this was of utmost importance to Marvin Creed.

It struck Cullen as rather odd that his role in this battle

between the Crooked-T and Reid's Mill had been simply to have come here to observe, then make recommendations to the governor. The series of events that had occurred since he first rode in, somehow managed to cast him into the role of antagonist when it came to the Crooked-T. The thought struck him that maybe he was not called upon to single-handedly do battle to save the town of Reid's Mill. Maybe in his capacity as special agent for the governor of Texas, he was required only to withdraw to Austin and present his report. On the other hand, if he agreed to face Roper with pistols, and won, it might destroy Marvin Creed's plans to capture the town as his own kingdom. On the other side of the coin, if he faced Roper and lost, it might mean the worst of the town's fears would become reality. *So I reckon I'd best win,* he decided. His own death was of no real concern to him. It never had been, ever since his wife and children had been brutally murdered. His indifference to death was one of the major reasons he accepted the governor's offer to work as his special agent.

"What are you gonna do?" Jim finally pressed when it appeared that Cullen's mind had wandered off somewhere else.

"Sorry," Cullen said. "I was just thinkin' about something else there for a minute or two. What am I gonna do? Why, I reckon I'll finish this fine plate of stew, and then I'll go see if I can find Roper and we'll discuss whatever he wants to talk about. This stew's good, I recommend you eat yours before it cools off too much more."

"Damn it, Cullen," Jim swore. "That man's a fast gun. It's wrote all over him. He ain't got but one thing in mind and that's to get you to face him man-to-man. I know you handle yourself pretty well, especially for a man your size.

You're quick, but I'd bet any amount of money that Roper's a professional. If he wasn't, Creed wouldn'ta hired him." He paused, waiting for a response, but Cullen just continued eating. "You're the one who told me not to do any duels with an outlaw. You said sheriffs don't fight duels."

"That's a fact. I did say that, and I meant it," Cullen said. "But I ain't no sheriff." He knew Jim's argument was a sound one and he was not presumptuous to the point where he thought he was the fastest gun around. Quicker than some, slower than others, was the way he saw himself when it came to drawing his weapon and firing. No matter who was the quickest, he didn't plan to lose in the competition. "Besides," he concluded, "maybe a face-off is the last thing Roper's got on his mind." He held his cup up and looked around for Becca.

She came to the table, carrying the pot. "You gonna try a piece of pie?" she asked as she filled his cup. Then to Jim, she asked, "Something wrong with your food? It doesn't look like you've touched it."

"What kinda pie is it?" Cullen asked. When she told him, he said, "Apple pie, that's my favorite. I think today's a good day to eat a slice of apple pie." Both Becca and Jim looked at him as if he had suddenly been struck silly.

When he had finished his dessert, he paid Becca for his meal and walked over to the weapons table to strap on his gun belt. Jim got up with him, although he had not eaten half of the stew on his plate. "I'm goin' with you," he announced. "Where we goin'?"

"Thought I'd go down to the Whiskey Mill and buy me one of those cigars Harman Gill likes to smoke. You want one?"

"No, but I'll go with you," Jim said. He glanced at

Becca and shook his head. She answered with a shrug, having picked up on more of what could be considered strange behavior for the usually somber McCabe.

"Have you seen any other Crooked-T hands in town today?" Cullen asked Jim as they walked down the street. Duncan answered, saying that Roper was the only one he had seen. That was interpreted by Cullen as meaning there was no plan to shoot the sheriff at the same time Roper did away with him. So that was one less thing to be concerned about at the moment.

When they walked into the Whiskey Mill, there were only half a dozen customers and four of them were in a card game. There was no sign of the Molly-Maes, probably because most of the customers were past the age of wasting money on what they had to offer. Cullen and Jim walked up to the bar, where they were greeted by Archie. "Rye?" he asked automatically when addressing Cullen, since that was his preferred whiskey.

"I believe I will," Cullen answered. "And I'll buy one of those fancy cigars your boss likes to smoke, if you've got some to sell."

"I've got some," Archie said, "but they'll cost you more than the whiskey."

"I'll take one, anyway, since this will most likely be the only one I'll ever smoke. How 'bout you, Jim?"

"I'll just take the whiskey," the sheriff said.

Inside Harman Gill's office, unaware of the two men who had just walked into the saloon, Shane Roper was in the midst of explaining why it was important that he challenge Cullen McCabe to a duel, instead of simply putting a bullet in his back. "If it's done right, with both parties with a second to make sure it's a fair contest, then nobody can complain about it. And when I'm named sheriff, nobody can complain that I murdered McCabe."

"What about Sheriff Duncan?" Gill asked.

"That's simple," Roper replied. "He'll have an accident. First we'll take care of McCabe."

"You sound awful sure of yourself. How do you know you're faster than McCabe? He was quicker than Clive Dawkins."

Roper's face broke out with a confident smile. "Clive was fast for a bumbling farmhand, but he never came up against a professional. I have no concerns about being beaten to the draw by any man, especially Cullen McCabe."

They were interrupted then when Archie opened the door and stuck his head in. "Just thought I'd let you know Cullen McCabe is settin' at one of my tables, smokin' one of your favorite cigars."

Roper jumped to his feet, anxious to see that McCabe didn't walk out again. He pushed past Archie, who was still standing in the doorway. Archie and Gill followed along behind him. "There's a man I wanna see," Roper announced as he walked up to the table. "I see you brought the sheriff with you. Do you feel like you need protection?"

"No, I don't," Cullen answered. "Is there some reason I should?"

"That depends on what kind of man you are. I've been lookin' for you because I take a strong objection to the sneaky murders of several of my men by your hand. And I'd like to see if you're man enough to stand behind your word. So I'm asking you now, do you deny the cold-blooded murder of Jake Williams?"

Cullen got to his feet. "Was that the yellow back-shooter's name? Yeah, I deny murderin' him."

"Then, you, sir, are a damn liar," Roper snarled.

"Well, this ain't the first time I've been called one and, so far, it ain't hurt me none. So I reckon you've got your-self all worked up over nothin'. Your man Jake was a sneakin' dog slippin' around behind the back of the stable, trying to get a shot at somebody's back."

Roper stepped up almost in Cullen's face. "And I'm callin' you a liar." He reached in his pocket and pulled out a glove. Looking Cullen in the eye, he suddenly reached up and slapped him across his face with the glove. Hardly versed in the gentlemanly way of accepting a challenge to duel, Cullen reacted automatically, anyway. With a hard right hand, he planted a haymaker on Roper's jaw that knocked the surprised duelist backward over the table and onto the floor. Stunned, he lay there on his back for several long moments before he seemed to regain his senses. At that point, he reached for his pistol, only to find Cullen standing over him, his six-gun already drawn. With little choice, he rolled over to get on his hands and knees and remained in that position long enough to remind him of the importance of a formal duel. "I'm going out in the street. If you're not a yellow coward, you'll come outside and face me and we'll settle this once and for all." He got to his feet then, picked up his hat, and headed toward the door, his steps still a little unsteady. Nodding toward Harman Gill, he said, "Come on. Since he brought the sheriff, you can be my second."

"You gonna face him?" Jim asked Cullen.

"I reckon so, 'cause I think Marvin Creed is figurin' on puttin' him in your job," Cullen said. When they walked outside, they found Roper waiting, his coattail tucked behind him. Cullen took his coat off and handed it to Jim. "Make sure the street is clear behind us, so nobody catches a stray bullet." A small group of spectators had already gathered when it became apparent what was about to happen. So Jim yelled for everyone to stay on the sides of the street. That caused more spectators to come from the stores to watch. Cullen looked at Roper standing almost casually now while he waited. It appeared that he had recovered his balance and steadiness, confident in his knowledge that there was no one faster in a quick-draw contest. There was even the hint of a smile, evident in spite of the rapidly growing lump on one side of his face and the blood running out of the corner of his mouth.

"How you wanna do this thing?" Jim asked. "First blood drawn, declared the winner?"

"No," Roper answered. "To the death. Last man standing is the winner."

Jim looked quickly toward Cullen, sure that Roper had done this before. "Whatever he wants," Cullen said. The two combatants were standing ready, about forty paces apart.

"All right," Jim called out. "You both ready?" Both men said they were ready. "You want me to count to three or somethin'?"

"No," Roper answered him. "We'll just leave it up to you, McCabe. Whenever you feel like you've got a chance, go ahead and reach for it."

Cullen took a square stance. He knew he was going to have to be faster than he had ever drawn his weapon before. He knew what he had to do and he was determined to keep his concentration on the task to be done. When he felt he was ready, he made his move. With the speed of a bolt of lightning, Roper pulled and fired, his bullet striking Cullen before he raised his weapon high enough to aim. Ignoring the impact of the slug against his upper-left chest, Cullen continued to raise his six-gun, taking dead aim while Roper, surprised, quickly cocked his pistol. He was not quick enough, however, to raise it again before Cullen's bullet struck him in the forehead. Killed instantly, the dead man's reflexes shot a final round into the ground before he collapsed.

Jim Duncan rushed to Cullen's side. "Oh, damn, Cullen! You all right? You been shot! We got to get you to Doc Stevens. Are you all right? Can you make it to Doc's? That's the damnedest thing I've ever seen. You just stood there and took aim after he'd already shot you."

"I figured he was most likely faster than I was, so I knew the only chance I had was to take dead aim and make sure I stopped him before he could get another shot off," Cullen said as they walked toward the doctor's office.

"Man, you were lucky as hell he didn't place that round in the center of your chest," Jim said, continuing to marvel over Cullen's survival.

"I expect he meant to do that," Cullen surmised. "But he mighta still been a little unsteady after goin' over that table and landin' on his back. Didn't hurt his speed any, though. He was the fastest I've ever seen."

Like others on the street, Dr. Ronald S. Stevens heard the shots and looked out his door to see what the shooting was about. "I swear," he called to his wife, Doris, "it's that big gunman, McCabe. Looks like he's shot and he's coming this way. Jim Duncan's with him. Moving along on his own, though. Better get me some water heated up." He stood up front, holding the door open for them. "What happened, Jim?"

"He got shot!" Jim answered. "We had us our first duel in the street and Cullen won. Stood like a statue and took a bullet before he put a round right in Roper's forehead. When Doc asked who Roper was, Jim said, "He's Marvin Creed's foreman and he came into town to kill Cullen."

"Well, come on, let's have a look," Doc said to Cullen. "Let's get that shirt off. Looked to me like you were walking all right. Must not have hit a major artery or organ." Doris brought in a pan of hot water and Doc started cleaning Cullen's chest and shoulder. "You were pretty lucky, mister. That bullet struck you right in the muscle and soft tissue, just shy of your shoulder. We'll get that outta there without much trouble a-tall and you'll be back ready for another duel in no time."

As the doctor predicted, the bullet was removed and Cullen was out of there in less than an hour's time. When he left Doc's office, he went straight to see Joe Morrison and found Jim there after helping Joe cart Roper's body to Joe's combination jailhouse-mortuary. "I wanted to catch you before you did anything with that body," Cullen told him. "That's another one I'd like to return to sender. I think we need to send a message to Marvin Creed. Keep whatever you found on him for your trouble, but I'd like to take him back to the Crooked-T in the mornin'."

"Shoot, Cullen," Jim remarked, "you ain't in no shape to take that body out there to the Crooked-T."

"I think Creed needs to know Roper failed and maybe

he'll finally see he's beat when he thinks he can take over this town."

"Maybe," Jim said. "But if you still feel like you can make a trip out there in the mornin', then I'm goin' with you. It might be better if the sheriff was to go out there and give that ol' man the word to keep his claws outta Reid's Mill."

"You might be right," Cullen allowed. "It would be the first time he got an official warnin' from the town." He was encouraged to see someone in the town take on some responsibility for defending it. Another thought crossed his mind at that point, so he expressed the concern it brought to mind. "On the other hand, it might not be too smart for both you and me to ride into that ranch together. If Creed was to take a notion, he might decide to kill us both while he had the chance." He looked directly at Jim. "And it's important that the town has a sheriff. Otherwise, there ain't nobody to keep him from takin' over the town."

"I understand what you're sayin'," Jim replied. "But I think it's time Creed finds out that the sheriff of this town ain't afraid of anybody. I'm goin' with you."

Cullen shrugged. There seemed to be no room left for argument. "I reckon so." He saw that as another healthy sign for the town, so he turned his attention to the practical aspect of hauling the body then. He questioned Joe Morrison as he stood gazing at Roper lying on Joe's worktable. "Has he gone stiff already?"

"No, he ain't stiff yet," Joe answered, then explained. "He won't start gettin' stiff until about three or four hours. They call that rigor mortis," he added, hoping to impress them with the term. Cullen was thinking about Clive Dawkins. He had thrown his body over his saddle right after he shot him and it wasn't stiff when he left it at Marvin Creed's front porch.

"After he gets stiff, how long before he'll loosen up again?" Cullen asked.

"He'll stay stiff as a board for a day or two before he starts to limber up again. That's what I've heard. I know everybody I've put in the ground was still stiff when I covered 'em up."

Cullen nodded his understanding. "How 'bout we take him off that table and set him up in that chair over there. Then when he stiffens up, he'll be in a bent position and he'll ride a lot easier bent over the back of his horse when we pick him up in the mornin'."

"That makes sense," Jim said. "It'll be a lot easier to tie him on the horse." So the three of them picked Roper up and sat him in the chair.

Cullen stepped back and looked at the corpse, trying to picture it draped over the saddle. "It'd be even better if his arms were stickin' straight out. Then it'd be real easy to tie his hands and feet together under the horse's belly."

"Even though he's stiff, if you work at it, you can get his arms in another position," Joe offered. "It takes a little rubbin' and bendin', but you can change his position some. I have to do that sometimes to get 'em in the coffin."

"How 'bout if we move that sawhorse over there in front of him?" Jim asked. "We could prop his arms out in front of him on that and then we wouldn't have to work him a-tall."

"That would work," Cullen said. "We need to pull his legs straight out in front of him, too, so his knees ain't bent."

When they were finished, they took another look at

their handiwork, satisfied with the cargo to be hauled out to the Crooked-T. "I reckon it's a good thing we ain't usin' my barn as a jail right now," Joe commented. "It might be hard to keep a prisoner in the barn with something like that lookin' at 'em."

"You'd best tell Hope not to go in here tonight," Jim advised with a chuckle.

"Ain't no worry about that," Joe replied. "She won't go anywhere near this shop, anyway, whether I got a guest in here or not."

CHAPTER TWENTY

Cullen and Jim met for breakfast at Stoddard House as soon as Becca opened the door to the dining room. "Good mornin', fellows," Becca greeted them. "You're gettin' an early start on the day."

"Yep, we've gotta take a little trip," Jim Duncan responded.

"You can still change your mind about goin' with me," Cullen said. "I wouldn't think nothin' about it a-tall. You've got the town to be responsible for and I can understand that."

"Nope, I ain't changed my mind," Jim said adamantly. "That crowd out there at the Crooked-T needs to hear it from the sheriff that we're tired of puttin' up with their aggravation. Maybe you've forgot about it, but I remember you got shot yesterday. Are you sure you're up to ridin' out there with that body? Might be, I'd best go alone."

"The wound ain't botherin' me a-tall," Cullen insisted. "You can't even see the bandage under my coat and it doesn't hurt to move my arm, if I don't do something crazy with it."

"You know, you already took a chance when you went

ridin' in there with Clive Dawkins's body," Jim reminded him. "This time, they just might take a shot at you, if you go in there alone again, so it's best I go with you. Probably, neither one of us has got any sense for goin' anywhere near the place. But the more I hang around with you, the crazier I get. I don't know what your excuse is."

With that settled for good, they finished breakfast and went to the stable to saddle up. When Moss asked about Roper's saddle, they told him they had decided to return the saddle and the horse, certain that Creed would claim they were his property. From there, they went to pick up their delivery at the barbershop. Even with Roper's body bent to hang over a saddle, it was an awkward chore to load. Hearing them talking to one another out back of the house, Hope Morrison looked out her kitchen window when they were halfway to the waiting horse. One look at the grotesque burden they were transporting to the horse and she immediately recoiled and pulled the curtain closed.

The dull clang of a cowbell rang out from the kitchen door of the Crooked-T headquarters. It brought an immediate response from the men sitting around the bunkhouse table in the form of teasing remarks. "Hey, Juan," Blackie japed. "Your wife's wantin' you. You oughta take better care of her and she wouldn't bother you when you're eatin' breakfast."

"Yeah, Juan, women need that special attention," Sam Culver waded in. "Ol' Herman can help you with that. He's been drivin' women crazy for over a hundred years. Ain't that right, Herman?"

"You go to hell, Culver," Herman responded.

Juan got up from the bench where he was sitting, took his plate to the tub by the pump, and dropped it in the dingy dishwater, then went out the door. The cowbell was used to summon him to the house, saving Lola the trouble of walking to the bunkhouse to fetch her husband. "Tell her to ask for me next time, Juan," Lem Trask hollered. "I ain't as rank as the rest of this crew." As he always did, Juan ignored the crude remarks and hurried up to the kitchen door.

Lola was waiting for him when he went into the kitchen. "Señor Creed wants to see Señor Roper as soon as he comes back from town. Did he not come back last night?"

"No, he did not and he is not back this morning. Tell Creed I'll tell Roper as soon as he comes in. Is that all you wanted to tell me?"

"Sí," Lola answered. "Señor Creed is very anxious to see him. What are the men doing?"

"What they always do when they are not stealing cattle," Juan said, making no effort to hide his disgust. "They sit around and play cards and drink whiskey, if they have any."

"Maybe Señor Roper will put them to work when he comes back, but you need to cut more wood for Señor Creed's study." He nodded, turned around, and went back out the door.

He was still at the woodpile, splitting wood for Creed's fireplace, when he spotted the riders approaching from the west. There were two of them and they were leading a third horse with an odd-shaped load on its back. His natural reaction was to run to the bunkhouse to alert Roper.

Since Roper was not there, he hesitated, trying to decide where to run, to the bunkhouse, or to the ranch house. There was not one of the men who might be in charge in Roper's absence, so he thought it best to alert Marvin Creed. He dropped his ax and paused to take one more look at the riders before running to the house. He stood confused for a moment when he realized that the odd-shaped load was a man. He felt his heart stop when he recognized the fearsome figure riding the dun horse. *Cullen McCabe!* He turned then and ran to the house. Up the kitchen steps he scrambled, into the kitchen without the customary requirement of knocking first. Startled, Lola looked at him as if he had lost his mind. "Cullen McCabe!" he blurted. "I think he bring Roper home."

She ran to the door, which Juan had left standing open, to see for herself. When she spotted the two riders, they were already past the barnyard and were heading toward the house. She turned at once and ran through the kitchen, into the hall screaming, "Señor Creed! Señor Creed!"

"What the hell is wrong with you!" Creed roared, coming from his study. In breathless gasps, she told him what she had seen approaching the house. Stunned momentarily, he tried to think what to do, then he ran back into his study to strap on his sidearm and take another moment to regain his composure. He started toward the front door, but stopped, flustered. "Where's my hat?" Lola ran in the study, picked up his hat from his chair, and brought it to him. He put it on, then walked to the front door, pausing before the hall mirror to adjust his hat, before opening the door and walking out on the porch. He stood there and waited for the riders to pull up before the porch. "Mr. McCabe," he said, speaking in his customary commanding tone. "And if I had to guess, I would say that the man with you is Sheriff Jim Duncan."

"Creed," Cullen acknowledged. "We brought you some more of your property that we had to clean up outta the street in Reid's Mill. I believe you know Mr. Shane Roper. It seems he was another confused soul who came to Reid's Mill to commit suicide." He motioned toward Jim. "You guessed right. This is Sheriff Duncan and I expect he'd like to say a word or two to ya."

"That's right, Cullen. I've never had the opportunity to meet you, Mr. Creed. I'm right sorry it has to be under circumstances such as these. But as long as we rode all the way out here, let me tell you that the town of Reid's Mill will no longer put up with the unacceptable conduct of the men on your payroll. From now on, your men will be treated just like everyone else in Reid's Mill. If their conduct is acceptable, then they're welcome. If they break our laws and disturb the peace, we have a nice new jail now being completed that'll be waitin' to take care of 'em." He paused and looked at Cullen, who couldn't hide the look of surprise on his face. "That's all I wanna say."

"Now that you've said it, you can get the hell off of my land," Creed demanded. "I'd ask you how Shane Roper was shot, but I doubt I'd get a truthful answer. Probably shot down from a dark alley by a cowardly assassin."

"When you take him off his horse, you'll see the shots that killed him, one in the gut and one in the head. Both of 'em were front-entry wounds, which'll tell you he was lookin' at his shooter at the time." Cullen paused to make sure that sank in before continuing. "It was Roper's idea for me to face him in a contest to see who ruled Reid's Mill. He lost, so I reckon you oughta be able to tell your men they've got to learn to behave like civilized adults from now on, if they wanna drink in Reid's Mill."

"You've got a helluva lot of gall, coming here on my land to tell me how to handle my men," Creed spat. "I hire them to work on this range. I don't care what they do when they're on their own time. That's none of my business. Now, suppose you turn yourselves around and get off of my range." He pointed a finger at Jim. "And it looks like nobody's told you that you're the sheriff of Reid's Mill, not Bosque County. You don't have any authority to do anything where you're sittin' right now unless I say so. You're trespassing and I shoot trespassers, so you'd best get outta here before I lose my patience and call out my men to escort you off."

"Maybe that ain't a bad idea," Cullen said. "Let's call 'em out." He drew his six-gun and fired two quick shots into the air. Startled, no more than Jim or Juan, who was standing at the corner of the porch, Creed wasn't sure if he should reach for his gun or not. In his moment of hesitation, he decided not to when Cullen smiled at him, his six-gun still in hand.

In a matter of seconds, the bunkhouse emptied of all the hands, including Tater, the cook. In the confusion the shots created, the men just stood and gawked toward the house. With no one to conduct them, they weren't sure what to do, if anything. Blackie was the first to state the obvious. "That's Roper on that horse!"

"Yeah," Shorty exclaimed, "and that's McCabe and the sheriff that brung him in. I knew Roper was makin' a mistake when he went after McCabe. That man ain't like other men."

"Reckon what we oughta do?" Sam Culver asked.

"What the hell can we do?" Herman Thompson answered him. "Are you thinkin' about runnin' up there with our guns a-blazin'? I'm thinkin' that'd most likely cause him to shoot Mr. Creed and half of us. There's two of 'em and we'd be easy targets runnin' across that open yard."

"Well, whadda we do, then?" Lem Trask asked. "I wish to hell that Roper was here."

"He's here," Tater said cynically. "Maybe you ain't noticed."

"You know what I mean," Trask came back. "He always told us what to do."

Back at the front porch, Creed gaped at his crew of outlaws shuffling around in front of the bunkhouse, with no sign of knowing what to do. With his whole body on fire with the helpless frustration he felt to have his assassination plan thrown back in his face, Creed was determined not to show any weakness. "Now that you've had your little circus with my foreman's body, I'll tell you once again to get off of my land. One signal from me and my men will help you off the property. And it won't be to your liking, I guarantee it."

"We'll be leavin' now, Creed," Cullen replied to his threat, "not because of your threats, but because we've delivered the message we wanted you to have. I think you oughta have enough sense to know that any signal you gave your men would cost you your life and the lives of about half of the men, too. That would leave Juan, there, to run the Crooked-T, I reckon, and only two or three men to work it. So, just remember, the town of Reid's Mill ain't gonna be taken over by you or any other crooked cattle rustler." He glanced over at Jim. "You ready, Sheriff?"

"I'm ready," Jim replied.

Cullen motioned Juan away from beside the back corner of the porch and held out the reins of Roper's horse. When Juan stepped up and took the reins, Cullen backed Orphan away from the porch. Following suit, Jim backed his horse away as well. When they were a good distance from the porch, they wheeled their horses and loped across the barnyard to the trail they had ridden in on. With a sharp eye toward the group of men standing in front of the bunkhouse, they left the Crooked-T behind them.

They were past the notch in the line of hills west of the Crooked-T when Jim asked Cullen why he had shot up in the air and consequently alerted Creed's men that their boss was in trouble. "I wanted to see how many men he had left," Cullen answered. "I counted six. How many did you get?"

"Uh," Jim answered. "I didn't count 'em. I just saw that there was more of them than there was of us."

"I wanted to get a look at 'em, too, so I might recognize 'em, if they were to ride into town. They were hardly in a position to do much to help Creed without runnin' a big risk of gettin' him shot. Just like I told him," Cullen said.

"Take him somewhere and bury him," Creed ordered angrily, sickened by the grotesque shape of Shane Roper's body. He had counted on Roper to force McCabe into a shootout, knowing that Roper would surely win. And yet Roper failed him. He was already down to six men, and not one of them with the brains to take Roper's place as his foreman. His great plan to take over the town of Reid's Mill had no place in it for the simple outlaws left in his bunkhouse. The plan had been to eventually kill them all by Roper's hand for the people of Reid's Mill to see he had cleared the town of troublemakers. The thought of what had actually happened made him clench his fist and grimace. Aware then that Juan was still standing there, holding the horse's reins, he roared, "Go bury that damn body!" He turned to go into the house but stopped to say, "Go by the bunkhouse and tell Tater I want to see him."

"He don't wanna see nobody else?" Blackie questioned Juan when the Mexican delivered Creed's instructions. "Just Tater?"

"*Sí*, that's all he say, 'Tell Tater I wanna see him.'"

"We shoulda gone up to the house," Herman said. He was standing by Roper's horse with the others, gaping at the strange shape their former boss was in.

"He looks like a damn monkey or somethin'," Lem commented, standing next to Herman.

Sam heard the comment and quipped, "You might have to dig a round grave for him. Be easier than tryin' to straighten him out."

Knowing he would get no volunteers to help him dig the grave, Juan led the horse to the same little rise where he had buried Clive Dawkins. *Two just alike,* he thought, *belong together*.

Tater rapped on the kitchen door and when it opened, he told Lola that Creed wanted to see him. *"Sí,"* she said. "I tell him you are here." In a few seconds, she came back to the kitchen to tell Tater to go into the study.

"You wanna see me, Mr. Creed?" Tater asked when he walked into the study. He looked all around him at the desk and the leather furniture, trying to see everything, so he could remember it when telling someone about his first visit to the study.

"Yes, Tater, come on in." Creed had managed to calm himself after a glass of his favorite brandy. He had too much invested in Reid's Mill to simply give up on it. "We've suffered a serious loss with Shane Roper's death," he began. "Roper seemed to have a good bit of faith in your judgment, so that's why I sent for you. We've got to approach Reid's Mill in a different direction now that Roper's gone. Of the men we have left, who comes to your mind as the one with more leadership qualities?"

Tater didn't respond with a name at once. Thinking of the five men back inside the bunkhouse, there was not one that came to mind at once as a leader. Herman Thompson was the oldest but commanded no respect from any of the others. Blackie Welch was the biggest talker of the bunch, but that was all he was, just talk. He thought of Shorty Taylor and how he preached the gospel of fear for Cullen McCabe. That left only Lem Trask and Sam Culver. Lem didn't have a spoonful of brains in his head, so that left one. "Sam Culver would be the best, I reckon," Tater declared. "And I ain't sayin' he's another Shane Roper," he was quick to point out. "Ain't none of us ever done nothin' but whatever somebody told us to do."

"We're going to have to work with what we have now," Creed said. "With Cullen McCabe in that town, I don't have the time to build up our crew to the size it was. We've got to make our move now."

"Yes, sir, that's a fact," Tater said, although he had no idea what Creed had in mind.

"Good," Creed said. "You go on back and send Sam Culver up here."

"Yes, sir," Tater replied, and went back to the bunkhouse. When he walked in, the men gathered around him expectantly. "Sam, go up to the house. Creed wants to talk to you," Tater told him.

"What about?" Sam asked, leery of any meeting with Marvin Creed.

"I reckon you'll find out when you talk to him," Tater answered. Sam shrugged and walked out the door, confident that he hadn't screwed anything up that he could recall.

"What does Creed want with Sam?" Blackie asked. "Is he gonna call all of us up there to talk to him?"

"Nah," Tater said. "He just wants to talk to Sam. That's all he said."

"With Roper gone, seems to me like he might be thinkin' about a new foreman," Herman speculated aloud. "You think he's gettin' ready to make Sam the new foreman?"

"No, hell no," Blackie blurted. "I hired on before Sam did." He turned to point his finger at Tater. "Did you tell him Sam was the best man for a foreman?" He looked around at the others to see if they were as outraged as he. "Hell, Sam has trouble findin' the outhouse, if there ain't a full moon."

"I didn't tell him nothin'," Tater lied. "That's just Herman talkin' and you swallowed it. I ain't got no idea what he wants with Sam."

"He had to call you up there for some reason. You musta told him somethin'," Blackie insisted. "Else there wouldn't be no reason for him to call Sam up there to talk. You got a habit of thinkin' you know more'n the rest of us."

"Maybe you're right, Blackie," Herman commented. "Maybe Boss shoulda picked you, somebody that ain't got no more sense than to pick a fight with the cook."

"Shut up, ol' man," Blackie came back at Herman. "Ain't nobody asked for your advice."

While the inane discussion over who would be the best foreman continued in the bunkhouse, Marvin Creed was trying to delve into the simple mind of Sam Culver, hoping to find some indication of leadership. He finally surrendered to the idea that the men he had left were clay figures that would have to be set in place by him. He discovered that Sam was not afraid to do whatever he was told. And since these men he had left were going to be sacrifices to his plan in the end, he was probably the best choice as foreman. He was big and strong, so he was not likely to be intimidated by any of the others. When the meeting was finished, Creed said, "I'm making you my foreman, taking Roper's job. You think you'll have any trouble from the other men?"

"No, sir," Sam replied. "I won't have no trouble, and if I do, I know how to handle it."

"Good man, that's what I wanted to hear. You go on back and tell the men they need to get ready to earn their pay."

CHAPTER TWENTY-ONE

Cullen was anxious to see what difference Shane Roper's death would make in the town's problems with the Crooked-T. Creed had lost his foreman, the man who carried out Creed's instructions, and he was down to about half the men who had once ridden for him. The question in Cullen's mind was, has Creed had enough? He hoped the loss of Roper would discourage him enough to cause him to give up on the idea of owning a whole town. He could understand Creed's original plan, to sweep in and run all the troublemakers out of town. Establish a strong sheriff who would keep the trouble out of town, all this single-handedly. He would be king. But now, that plan was no longer workable.

Cullen was smart enough to know that, if Creed hadn't given up, then one of his next steps would be the elimination of him. So he figured he'd best develop some eyes in the back of his head. He had been concerned about Jim Duncan's safety as long as Shane Roper was alive. Now that may have changed, dependent upon whether or not Creed had another candidate for the job of sheriff. Cullen thought that unlikely. It was possible that Creed would now attempt to buy Duncan and keep him in the job. Even if that was his new plan, how could that give him any leverage to take over the town? It was a question Cullen had no answer for, so he figured there was nothing left to do but wait and see if the problem with the Crooked-T men would continue.

Marvin Creed had no intention of giving up on his plans for Reid's Mill. In fact, he had decided he would go ahead with the next step, in spite of the loss of his ideal candidate for sheriff. One item on his plan that had not changed, however, was the elimination of Cullen McCabe. This time, it would be a simple assassination. He would talk to his new foreman, Sam Culver, about that soon. But for now, he decided it was time he paid a visit to the Whiskey Mill Saloon. "Lola!" he called out. "Tell Juan to saddle my horse and lay out my black riding suit. I'm going into town."

"*Sí*, Señor Creed," Lola responded. "Will you be overnight?"

"No, I've got one short chore to do, then I'll be back before supper."

"Should Juan tell Sam Culver to send someone in with you?" Lola asked because he never went to Reid's Mill.

"No, I don't need protection," he replied, irritated that she would ask. "I can take care of myself."

"*Sí*, sir, I call Juan." She went to the kitchen door and rang the cowbell to summon her husband. Then she hurried into Creed's bedroom to lay his riding clothes on the bed. By the time she was back to the kitchen, Juan was there, so she told him what to do.

When Juan returned with his horse, Creed stepped up into the saddle. He turned the red roan gelding and rode to the bunkhouse, where he pulled his horse up in front. "Sam Culver," he called out, and in a few seconds, Sam ran out the door.

"Yes, sir, Mr. Creed," Sam blurted. "I was just at the other end, movin' my possibles into the foreman's room."

"I'm going into town for a short meeting. You're in charge until I get back. It might be a good idea to find some work for the men to keep them occupied. I don't want to see any of them in town tonight."

"Yes, sir, I'll see to it," Sam replied, then stood there until Creed rode out to pick up the westward trail to Reid's Mill. "I wonder what that's all about," he murmured to Shorty, who came out to stand beside him.

"Did I hear him say he's ridin' into town?" Shorty asked. "Reckon why he's goin' to town. He don't never go to town."

"Ain't none of my business," Sam said. "I reckon you heard him tell me to get you boys off your lazy asses and get some chores done."

Shorty grinned. "Nah, I didn't hear him say that."

"Well, he did, so I reckon some of you can split some more wood for the bunkhouse and a couple of ya can throw some fresh hay down from the hayloft." He followed Shorty into the bunkhouse to give the others his instructions.

"Yes, sir, Mr. Bossman," Blackie replied sarcastically. "Gimme that ax and lemme split some of that wood for ya."

"What's it gonna take, Blackie?" Sam asked. "Am I gonna have to whip your ass for you, before you can get over Creed not makin' you the foreman?"

"I expect that's what it would take to convince me he made the right choice," Blackie responded. "Anytime you feel like you're ready."

Without warning, Sam threw a sucker punch that landed flush on Blackie's jaw, knocking the unsuspecting Blackie sprawling to the floor. "How 'bout now?" Sam asked. When Blackie tried to scramble to his knees, Sam was on him with a series of rights and lefts, driving him back flat on the floor until he was finished. Sam stood over the fallen man to make sure he had had enough. Then he looked around him. "Anybody else wanna say somethin' about me takin' Roper's place?"

"No, don't nobody else wanna complain," Tater answered for them. "We can't afford to lose any more men." He stooped down beside Blackie to help him sit up. "You ain't never gonna learn when to keep your mouth shut, are you?"

Cullen was sitting at the big table, across from Jim Duncan, when Marvin Creed walked into the dining room at Stoddard House. Jim was in midsentence about the way his mother used to fry potatoes in bacon fat when he stopped, astonished to see the owner of the Crooked-T. "This oughta be interestin'," Cullen remarked as both men watched Creed pause at the weapons table for only a second before passing it by. When Becca started walking toward him, he opened his coat to show her he wasn't armed. He showed only a flicker of surprise when he saw McCabe and Duncan sitting at the table. Recovering at once, he strode over to their end of the table and paused.

"Well, gentlemen, I find myself in your territory now.

So I'll ask if I can sit here at this end of the table with you." He waited for an answer.

Jim wasn't sure what to say, after Creed had ordered them off his land, but Cullen gestured toward the bench next to the sheriff. "Have a seat. This ain't nobody's private territory you're in now. Harvey Stoddard owns this place, but nobody owns the town it's settin' in. Come to think of it, I believe I owe you a meal, so this one's on me."

"I graciously accept your offer," Creed replied.

By now, Jim was getting over his astonishment and managed to find words. "I'd always heard that you had some interest in the Whiskey Mill. I'da figured you to eat dinner down there."

"That would seem logical, wouldn't it?" Creed responded. "But fortunately, I've heard too many reports from my men on the quality of the food prepared at the Whiskey Mill. So I decided I might be better off eating here at the Stoddard House."

"What brings you to town, Mr. Creed?" Cullen asked. "This is the first time for you, ain't it? At least, that's what I've heard, that you never come to Reid's Mill."

"Business, Mr. McCabe." He nodded toward the sheriff. "You're right, Sheriff, I have a business interest in the Whiskey Mill." He paused when Becca filled his cup. "I expect you'll be seeing me here in town a great deal more in the future. So I think it would be a good thing if we forgot about our disagreements and started fresh to work together to develop this little town to its full potential. I'm willing to forget any complaints I may have had. What do you say, gentlemen?" He aimed a thin smile at Cullen and thought, *and I hope there are enough people overhearing this, so when my men shoot you down, they'll remember I said it.*

"Keepin' the peace is always a good idea," Cullen replied. "Like the sheriff told you this mornin', the citizens of Reid's Mill intend to have a peaceful town where their women and children don't have to worry about gettin' shot by a stray bullet. If you have the same intention, then I can't see any reason why we can't all work it out together. I expect it wouldn't be a bad idea to meet with the mayor and let him know you're willin' to control your cowhands."

Creed smiled patiently. "That would certainly be my intent, even though I'm sure you both know it's impossible to monitor every one of my men, if they've been drinking."

"That ain't no problem," Jim spoke up then. "From now on, if they get a little rowdy, they go to jail."

"I see," Creed said, "and I suppose there would be a sizable fine to bail them out."

"That would only be fair," Cullen replied, "to cover the expense of feedin' 'em."

The verbal sparring continued through dinner until Creed finished and bade them good day. Cullen and Jim lingered over coffee after Creed left, still scratching their heads over the chance meeting with the owner of the Crooked-T. As soon as Creed went out the door, Becca came over to ask, "Was that Marvin Creed?" She had overheard enough of their conversation to piece that fact together. Jim assured her that it was none other and she, of course, wanted to know if there was a possibility of a truce between the Crooked-T and Reid's Mill.

"Anything's possible," Cullen told her. "I reckon we'll

just have to wait and see what happens in the next few days and hope for the best."

When Becca returned to the kitchen, Jim looked at Cullen and asked, "You really think that sly ol' dog has given up his ideas about takin' over the town?"

"Well, no, I don't," Cullen answered frankly, "but I'm hopin' I'm wrong."

Down the street from Stoddard House, Marvin Creed reined the red roan to a stop before the little bridge that spanned the river separating the main street from the Whiskey Mill. He remembered thinking it a ridiculous location for the town's lone saloon. Now, however, he thought it ingenious. It was a perfect location for the larger saloon and gambling house he and his partner, Ford Wyatt, envisioned. With the narrow river separating them from the main street, it would be like a grand city of all the sinful things a man desired. Whiskey, gambling, prostitutes, plus a first-class hotel, all that would be available on the other end of this little bridge. And his would be the hand that held the scepter.

He nudged his horse forward, and as the roan stepped across the narrow bridge, he thought that one day the bridge might have to be replaced to accommodate a carriage. He pulled up in front of the Whiskey Mill and sat there for a few moments before dismounting. This was the first time he had seen the saloon since it was first under construction. At that time, he had preferred that the town not know that his was the money behind the saloon. Looking at the building now, he wondered if he should not have taken a controlling hand from the start. It had a look of excessive wear that disappointed him and one of the front windows was boarded up where the glass had been broken out. He nudged his horse forward to the hitching rail.

Inside, he paused at the door to look the room over, disappointed again to see only a few customers. "Howdy, stranger," Archie offered a cheerful greeting when he walked up to the bar, taking note of Creed's gentlemanly attire. "What's your pleasure?"

Creed paused a second to take a good look at the bartender before responding. "You can tell me where I might find Harman Gill," he said.

"Harman's in his office," Archie told him. "Ain't nothin' I can do for you?"

"I need to see him," Creed replied impatiently.

"I'll tell him," Archie said. "Who can I tell him is lookin' for him?"

"Marvin Creed."

That stopped Archie in his tracks. "Marvin Creed!" Archie blurted, his eyes growing wide open. "Yes, sir, Mr. Creed, I'll get him right away." He hurried off to the office.

In less than thirty seconds, the office door opened again and Harman Gill rushed out with Archie following. "Marvin, I swear, what are you doin' here? What can I get you?" He turned to the bartender behind him. "Archie, get Mr. Creed a drink."

"I don't want a drink." Creed held up his hand to stop Archie. To Gill, he said, "Let's go in your office."

"Right," Gill responded. "See that we're not disturbed, Archie." He led the way and held the office door open for Creed. "You want coffee? Something to eat?" Gill continued.

"Calm down, Harman, I just thought it was time for me to drop by to see how my investment is coming along."

"I think we're doin' just fine, considerin' the area we've got to draw customers from," Gill replied. "It was a damn shame about Shane Roper, a real piece of bad luck. I'm worried about what that might do to our plans. But the saloon is makin' it all right, if that's what you're concerned about."

"It looks like it needs some repairs," Creed commented.

"Oh, you must have noticed the window out front," Gill quickly replied. "I'm gonna order a new sash for that window. I have to keep up with a lot of that kinda repair, but you know, it all comes from your boys from the Crooked-T. I understand the plan, though," he added quickly. He paused then, hesitating to ask, "How's that plan gonna work now that the town's put a new sheriff in office?"

"That's just a minor setback and it will be solved shortly. In fact, one of the reasons I came here today was to make you aware of bigger plans I have for Reid's Mill. I had a meeting with a business associate of mine in Fort Worth and we've decided to build a bigger saloon and gambling house here."

Gill was surprised to hear that. "I thought the plan was to clean out all the troublemakers in town, so you could put your own man in as sheriff and eventually run the town."

"That was the plan, but now the plan has changed. We'll build a place so big, it will satisfy every need a man might have. We'll be the biggest in Texas."

Gill couldn't believe what he was hearing. He had to express his doubts. "I'm not sure this is the spot for a place like that. We're havin' trouble drawin' in customers just for this saloon. There ain't nothing for miles around here but small ranches and farms. The kinda place you're talkin' about would have a better chance in Fort Worth, or even Waco, than it would here in Reid's Mill."

Creed didn't want to hear that kind of talk. He was not willing to admit that his original plan to terrorize Reid's Mill with his gang of outlaws, then sweep in and save it by banishing the outlaws, was not going to work. Only a grander plan, on a bigger scale, could make the setback seem unimportant. Ford Wyatt had seemed interested in a project like the one Creed now envisioned, but he had committed only to come to Reid's Mill one day to look the area over. So far, much to Creed's chagrin, Wyatt had not made time available to come.

When Creed seemed to have gone mute after his response to his grand plan, Gill sought to repair the damage done. "It sounds like a great idea, but you'll do better in a broader marketplace. We can still accomplish what you started out to do right here in Reid's Mill. All you have to do is get rid of Jim Duncan and Cullen McCabe, and you're right back where you started. I like that idea."

"We're going to get rid of those two, no matter what we decide to do," Creed declared. "I'll let you know about any other plans after Ford Wyatt and I talk this area over. I'll be going now."

"If you wanna stick around awhile, I'd have Callie Belle cook up somethin' special for supper," Gill offered, hoping Creed would refuse.

"No, thanks. I told Lola I'd be back for supper." He stood up abruptly and started to leave.

"Are you sure you don't wanna rest your horse before

you start back?" Gill asked. "You could sit here and enjoy a drink or two while he's restin'."

"No, the horse hasn't worked that hard. I need to get back." Still deflated by Gill's reaction to his grand gambling project, he wanted to get back to the ranch and get his plan to eliminate McCabe and Duncan under way. At this point, that could at least bring him some satisfaction. As Gill walked him out to the front door, Creed asked, "What do you know about this McCabe drifter?"

"Not much," Gill answered. "And neither does anybody else. He just showed up one day and started hangin' around. Said he was just passin' through, but he's still here."

"He seems to enjoy killing my men," Creed complained.

"He's a tough son of a gun," Gill allowed. "But I gotta be honest about it, Marvin, they were the ones who started it with him." He went on to describe the face-off between McCabe and Roper, which Creed was very much interested in learning.

"Well, what's he hanging around for? He sticks his nose in the town's business like he has some kind of interest in it. He brought Shane Roper's body out to my ranch this morning with Sheriff Duncan. What's he doing riding with the sheriff?"

"I swear I don't know, Marvin. Ain't nobody figured him out yet." He stood on the porch while Creed climbed up into the saddle and watched him as he rode back across the bridge. An unusual visit, he thought, after all this time without one. Gill couldn't help wondering what would happen to him if Creed ever decided to move into town and take over the saloon he rightfully owned. *Maybe he'll catch up with McCabe one day, face-to-face.* It was more a wish than speculation.

* * *

As Creed had told Lola and Juan, he was back at the Crooked-T before supper. He rode the roan up to the corral and left it there for Juan to take care of. Before going to the house, he went into the barn when he saw his foreman through the tack room window. In the tack room, he found his foreman sitting on a keg, replacing a frayed cinch strap on his saddle. "Sam," Creed spoke out, startling him. "I've got an offer I want you to present to the men for me."

"Yes, sir, Mr. Creed," Sam responded immediately.

"Actually, the offer is open to you, as well," Creed said. "I want you to tell the men that I'm putting up a two-hundred-dollar reward for the man who kills Cullen McCabe, face-to-face, in a shootout."

"Two hundred dollars," Sam repeated. "Damn! I'll tell 'em."

"Here's something else you can tell them," Creed continued. "Harman Gill told me that Roper was faster than McCabe. The only reason McCabe beat him was because he stood there and took dead aim after Roper's bullet struck him. He's wearing a bandage under his shirt."

"Is that a fact?" Sam marveled. "So Roper was faster. We've been talkin' about that."

"You tell the men that the two hundred is for a face-to-face contest. If you shoot him in the back, I'll give you twenty dollars and my thanks for a job well done."

"Is it all right if the men go into town tonight?" Sam asked, knowing there would be some anxious for the hunt to begin.

"Half of you tonight and half tomorrow," Creed said. He turned and headed for the house, while Sam hurried to the bunkhouse to tell the others about the reward. As he walked, he considered his own chances against McCabe. Creed said McCabe wasn't as fast as Roper. Sam knew he wasn't as fast as Roper, either, but he didn't know how fast McCabe was. Was it a matter of a split second, or enough time to wind your watch? He wasn't sure he wanted to risk finding out. Another thought struck him just as he approached the bunkhouse door. He knew Creed had been planning to make Roper the new sheriff in Reid's Mill. With McCabe dead, Jim Duncan was bound to be next on the list. And since Creed had picked him to replace Roper, it stood to reason that he was going to name him the new sheriff. In the long run, that would be worth a hell of a lot more than two hundred dollars. Feeling fortunate that he had thought of it, he went inside and told the men about Creed's offer.

"Half of us tonight and the other half tomorrow," Sam said, repeating Creed's instructions. As Creed had, he emphasized the face-to-face condition placed on the two-hundred-dollar prize. "To show you I ain't givin' myself no special privileges, I'll stay here tonight."

To no one's surprise, Tater spoke up right away and said, "I ain't gonna face nobody in a shootout. So I'll be stayin' here, too. I'll pass on the chance to make twenty dollars for shootin' him in the back."

"Then I reckon the four of you can draw straws," Sam said. "Two short straws go into town tonight. The other two can go in with me tomorrow. Fair enough?" Everybody nodded. "Tater, you cut the straws."

Tater pulled some straw out of one of the mattresses on an empty bed and cut them to the proper lengths. Then he held them so as to hide their length and the drawing took place. Blackie Welch and Lem Trask were the lucky winners of the short straws and with a chorus of razzing for the losers, they hustled to get ready to leave for town. "The only rules you've gotta worry about, other than the one about face-to-face shootin', is you've gotta be back here for breakfast in the mornin'. If you get a shot at McCabe, but you don't get back here when Tater's got the chuck ready, you lose, even if you shoot the son of a buck. That's so everybody gets a fair chance."

Lem and Blackie saddled up in a hurry and were soon heading out of the barnyard amid a fanfare of hooting and hollering and speculations about their chances. Up at the ranch headquarters, standing on the front porch, Marvin Creed watched the two would-be assassins and silently wished them good hunting. He went back into the house then and called out, "Lola, I'm feeling tense and tired. I need to have you message my shoulders." It was a notice that the quiet little Mexican woman dreaded to hear, for it never stopped with a simple massage and always led to his groping exploitation of her helplessness. Her greatest fear was that her husband would someday realize the sickening episodes she was forced to endure. But she had been warned by her abusing master that, in the event Juan found out, it would simply lead to his death, should he try to avenge her.

CHAPTER TWENTY-TWO

"Looks like you fellows have had a busy day," Becca Stoddard commented when Cullen and Jim walked into the dining room for supper. "You were both here for breakfast and dinner, and now you're back for supper. The food must be pretty good here."

"We thought about eatin' at the Whiskey Mill for supper," Jim teased. "But we figured you needed the business more. Callie Belle Sykes has folks comin' from all over Texas to eat her cookin'."

"I'm gonna tell Cora what you just said," Becca threatened. Then she smiled at Cullen and said, "Don't worry, I'll be sure I don't get your plates mixed up."

"I 'preciate it," Cullen grunted, thinking she had no idea what a full day the two of them had already had. And the night was young. The way things had gone that day, he halfway expected Marvin Creed to show up in town before the night was over. Things were bound to come to a head any day now and there was nothing to do but wait to see what Creed's next move might be. He knew Jim was looking to him to anticipate Creed's next move, but it was hard to predict what a crazy man might do. And at this point, Cullen considered Marvin Creed to be certifiably crazy. As if in tune with his thinking, Jim asked a question.

"Whaddaya think Creed is gonna do next?" Jim asked.

"I wish to hell I knew," Cullen answered him truthfully. "He ain't likely to give up and come to your church Sunday mornin' to confess his sins. But he might decide he ain't gonna have it the way he wants it and try that other approach he showed us when he sat down at dinner with us today."

"Yeah," Jim recalled . "He sure changed his tune, didn't he? He was downright friendly. I declare, I think you're right, we're dealin' with a crazy man."

"I'm thinkin' you might want me to help you keep an eye on the town tonight and maybe a few nights after tonight, just to give you a couple more eyes. I'm just offerin'. You're the sheriff and you might rather have me just keep outta your way."

Jim responded with nothing more than a look right away. But it was a look of pure gratitude. He hadn't been a sheriff for very long and he was not sure he was ready to handle whatever response the Crooked-T made after today's activities. "I'd appreciate any help you wanna give." He paused, hesitating to say what was in his mind, then decided to spit it out. "I reckon you know that Paul Dickson and some of the other council members are not sure you're on the up-and-up with the way you've gotten yourself involved with the town's problems. Since you were just passin' through town, they're wonderin' why you bother to trouble yourself with our problems."

"I can understand that," Cullen said. "It really ain't

none of my business. I know they're concerned that I might have the same ideas Marvin Creed has. How 'bout you? Are you worried about what I've got on my mind?"

Jim gave him a frank look when he answered. "No, as a matter of fact, I ain't. I hope I don't turn out to be the biggest fool of all, but I don't think you've got anything in mind but lendin' a helpin' hand to keep the town from bein' run over by Marvin Creed. And I've got enough sense to see that you know a helluva lot more about what's goin' on here than I do. So damn right, I want your help."

"Well, the first thing we've gotta do is watch each other's backs," Cullen suggested. "Creed sent Roper in here to take me out. I'm sure you woulda been next. So I expect we're still on his list of chores. I reckon we're gonna be keepin' our eyes open for most of the night, so we'd best take advantage of this big plate of beef and potatoes before we think about anything else."

"We're thinkin' alike already," Jim said, and attacked his steak with knife and fork, unaware of the two Crooked-T riders approaching Reid's Mill as they spoke.

"Let's let the good folks of Reid's Mill know we've come to visit 'em," Blackie said when they reached the main street.

"The last time I did that, I was with Jake and Shorty," Lem said. "The sheriff stopped us and said he was gonna throw us in jail if we shot our guns off when we hit town. That was the night Jake got killed. You wanna take a chance on that?"

"Yeah, I'll take a chance," Blackie said. "Hell, he ain't never told me not to shoot my gun, so maybe he'll just warn me, like he did you. If he tries to put me in jail, then I reckon I'll just dare him to try it and I'll collect my two hundred dollars."

"Sam didn't say anything about a face-off with the sheriff," Lem reminded him. "He said to shoot Cullen McCabe."

"Yeah, but you know he's gonna want the sheriff next, so we might as well take whichever one shows up. It'd just be his tough luck 'cause I ain't lettin' no sheriff take me to jail." To emphasize his intention, he promptly pulled his .44 and fired a couple of shots in the air. Lem shrugged, pulled his weapon, and fired in the air as well. They looked at each other and laughed. "Yeeee-haw," Blackie yelled, and galloped his horse down the middle of the street. Inspired, Lem went in the opposite direction. They galloped, yelling and shooting, to the ends of the street, then turned around and galloped back to meet at the bridge across to the saloon. Their entrance announced, they proceeded to the Whiskey Mill to celebrate it with a drink of whiskey.

"I thought we was under an Injun attack," Archie joked when Lem and Blackie ambled into the saloon. "Ain't you boys afraid you're gonna spend the night in the temporary jail Sheriff Duncan's got all fixed up for you? The word around town is that they're gonna call it the Crooked-T Bosque River Bunkhouse."

"Pour me a drink of likker while you ain't doin' nothin' but standin' around flappin' your jaw," Blackie replied.

"What happened to your face, honey?" Mae Davis said, and reached up to feel it.

Blackie caught her hand before she could touch it. "Just a little tussle with a feller who caught me by surprise. It ain't nothin' but a scratch or two."

"It looks like you got run over by a train," Mae said.

"You oughta see the other feller," Lem declared from across the room, chuckling. "He's got a sore knuckle on one of his fists."

"He hit me when I weren't lookin' and you know it," Blackie protested. "And that story ain't ended yet."

"I'm gonna ask you to put both your hands on that bar facedown."

"What tha . . . ?" Blackie protested, not even aware the sheriff had come in the door. He started to turn around.

"I'm not gonna tell you again," Jim Duncan threatened, and cocked both hammers back on the shotgun he carried. "Both hands flat on the bar," he ordered again.

"All right, all right!" Blackie blurted. "Take it easy with that shotgun. If you got a beef with me, why don't we take it outside and settle it man-to-man?"

"I told you fellows about raisin' hell in town, so I'm gonna let you be the first guests in our temporary jail. Get those hands flat on that bar." Blackie reluctantly placed his hands palms-down on the bar and Jim stepped quickly up and pulled the .44 from his holster.

"We could take this outside and settle it face-to-face," Blackie said. *What the hell are you waiting for?* he thought, waiting for Lem to take the twenty-dollar shot.

Lem had drawn his revolver only halfway out of his holster when he heard the solemn voice of Cullen McCabe behind him. "Draw that weapon and you're dead." He immediately released it and held his hands up over his head. Cullen pulled the weapon out of the holster and stuck it in his belt. "All right, now you can march over to the counter with your friend." When they crossed the room, Cullen said, "You can put your handcuffs on 'em,

Jim, I'll watch 'em while you do." The small crowd in the saloon were muttering in astonishment over the apparent ease of the arrest of the two boastful outlaws as Jim cuffed both prisoners and he and Cullen walked them to the door. "Sorry to disturb you folks," Cullen said as they left the saloon.

Once they were outside, it was easy to determine which horses belonged to their prisoners because there were only two at the rail. Cullen took the reins and led them when they walked across the bridge and down the street to the barbershop and the temporary jail behind it. They marched the two men all the way to the barn before Blackie started to protest. "You got no call to lock us up. We just rode into town and nobody ain't ever told me I ain't supposed to shoot my gun in the air. I weren't hurtin' nobody."

"Your partner, here, knew it," Jim answered him. "And I expect he told you about it. We're not gonna have any more of your wild nonsense in this town. You've been warned and now you found out we weren't foolin'. We hope you'll remember next time. Don't worry about your horses. We'll take 'em to the stable and they'll be taken care of just the same as for civilized men."

"You can't keep us in here," Lem complained as he watched Jim unlock the padlock on the heavy door. "This ain't no jail. It ain't even got no windows."

"You can call it a hotel, if you want to," Jim replied. "But I'm pretty sure it'll hold you and there ain't nothin' to look at, anyway. So you don't really need windows. There's a water bucket and a slop bucket and some bedrolls in a pile over yonder." He pointed each item out.

"I'll feed you some breakfast in the mornin', and if you behave yourselves, I might let you go tomorrow sometime." Cullen covered them while Jim unlocked their cuffs, then they were locked up for the night.

Cullen and Jim led the horses down to Moss Pringle's stable and on the way, Jim asked Cullen a question. "You helped Joe Morrison get that barn ready for prisoners. Do you think you could break outta there?"

"I reckon," Cullen replied. "But I'd have to have an ax inside with me and then it would take me a helluva lotta work to chop a hole through that heavy timber. Joe musta been afraid those dead people he works on might get outta there."

"Hope Morrison mighta had somethin' to do with it," Jim said, and chuckled.

They walked Lem's and Blackie's horses down to the stable and helped Moss unsaddle them. Then they went back to catch Becca Stoddard before she left the dining room for the night to let her know she would be fixing two extra breakfasts in the morning. Her first question was to joke, "They're in jail, aren't they? Why didn't you get their breakfasts cooked at the Whiskey Mill?"

"'Cause they ain't done nothin' real bad yet, just shot their guns in the air," Jim said.

They left the rooming house to take a look around town, in case the two they locked up weren't the only Crooked-T men in town that night. "I'd best give you a hand in the mornin' when you feed those two. It'll be a lot easier to handle your prisoners by yourself when they finish the jail and sheriff's office and you're keepin' 'em in a regular cell room. But in that barn, it might be hard to keep your eye on both of 'em at the same time. So, if you want, I'll just be your deputy, till you can handle everything on your own."

"I 'preciate it, Cullen. I was thinkin' about that very thing when I was takin' their cuffs off inside just now." He shook his head as if perplexed. "I ain't sure I'm cut out for this job or not."

"You're doin' fine," Cullen encouraged. "It won't take long for you to settle in, and then you won't want nobody to be in your way when you're doin' your job."

Tater Owen plopped a generous spoonful of fried potatoes down on the strip of sowbelly on Sam Culver's plate, Sam being the last of the three men in the grub line. Tater gave him a look, then shook his head. He didn't have to say anything. All four men left in the bunkhouse were thinking the same thing—breakfast, and Blackie and Lem hadn't shown up yet. After Sam took his plate to the table and sat down with Herman and Shorty, Tater walked outside and stood for a few minutes, peering off toward the notch in the hills west of the ranch. "They ain't gonna make it," he finally announced to no one, and went back inside. He poured himself a cup of coffee and sat down at the table with the other three men. "Looks like that two-hundred-dollar reward is still out there for somebody to claim. Reckon you fellers can have a shot at it now."

"Reckon it'll be one of you two," Herman commented. "I'm gettin' too long in the tooth to be challengin' anybody to a showdown. My reflexes ain't what they used to be." He looked over at Shorty, thinking of his reluctance to any meeting with Cullen McCabe. "How 'bout you, Shorty? You goin' into town with Sam?"

"I don't know," Shorty said, hesitating. "I ain't cravin' a drink of likker, but I'll ride in with you, Sam, if you need some company."

"Well, I've gotta ride into town just to find out what happened to Blackie and Lem," Sam said. "Mr. Creed is gonna wanna know right away this mornin' if they cornered McCabe. If they didn't, we might be missin' two more men." He looked at Tater and he was concerned to the point of commenting, "Tater, you've been workin' for Mr. Creed longer'n any of the rest of us. Whaddaya reckon he's gonna do if somethin's happened to Blackie and Lem? There ain't but four of us left. And I ain't smart enough to know what his plan is, but it sounds like the whole damn town is gettin' their backs up against us. It ain't just McCabe anymore."

Tater had no answer for him. Sam was right, Tater had been with Creed from the first herd of cattle he rustled, back before the idea of taking over an entire town got into Creed's head. So he felt a sense of loyalty to Creed and he would risk his life to defend him should anyone attack him. But he also recognized the danger in the course his boss was pursuing. "I ain't got no answer for you, Sam," Tater finally answered. "I reckon we'll know for sure after we find out what happened in town last night." He shook his head slowly. "You know, sometimes I think how nice it would be, if we was just workin' this ranch like a legitimate cattle ranch and wasn't tryin' to take over a whole town."

"Sure would be a lot more peaceful life, wouldn't it?" Herman remarked.

"You'd best be careful," Tater cautioned Sam. "If they tried somethin' and got caught, they mighta strung 'em up. And they might be lookin' to hang every Crooked-T hand that shows up in town." He could see that Sam was turning that possibility over in his mind. "You'd best report to Mr. Creed before you go. It's a wonder he ain't showed up here at the bunkhouse already."

"Yeah, I was goin' to," Sam said, "soon as I finish my breakfast and saddle my horse." Conversation was lacking at the breakfast table after that, a direct contrast to the raucous send-off that Blackie and Lem had received the night before. When he finished, Sam went out to saddle his horse. Shorty, as had been his habit lately, went out to help Sam saddle up, and warned him to beware of Cullen McCabe. "Yeah, I will," Sam told him, thinking Shorty was getting as crazy as Creed lately.

When he knocked on the kitchen door, Lola told him to come inside, that Creed wanted to see him and was about to send for him. "Wait here, please, Señor Culver. I tell him you're here."

In a few minutes, Creed came into the kitchen. Sam was surprised to see Creed was still in a bathrobe. He addressed Sam with one word, "Well?"

"They ain't come back yet, Mr. Creed. I'm fixin' to ride into Reid's Mill to find out what happened to 'em."

A deep frown of anger formed rapidly on Creed's face. "Those worthless drunks," he spat with no concern for what might have been their misfortune. "You go on into town, and if you find them, tell them they're fired. You understand?"

"Well, sir," Sam replied. "They mighta got arrested or shot or somethin'."

"You tell them they're fired," Creed repeated.

"Yessir," Sam said again, and turned to leave. He caught a distressed glance from Lola, who was holding the door open for him.

"And Culver," Creed said, "you find that damn McCabe for me and shoot him down like a dog."

"Yessir," Sam answered once again, and hurried away, not sure if Creed was in his right mind or not. He started to go back to the bunkhouse and tell Tater about the boss's wild behavior, but he decided that wouldn't accomplish anything. He got on his horse and headed to town, thinking he needed to at least find out what happened to keep Blackie and Lem from returning to the ranch.

Sam did a lot of serious thinking during the fifteen-mile ride to Reid's Mill. And for the first time in his life, he wondered if he had not made a grave mistake when he chose the path of life that looked to him to be the easier. He had never felt any remorse for stealing another man's cattle. But now, things were different. Instead of just stealing cattle or horses, now killing had entered into his daily duties. Today, as he rode into town to check on the progress of a planned murder, he wondered that he had come to this point in his life. It was easy to lay all the blame on Marvin Creed, but he had accepted Creed's money and consequently agreed to commit any crime he was ordered to. Worse than that, he was now Creed's foreman, and as such, his job was to order others to commit murder without any more conscience than killing a chicken for supper.

He entered the town of Reid's Mill at a slow walk. Still early in the day, there was very little activity on the street as he guided his horse across the bridge to the Whiskey Mill. When he walked inside the saloon, there was no one behind the bar and he glanced around the almost-empty room. In the very back corner, near the office door, he saw Archie Wells sitting at a table with the Molly-Maes. They were drinking coffee and eating some kind of hash. "Howdy, Culver," Archie called out, and started to get to his feet.

Sam waved him back down. "Keep your seat. I don't want nothin' from the bar." He walked back and sat down at the table with them. "I wouldn't mind a cup of that coffee." Molly jumped up and volunteered to get him a cup. While she was gone, Sam looked at the plate of food in front of Archie and asked, "What's that you're eatin'?"

"Somethin' Callie Belle mixes up. She calls it breakfast hash. There ain't no tellin' what she puts in it and I'm afraid to ask. It tastes pretty good, though, so I figure if I don't know what it is, it won't hurt me none. You wanna try some?"

"No, I et breakfast before I left the ranch this morning. I was just wonderin' what it was 'cause I'd never seen anything like it before."

"You come in to see about gettin' your boys outta jail?" Mae asked.

"Jail?" Sam exclaimed. "Is that where they are?"

"Yep," Archie replied, then waited while Molly set a cup of coffee down before Sam. "Yep," Archie repeated, "the sheriff and Cullen McCabe jumped 'em in here last night before they'd even had time for a drink. Hauled 'em outta here and locked 'em up in that barn behind the barbershop."

"What did they do? What did they lock 'em up for?"

"They rode into town, shootin' off their guns, racin' up and down the street, just raisin' a lotta hell. And the sheriff had already told Lem he was gonna throw him in jail, if he did that again. Him and McCabe slipped in here and got the jump on both of 'em before they knew what was happenin'."

"Speak of the devil," Molly interrupted. She nodded toward the front of the saloon. They followed her gesture to see Sheriff Jim Duncan standing in the doorway. He was carrying his shotgun across his arm, as had become his habit over the last few days.

"Good mornin', Sheriff," Archie sang out. "You lookin' for a drink, or is this a business call?" Sam sat still but couldn't help thinking that one shot and he could be two hundred dollars richer if Creed had put a bounty on the sheriff's head, too.

"This is a courtesy call, I reckon," Jim answered. "I recognized that young fellow there as a Crooked-T hand and I thought he might be lookin' for two of his friends. So I thought I'd tell him they're locked up for disturbin' the peace and reckless handlin' of a firearm. I think they mighta had enough time to think about it, so if you wanna take responsibility for 'em, I'll turn 'em over to you. Is that what you want?"

"As a matter of fact, it is," a surprised Sam Culver replied.

"There's a catch, though, they gotta leave town right away."

"You sayin' they're banned from comin' to town again?" Sam asked.

"No, I ain't sayin' that. They're welcome to come back after today anytime they want to, as long as they don't come roarin' in here again, scarin' women and children. By the way, the town appreciates the way you rode in this mornin', nice and quiet. I expect you wanna rest your horse before you start back to the Crooked-T, right?" Sam said that he would. Jim continued. "I'll tell you what, why don't you go ahead and drink your coffee and whatever you're fixin' to do and I'll meet you at the barn behind the barbershop in about an hour. And I'll turn your men over to you. Is that all right?"

"Yes, sir, Sheriff," Sam responded, "that's fine with me. I'll meet you over there." He hesitated, still stunned by the courteous attitude of the sheriff. "And thank you," he managed to sputter, giving no thought to Jim's cautious withdrawal from the saloon. After he was gone, Sam looked at Archie and the women, all with eyes wide in surprise and speechless. "Why is Marvin Creed complainin' about the way his men are being treated here in town?"

"Danged if I know," Archie answered.

"Well, his friend Cullen McCabe has been shootin' 'em right regular," Mae saw fit to remind them.

CHAPTER TWENTY-THREE

Cullen brought Blackie's and Lem's horses to the temporary jail behind the barbershop, then he waited with Jim for Sam Culver to show up. Sam was prompt, anxious to transport the two prisoners back to the Crooked-T. Still somewhat puzzled by the courteous reception he received from the sheriff, Sam was not at all certain this was not a trick to throw him in the barn with Lem and Blackie. This was the first time he was actually in the presence of the big stranger called Cullen McCabe and he could not deny a slight feeling of intimidation, even though Cullen said nothing to him directly. Sam stood, silently watching while Jim took the precaution of unloading the pistols of both Blackie and Lem and placing them in Sam's saddlebag. "Reckon you boys are free to go," Jim said then, and stepped back beside Cullen.

Unable to forget about the two-hundred-dollar reward, Blackie paused before climbing up into the saddle. "I'm callin' you out, McCabe. Let's you and me get it on right now. I wanna see how fast you are."

"Shut up, Blackie!" Sam commanded. "Get on your

horse and let's get outta here. I wanna be back at the ranch in time for dinner." He looked quickly at Cullen, whose stoic expression never changed. "We're on our way," he said.

"Obliged," Cullen replied.

Cullen and Jim got on their horses and followed the three Crooked-T riders until they saw them turn onto the trail to the east. "That Culver fellow didn't seem like he was cut outta the same tree as the rest of those monkeys out at the Crooked-T," Jim commented.

"I thought the same thing," Cullen said.

"What the hell's got into you?" Blackie demanded of Sam. "You gettin' a little yellow streak startin' to grow down your back? I coulda took care of that big jasper right then and there, if you hadn't been so quick to do everything he said. I don't know why in the world Creed picked you to be the foreman. You'll play hell tryin' to follow Shane Roper's footsteps."

"Blackie, you're gonna let that mouth of yours earn you another whuppin', if you keep on jawin' at me. If you'da shot McCabe, you wouldn'ta got the two hundred dollars 'cause you didn't get it done before breakfast this mornin'."

"You can mark this down," Blackie replied. "You ain't never gonna give me another whuppin' and that's a fact."

"I swear," Lem remarked, "that's what we need right now. Let's all start squarin' off against each other. I'll bet ol' McCabe would be tickled to hear you two goin' at it. He'd figure we're gonna wipe ourselves out and him and the sheriff won't have to bother with us no more."

"Lem's right," Sam said. "There ain't but six of us left

in the bunkhouse and I ain't too sure Mr. Creed is thinkin' straight lately." He went on to tell them of Creed's orders to him to shoot McCabe down. "Never mind what happened to me after I shot him, he just wants McCabe dead. I'm thinkin' the six of us had best talk it over and decide where we stand with this business of takin' over the town of Reid's Mill. 'Cause it looks to me like there ain't a snowball's chance in hell of us takin' that town over."

"Whaddaya think we oughta do?" Lem asked, surprised that Sam had said what he did but ready to admit to himself that he had harbored doubts about Creed's grand plan.

"I don't know," Sam answered truthfully. "That's why I think the six of us need to talk it over and decide where we stand. One thing that bothers me is how Creed said he was gonna take the town. Our job was to raise so much hell in the town that they'd welcome Creed in to clean it up. That meant he'd get rid of the hell-raisers, meanin' us. Then he'd put Roper in as sheriff to keep us out. Well, I'm askin' myself now, how's he gonna get rid of us hell-raisers? I don't think he's fixin' to make us all deputies. I think he's got somethin' else in mind."

"Damnation!" Blackie exclaimed. "I ain't ever stopped to think about it like that. Maybe we'd best have a little meetin' as soon as we get back." Thoughts of settling with Sam were forgotten in light of this new worry. "We'd best be careful how we go about it, though. You know Tater is like a loyal old hound dog when it comes to Creed."

"You're right about that," Lem said. "He might take some convincin', if we decide we're gonna do somethin'."

* * *

They arrived at the Crooked-T in time for Tater to slice some more sowbelly to go with the pot of beans on the stove. "Well, they ain't dead," was the greeting they received from Herman Thompson when they rode into the yard. With nothing to do, he and Shorty had been sitting around the bunkhouse keeping Tater company.

"Where'd you find 'em?" Tater asked Sam. He was told they had spent the night in jail. "Well, I'll be . . ." Tater started, then said, "You need to get on up to the house. Mr. Creed wanted to see you as soon as you got back."

"Right," Sam said. "I figured that. I'll go up as soon as I take care of my horse."

"You'd best go see him now," Tater insisted, "then take care of your horse."

"I'll unsaddle your horse for ya," Lem volunteered. "You'd best do like Tater says."

"All right, I 'preciate it," Sam said, dreading the meeting with Creed. "I reckon I'd best not keep the boss waitin'." He went out the door of the bunkhouse and walked across the yard to the house. It was a minute or two after he knocked before Lola opened the back door. It struck him that she had a weary look about her, even more pronounced than usual. "Mr. Creed wanna see me?" Sam asked.

"*Sí*, Señor Culver. Come in. I tell him." She left him standing just inside the kitchen door while she went to find Creed. In a few moments, he stormed into the kitchen with Lola behind him.

"Did you kill him?" Creed demanded. "McCabe, is he dead?"

"Well," Sam hesitated, "no, he ain't dead." He saw Creed's eyebrows dip in anger. "But I found our two missin' men. They're both all right. They were in jail and that's why they didn't come back this mornin'." He could see that this intended welcome news was of no interest to the irate man.

"Where was McCabe?" Creed asked. "Was he in town'?"

"Yes, sir, he was in town. He was right there at that barn they're usin' for a jail when they turned Blackie and Lem over to me, him and the sheriff, too."

"Why didn't you shoot him, like I told you to?" Creed demanded. "Why didn't you shoot them both?" He exhaled through clenched teeth, clearly boiling over with anger.

"Well, sir," Sam stumbled, trying to think of an answer that might seem reasonable to a man who was obviously not thinking straight. "I knew you wouldn't want it to look like outright murder 'cause you mighta wanted to make me the sheriff after they were both dead. So I thought you'd want me to wait for a better chance to shoot 'em when nobody would see me."

His explanation only seemed to make Creed angrier and more frustrated. His plan to rule Reid's Mill had crumbled piece by piece with the arrival of Cullen McCabe. So, at this point, McCabe's death seemed to him more important than the takeover plan. Sam stole a quick glance at Lola Lopez, who returned his gaze with eyes filled with terror. After what seemed a long pause, Creed finally spoke again, his voice low and deadly. "I guess I was mistaken when I made you my foreman. Get out of here."

"Yes, sir," Sam responded, then promptly did an about-face and went out the door. It was obvious there was nothing to gain in an attempt to reason with a crazy man.

When Sam was gone, Creed turned to look at Lola. "Tell Juan to saddle my horse and bring him to the back door." She went immediately to the cowbell to summon her husband.

Hearing the cowbell, the men eating dinner in the bunkhouse paused to wonder what it was about. And when Sam walked in a few moments later, they looked to him for information. "I don't have any idea," he said in answer to their questions. "The only thing I can tell you is I think I just lost my job as foreman because I didn't shoot McCabe down this mornin'." He gave Blackie a hopeless glance. "Maybe you'll get the job now."

"I don't want it now," Blackie replied.

Almost half an hour later, they heard a horse lope across the yard. Shorty got up and walked to the door. "Where in the world is he goin'?"

"Who?" Tater asked, although it could be only one person.

"Mr. Creed," Shorty answered. "He's ridin' out on the trail to Reid's Mill."

"The devil you say!" Tater responded, and joined Shorty at the door to see for himself. "He ain't in his right mind. We need to go catch him before he does somethin' crazy."

"You catch him," Herman said. "I know you've been with Creed for a long time and he might be like a daddy to you. But to me, he's the owner of this ranch. He can do what he wants, so I ain't gonna tell him he can't go for a ride."

Marvin Creed's mind was in a swirl of confusion as he followed the trail west, but there were still rational thoughts of personal habits that registered. One of these was the thought to vary the pace between trotting and walking, so the animal could reasonably make the thirty-mile round-trip to Reid's Mill and back. He was sick and tired of waiting for the men he paid to carry out the simple orders he gave them. Now, his patience had run its course on the elimination of one man and he decided to do it himself. He was not insane to the point where he would challenge McCabe to face him in the street, for he was not a professional gunfighter. He was not intent upon having a reputation as a gunfighter, either. His goal was to end the life of one who annoyed him. So, for this task, he was going to use a Winchester rifle at a distance of somewhere in the range of two hundred yards or less. But not a great deal less, for he wished to have ample time to withdraw after taking the shot.

His pacing of the red roan's gait resulted in a gratifying time of a little less than two hours before reaching a small stream that Creed estimated to be 135 yards from the bridge that crossed over to the Whiskey Mill. *Perfect*, he thought. If McCabe or the sheriff was on the street, he would be able to spot them. If they went to the saloon, or their temporary jail, or the dining room, they would walk past that bridge. He tied his horse in the trees beside the stream, then found himself a comfortable position to watch the street. He took his army field glass and adjusted it for distance. Then he held it up to his right eye and watched the occasional passerby, as well as the random drinker who used the bridge. On the brink of discouragement, he pulled the glass away to rest his eye just as McCabe came into his view. In a panic, lest he miss the shot, he jerked the glass back to his eye. *It was McCabe!*

He definitely recognized him and he stopped right in front of the bridge. His fingers trembled as he sighted his rifle on the broad back of the man who had come to interfere with his plans.

Cullen had paused at the bridge leading to the saloon when he heard Jim call from behind him. "Where you headed?" Jim asked.

"Goin' to pick up my horse and take him to the stable," Cullen answered. "I left him at the jail. Then I reckon I'll meet you back at the saloon and we'll see if we're gonna have more guests from the Crooked-T." Both men heard the snap of the bullet as it passed between them and neither waited to be told to dive for cover below the bank of the river.

"Where'd it come from?" Jim asked, then got another shot that dug into a plank of the bridge.

Cullen worked his way along the bank, trying to get a better place to look from as a third and fourth shot snapped by. "He's gotta be back on that trail to the east," he called out. "Else he wouldn't have an angle between the buildings to see this bridge." Certain now, he said, "He's back yonder by that stream!" Then to confirm it, he saw a muzzle flash and another shot. "I'm goin' after him!" As quickly as he could make his way through the bushes along the bank, he worked along the river until he reached the barbershop and his horse tied at the barn behind.

He came out from behind the barbershop at the gallop, hoping to circle the spot where he had seen the flash. But as he circled back toward the trail, he saw a rider galloping away from the stream, heading straight back east. Cullen had no doubt that he was following another Crooked-T outlaw and he was determined to run this one to ground. He came out on the trail and he could see the rider ahead of him approximately one hundred yards. The sniper held his horse to a hard pace, forcing Cullen to do the same, if he wanted to keep up with him. Afraid he was going to break Orphan's wind, Cullen slowed the dun to a walk. Ahead of him, the gap widened at first, then locked on to Orphan's pace.

The chase continued on that way, with Cullen unable to close the gap between them without killing his horse. He finally conceded the race, but he knew he would find his sniper at the Crooked-T. The problem was going to be finding the right man if they put his horse in the barn before Cullen got to the ranch. A bigger problem was going to be the probable gunfire from half a dozen ranch hands as soon as he showed his face. It didn't make sense to ride into all that gunfire, so he had to admit defeat. Still, he continued to walk his horse toward the ranch. He was so close now and the light of day was fading away. He might be able to get close without being seen in the twilight, so he continued on until he reached the outer edge of the barnyard. There were lights burning in the house and in the bunkhouse and he saw no one in the yard. He realized that the crew were still eating supper in the bunkhouse. So, he rode a little closer before stopping to take a good look around him. It was then that he saw the horse, standing broken, at the kitchen steps. *It was Creed!* The man he had been chasing was Marvin Creed!

What fit of madness had pushed Marvin Creed to ride to Reid's Mill to try to kill him at long range? *He's still got a bunkhouse full of men down there,* he thought. *If I arrest him, I'll never get out of this place alive. But if I do manage it, it'll put a stop to any threat of Reid's Mill becoming a hangout for outlaws.* He nudged Orphan, and the dun gelding walked slowly across the yard to the house. Behind him, he could hear the loud talking and laughing coming from the bunkhouse.

When he stepped down from the saddle, he took one look at the roan standing, his muzzle touching the ground. Creed was going to have to find another horse and Cullen told himself to get on Orphan and ride like hell outta there while he still could. But he was standing on the back step of the house, and the man who had tried to kill him and Jim was just inside. *I'll just play the cards I'm dealt,* he decided, and went up the steps.

The kitchen door was not locked, so he pulled his six-gun and slowly opened the door. There was no one in the kitchen, but he heard voices in another room. He recognized Creed's voice. It sounded as if he had issued a sharp command. Then he heard the Mexican woman cry out as if she was being hurt. Cullen walked quietly through the kitchen to a hallway door. He followed the sound of the voices to another room where the door was partially open. He could see the woman standing on the far side of the room, her blouse torn from some obvious rough handling.

Cullen looked through the crack of the door by the hinges to make sure Creed wasn't hiding behind the door. When he didn't see him, he swung the door open wide and walked in to face the terrified woman. "You don't have to be afraid of me," he told her. "Where is he?"

"I'm right behind you, Mr. McCabe, and this shotgun

is aimed right at your back," Creed said, stepping behind him into the room. "So I suggest you drop that weapon on the floor. I've enjoyed the chase we had together, although I'm sorry I missed you and that damn sheriff back in town. Go ahead and drop that gun, or I'm gonna open up your back with this twelve-gauge shotgun."

Stunned to think he had been so careless that he failed to check the dark hallway before entering the room, Cullen froze. "What's the use of droppin' my gun? You're gonna shoot me, anyway, right?" His options were slim. To turn and fire was the only one he had and he was under no illusion that he could do that fast enough to keep from getting blasted by the shotgun. His only hope was to keep Creed talking and hope he got careless. The odds were still not good, but they were all he had.

"If you don't drop it, I'm going to be forced to send you to hell right now. And I would have liked to find out a little more about a supposed drifter who took it upon himself to interfere with my plans. But if you insist . . ."

"Hold on!" Cullen reacted. "I'm puttin' it down. Mind if I turn around?"

"No, I don't mind, but get rid of that gun first, else I'm gonna blow a hole in you."

"It was worth a try," Cullen said, bringing a chuckle from Creed.

Creed watched him closely as he bent down and laid his weapon on the floor. "Now you can turn around and we'll talk a bit. Slowly," he cautioned as Cullen stood up and turned to face his executioner. "That's better," a smiling Creed told him. "You know, you really should have taken my offer when I gave you a chance to join my crew.

And I know you've probably figured as much, so I'll tell you that I did send Juan after you to kill you that night. The bumbling fool fell off his horse. So," he said, changing the subject, "who do you work for, McCabe? Who sent you to Reid's Mill?"

"Like I told you," Cullen answered, "nobody sent me. The town just looked like they needed some help and I decided I didn't have anything more important to do. So I hung around awhile."

"Do I look that stupid?" Creed challenged. "You had to have good reason to try to kill me."

"I didn't know it was you takin' potshots at me back in town. And I didn't plan to kill you. I was plannin' to turn you over to the court in Waco and let them decide what to do with you."

"What a noble thought," Creed scoffed. "Maybe I've had the wrong impression of you, McCabe. Maybe you're really a good man and you're trying to do what's right. But I've killed a lot of good men who got in my way. And you've gotten in my way more than most. I'm tired now and I need some supper, so we'll end our little chat right here." He raised the shotgun to his shoulder.

Cullen braced himself for the moment of impact, even though he knew he could not withstand the blast. He heard the shot, but there was no sensation of pain. Confused, he watched helplessly as Creed doubled over in agony, only to stagger backward to fall on the floor when a second shot slammed into his chest. Recovering quickly, Cullen turned to face the fragile Mexican woman, obviously in shock, as she held the revolver in her hand. She looked about to faint, so Cullen moved quickly to support her. When she felt his arm around her waist, she became almost limp. He gently took the pistol from her hand and stuck it in his belt. "Let's sit you down in this chair," he said, and led her to one of Creed's easy chairs.

"I couldn't let him do it," she pleaded softly as he lowered her into the upholstered chair. "He's an evil man and I know you are a good man."

"You did the right thing," Cullen calmed her, knowing that every man in the bunkhouse would be on the way to the house after hearing those shots. He could not be sure how strong any feelings of loyalty for Creed might be. So, rather than risk any retaliation against the woman for shooting him, Cullen offered her the option. "If you're afraid of what the men might think, you don't have to tell them you shot him. You can let them think I did it. No one will ever know." With tears streaming down her cheeks now, she didn't speak but nodded her head rapidly. "Now, I'd best get ready for company," he said, and picked up his six-gun from the floor. Looking back at her, he pulled the revolver she had used from his belt, held it up, and asked, "Where does this go?"

She pointed to a table beside a sofa. "In the drawer," she said.

Hearing the first footfalls on the back steps, he moved quickly to replace the pistol in the table drawer. Then he picked up the shotgun Creed had held on him and positioned himself in the corner of the room, opposite the chair where she sat. Standing behind Creed's desk, he had partial cover. He waited, and in a minute or two, he heard them calling out Creed's name. A few moments later, they appeared at the study door, led by Tater and Blackie.

The first thing they saw was Lola sitting in the chair in the corner of the room, but immediately after, they were aware of Cullen in the opposite corner, his six-gun in hand and the shotgun lying on the desk by his other hand. Without waiting, Juan pushed through the others, stepped over Creed's body, and rushed to his wife's side. Tater and Blackie were stopped immediately by the sight of the body. The shock of seeing the absolute master of their fortunes lifeless on the floor of his study served to block out thoughts of immediate reaction. So, instead of guns blazing in angry reaction, Creed's soldiers stood staring in disbelief. "So, what's it gonna be?" Cullen finally broke the silence. "Is this enough killin'? Or do you need some more?"

"Did he ride into town, lookin' for you?" Tater asked calmly.

"He did," Cullen answered. "But he didn't come all the way into town. He hid just outside and started shootin' at the sheriff and me walkin' on the street. I followed him back here to arrest him, but he didn't wanna be arrested."

Tater shook his head sadly. He had once believed in the man, but he had not been unaware of a growing disregard for the men who rode for him. "He ain't been right in the head lately," he muttered. "Ain't no use for anybody else to die over this."

"Maybe just one more," Blackie suddenly blurted, and took a couple of steps to the side to give himself an angle at the man behind the desk. "From where I'm standin', I see a sneakin' dog that slipped into the boss's house and shot him down, right in front of that woman settin' there. I say you need to answer for that, big man, and this time you ain't got no choice 'cause I'm fixin' to shoot you down where you stand." He reached for his .44 a fraction of a second before the slug from Cullen's six-gun struck the center of his chest.

No one else drew their weapon. The room was left in shocked silence, the only sound heard was a soft comment from Juan, meant only for his wife's ears. "Now I have two holes to dig."

Cullen stood ready to deal with whatever followed, even though he sensed an air of surrender on the part of the remaining members of the Crooked-T gang. Herman Thompson took the lead and expressed what was on everyone's mind. "Since I'm older than the rest of you boys, I'd like to say I've had enough of the outlaw side of life. I think we'd all agree that poor Blackie, there, is the only one of us left here who enjoyed the kind of life we were leadin'." He looked around him at the others. "Am I right about that? Ain't that what we were talkin' about earlier today? See if we couldn't run an honest operation for a change?"

"How do we know the people of Reid's Mill will let us be, after what we done to them?" Lem asked.

"I don't think you'll have any problem with the folks in Reid's Mill," Cullen was quick to assure them. "They were just sick and tired of the constant fighting and troublemakin' that was goin' on. Once you convince the sheriff and the mayor you're on the up-and-up, they'll welcome you to town."

Sam Culver could not resist asking the one question that had caused some suspicion about Cullen's presence in Reid's Mill. "And you ain't workin' for nobody that's lookin' to do the same thing that Creed was? 'Cause it looks like you got a wide-open door now."

"Nope," Cullen answered. "I give you my word, you'll be seein' the last of me in the next day or so."

"How do we know your word's any good?" Tater asked, causing a few chuckles.

"You don't," Cullen replied. "Tell you what, why don't you pick a couple of ya to act as your representatives. Come on into town tomorrow and I'll get the sheriff and the mayor and anybody else that's interested, and you can have a peace treaty, just like the Indians."

"That sounds good to me," Sam said, and looked around at the others, who nodded in agreement. "When and where?" he asked Cullen.

"How about dinnertime?" Cullen answered. "Twelve noon at the Stoddard House dinin' room. All right?" They all agreed. Cullen shook hands with each of the men. "Now, I expect I'd better make some tracks. I've got a fifteen-mile ride."

CHAPTER TWENTY-FOUR

It was late when Cullen guided Orphan across the bridge at the stable. Knowing the dining room was closed, he took care of his horse first, then walked up to the Whiskey Mill to see if he could find something fit to eat there. Much to his surprise, he found Jim Duncan sitting at a table near the back of the room. Jim waved him back as soon as he saw him. "I figured you might show up here," Jim said. "I knew you missed supper and a feller big as you has to graze on somethin' before you turn in."

Cullen looked over to see what was in Jim's cup. "Is that coffee you're drinkin'? Is it fit to drink?" He would have suspected not, this long after supper.

"Yep," Jim said. "I talked Cow Bell into makin' me a fresh pot, since I knew you'd be late. She's still got some cold biscuits left, too, and they ain't bad if you pour a little molasses on 'em." So that was his supper, and at the time, it seemed to hit the spot. He gave Jim his full report on the occurrence at the Crooked-T and Jim was eager to help organize the noon meeting with the mayor. The result of Cullen's pursuit of the sniper was a far cry from what Jim had expected. "If this meetin' with a couple of those

Crooked-T men works out, that might be the end of most of our problems."

"I expect so," Cullen said, "but it'll only stay that way if you keep a strong sheriff's department, so don't let 'em cut you back just because things get peaceful for a while."

"I reckon I'll do all right as long as you're around to give me some help when I need it."

"I ain't gonna be around," Cullen said. "It's time I moved on outta here. I've about wore out my welcome and I need to see how bad my cabin south of Two Forks is. I figure I'll cut out tomorrow after your meeting with the Crooked-T."

His announcement obviously upset Jim. He had become used to having Cullen around. "Hell, now that you might not get shot every time you come in this saloon, you oughta stay awhile and enjoy it."

"I never was gonna stay as long as I did," Cullen reminded him. "I was just passin' through town before I got caught up in helpin' you a little bit."

"Well, hell . . ." Jim exhaled. "Don't go till day after tomorrow. That's the official openin' day of my jailhouse and office. Paul Dickson got in touch with the sheriff's department over in Waco and he's gonna come over to help us celebrate. Bosque County was supposed to send the commissioner or somebody, too. But I ain't too sure about him. But you've gotta be there, you're the spark that started this whole thing."

"Well, congratulations, then," Cullen said. "I reckon it wouldn't hurt to hang around one more day." He looked across the room to a table where Harman Gill was sitting with Molly Dugan. "Reckon we oughta go over and tell Gill his partner died?"

"That would be the responsible thing to do," Jim replied with a grin. "You ready to go?" Cullen said that he was, so they got up from the table and crossed over to Gill's table.

"McCabe," Gill acknowledged with no show of enthusiasm.

"Have to bring you some bad news," Cullen said.

"Oh?"

"Yep. Your financial partner has passed on to his reward. Marvin Creed passed away earlier this evenin'. Died of lead poisonin', once in the gut and once in the chest. Sorry for your loss."

Gill's eyes began to expand until they looked as big as silver dollars. Then the corners of his mouth turned up to form a wide smile. "You ain't japin' me, are you? Is Creed dead?"

Cullen nodded. "Sorry to see you're takin' it so hard," he commented sarcastically.

"Are you kiddin' me?" Gill responded. "Now, I don't owe the son of a gun a dime and I'm soul owner of this saloon! Molly, that calls for a drink! It's on the house, boys!"

"Thanks just the same," Cullen responded. "We were just leavin'. I've got to get some things ready to travel."

"You leavin'?" Gill asked. When Cullen said that he was, it brought an even wider smile to Gill's face. "Well, that's too bad, just when we was all gettin' used to havin' you around." Cullen responded with a smile to match his. Then he and Jim walked out, Jim to check on some things at his new accommodations, and Cullen back to the stable to see what supplies he had left in his packs for his trip back home.

* * *

Cullen was up early the next morning and one of the first in the dining room when Becca opened the door. "You must be hungry this mornin'," she greeted him. "You all ready for the big meetin'?"

"I expect so," Cullen answered. "But I reckon I'll be more of a spectator. Jim and the mayor will be makin' the treaty with the Crooked-T men."

"Do you really think it'll be any different than it was before Creed was shot?" Becca asked. "It's still just a bunch of horse thieves and outlaws that's left out there. Ain't that so?" She paused to fill his coffee cup. "You know, you ain't said who shot Creed."

"That's right," Cullen said, then moved on to her first question. "You might be surprised. The real hard-core guns in that gang aren't there anymore. The last one was Blackie Welch and he's gone now."

"What happened to him?" Becca asked.

"He got shot," Cullen answered simply. "I really believe the rest of the men are ready to try to make a go of that ranch they're left with. It'll be hard work, but it'll be well worth it, if they make it pay off. Ain't that what you say, Jim?" he said when the sheriff walked into the dining room.

"Don't believe anything he tells you," Jim shot back. "He's just another drifter passin' through town. Ain't that right, Cullen?"

"I reckon that's about the size of it," Cullen said, and left some money on the table for his breakfast.

* * *

The next day started pretty much like a duplicate of the prior day with Cullen opening up the Stoddard House dining room for breakfast. The only difference being that this morning was to be his last visit to enjoy Cora's cooking. Stumpy Morgan and Johnny Mitchell showed up for breakfast on this morning, planning to attend the official opening of Jim Duncan's jail. Stumpy insisted his only interest was to see what kind of accommodations might be available for him, if he should happen to have to sleep off a drunken arrest one night. Johnny, on the other hand, was excited over the opportunity to have an item of news for his monthly newspaper. The conversation at the breakfast table naturally rehashed the meeting the day before with Sam Culver and Herman Thompson, and the general opinion that it was a historic day for the town of Reid's Mill. Before breakfast was over, Paul Dickson brought Sheriff Edward Rice from Waco in to eat. The official opening of the jail was to be held at eleven that morning, to be followed by another dinner in the Stoddard dining room after the ceremony. Everyone at the breakfast table planned to be there.

The opening went well as Sheriff Rice performed an inspection of the building, especially the cell room and the cells. He gave it a high rating and everybody cheered. After it was over, Cullen made it a point to shake Jim's hand and wish him success in his job. "Don't forget," Jim reminded him, "we've got another feed comin' up at Becca's."

"I won't," Cullen said, although he didn't plan to stay for that event. His horses were ready and so was he to get started back to Austin. His job was finished as best he could tell. He'd make his report to the governor and see what he thought of it. *Too bad that fellow from the county didn't make it,* he thought. It would have helped Jim feel like he was considered a key figure in Bosque County.

Cullen would have been pleased to know Raymond Schwartz from the county commissioner's office did show up for the opening, although it was after most of the people had drifted over to Stoddard House. He, nevertheless, was greeted warmly when he presented Jim with an official sheriff's badge. After the applause, and a crack from Stumpy that he liked Cullen McCabe's jail tree the best. "It was just the thing to hang jailbirds in," Stumpy japed.

"Where is Cullen?" Jim Duncan questioned aloud. "I want him to see this badge." He looked around the crowded dining room, just then realizing Cullen was missing.

"Cullen's gone," Stumpy told him. "Right after we left your new jail, I saw him leadin' his packhorse out the south road."

His remark brought a sudden silence to the jovial conversation. "I ain't had a chance to thank him proper for what he done for this town," Jim said softly. "I owed him more'n a simple thank-you."

Then another regret was voiced when Raymond Schwartz spoke. "I'm sorry I missed Special Agent McCabe, too. He seems to be so important to the governor and I wanted to meet the man."

"Say what?" The words just seemed to fall out of Stumpy's open mouth. No one else could think of anything to say. But that wouldn't last for very long.

TURN THE PAGE FOR AN EXCITING PREVIEW

Three men of honor. One impossible mission.
No turning back. The Jackals ride again—in the
Johnstones' gun-blazing chronicle of the wild and
lawless West . . .

JOHNSTONE JUSTICE.
RELEASE THE JACKALS.

In Texas's Big Bend country, every man has a price.
For crime lord Harry Holland and his ruthless gang of
cutthroats, that price is $20,000—a ransom demand for
the kidnapped daughter of a retired army colonel. So far,
neither the army, the Rangers, nor bounty hunters have
been able to penetrate Holland's guarded fortress.
In desperation, the colonel turns to the Jackals. As a
longtime friend, retired cavalry sergeant Sean Keegan
is determined to bring the man's daughter back alive—
with or without the ransom money—but first he needs
to convince his partners, former Texas Ranger
Matt McCulloch and bounty hunter Jed Breen.

THIS IS NO ORDINARY JOB.
THERE'S A GOOD CHANCE IT'S SUICIDE . . .

When word gets out that the Jackals are on the case,
all hell breaks loose. They're up against trigger-happy
mercenaries, marauding Apaches, and one final, jaw-
dropping surprise—a kidnapping victim who doesn't
want to be rescued. This time, the Jackals have
no one to save . . . but themselves.

THE JACKALS
EVERY MOTHER'S SON
by NATIONAL BESTSELLING AUTHORS
WILLIAM W. JOHNSTONE
and J. A. JOHNSTONE

ON SALE NOW WHEREVER PINNACLE
BOOKS ARE SOLD.

PROLOGUE

Letter to Captain J.J.K. Hollister,
Texas Rangers, Purgatory City

Captain Hollister:

This letter was never written. If anything in this letter ever is mentioned publicly, by you, the press, your men, or by the biggest wastrel and drunk in West Texas or anywhere in Texas, Mexico, the Southwest, the United States and Her territories—or anywhere in this world, for that matter—your reputation, your career, your life are officially over.

This letter and envelope are to be burned immediately after you have finished reading it. The terms of the preceding paragraph apply to this order, too.

Having read your report to Austin on the 7th inst., I have met with Major McDonald, Attorney General Eubanks and Brigadier General Marshall, commander of the Department of Texas, and we have reached this conclusion:

Leave Harry Holland alone.

While Holland is a notorious cutthroat, whose crimes rival those of the most desperate felons in the annals of Texas, as well as our nation, the fact is that Holland and those thirty banditti that ride with him confine most of their crimes south of the border. General Marshall and Major McDonald agree that harassing those greasers keeps them from raiding our ranchers and villages in the Great State of Texas. Everyone in Austin believes that the Mexicans would love to reclaim Texas as one of its provinces, or at the very least reset the international boundary at the Nueces River instead of the Rio Grande, and I will not let that happen on my watch, So Help Me GOD!

But as our lily-livered president in Washington, District of Columbia, does not want to provoke a war, we cannot send Army troops or Texas Rangers across the Rio Grande. So the consensus here is to let Harry Holland carry out the war for Texas and the U.S. Army.

Is that clear?

Yes, I know, Captain, that the Texas Rangers never shirk duty, that they, like those abysmal Mounties in that frozen tundra of Canada—which also should be part of our United States—always get their man. By thunder, the Texas Rangers even caught that notorious evildoer John Wesley Hardin—by pursuing him all the way to the Florida Panhandle. Boundaries are not our concern. Justice is.

But let us face the facts, Captain. Holland and his men have built an impenetrable fortress in the Big Bend country. Your last pursuit of a band of Holland's hellish marauders was unsuccessful. Having read your report, allow me to point out how vain it was:

1. You led your entire battalion, except for ten men left to keep the peace in Purgatory City and the westernmost extremes of our state, after

six of Holland's men wounded one cowboy and made off with forty head of Lazy H beeves. (I suppose Holland and his men had grown tired of eating javelinas for supper.) This makes me ask why you thought a crime of rustling fewer than one hundred head was worth risking almost your entire command. Could the $12,500 reward the U.S. government and the state of Texas has put up for the capture or killing of Harry Holland have motivated this campaign?

2. Three of your men had to turn back and walk—walk!—leading their horses all the way to Mr. Ben Madison's ranchero—as their mounts went lame riding over this harsh country. It was Mr. Madison's beeves that the raiders rustled, and now Mr. Madison had to loan your three Rangers horses so they could return to Purgatory City. Your commander, Major McDonald, has informed me that he just received a bill for those horses, since they have not been returned, for $150. You and your three footsore Rangers can only be relieved that the rancher did not swear out a complaint for horse theft.

3. Two civilian scouts, hired without authority for Major McDonald's office, apparently got lost in the rugged country. According to your report, after three days of searching the scouts were given up for dead.

4. On the seventh day in the Big Bend, according to this report, having ridden into dead end after dead end, and barely finding your way back to

the main trail yourselves, this Ranger expeditionary force was attacked by what you call hostile Apaches. As Brigadier Marshall so succinctly put it: HOSTILE APACHES is redundant. Were you unaware that a band of Apache warriors is also holed up in the Big Bend? Colonel John Caxton at Fort Spalding near Purgatory City has had no luck flushing those Apaches out of that godforsaken country, either. But since the Apaches also seem to prefer raiding south of the Rio Grande, Colonel Caxton at least has the brains not to send his troops into the Big Country on what amounts to a suicide mission.

5. The ambush by the Apaches cost you a mule laden with food stores, and a mule laden with ammunition. Captain, I must commend you for giving arms and food to an enemy of the people of our state, and even an enemy of those peons below the Rio Grande. To your credit—and I remember how gallantly you served in the late Rebellion under General Hastings, God remember his name and the glory he reaped at Fredericksburg—you suffered only four casualties, of which only one was killed. Killed, by your best estimation, by friendly fire.

6. Over the next two days, you sustained one more casualty when a young Ranger fell into a hot spring and was severely scalded. You said in this report that he is expected to recover although his face will no longer be admired by his

sweetheart and that he still screams whenever
he rolls over.

7. A rabid coyote ran off two more horses, leaving
   two more Rangers afoot. They were ordered to
   ride double, until one slipped off his horse and
   broke his left leg in three places after tumbling
   seventy-seven yards down a rocky slope. He
   had the good luck, I assume, to at least be able
   to ride in a travois with some comfort—once all
   the cactus spines had been removed from his
   body. This begs the question: I assume the
   whiskey rations you mentioned in your expense
   report might be the blame for a Texas Ranger
   falling off his horse!

8. After two weeks without getting no closer to
   Harry Holland and his marauders than finding
   ancient tracks and horse droppings that were
   dried, you decided that you had "put a scare"
   into Holland as he must be hiding. Let me
   repeat that phrase —"put a scare"—into an
   outlaw who you never saw, not even dust from
   his ponies, and for all you know, neither Harry
   Holland or any of his nefarious associates ever
   knew you were in the general area of his hidden
   compound. The only ones that knew of your
   existence, in my estimation, were some
   Apaches and a coyote, and I can imagine the
   ravens circling over your heads laughing, CAW,
   CAW, CAW, CAW.

9. While figuring the way out from the maze that
   is Texas's Big Bend, you ran out of water at the
   time you found the main trail again, and headed

north for Apache Springs. Apache Springs is twenty miles away, according to the Major, but the Rio Grande was probably a quarter mile south? Can we blame this on sunstroke?

10. Luckily, a severe thunderstorm drenched you and your men that afternoon, bringing some comfort to your command but not to the pack mule that was struck by lightning.

11. Four days later, you returned to the Rangers headquarters in Purgatory City, having lost only one Ranger—so far, unless the two men who came down with pneumonia after the monsoon have not succumbed by the time this letter reaches you. I assume you do not consider your guides left behind and presumed dead as part of your command since they were not sworn in as Texas Rangers.

Well, Captain, I think these facts sum up why you are to leave Harry Holland alone. Colonel Caxton, according to the Brigadier, believes the same. Unless Holland is foolish enough to attack Purgatory City or Fort Spalding en masse, forget he exists. Leave him to the foolish bounty hunters who think they can find his hideout and not be staked out beside an ant bed with honey poured over their faces by Apache Indians. If Holland is killed by Mexican Rurales or Apaches or by his own men, good riddance. As far as you are concerned, Harry Holland does not exist. You may send out a SMALL patrol every now and then, just to save face, but that patrol should not venture beyond the outskirts of the Big Bend.

If the press were to find out about this, the embarrassment would raise Sam Houston from the grave and his wrath would be worse than that of Apaches and Holland's marauders combined.

Remember your orders. And remember that if you disobey my instructions, the points I made in this letter regarding your stupidity can be made to every newspaper in our glorious state.

Sincerely,
David X. Cumberland IV
Governor of Texas

P.S.: Speaking of nuisances and blights on Texas's Good Name, is there any word on "The Jackals?" You could start your return to my good graces if you were to inform me that Matt McCulloch, Sean Keegan, and Jed Breen are now dead.

CHAPTER ONE

Jed Breen damned well knew how much trouble he was in. Stuck in the middle of the salt fields, his horse dead a hundred yards away, buzzards circling, and those big black birds likely knew they'd have more than a roan gelding to feast on before too long. Two men had Breen pinned down. The baking sun beat him down, too. His canteen lay underneath the dead roan. So did Breen's Sharps rifle. The only thing Breen had to defend himself was a .38-caliber Colt Lightning revolver, and the two men who wanted him dead positioned themselves far, far away. Out of pistol range, they were, but Breen pulled the Colt from the holster, and cocked it anyway.

At least, he tried to cock it. The casehardened iron would not budge. The Lightning being a double-action, Breen tried to pull the trigger, which should have brought the hammer back, but no matter how hard Breen squeezed, neither trigger nor hammer moved. He jostled with the cylinder. Nothing. Not a movement, not a creak. He jammed it on the dead junk of juniper he hid behind, then worked hammer and trigger again. His end results? A string of silent curses.

Breen had yet to catch his breath after running for the nearest shelter he could find—this one dead juniper in the middle of a sea of white. His heart thundered, and Breen wet his tongue while he re-evaluated his situation.

No rifle. No horse. No water. And a jammed revolver.

Well, he thought, if those two hombres get close enough, I can always blind them by throwing salt in their eyes.

Breen tested the Lightning once more, only to see the same results.

No rifle. No horse. No water. No revolver.

He sighed.

No chance.

He took off his hat, ran his fingers through his bone-white hair, and briefly checked the position of the sun. Dark was a long ways off. Mountains rose off to the northwest a ways, but Breen would have to run more than three-tenths of a mile before he reached the end of the salt flats in that direction. Southwest and west would take him another mile before he left the white desert for the tan one. It would also take him farther and farther from the water of the river to the east. And if he ran west, his back would provide an inviting target for the two assassins.

Never wanted to cash in my chips with a bullet in my back. Unless I was making love to a jealous husband's wife.

His smile didn't last long.

The only directions, heading east, would mean covering two hundred yards or more, and he would be moving straight to two men waiting for him. Two men who had already proved themselves to be pretty good shots with rifles.

Jim Kincaid. That's who brought Breen to this country.

That's who got Breen in this fix. Kincaid. And that $400 price on his head.

Kincaid had made a name for himself robbing trains in the Indian Nations. Deputy United States marshals had been hunting him for two or three years with little to show for it except three wounded and one dead deputy. The KATY railroad had put up a $200 reward on Kincaid, the dead deputy's widow had offered another $100, and the state of Texas figured he was worth $100 for being a general nuisance and for the fact that the KATY— nickname for the Missouri-Kansas-Texas Railway—had finally reached Texas a few years back.

With the pressure and noose tightening, Jim Kincaid had left the Nations and had last been seen in El Paso. Breen saw the latest reward poster on Kincaid in Mesilla, New Mexico Territory, where he had just deposited a murderer for a $150 reward. Heading back to his home in Purgatory City, Texas, Breen stopped in at a saloon in El Paso, where he learned that Jim Kincaid had just moseyed out of town and was making his way to Lincoln in New Mexico Territory where he figured he might as well sell his gun to the highest bidder in this range war going on up there.

This time of year, hot as things were getting in Texas, Breen figured that he might as well head to Lincoln, too. Pretty country, that part of Southern New Mexico Territory, and if a man like Jim Kincaid wanted in on the action, chances were other desperadoes would be joining the rival forces in Lincoln, too. Desperadoes with their descriptions on all sorts of wanted posters. If Breen could collect enough bounties, well, he might have enough money to last him till fall.

What Breen had not counted on was that Jim Kincaid would run in to John Murrell on the ride up to Lincoln.

Murrell was wanted for three murders, two assaults, one rape, and six or seven stagecoach robberies. The last poster on Murrell that Breen had seen said his bounty totaled $300, which did seem a tad low for a man who had killed three men and raped a woman, but Breen didn't think about that until he was trapped in the salt flats.

He saw where Murrell met Kincaid, just northeast of Howell's Tanks. Neither men had stopped at the rough-shod station run by Lucius Howell—at least that's what rawboned, tightlipped Howell had told Breen, but most smart men knew better than to drink Howell's rotgut or play cards with any gambler operating there. That meant Murrell must have ridden in to Kincaid's camp, shared some coffee, then camped there for the night, and that morning, Murrell rode east, and Kincaid kept on the trail to Lincoln.

What Breen didn't figure on was that John Murrell had been in El Paso, too, and had seen Breen ride off after Kincaid. Probably the same bar fly who confided Kincaid's plans to Breen—for $10—took money from Murrell to learn of Breen's idea. Breen didn't even know Murrell and Kincaid knew each other. Maybe they didn't until then.

A few miles past Howell's Tanks, the trail went through the salt flats. Breen stopped to rest his horse, drink water from his canteen, and scan the country with his binoculars. Kincaid's hoof prints revealed a man in no particular hurry still riding along at a leisurely pace, it being hot, and Lincoln County being a good distance away.

Satisfied, Breen rode through the country, and made a careless mistake. He left his Sharps rifle with the fancy telescopic sight sheathed in the scabbard. Two rifle shots rang out, one punching a hole through the bedroll behind the cantle, another slamming into the roan's head. Breen barely managed to clear the stirrups. Landing in the sand, two other shots kicked up white dust a few feet from Breen, who climbed to his feet, felt a bullet tug on his bandana, and another slug buzz past his left ear.

He took off running before the next two bullets sounded, seeing the juniper, and figuring that his luck would not hold. Yet it had. Breen dived to his right, as two bullets clipped the brittle branches of the dead tree, and that's where Breen pulled himself up into a ball and started figuring his options.

"Señor Kincaid," a voice called back from the rocks, "that *bouledogue* of a *chasseur,* he runs like a *pura sangre,* and is *uno hombre con suerte.*"

"Keep quiet, Murrell," Kincaid rang out from his position. "And if he raises his head, blow it off."

That was when Breen understood that the second gunman was John Murrell. He was the only outlaw in these parts who could not complete a sentence in one language. It always came about as a mix of English, French, and Spanish.

While he beat on the Lightning some more, Breen did some backtracking in his mind and came up with his theory about how Kincaid and Murrell met.

"*Cazador, mi amigo,*" Murrell yelled, "you should have remained in that *salon pas cher* in the *ville* of El Paso."

"Shut up, Murrell. Keep your rifle sights on that mad-dog killer."

That exchange just confirmed Breen's theory.

"You should have kept running, bounty killer!" Kincaid

yelled. "Might have made it. But not now. We've found our range, right, Murrell?"

A bullet shattered a limb on Breen's right, bathing the brim of his hat in bark.

"*Bueno,* my new friend. Now . . . *regarde ça.*"

The next shot thudded into the lower trunk. Had John Murrell carried something more powerful than his repeating rifle—like Breen's Sharps rifle—the slug probably would have torn through the juniper and punched a massive hole through Breen's back.

Once the echoes of the bullets drifted away over the white vastness, the two killers started laughing.

Breen wiped the salt off the palm of his left hand, and used the right to try to get that Lightning to work again. All he needed was two shots. If he could somehow get close enough to the outlaws.

"Bounty killer!" Kincaid's voice thundered again. "I'm enjoying a cold sip of water from my canteen right now. I reckon your canteen is keeping your hoss company."

"And I, *mon nouvel ennemi,* I sip from this *bota* that contains *un excelente vino blanco.*"

"Come join us!" Kincaid yelled after another round of laughing. "Because that sun must be frying your head right about now. And I don't see a cloud in the sky."

The laughter continued, and Breen stared across the salt flats, saw the heat waves rippling across the white expanse of nothing.

Hell, he quite realized, *I never knew just how salt could make a body thirsty.*

Connect with U s

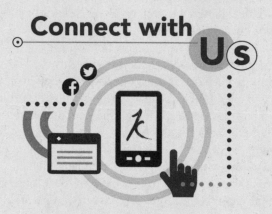

Visit us online at
KensingtonBooks.com
to read more from your favorite authors, see books
by series, view reading group guides, and more.